NATIVES
AND
STRANGERS

NATIVES
AND
STRANGERS

Louisa Dawkins

HOUGHTON MIFFLIN COMPANY

BOSTON

Library of Congress Cataloging in Publication Data

Dawkins, Louisa.
Natives and strangers.

I. Title.
PS3554.A946N3   1985   813'.54   85-171
ISBN 0-395-36553-8

Printed in the United States of America

A 10 9 8 7 6 5 4 3 2

This book is for Anna with love and gratitude

PART I

1956

1

Galana

"I wish I could take you home to England with me," Virginia Hamilton said to her daughter, Marietta, before supper in the office at the beginning of the rains. "But Aunt Sophia only sent money for the one plane fare. The Wiltons will be looking after everything while I'm away. We met them in Arusha. They had an Airedale called Hercules. Surely you remember him? I'll only be away three months. I bet the time will fly. For you, I mean," Virginia added hastily, "as well as for me."

"England may be *your* home," Marietta remarked, "but I've never been there. How can it be mine?"

Although she'd left as a babe in arms, at least Virginia had been born in England. But Marietta had been born in Tanganyika Territory, at Songo in the Great Rift Valley, which runs all the way north from the Zambezi to the Sea of Galilee. Not that she remembered anything about Songo, because before she was two they'd gone to Mutheo and from Mutheo to Luganga, and just last August, in the week of her ninth birthday, they'd come to Runga on the southern shore of Lake Victoria. One of these days they'd be moving on again. Virginia Hamilton wasn't one for staying put.

Virginia was a manager. She managed rest houses that the government provided for touring officials in remote places where no one in his right mind would dream of starting a hotel. Such places appealed to Virginia, though, and the rest houses presented a challenge. The more run down the better, so far as she was concerned. She'd arrive somewhere that was utterly inhospitable, and in no

3

time at all she'd transform it. From the bar, where just a little while ago you could have heard a pin drop, would come wave upon wave of laughter, and from the dining room, exclamations of delight at the miraculous improvement in the food; on the veranda, someone would be doing wonders on the ancient missionary piano — and in the middle of all this, young Mrs. Hamilton would be tossing her remarkable dark blond hair. She attracted the care-worn the way a lamp attracts moths. "Whatever's such charm and talent doing in a place like Runga?" her guests asked themselves and one another. But Virginia preferred the bush to Dar-es-Salaam or the Highlands or even the Kenya Coast. Once she'd had the chance to run a hotel in Malindi and she'd turned the offer down. She liked the edge of the world, she said, so long as one could keep on moving. England, which she'd been back to less than half a dozen times in over thirty years, was home enough for her.

But not for Marietta.

Every single person Marietta knew, with the sole exception of herself, had a home. Whether or not they lived there, they always had it in reserve, to return to now and then, and the rest of the time to bear in mind. Her friend Violet did. Violet's home was on Galana Island in the Kavirondo Gulf, and even though she didn't go there often, she talked about it constantly. Things were infinitely better at Galana than at any other place she'd been. "Then why d'you stay here?" Marietta would yell, whenever they had a falling-out. "This time I'm leaving, you'll see!" Violet would yell back. But she never left. Although once they hadn't spoken from Tuesday afternoon to Thursday morning, half an hour was generally as long as either could hold out.

Their friendship had begun one day when Marietta and her mother were living at Mutheo, which came after Songo and before Luganga. Marietta was stalking lizards on the veranda when suddenly a woman appeared with a big baby on her back and a small, bright-eyed girl at her side. Boremo, the woman said her name was, and she was looking for her husband, the Ruba man Justin, who worked for the white people at the rest house. But Justin had gone to buy charcoal at the market, so Boremo sat down to wait in the shade, and in no time her bright-eyed daughter was stalking lizards, too.

Boremo had come to Mutheo for the purpose of getting pregnant, and a few weeks later, when she'd achieved this goal, she an-

4

nounced she was going back to Galana. But meanwhile Violet and Marietta had become inseparable — and when, arms round one another, they'd pleaded and begged and begged and pleaded, Boremo had given in. She'd get her sister's daughter as a baby-nurse instead, and Violet could remain with her father until September, when he got his leave. Violet had been about six then — old enough, Boremo agreed, to be away from her mother — and Marietta had been four and a half. When September came, Violet went off to Galana as agreed, but a month later she was back with Justin. So it went every year, because she refused to be parted permanently from Marietta. As for Marietta, she couldn't imagine life without Violet, who'd taught her everything of importance. How to climb trees and swim and cook *ugali*. How to remove jiggers from her toes and tie the laces of her tennis shoes.

Apart from having a home and being so very clever, Violet had another great advantage. She had a father.

"Yours is dead," Virginia had told Marietta when the notion that you had to have a father had first occurred to her and prompted her to ask. "He died before you were born."

"Do I look like him?"

"Like *him*? Thank God, no!"

"Have you got a snapshot, then?"

"No snapshot. Nothing. Except you, Etta," Virginia had added, walking away. She didn't intend to talk about the late Charles Hamilton. Not now. Never.

Once, when Justin had found Violet and Marietta behind the servants' quarters at Luganga fighting like jackals, he'd said in disgust, as he pulled them apart, "What is it for that you scratch each other's faces and scream and roll on the earth?"

"She's jealous," Violet replied, wiping her nose with the back of her hand. "She's a wicked girl. She wishes I were dead."

"What did you do to her, then?" Justin said, but quite gently. He wasn't one for blaming. Generally he could see both sides of an argument.

"It's not what I did, it's what I have and she hasn't."

"What's that?"

So then Marietta had to explain. After a moment's thought, Justin said, "I have three sons, Samuel, Isaaka, and Nelson, and besides them, Violet and Mari. Both are my girls." Looking Marietta straight in the eye, he added, "I have watched you always, haven't

5

I? Have I not taught you my language, so that, white as you are, to hear you with the eyes shut a person would take you for a Ruba girl? What more is there?" Surely there's something more, Marietta thought — though what, she didn't know. "One day soon you will be coming home with us," he finished, "but now you must bathe and change your dress before the memsahb sees your condition."

Each year Marietta would ask to go to Galana with Violet and Justin, and each year Virginia would say, "It's too far and too dangerous on those buses. God knows what would become of you!"

"Nothing's become of *them*. They always get back safe."

"But, Etta, if you went, I'd miss you so!"

Marietta had to wonder about that. Virginia had so much to do and so many other people to think about that quite often she seemed to forget her daughter existed. In those odd moments here and there when Virginia didn't have to be busy or gay or charming, Marietta had seen her grow abruptly sad. She didn't share her secrets with her daughter, though. She kept herself to herself, and now she was going away from the beginning of July to the first day of October. This year, Marietta decided, absolutely nothing would stop her from going to Galana.

It wasn't too difficult to persuade Dick and Susan Wilton. After all, Virginia hadn't told them *not* to let her go. She hadn't said anything about trips at all, actually. Once they got down to thinking about it realistically, the Wiltons, who were getting on for seventy, weren't sure how well they'd manage with Marietta. When Virginia had asked them to fill in for her while she was away, she'd been looking for people who knew about rest houses, not children. And entertaining children was definitely not their forte. Why not let Marietta go? She wanted to so badly, and really, what harm could come to her with the man who had looked after her virtually since birth? Of course there must have been an ayah to begin with, the Wiltons guessed, but later on, what with Virginia being so busy, Justin was the one who'd been in charge. Years ago, when Marietta came with her mother and the houseboy to Arusha, the Wiltons had wondered if the child could even speak English. They'd both quite disapproved of what Virginia was doing, letting her daughter grow up like a native. But it was a very tough life she led, off God knows where, with no husband. Really, it was her business, not theirs, how she brought up her child. Anyway, one had to admit that the child seemed perfectly cheerful despite her unusual family life. So why *not* let her go to Galana? Justin had promised to dose her regularly with medicine for malaria and worms.

On the first day of September, Justin, Violet, and Marietta took one bus and then another, and slept that night in a market. In the morning they got on a third bus, grinding along the track beside the lake shore and across the border into Kenya.

When she was small Marietta had gone up with her mother every year to stay with Virginia's great friend Daphne Dawson and her husband, Peter, in Katari, just outside Nairobi. The Dawsons lived in a very grand way in a mansion with turrets and a dozen servants. They were at the very center of the Nairobi social whirl, and a week with them provided Virginia with a lovely change from Luganga or Mutheo, as well as a good six months' worth of gossip. After the State of Emergency was declared at the start of the Mau Mau Rebellion, Virginia announced that a few Bolshi Kikuyu weren't going to deprive her of her Rest and Recreation. Besides, Nairobi was swamped with British soldiers and special police and paratroopers and tracker dogs; there couldn't be any trouble there. Off they went as usual that November. On the third day of their visit, a Settler couple, John and Barbara Graham, were murdered during dinner in the pleasant house they'd built themselves, half a mile down the road from the Dawsons'. It turned out that their cook, kind old Kimathi, who'd been with them twenty years, was a high-ranking Mau Mau organizer; he'd extorted money from all the servants in Katari, including the Dawsons', and salted it away in boxes in the Grahams' garage, and when the murderers arrived he'd unlocked the kitchen door and ushered them right in. The next time Virginia had gone for her Rest and Recreation she'd left Marietta behind in Tanganyika, and although there hadn't been any more terrorist incidents in Katari, she hadn't taken her daughter up to Kenya since.

But Marietta, Violet, and Justin weren't going anywhere near Katari. Galana was hundreds of miles over unpaved roads to the west, and if, four years after the Declaration of Emergency, the Kikuyu were still quarreling with Queen Elizabeth, that was their affair. It didn't concern the people of Galana, most of whom had never laid eyes on a Kikuyu and had no wish to go to Kikuyuland, which they'd heard was high and cold and very overcrowded.

A few miles past the Kenya border a range of ragged mountains came into view. Justin said that beyond them lay Rubaland; soon they'd reach the ferry to take them to Galana. The mountains were desiccated, copper-colored, jutting thousands of feet up against a glaring sky. In the dawn of the world they had been volcanoes.

"Can we get out and climb them, Justin?" Marietta shouted, over the roar and clatter of the bus. "From the top you must be able to see Uganda."

"You'll see nothing up there but snakes and vultures," Violet said.

"And thieves," Justin added, "who take our cattle and drive them to the hills and slaughter them. And when they've eaten, they sleep, and when they awake, down they come again. They don't know how to herd as we do, only how to steal what others breed and raise. And the government does nothing. They're too busy in Central Province, fighting the Kikuyu. They have no time for Luo thieves."

"Why don't they raise their own cattle?"

"They're lazy, Mari."

"But thieves aren't lazy," Marietta persisted. "They're quick and cunning. Otherwise they'd be caught. What they're after is the excitement. It's more exciting being a thief than an honest man." But she didn't get a rise out of Justin, who cracked his knuckles and fastened his eyes on the back of the bus driver's head.

They rattled round the bottom of the long-extinct volcanoes, stopped at a crossroads, and waited while the overheated engine cooled; then they set off once more and reached their destination as the sun was sliding into Lake Victoria. And there across a narrow channel lay Galana Island, green and brown and golden on dark blue evening water. Marietta raced with Violet to the beach, where they shook off their sandals, tucked up their dresses, and waded in near the dock. The fish darting past their ankles were brighter by far than any they'd seen at Runga. They tried to catch the fish with their hands, but all that happened was that their skirts got soaked. They laughed and plunged their hands in again and again. Their laughter roused a flock of large, white water birds, which rose from a nearby reed bed, circled once, twice, a third time, and wheeled away into the setting sun. On the far side of the channel half a dozen men were bathing in the shallows. They soaped and splashed themselves and called to one another, and the sounds traveled back across the water to the children wading by the dock.

Eden was within sight and earshot. How to get there was the question, since the ferry had broken down a week ago, and the ferryman, who'd gone off to Homa Bay to get a fan belt, hadn't yet returned.

In the quiet water on the mainland side were a handful of long, light fishing boats painted scarlet and yellow. From the beach Justin hailed the nearest fisherman by name. The man shook his head and bent close to his nets again, but another man a short distance further on took up his paddle. Seven cents, he shouted. Five, Justin shouted back. It was five a year ago. But last year isn't this year, is it? — and they settled on six.

They were reaching Galana just after the millet harvest, a time for celebration and for greeting relatives, and Justin's were extremely numerous. Boremo's relatives had to be greeted, too. And every one of these people — the uncles, the cousins, the grandfathers' brothers' wives, the grandmothers' sisters' husbands — were Violet's relatives as well. Whole lineages, four generations, made up Violet's family, not to mention ancestors, all known, remembered, honored. Marietta's family consisted of exactly three people: herself, her mother, and her Aunt Sophia, whom she'd never seen, but who (so Virginia's postcards said) was as full of pep as ever. But however peppy the fabled Aunt Sophia might be, however easily she ran you off your feet, when all was said and done she was only one person; she wasn't a household, a lineage, a clan.

Boremo was expecting a baby soon, the outcome of a February visit to Runga. The last baby, Violet's only sister, had died. Of witchcraft, Violet whispered. Because of measles, Justin said firmly. (He'd gone to the mission school at Kendu Bay and refused to talk about magic.) Although they ate in Boremo's house, Violet and Marietta didn't sleep there. You couldn't sleep in your mother's house if your father was there, no more than you could sleep in your father's house when your mother was there. Once when Virginia and Marietta were living in Mutheo and Boremo had brought Violet to visit Justin, Virginia had found a small black head next to her daughter's blond one when she went in to say good night. "How in heaven's name did *she* get in?" Virginia asked.

"Last night she slept on the veranda and she was scared. So tonight I brought her in here," said Marietta.

"But why can't she sleep with her parents?"

"Because she mustn't. She has to show respect to her mother and father, now that she has sense." Sense had come, Violet had explained to Marietta, at the end of the dry season, when she'd begun to notice certain adult behavior that she'd never noticed before.

Virginia shook her head and for form's sake grumbled, but it was mild grumbling and soon she gave in. Why should anyone know if Marietta slept with the houseboy's daughter, and supposing anyone did, would it matter? When Boremo had finally gone home, leaving Violet, this arrangement was already well established. On occasions when they were forced to sleep apart, both children had bad dreams. So when Boremo offered Marietta a choice between sleeping in her house and going with the other children to the grandmothers, naturally Marietta went with Violet.

There were two grandmothers — Sara, who was Justin's mother, and her co-wife, Bosibori, formerly known as Ruth. They were sisters. Ruba people preferred to marry sisters; it made for much less trouble than if you married women who were unrelated. After all, sisters had already spent a childhood negotiating who stood where and who had what. Jealousy was an ordinary part of their lives. They, unlike most co-wives, had the chance to be friends and not just enemies. Indeed, often they were rather better friends with one another than either was with their husband. This was the case with Sara and Bosibori. For forty years their husband, Obiri, who was something of a fisherman and much more of a trader, had taken donkey-loads of salt into the Nyanza Hills, and for long stretches the two women had lived contentedly without him. Recently, however, when their husband had shifted the burden of the salt trade onto one of his sons and come back to Galana for good, Sara and Bosibori had discovered that two was company but three was a crowd, and they made no secret of their feelings. A wise man, Obiri began spending more and more time in his fishing boat, and gradually things settled back to normal.

Bosibori was the older of the two. In her girlhood she and her sister had renounced their Ruba names, stepped into the baptismal waters, and emerged as Ruth and Sara. Thereafter they'd gone every Sabbath to the Adventist church near the middle of the island. Ruth had married first, three years before her sister, and then she'd given birth every other year. But her babies kept dying. The ancestors soon let it be known, through a celebrated diviner on the

10

mainland whom Obiri consulted, that they had been sorely neglected by Obiri's family. They demanded that an ox, seven goats,
and four sheep be sacrificed, and worse yet, that Ruth renounce
her faith and undertake training as a diviner. This she refused to
do, despite the entreaties of Obiri and his relatives, because she
loved her God and believed in His coming.

But after the fifth child died, the ancestors became insistent.
There were omens everywhere: owls flew by in daylight; clay pots,
standing alone, cracked and fell to pieces; a goat was struck by
lightning. Ruth had no choice but to leave the church, resume her
old name, Bosibori, and however arduous and costly it might be,
begin her apprenticeship in divination. For this she was in the end
richly rewarded. By the time she reached the change of life she'd
had five sons, four daughters. And it turned out that the role of
diviner suited her well. Her understanding of the ills that sundered
families and set ancestors against descendants was nothing short
of extraordinary. From the start her diagnoses were consistently
accurate, her prescriptions efficacious; people flocked to her from
all over the island and from the mainland as well. The pain of her
personal sacrifice dimmed as her exceptional talents for negotiating between the living and the dead gained recognition. As her reputation grew, so did her wealth. Now she lived in a concrete house
with many luxuries in it, including a massive Leatherette sofa that
she'd bought from Father Rider of Saint Thomas's, Ubithi, when
his order had recalled him from Galana, after a scandal involving
a female layworker. Bosibori's house was painted blue, and the one
she'd built thirty yards away for her sister Sara was forest green.
Sara's had no sofa but did have six cane chairs from Father Rider's
dining room.

Both sisters lacked two front teeth. Bosibori had lost hers many
years before, when a crazed client had attacked her in the middle
of a divination session. Sara had knocked hers out herself when
she'd slipped in the rain on the path from the lake and hit her teeth
on the rim of her water pot. Both loved to talk. They tended to
share sentences; one would start, the other finish. Obiri had long
since surrendered center stage to them. Perhaps another man
would have taken a pliable young bride for pleasure and, almost
as important, for protection against the alliance of the two old
women, but Obiri couldn't afford another wife: however pliable
she might be, inevitably she would produce more sons. He already

had eleven to provide with land and cattle. So he continued to divide his time between the sisters — one week with Bosibori in the blue house, the next with Sara in the green. No one quite knew if the attentions he paid them were sexual or merely diplomatic or both, but whatever their nature he kept to the schedule.

The week in which Marietta arrived at Galana was Sara's week with Obiri. This meant that the two girls, and Violet's brothers Samuel and Isaaka, who now had sense as well, were sent across the yard to Bosibori. In addition to the Leatherette sofa, Bosibori had a great brass bed, which she'd bought from a departing missionary of the Church of God. All four children slept in it with the old lady. Marietta, as the visitor, had the place of honor between Bosibori and the wall. She discovered early on that if she poked a finger between Bosibori's first and second ribs, her snores faltered and ultimately died away, and everyone could sleep soundly until morning. More often than not they were awakened by a supplicant who had come hurrying through the bush by night with coins knotted tightly in a rag, to tell of terrible afflictions and to pay for Bosibori's wisdom. Roused by the urgent voice and the banging on the door, the old lady would send the children tumbling off the bed; she'd grope past them for the faded purple bag in which she kept the beads and rings and knucklebones by which she understood the past, construed the future. Daybreak; it was time for her to go to work.

The children spent their morning working for Boremo. Slow and heavy with her pregnancy, she complained to those in earshot about her aching back. The girls washed clothes at the lake shore and spread shirts and pants out to dry on the grass. And they fetched and carried, water mostly, balancing the clay pots carefully on their heads as they came up the same rise where long ago Sara had lost her two front teeth.

Samuel, whose job was herding goats, mocked the red, perspiring Marietta during her first few days at Galana. "You're only a *mzungu*. Can a white girl carry pots?" And then he'd drive his goats headlong across her path. He was a year younger than Marietta and half a head taller, and strong and lithe and inordinately pleased with himself. Marietta detested his grin, his swagger. She decided to give him something to remember her by. On the fourth day, when Boremo had gone to the market, Marietta hid behind a tree just outside the compound and threw herself on Samuel as he came ambling past. He recovered almost instantly, pushed her off, sprang back and then forward again. He pulled out a handful of her hair and tore one sleeve off her dress, but she managed to give him a swollen eye and a long, red scratch down the middle of his back. After that he didn't call her *mzungu*, and by the middle of the month they were friends. To her delight, Marietta could swim six yards farther under water than Samuel could.

Often in the afternoon Justin took them to greet his relatives. Violet's relatives. "Yours too," he assured Marietta. "You're both my girls." At first suspicious of Marietta, the relatives warmed to her the moment they heard her speak Ruba. The men took both girls out in their boats, the women teased them, roasted new maize for them, told them stories. But Boremo was the best storyteller, Marietta thought. Despite being tired, she put every ounce of her attention into telling her stories. She told all the ones she remembered from her childhood, and others she'd made up. Violet, who already knew them, would wander off, but Marietta was enchanted. Among the Runga regulars Virginia had a reputation as a raconteur, but her stories all dated from Songo at the earliest. She never told stories about her childhood. For her, time that counted began on the day of Marietta's birth; everything earlier she had consigned to darkness. She'd had parents and lived in Kenya on a farm in a place called Rumuruti, but her parents had died and the farm had been sold, and that was that. Marietta didn't even know how Aunt Sophia was related, though she must have been somebody's sister once.

The high point of the visit, the wedding of Sara's youngest daughter, came almost at the end. The girl, Zipporah, was shadowy and silent, having grown up in a household with two such forceful women. Violet thought her stupid. She said to Marietta when they were washing underclothes, "Her husband will be tired of her by Christmas, just you see!" But the grownups thought Zipporah perfect. She was shy and respectful, she made excellent *ugali*, and she was still a virgin.

As the oldest son and brother, Justin had to inspect the cattle the bridegroom offered; if they proved acceptable, Zipporah would go to her new home the following day. The day the cattle were to be brought was one of high excitement. Ten head had been promised — four Brahma, five native, and one European. Dozens of relatives were assembled in Obiri's homestead, watching carefully for the cloud of dust that signaled the cattle's arrival. When it came, a cry arose and the children pelted up the hill to get the first glimpse. How many bulls? How many cows-in-calf? How many heifers? Was the European brown or black or white or yellow? All this the children saw before the grownups; grownups had to control their impatience and wait with composure. After the cattle were penned, Justin came forward with his father. His head was newly shaved and he wore his best khaki trousers and bush jacket. He greeted the visitors gravely and then looked at the animals, speaking quietly with Obiri about each in turn. How smart Justin looks, Marietta thought, and how important! At last, almost imperceptibly, he nodded. And then it was time for the feast.

Sara, the Christian, had contributed the meat; two goats slaughtered early in the morning were roasting, each over its own fire. Bosibori, the pagan, was in charge of liquid refreshment; beer bubbled in *her* kitchen. Obiri had provided fifteen *talapia* fish, weighing more than four pounds each, and there were greens besides, and sweet potatoes, and red beans, brown beans, huge pots of *ugali*. The children stoked the fires and helped to turn the meat. They carried mugs of beer to the guests and refilled them as soon as they were empty, which was almost instantly.

As Marietta slipped by with beer for Obiri's youngest brother's wife, who'd come down from Kisumu for the occasion, Justin turned and pulled on one blond braid. "Little hummingbird," he laughed. "Ever hither and yon!" He was pleased.

But Violet, a few steps behind, heard what he said, and later, when the sun had set and the guests, or those who were still ambulatory, were wandering off towards home, she turned on Marietta. "Hummingbird! You're his favorite! It's always you, not me!"

Marietta, startled by her fury, answered, "The hummingbirds here are yellow. That's all Justin meant."

"And not black!" She hoped Marietta would drown, that she'd be trampled by a hippo, be poisoned by a snake, die of smallpox, catch scarlet fever. For stealing her father, Marietta deserved to die not one but several dreadful deaths. Violet wept huge tears.

But in the morning as they watched the bridegroom with his age mates taking Zipporah away, Violet threw one arm across Marietta's shoulders and whispered, "His nose is flat. He looks like a monkey. The husband they choose for us will have to be ever so much more handsome!"

14

"Husband? But there are two of us."

"Yes, we're like the grandmothers. We'll marry the same man. I'll go first and you'll come later."

And Boremo, overhearing, laughed. "Of course, Mari. This is your home, so where else should you marry? And I'll bring meat and flour at the birth of your first child."

This is your home, she'd said. Surely, thought Marietta, England couldn't be more beautiful or the people kinder than at Galana, and of course she wouldn't be separated from Violet, ever.

Suddenly one evening Justin told them the memsahb was returning to Runga at the end of that very week, and it was necessary for them to get back in good time. They said good-bye to everyone the night before and got up in the dark to walk the four miles to the ferry. As the sun rose they crossed to the mainland, climbed into their bus (the first of many), and began the journey back to Runga.

In the middle of the first morning the bus broke down irreparably, and they had to wait till late afternoon for another one to pass and pick them up. Back in Tanganyika they had better luck. There were delays because of arguments between the driver and the passengers over fares, and they had a three-hour wait in a place called Kuta where the mango trees were very numerous — but alas, it was long past mango season. They reached Runga on the evening of the second day. Lifting their bundles to their heads, they set off in the dusk to walk the last half mile. Walking briskly after long hours of being cramped in the bus, Justin carried a large cardboard box with "Kiwi Shoe Polish" stamped in dark red letters on all sides; Violet and Marietta carried their clothes inside gunny sacks tied at one end with string. They went in single file along the edge of the unpaved road, past the *dukas*, many of which were already closed up for the night, and on into the residential part of the town. The rest house stood on a large piece of land between the gardens and bungalows of the better-off Indian traders and those of the British government officials. Directly behind it was the Ismaili mosque and in front was the lake. Except in the hottest part of the year, one could count on a breeze off the water. At seven o'clock in the evening the air was cool. They were back with three days to spare. They'd have plenty of time to settle in before Virginia arrived from England.

But when they turned in at the gate, the Wiltons' Land-Rover wasn't in the parking space reserved with a neatly painted sign for the rest house manager, to the left of the front door. The Wiltons' vehicle was over to the right, next to the district commissioner's, and Virginia's Land-Rover was in the manager's space. Justin stopped so suddenly that Violet walked right into him and Marietta into her, and the gunny sacks went tumbling to the ground. Justin gave one long, deep sigh, straightened his box, and marched on up the steps into the rest house lobby. Violet and Marietta picked up their bundles and followed him.

The judge was up from Mwanza for the quarter sessions, and he and the district commissioner and the assistant district commissioners and all the British bigwigs and most of the little ones as well were congregated in Mrs. Hamilton's bar, congratulating each other for the thousandth time on the fact that they hadn't been posted to Kenya. By now, memories of the horrors that had marked the announcement of the Emergency were beginning to dim, for in 1952 the colonial government had sent in the army in full force, including troops seasoned in the long struggle against communism in Malaya and against fascism in the Second World War. Their job had been to teach the Kukes a lesson, and for the most part they'd done it. The butchering of isolated Settler farmers had long ago been stopped; in all, the headcount came to thirty-odd Europeans. Bad enough, but if Whitehall had acted with any less alacrity and single-mindedness, Kenya might well have got the bloodbath that everyone, back in October 1952, had so much feared. Of course, in the reserves of Central Province, African losses had been vastly greater. Fifteen, twenty thousand dead. Who knew exactly? All the same, the mass of the Kikuyu people were now pacified — "decontaminated" was a favorite expression. They'd been moved out of their traditional homesteads into villages where the police and the King's African Rifles kept a very close eye on them. In all fairness, it hadn't taken most of them that long to learn the error of their ways, and as a reward Whitehall was talking about, if not quite yet promising, self-rule in the foreseeable future. When the British left, of course, the Africans were to understand, it would be of their own accord, not because anyone was forcing them out.

Yes, life up in Kenya was so quiet these days that one might even be lulled into thinking the war was over. Unfortunately this was not at all the case. A hard-core group of so-called Nationalists had holed themselves up north of Nairobi in the Aberdare Mountains,

16

from which they continued to fight a small, nasty, and hugely expensive guerrilla operation that might go on indefinitely. Despite the millions spent, the lives, both white and black, lost, the lessons learned (if too late in the day to make much difference), the war dragged on. Why would anyone in his right mind want to live with that sort of uncertainty?

In comparison Tanganyika was a pretty nice place to be. Here there were reasonable natives, few people of the arrogant Settler type (a specialty of Kenya), no General China, and last but not least, no Jomo Kenyatta. Seeing that they didn't have enough on him to hang him, the least Her Majesty's Government could've done was ship Jomo off to some island in the South Atlantic. But the fools had imprisoned him right there, in his own country, and instead of forgetting him, the bloody Kukes had turned him into God! The great good fortune of the men in the rest house bar at having escaped the Kenya quagmire provoked gales of self-congratulatory laughter and another round of drinks.

On the opposite side of the lobby Mrs. Hamilton was in her office with the door shut, giving Dick and Susan Wilton the rocket of their lives.

Viginia had met a man in England, and at first they'd had great fun. They'd talked about his coming out to Africa to see if he could live there. They'd even talked about living together up in the Highlands, at Arusha maybe, or somewhere else a bit cooler than Runga. But in her usual fashion Virginia got cold feet, frozen feet, a week ago Monday in the Palace Hotel in Eastbourne, and the only way to get the circulation going again was to pack up and ring for a taxi and take the next train to London. From there she'd called Aunt Sophia in Wiltshire to say she'd decided to catch the Tuesday plane, not the Saturday, because she was missing Marietta. She'd come bumping over Europe and the Mediterranean, then up the Nile, and at each stop she'd felt just a little warmer, so that by the time she reached Nairobi she was her normal self again. She'd had a good laugh with Daphne and Peter Dawson, and after a night's sleep, picked up her Land-Rover and driven southwest three long days, until at six o'clock that evening she'd reached Runga and found her daughter gone.

Justin put down his box and listened a moment at the office door. The memsahb's mood was unmistakable. He sighed deeply again and knocked. There was a brief silence, then *"Karibu."* Justin opened the door; the Wiltons, dazed and flushed, were huddled very close to each other in the middle of the room. Beyond them was Virginia, dust stained, in khaki shirt and dungarees, her hair in wisps about her flushed face. If she was angry at the Wiltons that was nothing compared with the rage that she now unleashed on Justin. Savage, she called him, thief and bloody wog, and she was going to go into the bar this minute to get Judge Hever to arrest him and send him to prison for life for kidnaping.

She was so enraged, in fact, that it was quite some time before she noticed her daughter lurking behind a wooden pillar in the lobby. Then she bounced out, seized Marietta by the arm, and pulled her back into the office, where she shook her very hard, shouting, "You dreadful little sneak, running off like that! It could've been the end of you! Don't you ever *think!*" But the next moment she was hugging Marietta and saying, "It's my fault. You don't know what you are. You're not English and you *can't* be African. So what in the hell are you? Oh, Etta, I'm so sorry, really I am," and she buried her face in Marietta's tangled tow-colored hair.

"Sorry for what?" Marietta said, wriggling a little. "I had a very good time. The best I've ever had. Why be sorry about that?"

Her mother said miserably, "This is such an awful, seedy place, such a narrow life, there's no one here for you at all."

Eventually Virginia got over the illicit visit to Galana, more or less, the Wiltons departed for Arusha cheerfully, and Justin went not to prison but back to washing the clothes and helping out in the dining room. And after a few days of being "grounded," the children had the run of the town again. But Virginia couldn't let go of this new idea that there wasn't anyone in Runga for Marietta, which was just the same as saying that Violet wasn't a person, and that couldn't have been further from the truth.

What Virginia meant was that there weren't any European children Marietta's age. There were one or two babies and a few a bit older than that, but once they were six or seven the British sent their children "home," or if not that far, at least to Arusha to boarding school. Arusha was up on Mount Meru. It was cool and healthy and as much like "home" as you could find in Tanganyika. You could play hockey and football and lacrosse and conjugate Latin verbs and make believe you were in Winchester or Cheltenham.

18

Unlike the other British parents, Virginia didn't send her child away. "I can't afford it" was the official reason she gave to those who asked. "I never set foot inside a school myself," she'd say with a laugh. "When I've made my fortune, I'll send her to Paris to be finished off!"

Meanwhile, Marietta did a correspondence course. Every fortnight a new assignment arrived for her in a large, reusable yellow envelope from Dr. Bram Vorster's Academy in Pietermaritzburg, South Africa, and every fortnight Justin would stand over her while she collected her sums and exercises together and sealed them in the same yellow envelope. Then Justin would tramp through the town to the post office to send it back to Dr. Vorster.

Parents were supposed to supervise, but Virginia was generally too busy, so Marietta did her course largely unsupervised — and with a great deal of assistance from Violet. Violet hadn't ever been to school either, but she'd joined the household just at the point when Virginia, in a rather haphazard fashion, was teaching her daughter to read, and Marietta had insisted on Violet's being included in the lessons. Once Marietta had achieved literacy, she — and Violet, too, of course — had been handed over to Dr. Vorster. Two agile brains accomplished more in a much shorter period than one alone could ever have done. Marietta was good at writing and even better at drawing, but the course didn't stress creativity, so she kept her pictures to herself. Violet was only average at writing but excellent at geography and arithmetic. Together they got very good marks indeed. Once they'd done a whole year's work in six months and Marietta had received a note of congratulation and encouragement in Dr. Vorster's own hand. The correspondence course was part of the natural order of things — or it had been, until Virginia exclaimed in rage and sorrow that the life her daughter led was narrow.

Narrow? But there was so much going on! Almost everything that happened in Runga Marietta knew about. Who was born, who died, and why. Who lied to whom, who got caught, and who got away with it. Some of this came from eavesdropping and observation in the streets and markets, and some of it came from servants. Servants willingly told you what their employers were up to. In the European bungalows there was a lot of drinking of gin and whiskey, so much cheaper in the colonies than in the U.K. — poor blighters, taxed to the hilt. And there was a good deal of "playing" together by people who weren't married, and by the

19

bwanas with local boys. This last was an abomination, inviting terrifying consequences if you didn't sacrifice in time. The boys, though, were young and greedy; they were prepared to take that risk for money. They thought they could escape the wrath of the ancestors. In time it would catch up with them, of course, but by then they would be less beautiful and past the age for play. The goings-on in the Indian bungalows were another story. Indians hardly ever drank, and they didn't seem to play so much with one another's wives or with boys either. But there was a tremendous amount of fighting between old women and their daughters-in-law. In the Indian bungalows, that was where the excitement was.

Often Marietta and Violet had so much news to digest that their heads ached. They couldn't possibly have room for any more. Runga was world enough for them. On the other hand, Violet was beginning to have breasts (only nipples so far, actually) and both of them were starting to think about their appearance. When the dry season came that year, they rubbed their legs and arms assiduously with Vaseline to stop the skin from flaking and to make it shine. Violet's skin shone beautifully. Marietta's just felt sticky and attracted dust. And they began to feel a bit self-conscious, too, about the dresses that came as hand-me-downs from the daughters of the woman who lived next door to the Dawsons in Katari, or sometimes from the second-hand clothes seller in the Runga market. Mightn't a wider life mean smarter clothes?

In the compound of the Ismaili mosque across the road from the rest house was H.R.H. Aga Khan Primary School. Four times a day Indian boys and girls passed through the high stucco archway. They wore gray trousers and skirts and neat white shirts with badges appliquéd over their hearts. Violet and Marietta took to positioning themselves in the drainage ditch opposite. They were charmed by the way the girls' pleated skirts swung, and especially by their shiny patent leather shoes.

Once at midday, when Virginia dashed out into the road to supervise the unloading of seventy-five crates of beer that had come two weeks late, she noticed her daughter sitting with her dress up and her underpants clearly displayed (Violet's legs were together and discreetly covered with her skirt). Marietta's hair was tangled from playing in the guest house shrubbery (Violet's head was shaved). "Whatever are you doing there?" Virginia cried. "Heaven knows what's in that ditch! Indescribable things!"

20

Marietta scrambled up. "They wear shiny shoes," she said, in explanation. "Couldn't I have a pair, Mum? They sell them on Lugard Road."

"And where would you wear them?"

"Couldn't Violet and I go to that school, too?"

In the November heat Virginia mopped her forehead. "Those children are Indians," she said, frowning. "You can't go to their school. Europeans go to European schools, Africans to African schools, Indians to Indian schools. That's the way it is."

Marietta got her patent leather shoes, and wore them twice, at Christmas and on New Year's Eve, but the question of school supplanting the correspondence course, and leading, possibly, to a wider life, was dropped until Neville brought it up again.

2

Itep

Neville passed through Runga on his way south to Kungwe in search of very special butterflies. He'd be staying only one night, he said. He had to get on to Kungwe before the butterflies emerged from their chrysalises and flew away. This was due to happen any day soon. Neville had a long, lean, elegant face. When she looked into the bar, Marietta noticed him listening to her mother. This was unusual. Men usually talked while Virginia listened. Neville stayed two nights that time, after all.

Marietta was building a house of cards on the reception desk when Neville got back from Kungwe. He said, "How many cards have you used so far?"

"Thirty-two."

"Have you ever used the lot?"

"No. Have you?"

"Only once. Then someone opened the door of the room I was in and the whole house came down. I've tried many times to repeat that feat, but I've never managed to."

Virginia came into the entrance hall. She was wearing a frilly white blouse and a sweeping orange skirt. Marietta saw that her toenails were shiny pink. "You came back exactly when you said you would," Virginia said, laughing. "How was your safari?"

"The road was appalling but I got down in time. The chrysalises opened before my very eyes!"

"How long can you stay?"

"That depends," Neville said, laughing back at Virginia over Marietta's head.

The next morning Marietta and Violet were on the veranda playing hopscotch. Neville strolled over and leaned against a pillar, hands in his pockets. He had all the time in the world, it seemed, to watch the children play. Balancing on one foot in the last square, Marietta leaned over to pick up her pebble. She felt Neville's eyes on her back, wobbled, and lost her balance. "Hell!" she exclaimed. "Violet, you won."

"Let's play again."

"No, you always win. Let's do something different," Marietta said crossly in Ruba, and turned away.

"Would you like to see what I got at Kungwe?" Neville said.

Reluctantly Marietta looked up at him. Having to be polite to the guests was a nuisance, by and large. "Well, what *did* you get?"

"Butterflies."

"We don't know much about them."

"I could teach you, if you like."

Marietta glanced at Violet and Violet nodded. So they went with Neville to his room, which was the biggest in the rest house. Virginia called it the bridal suite, though it was just one room, and you had to share a bath. And honeymooners didn't come to Runga ever, though twice men had come with women they'd run off with (Justin said they'd eloped) and Virginia had put them in the bridal suite. Now she'd given it to Neville. There was a huge bed, a couch, and a large table with carved legs by the window. Neville had laid his boxes out on the table.

"Come on, I'll show you," he said, and opened the first box. "We'll have to be careful not to damage the wings. We could easily knock the colors off. But you can use the magnifying glass if you want to see up close."

"Is this how you earn your living?" Marietta asked. "Catching butterflies?"

"Not exactly. It's my hobby. I've collected them for years and years. Since I was younger than you."

"You don't know how old I am."

"Won't you tell me?"

"Guess."

"Well . . ." Neville's eyes narrowed. "I'd say you were eight."

"And what about Violet?"

"She's about eight, too."

"She's not. She's twelve. And I'm ten. You're a pretty bad guesser. Haven't you got children of your own?"

"Unfortunately, no."

"Have you got a wife?"

"I did once; not now, though."

"Have you got a dog?"

"No."

"Who d'you live with, then?"

"By myself."

"Aren't you lonely?"

"I am quite often."

Marietta turned back to the table. "What will you do with these once you get home?"

Just before tea that afternoon Marietta noticed her mother coming out of the bridal suite. "Did he ask you in to see his butterflies?" Marietta called down the veranda. "Didn't you like the huge purple one?"

"Purple? I didn't see it."

"But it's the biggest one of all! You were in there long enough, Mum. You went in at two and now it's half past four. You must be blind!"

Virginia liked short friendships. She didn't care for long, drawn-out affairs involving claims and obligations, and so although she generally had someone, no one ever lasted. Marietta, who was used to her mother's friends coming and then going, expected Neville, too, to fade away. But a month later he was back, and again three weeks after that. He liked Virginia very much, obviously, and seemed to like her daughter as well. He brought Marietta dolls from Nairobi (she considered herself too old for them) and a pullover with a cable pattern up the front. This he brought to Runga on the lake shore, where the temperature hovered between 90° and 110°. Neville was no fool, though. He beat Marietta at Scrabble, and Marietta had a vocabulary like no ten-year-old ever had, at least no ten-year-old in Runga. He also knew a great deal about lake birds, more than Marietta and Violet combined, and they'd lived all their lives beside lakes while Neville lived nine thousand feet up on a mountain in Kenya, where the birds were totally different. He certainly must have known that you didn't need a sweater in a place like Runga. So Marietta was suspicious.

24

At Easter Neville invited Virginia to his farm. "By the way, Marietta, I hope you'll come along as well."

"He really wants you," Virginia echoed.

"I really do. You will come, won't you?" Neville added to Marietta, who was building a house of cards with a new green pack Neville had given her.

"I don't know that I can," Marietta answered. Her face got hot suddenly and her house collapsed. Her mother's boyfriends never included her. She wasn't at all sure she *wanted* to be included.

"What's stopping you? You don't have school to go to."

"I'll get carsick," Marietta said desperately.

"Do you usually?"

"She never does," Virginia said.

"Then of course you'll come," Neville said, smiling, and that was that.

It turned out that Neville was Sir Neville Bilton, third baronet. He'd been christened not just Neville but St. John Robert as well, and he lived in a castle called Itep that he'd built for himself on the farm his father had left him on the slopes of Mount Elgon. Once, before the top blew off in one last apocalyptic eruption, it had been the highest mountain in Africa. It was still the longest and the widest and you got your first glimpse of it when you were more than a hundred miles away. It straddled the Kenya-Uganda border, dividing the rich wheatlands of Kitale from the banana plantations of Buganda. The summit, in the coldest part of the rainy season, was dusted with snow, and at those times the massive giant briefly challenged the majesty of Mount Kenya, across the Great Rift Valley to the east. Its dense forests were home to abundant elephant and leopard and more species of birds and reptiles than anywhere else on the continent. But at eleven thousand feet the forest abruptly halted and then came the tufted grasslands, dotted with giant lobelia, stretching upwards to the crater. Elgon was a true mountain of Africa, held in awe by the people and central to their myths. It wasn't fashionable, though, like Kenya or Kilimanjaro. It didn't feature in the fables of the white man, didn't seem to warrant literary attention. But it had caught the attention of Neville's father and continued to hold Neville's.

His castle was square and gray, with a castellated parapet. The windows were tall and thin, like Neville, and the front door was set into an arch with houndstooth carving round it. In the large, terraced garden there was a tower that Neville used as a study. He had a telescope on the roof, which you reached by a steep flight of outside stairs. From there on clear nights he studied the universe.

His parents' house hadn't suited him, Neville explained as they passed it, squat and whitewashed, to the right of the farm road.

"Whyever not?" Marietta wanted to know. "It's so cozy looking."

"I had elaborate ideas when I was young," Neville said, laughing.

"Are you old now?"

"Getting on." He was going to be forty-three next birthday, he said.

"What happened to your ideas?"

"They took a beating."

This was true. One summer his wife, Clarissa, had gone to France ahead of him. He'd had a lot to see to on the farm. When he joined her in Paris in mid-June, she told him she'd fallen in love with an Argentinian Grand Prix driver. Arturo lived by his wits, Clarissa said, and by verve and courage, not on his inheritance, the way Neville did and his father had before him. Neville's grandfather, Sir Samuel, had been an engineer, a nineteenth-century empire builder. He'd constructed docks and dams and bridges from Uruguay to Singapore, his pièce de résistance being the dam at Aswan on the Nile, which, unfortunately, had sprung a leak. For this he had been personally liable to the tune of two million pounds, but even so he'd made a fortune that relieved his descendants of the mundane need to earn a living. There was more to life than mere necessity, Sir George had believed, and so did Neville. Absolved from drudgery, father and son had turned their energies to farming the Kenya Highlands and to the pursuit of wildlife — bongo and roan antelope in Sir George's case, butterflies and birds in Neville's.

It had emerged rather late in the game that Neville's wife considered such activities mere pastimes, without significance or depth. Neville was only a gentleman; Arturo, a hero. So off she'd gone with her hero, and even though Arturo left her the following winter for a petroleum heiress, Clarissa had refused to come back. Instead she went alone to California. From there she wrote to Neville: "When you married me no doubt you hoped you'd found somebody so totally unaware of what she was or what she wanted that you'd be able to shape and mold her into whatever suited *you*.

26

Well, you were wrong, Neville. Young and ignorant as I was, I already knew I could never be interested in the Tanganyikan tiger moth or Romanesque architecture or any of your make-believe. For your sake I pretended I was. For seven years I kept up that pretense. But reality is what interested me, and for all your determination, you weren't able to change that."

Now Clarissa was experiencing reality in Cuernavaca; last year she'd been on the North Beach in San Francisco, and next year who knew where she'd be — but always at Neville's expense. Actually her alimony payments, as she reminded Neville often in her sprawling handwriting, came from far-sighted investments by his grandfather. Strictly speaking, therefore, she owed her liberation to Sir Samuel rather than to Neville.

Is that truly what he'd wanted, Neville had wondered, someone to mold and shape? He'd thought all along that he'd been sharing his interests with Clarissa because he loved her and she loved him. But supposing, setting her venom aside, Clarissa had been right and he really *didn't* know what life was about. Was it too late to learn?

For a year or two he'd looked for someone to learn from. Though all the women he met came in different guises, underneath they were more or less the same. Self-protective, unadventurous. All, that is, except Virginia. Virginia wasn't impressed by his title. It didn't matter to her that he was rich. She made her own way with style and zest. Even after close inspection, Virginia wasn't a bit like Neville.

Very early on the third day of their visit to Itep, Neville banged on Marietta's door. "Up you get, and bring that sweater I bought you. We're going to find those birds I've been telling you about."

In the forest it was dank and dark and the mist clung to the trees. They went some distance in the Land-Rover and then they left it and walked. At a slippery patch in the path, Neville took Marietta's hand, pulling her up after him. On firm ground again, Marietta tried to disengage herself. She felt his signet ring pressing into her fingers. She pulled, he resisted. She was caught. "I want to go back," she said.

"But we haven't seen anything yet, not one single bird."

"I don't care. I don't like it here. I'm scared."

"There's nothing to be scared of. I'm here. I'll take care of you."

*

27

At lunch on Easter Sunday, at the great dining room table, with the three of them all at one end, Neville said, "It'll be lovely for me having you and your mother here."

"We're moving up here," Marietta exclaimed, "and leaving Runga?"

"That's right."

"Are you going to run a rest house in this place?" Marietta turned to her mother.

"Oh, Etta," Virginia laughed, "of course I shan't. This is Neville's house. It isn't a hotel."

"What'll you do, then?"

"I'm sure I'll find plenty to do."

"Really," Marietta said.

"Things'll be a bit different from Runga, I admit," Neville said quickly. "More exciting."

"I never said Runga was dull! I *like* living in Runga," Marietta said. "Last night I saw bats here. There was one in the library flapping around. I'd rather stay in Runga, thanks."

"What Neville didn't tell you, Etta," Virginia said hurriedly, "is that he and I are getting married and that's why we're coming up here to live."

"Married!" Marietta choked on her rhubarb tart. She sprang up, head bent, napkin to her mouth. Neville rushed round to thump her on the back. Scarlet, she glared at her mother. "You don't *believe* in marriage! That's what you told *me!*"

"She told me the very same thing," Neville said, smiling. "But I'm pretty determined when it comes to arguing and I managed to change her mind."

Marietta frowned in disbelief. "How?"

"If we both sit down, I'll tell you."

"Oh, Neville, don't," Virginia said. "She's just asking for asking's sake. Etta, love, I hadn't met Neville when I said that, had I? You've got to expect people to contradict themselves sometimes."

Marietta pulled her chair up and sat down again. She pushed her dessert plate away and folded her napkin and laid it carefully beside her water glass. "All right, tell me how you changed my mother's mind."

"I told her I was on the lookout for someone quite extraordinary," Neville said. "But extraordinary women are very few and far between. Furthermore, they tend to come with children who, although they may eventually turn out to be extraordinary too, are at present obnoxious, spoiled, self-centered, absolutely set on having their own way."

"I am too, mostly," Marietta said.

"So I've gathered," Neville said, "but the difference between the rest I've met and you is that whereas their way and mine are diametrically opposed, you and I seem to have a fair amount in common."

"What, for instance?"

"You're always wanting to know, for instance. I like that. I've a sense we'll get along just fine."

"And that's why you and Mum are getting married?"

"That's part of it. Of course, your mother has her own very definite attractions. I told her all about those, too."

After a pause Neville asked, "Are you in the least bit pleased?"

"I'm used to there being four of us, not five," Marietta replied, head down.

"Four?"

"She means her and me," said Virginia, "and our houseboy and his daughter."

"If they don't move up here, I shan't either," Marietta said fiercely.

Neville raised one eyebrow. "In this big place, don't you think we could find room for them as well?"

"If so, it might turn out okay."

"It?" Neville said.

"Things. You and Mum and me."

Virginia said, "That's extremely enthusiastic, I must say!"

Neville grinned. "Well, she hasn't turned me down flat, has she? I've got one foot in the door. Now it's up to me to show her that it's worth her while to let me the whole way in."

Neville and Virginia decided to keep the wedding private. Later they'd give themselves a proper party up in Nairobi, or maybe Daphne would give a reception with a cake and champagne and dancing and pâté de foie gras at Katari and all their friends could come and behave as disgracefully as they wished. But for now, they both wanted to have getting married over with. The ceremony was performed ten days after Easter by the Runga district commissioner with two ADCs as witnesses and Marietta, Justin, Violet, and the Wiltons, who'd come down again from Arusha to fill in temporarily, as the only invited guests. A great many Africans were hanging in through the windows and stepping on one another's toes at the door that one of the ADCs was trying in vain to keep shut.

Virginia had on a new dress, run up by the wife of the Ismaili garage owner down the road. It was magenta crêpe de chine and in Marietta's opinion showed too much of her breasts. Marietta had chosen a gray pleated skirt that swung as she walked and a crisp white blouse to go with her patent leather shoes. Not too weddingish, Virginia had said doubtfully, but since for many months this outfit had been her daughter's heart's desire, she'd given in. Marietta picked a bunch of zinnias from the front border and took them with her to the DC's office. In the rush Virginia had forgotten about flowers. But then, she has even more to think about than usual, Marietta reminded herself, what with packing up and moving, too, as well as getting married.

In the days before the wedding, several times Virginia had said breathlessly, "You do *like* Neville, don't you, Etta?" and somehow disappeared before Marietta could reply.

But once, before her mother vanished, Marietta had had time to answer, "I'll have to see."

"You hold your cards close, I must say," Virginia said.

Marietta replied, "It's because I haven't decided."

She thought several things about Neville, as a matter of fact. She found his hands fascinating. Especially his fingers. He seemed to treasure whatever he touched. He must learn more than other people do from touching, Marietta thought. Though he was extremely purposeful, he wasn't in an endless hurry like her mother. Indeed, he seemed to be encouraging one to interrupt his train of thought; it was as if a diversion might even add to whatever he was thinking about. He smoked, but only a little, and hadn't any tummy, and though he sat up late in the bar with the paunchy, chain-smoking Runga regulars, he only got slightly red in the face and never drunk. But the most remarkable thing about Neville was that despite having so many interests and being about to marry her mother, he still had room for Marietta. This marvelous and terrible fact she found profoundly confusing. And of course she couldn't possibly tell Virginia that.

On the ride over from the rest house, Neville had said, "You're going to be the bridesmaid, the best man, *and* the father of the bride. You're giving your mother away, you know. We can't ask Dick Wilton because he's deaf and he wouldn't hear when the DC says, 'Who giveth this woman.' Hold onto this, will you," and he'd handed Marietta the wedding ring. "I'll let you know when I need it back."

Before the ceremony, Neville chatted calmly with the DC. They'd gone to the same English public school, though they hadn't over-lapped, and they both remembered the cricket coach with great affection. Then suddenly the DC cleared his throat and smiled and launched the proceedings, which joined Neville and Virginia in the eyes of God, the Queen, and H.E. the Governor of Tanganyika Territory. After champagne and *talapia* with a white sauce and trifle on the rest house veranda, they changed out of their wedding clothes, shook hands with everyone from the cook to the assistant *shamba* boy, climbed into Neville's Land-Rover, and set off.

They spent one night in the new Victoria Hotel in Kisumu with Virginia and Neville officially in the same room for the first time and Marietta down the corridor alone (Violet was in the boys' quarters with her father: she wasn't allowed to share Marietta's hotel room because she was black), and then they went on again, up the escarpment. They stopped once, for coffee and a pee at a shabby place in Baluga called the Wayfarer Hotel. The lobby floor was caked with dirt, the ashtrays were heaped with cigarette butts, the potted plants on either side of the front door were bone dry. Five of the eight wall fixtures lacked light bulbs.

"No wonder!" said Virginia, one eyebrow raised, as she spotted the manager drinking gin at twenty to eleven in the morning. There was lipstick on her coffee cup and on Neville's as well. They had to send them back. "This place'll collapse if something isn't done very soon. I wonder who owns it."

She stopped to ask the Indian clerk behind the desk. Mr. Muir, the man told her. From Mombasa. He had other properties. This was only one of many. "Looks like he's giving up on this one, then," Virginia said to Neville in disgust. "No soap in the W.C., and the toilet seat was broken. Quite apart from the lipstick on the cups."

After Baluga they passed through Eldoret and Kitale, and eventually, when the sun had set, they arrived at Itep to begin their new life.

*

Virginia was amused by all the grandeur. "It's like playing kings and queens," she said to Marietta. Justin wasn't amused, though. He had to fit in with Festus and Owangi, Neville's butler and cook, both of whom were Luos, and Ruba and Luo people had been enemies ever since the Ruba migration across the lake from Uganda in the eighteenth century. Justin wasn't about to change that state of affairs.

To Marietta, Itep was a place of enchantment. The games she and Violet played changed overnight from cattle raids and border wars to the Knights of the Round Table. Violet was skeptical. "If you don't want to be Sir Galahad, I'll be him and you be Guinevere," Marietta told her, but Violet didn't like the idea of Guinevere much either. She conceded, however, because the only other children at Itep were Luos and she didn't like Luos any better than her father did.

Although Neville was impressed by what Marietta had managed to get out of Dr. Vorster's correspondence course ("And Violet, too," Marietta reminded him — "I didn't do it alone, you know"), he saw that she'd missed a lot. Something fairly drastic should be done.

"Hold on," Virginia told him. "She's led a quiet life up till now. First let her get used to living in a proper house and sleeping under blankets with no mosquito net."

But Neville started writing for advice to those friends of his who had daughters, and sending off to schools, both in Kenya and abroad. Before too long, prospectuses began arriving by almost every mail. Some had pictures on their covers of Georgian or Tudor mansions. One had a photograph of a castle rather like Itep. That school was in Gloucestershire. There was a chateau, too, on Lake Geneva.

"They're too grand for my girl," Virginia said, "not to mention the expense. Where would I find that kind of money?"

"We can afford it," Neville said. "Marietta's the only daughter I expect to have."

Virginia had told Neville that she didn't intend to be a mother again. "It was difficult enough in my twenties," she'd said, "and that wasn't just due to poverty and widowhood. I wasn't cut out for it, d'you know what I mean?" They'd been in Runga in bed in the bridal suite after lunch on a Sunday at the time.

"You underrate your talents, Virginia. Marietta's quite a delightful child."

"Not much credit's due to me, though," Virginia had replied. "It's due to luck and Justin. Believe me, Neville, I know where my true talents lie."

Virginia wouldn't consider schools in Europe anyway. "Too far," she said. And she didn't care for the local ones much better. "Settler kids are even worse snobs than the kids in England."

"Marietta's too intelligent to be affected by a lot of little girls putting on airs," Neville said.

"Who are we to say she wouldn't be affected? After all the running about she's done with who knows what and hardly any of them white, in self-defense she could turn into the worst snob of the lot. Don't rush her, Neville. Let her go on with Dr. Vorster for a bit. There'll be plenty of time for your plans."

The people who farmed in the valley below Itep were terribly fond of Neville. Such a sweet man, they said in the Kitale Club. So why had he gone for Clarissa, who wasn't sweet at all, and far too pretty for her own good? Barbara Baker-Lyle, who remembered Virginia from a party at Daphne Dawson's, remarked, "By the way, this one's a smasher, too. Lovely skin. Then, what else would one expect of Neville? You know she's Harold Parkson's daughter? He came out after the First War and farmed near Rumuruti. Now *that* was a strange fellow for you! You could scarcely get the time of day out of Harold. Gave the distinct impression that he couldn't stand the sight of people, but of course up where he lived there weren't any. No whites, at least. Haven't thought about him in years. And Sylvia. Do you remember her, poor thing! Dragged out from London to the bush by Harold and marooned there. A pretty little woman, the type who's terrified of insects. Utterly unsuited to that kind of life. They're both long dead, of course." And what about Virginia? "Clearly very much alive! Had a rotten marriage and a little girl. Neville met her living by her wits in Tanganyika. Should be a sensible sort. Let's hope he has better luck with her than with the last one."

They couldn't wait to meet her but they were in the middle of long rains and it was difficult to get about, with the roads a sea of mud. For July, when things would dry up, the Nortons and the Bellevilles were planning dinner parties and the Hunts would have a dance for Neville and his bride.

Meanwhile, though, Neville's bride was having a change of

heart. Ever since the death of Charles Hamilton, Virginia had had a horror of intruders. For all her charm and gaiety, she had carefully erected barricades. Any man who took her vivacity as something more than a willingness to pass a short time pleasurably in his company had been confronted by a dense, intractable reserve. But Neville had come repeatedly to Runga, undaunted by her determination to keep herself to herself. She discovered he could guard her sleep. He could hold her terrors at bay.

And so he'd managed to persuade her that she wanted — and perhaps, after all her wanderings, deserved — to be treated well. It took marrying and moving lock, stock, and barrel to Itep for her to realize that the leopard hadn't changed her spots. Gentle Neville would asphyxiate her! She recognized the signs of her discontent, and they grew stronger day by day. She found she couldn't listen to her husband, so she'd watch his face and the way his mouth moved, hoping to decipher whatever it was he was telling her. But her inattention was intense. She simply didn't comprehend. The castle, which at first she'd found fanciful and charming, the archways, the massive furniture, the landscapes of the Norwich school on the master bedroom walls, were suddenly laughable. And her response to Neville's careful kindnesses and to his touch was visceral. In Runga she'd slept beside him. Now she lay awake.

Two months after the wedding Marietta found her mother in the library. Virginia was at the window with a view of the Cherangani Hills, fifty miles away, listening to the gramophone. When the record finished she turned to Marietta and laughed. "D'you see those hills, Etta? Aren't they beautiful? I'm so longing to explore them. Do let's go there soon, you and I!"

"Will Neville come as well?" Marietta said.

"D'you really think he'd want to?" Virginia frowned. "They're old hat to him, those hills. He's been looking at them since he was a boy."

"Still, he might want to come. I could ask him."

"It was only a passing idea." Virginia sighed as she put the record on again. "Don't bother about it."

But Marietta did bother, because she sensed from the slope of Virginia's shoulders that Neville didn't suit and that they'd be going somewhere else without him before long.

When Neville saw that he was losing Virginia, had already lost her, a familiar panic rose in him. But then he discovered to his great relief that the pain did not demolish him. He'd learned a little from Clarissa, after all, if not to stay away entirely from women who rejected the safe harbor that he offered them. But Virginia hadn't fled as yet, only set herself apart. She'd take a little time deciding where to jump and how. Meanwhile, she'd pay her dues by getting Neville's castle into tiptop shape.

So the months in which their marriage was petering out Virginia spent with carpenters and electricians and dashing down to Kisumu to see Ranjit Singh about replacements for the drawing room sofas. Mr. Singh promised them as soon as possible, but the materials, he pointed out, were not easily come by during the Emergency. Horsehair stuffing was an import of low priority while the war was on. Nevertheless, Virginia made headway. Walls were replastered, woodwork washed and varnished, plumbing fixed, and all the cushions on the library window seats re-covered. Once the inside had been seen to, more or less, Virginia went outside to the flower beds. She was busy all day long.

As his pain at his wife's disaffection eased, Neville turned his attention to her daughter. Marietta was delighted by his company, and he with hers. At first Violet was included. They all three spent long evenings in Neville's observatory, looking at the stars. He took the children through the universe, teaching them the names of the constellations, first in English, then in Latin.

"You won't remember," he said, "but they are lovely to the ear, I think."

"I shan't forget them," Marietta said, and with very few exceptions, she never did.

But gradually Violet was included less. After dinner Marietta found herself forgetting to go round to the boys' quarters to find her friend. "I saw you," Violet would say, deeply hurt, "climbing those steps. I called to you. You heard but you pretended not to. You didn't want me with you, did you? Don't you lie!" And later, as Neville's days were less encumbered with the farm, Violet would slide barefoot into Marietta's room, where she was brushing her hair before dinner.

"You left," Violet would accuse Marietta. "You did not tell me you were going. And you were away all day, forgetting me."

"We were fishing," Marietta would reply, guiltily. "At Igop. You don't like fishing, now do you?"

"I don't like to sit alone. How is it, Mari, that these days you forget your friend?"

"Fishing wearies you."

35

"Being by myself wearies me! But you don't care about that. Now you are only thinking about Bilton!"

Neville and Marietta would drive off early in the morning to where the river rushed out of the forest over sharp stones and into a deep green pool; it swirled and spun there, preparing to hurtle on again, down the mountain. They would boil water for tea on a headland jutting out above the river. Then they'd settle for the morning. Marietta had learned to fish from Peter Dawson long ago, below the Izaak Walton on the Fort Hare road. She'd caught perch mostly then. At Igop with Neville, she caught trout. At midday, they'd slit and clean and broil and eat them, with bread and plums from home, under an acacia tree, drooping long, brown pods. Then they'd listen to the crickets in the hot grass, and sleep a little, and wake and talk again and fish again until it was time to pack up and go.

At home they'd find Virginia on the terrace, her face streaked with earth and perspiration in the evening sun. She was making a rock garden in a difficult spot at the corner. The flowers would be all white and purple. "You do like purple, don't you?" she'd say to Neville. "Or would you prefer blue?" When that was done, she planned to start on the roses. They'd been neglected since Clarissa left. The *shamba* boy was useless if you didn't watch him, and Neville hadn't. There was so much work to do. But she was making headway, and by Christmas, perhaps, she'd be finished.

She rarely had the time or the inclination to go into town, so Neville and Marietta would drive the twenty miles down the mountain without her. On the way Neville often talked about England. Virginia had told Marietta that people in England spent their whole lives doing things the way they'd always been done and never considering any alternative. "And that's not much better than being dead. Three months of it every ten years is quite enough for me!"

But evidently Neville liked England better than Virginia did. His mother lived in London in a tall, thin house overlooking a square that was full of lilac and syringa in the springtime. Marietta had never seen lilac. "You will soon," Neville said. His mother lived with a housekeeper called Curtis. "Curtis can be ferocious," Neville said. "She once surprised a burglar in the middle of the night. He was twice as tall as she, and carried a leather cosh; he was poised to batter her brains out. 'Give me that instrument,' she said with a withering look, and he did, like a lamb; and having lectured him about the need to earn a living honorably, she opened the front door and sent him out into the square, into the arms of a policeman.

"Unfortunately," Neville went on, "Curtis doesn't approve of me. She thinks an Englishman should live in England, not at the end of the earth. I tell her, 'When I'm ready to, I shall.' But that doesn't satisfy her. 'You'll never be ready,' she says, and she could be right. I was thinking, you should go instead of me, Marietta. Curtis would approve of you."

"But I'm not English, really."

"Don't worry," Neville said, "you're English enough. Curtis will take you to all the parks. Once a fortnight she feeds every mallard in London. My mother doesn't care for ducks, so Curtis has to go alone. She'd enjoy having someone to go with her."

"What else do people do in England?"

"So much!" Neville cried, swinging past a flock of sheep. "There's so much to look at and hear and read; then, when you can't take any more excitement, and you're completely full, you come back again to Africa to sort it out. If you lived there all the time, you wouldn't have the chance to digest what you'd seen. It'll soon be time for you to go there; we'll both go."

"I wouldn't want to stay there. I might, of course, once I've been there, but I can't tell that ahead of time."

"At first, we'll go just to have a look."

"Shall we stay with Curtis and your mother?"

"No, we'd get in their way. They have a schedule, a set routine. They get quite cross if they're off a little. We'd better take a flat and have dinner with my mother now and then."

"What's she like, your mother?"

"She has bright green eyes."

"Like yours?"

"Brighter."

"Is she like you in other ways?"

"What am I like?"

"Comfortable," Marietta said, after a moment. "Is she?"

"I didn't always find her so. One's mother sometimes isn't, even though she might well be with other people. She expected a lot, as I remember, and didn't care for one's making a fuss." He laughed. "But I was her son! She might be quite different with you. Grandmothers can afford to spoil one. Mothers generally can't."

"Would she be my grandmother?"

"What else?"

They were down from the mountain now, driving between fields of young green wheat. "When we've seen London, then where shall we go?"

"Wales," Neville said. "You've got to see the border castles. Ludlow, Chirk, Chepstow. You do like castles, don't you?"

"I like yours. That's the first I've seen, except in pictures."

"They aren't so common in Africa," Neville said, nodding, "but in Europe you find them everywhere. There are some exceptional ones in Ireland. We'll go there as well, and then we'll go to France. My favorite's in Languedoc. Itep's a copy of it. Not exactly stone by stone, and it's less than half the size of the original, but it's what I had in mind."

"And after France?"

"I think we'd better come back here and take a rest."

"When shall we go?"

"One of these years. But this year we'll spend Christmas at Kilifi. We'll go out to the reef in a glass-bottom boat to watch the fish, not to catch them." There were several volumes on the marine life of the Kenya Coast in the library. They'd have plenty of time to look through them before Christmas. "The fish on the reef are indescribable," Neville said. "You've never seen them?"

"No. Then, according to you, I haven't seen anything. You're wrong, though," Marietta added, "you'd be surprised what I've seen!"

Neville smiled ruefully. "I'm always telling you this and that, throwing my weight about. I do apologize."

"You don't have to," Marietta said.

After they'd checked the mail and been to the bank and Jiwa Shamji's grocery store with the list Virginia had given them, they went to the Kitale Club for lunch. People greeted Neville as he walked in with Marietta at his side.

"How are you? And where's Virginia?" said Colonel Baker-Lyle. "We hardly ever see her. Just you and the little girl. She's too thin, Neville." Colonel Baker-Lyle nodded at Marietta. "I hope you'll fatten her up."

"I do my best," Neville replied, knowing perfectly well that Marietta consumed enormous quantities of food at every meal with no

38

observable effect on her appearance. Anyway, he liked her appearance, her narrow shoulders and her knees, habitually bruised from climbing and falling out of trees with Violet, on whom, being black, bruises didn't show. He liked the way she looked in the sweater he'd brought to her in Runga with the chill of Mount Elgon in mind, attacking with gusto her filet of Thomson's gazelle in the dining room of the Kitale Club. He imagined Christmas at Kilifi, and what she might say when she saw the crown jewels in the Tower of London or the view from Ludlow into Wales, in June, when roses ran riot in the keeper's garden.

But they weren't together at Christmas. They never went to Ludlow either, or even to the Tower. One evening, when she was kissing Marietta good-night, Virginia said, "Tomorrow you will have to be up early. We're going down to Daphne's and I doubt we'll be coming back. Neville and I aren't going to live together anymore."

"Why not?"

"Because we don't like each other as much as we once thought we did, at Runga." Virginia read from a script, one she'd rehearsed but not well enough, and her delivery was very poor indeed. She looked down at Marietta, sheets pulled to the chin. "I'm sorry, I honestly am," Virginia said bleakly.

"I like him, though," Marietta burst out, "ten times more than I did at Runga. Can't we stay?"

"No, we can't. It was a mistake coming here. You can't keep on with it once you realize something's a mistake."

Turning on her stomach, Marietta covered her head with her pillow. Through it she shouted, "Why do you always spoil things? You go if you like. I'm staying."

Justin loaded the Land-Rover before sunrise: three suitcases of Virginia's, a trunk and a canvas bag with Marietta's clothes, and the dolls and books Neville had given her. Then he threw in his and Violet's cardboard boxes tied with string. Last, he heaved a sack of maize onto the tailgate, pushed it into the vehicle, and closed up the back.

Neville stood in the doorway, hands in the pockets of his dressing gown, watching. Virginia kissed him on the cheek. "Sorry, old fellow. You're better off without me. You'll see. You know how to reach me, don't you? Marietta," Virginia called, "time to go."

Where *was* Marietta? Violet, hovering at the bottom of the steps, hung her head. Virginia pounced on her. "*You* must know. She's hiding somewhere."

They searched through all the rooms of the house and, in the dawn, through the garden. In the end Neville found Marietta among his London suits in the hanging closet in his dressing room. Knees pulled up to her chin, her back to the door, she huddled there defiantly. Neville stepped into the closet and squatted down beside her. He patted her shoulder.

"You're always welcome here, you know. I hope you'll come to see me sometimes. Up you get," he said gruffly. "They're waiting for you. You've got a long drive ahead of you."

"I'm not going." Marietta pulled away. "Tell the others for me, please."

They heard Virginia on the stairs. "Neville, where are you?" She sounded frightened. "She's not in the the garden." They heard her crossing the room beyond. She pushed open the dressing room door. "Etta, you scared me half to death!"

She came in amongst the suits, squatting beside Neville, all three of them huddled on top of shoes and boots and boxes on the floor of the closet, which smelled of moth balls and damp. Virginia's voice softened. "I should have planned this better. I have to go and I can't leave you here. You're my daughter, not Neville's. You belong with me. Besides," she said in a burst, as if she'd only just thought of it, "how would your old mum manage alone?" She took Marietta's hand. "Let's go. Violet's in the Land-Rover already."

The sun rose over the Cherangani Hills as they passed through the gate at the bottom of Neville's land, and Marietta, on the back seat with Violet, heard her mother start to hum. Virginia swung the Land-Rover into the road, heading east and away. "We never did get to those hills, did we? Never mind. There are others just as beautiful. We'll explore *them* instead."

As they bumped and skidded past country people carrying their headloads to the Friday market at Endebess, Virginia turned in her seat to smile at Marietta. "Better now, my poor girl? Won't it be fun to see Daphne? We've got so much to tell her, haven't we?"

Virginia and her little party pulled up in Katari after dark. The Dawsons' butler told them that the bwana was away on safari but the memsahb was at home, entertaining a house guest; he showed Virginia and Marietta into the drawing room, then disappeared.

There was a shriek, and Marietta, bone-weary from jolting down the interminable road from Kitale, glimpsed a pink figure flying along the gallery. Daphne, in a fuchsia negligee, swept past the mounted rhino and impala on the stairs and leapt into Virginia's arms.

"Darling!" she cried. "You took me completely by surprise!"

Indeed, it appeared to Marietta, perched on the edge of an over-stuffed chair, that Daphne's dark hair had not been brushed in a very long time and that she was naked under her negligee.

"This is a dreadful hour to arrive," Virginia apologized. "I tried to ring you from the Red Lion in Eldonia, but I couldn't get through."

"There's nothing dreadful about it. Peter's not here, though. He'll be sad to have missed you. He set off on Sunday with a pal. They'll be gone three weeks. Could you stay till he gets back? I'd love to have you keep me company."

"My dear, you don't look as if you *need* my company," Virginia said.

Daphne attempted to smooth down her curly black hair and grinned. "You have sharp eyes, Virginia. Well, it's Dick Muir, actually. You might know him."

"I've heard of him. Doesn't he own hotels?"

"Yes. I thought you must've run across him in your working days. Doesn't everyone in that business know everyone else?"

"The proprietors do. I was merely a manager, a dog's body."

"Come on, Virginia, you loved it! I remember that time we stayed with you at Runga. You absolutely raced about. Watching you I felt quite useless, and green with envy that you were enjoying yourself so much! Don't you miss work sometimes? By the way, where's Neville? Did you drop him off in town?"

"We came without Neville," Virginia said quietly. "I've left him."

"You've *what*?" Daphne clutched the mantelpiece. "My God, what did he do, bugger you?" She clapped her hand to her mouth. "Oh, Lord, not in front of the child."

Marietta went to the lavatory, where the toilet was ornately carved like a throne. She returned to find Daphne's friend, Mr. Muir, fully dressed in front of the fireplace. As she ate the cold ham and bread and butter that the cook had brought in on a tray, Mr. Muir held forth. He was tall and bony, with a high, bridged nose, and he wore a silk cravat. Maybe if he unwound the cravat his head would fall off. Marietta wished Peter Dawson were at home. Peter was her godfather, though she'd hardly ever been inside a church (but then again, neither had he). Between her visits he made collections for her, of things like wart hog tusks, which he presented to her on arrival. He'd also taught her how to ride years ago, when her mother had been out of a job and they'd stayed with the Dawsons for two months. Peter had a harelip that hadn't been repaired as well as it should have been. Perhaps that was why he was shy and why he loved Aunt Daphne so desperately, however badly she behaved, and why he was so kind to Marietta.

She didn't see Peter at all on that visit because by the time he came back from the Northern Frontier District she and her mother and Justin and Violet had already moved on. Having made the move north, Virginia decided to stay in Kenya, married or not; she'd had enough of Tanganyikan lake towns. She wasn't ready for Nairobi yet, though. She still preferred the bush. Before the war the Wayfarer Hotel at Baluga, with its twenty spacious rooms, Dartmoor stags' heads, English sporting prints, and acres of garden had been the *ne plus ultra* of western Kenya, but successive negligent managers had brought it to its knees. If you're willing to take it on, Dick Muir told her, then bless you! Virginia saw her task as being much more than fixing broken toilet seats and watering plants and wiping lipstick off cups. This was the challenge she'd been waiting for. She'd not only bring the Wayfarer back to life, she'd make it even better than it had been in the Good Old Days!

3

Keriki

At Baluga three roads converged — from Nairobi to the east, Tanganyika to the south, and Uganda to the west. At the top of the town the long, low brick buildings of the administrative headquarters of Keriki District faced onto a roundabout and a flagpole that flew the Union Jack between sunrise and sunset. Below the flagpole lay the market and two streets of shops and garages. The Wayfarer Hotel was at the bottom of the town. Old Muir, Dick Muir's father, had built it in the twenties and around it he'd planted a most remarkable garden. In fact, it was said to contain more varieties of flowering trees than any other place in Kenya except the Nairobi Botanical Gardens. Over the buildings Old Muir had grown creepers and vines of every sort.

Despite its charm and its cool nights, high above Lake Victoria, the Wayfarer had gone through such hard times with its slipshod managers that Dick Muir had thought seriously about cutting his losses and selling the property. Before Virginia appeared, he'd actually begun negotiations with Mattias Ongaki, the government chief, who was eager to move some of his wives — he was said to have fourteen on "active duty" and seven more who were "retired" — into the buildings and turn the shrubbery into a coffee farm.

Under Virginia's management the Wayfarer's finances were soon restored to their former health. Daphne had been right, of course. Virginia had missed her work terribly. "Yes, we used to live in Runga," Marietta heard her mother telling her guests, "and then we came up here." The Itep episode was an aberration, six months in an irrelevant world. "The Runga climate was so dreadful," Marietta heard her mother say, as if that was the only reason they'd left.

Virginia didn't talk about Neville, and for all one knew she'd forgotten him. But Marietta hadn't. Every day she expected him to come. One morning a month after they'd moved to Baluga, and still no sign of Neville, she burst out, "You've had the same father all your life. He's permanent. I wish I were you, Violet."

Violet replied sharply, "Since you were born you've lived with Justin. Why do you complain?"

"Justin isn't *my* father."

"But he takes care of both of us."

"I want a father of my own, one who doesn't disappear."

Violet said sadly, "What if no man is rich enough to take us both, Mari? In that case we'll have to marry separately. I'll go off to my husband's home alone. But when *you* marry, Justin will go with you and he'll wash and iron your clothes there just as he does now. You've heard him say so many times. I'm the one who should complain, not you."

"I don't want to share. I want a father of my own," Marietta repeated. "It was ever so much better when we each had one. We could both be favorites then."

Every morning when she awoke, Marietta thought, Today he'll come. When he didn't, she told herself, Oh well, he's got a lot to do today; he'll come tomorrow. Later on, she thought, His mother's had an operation and he went to London on account of her. In that case, though, he should have sent a postcard of the Tower. As the months passed and no postcard came, no sign, no word from Neville, her time on the mountain looking at the stars became more and more like a fairy tale. She belonged in a dusty African town, fitting into her mother's life, not in a castle, the center of attention.

She had an edition of Sleeping Beauty, extravagantly illustrated, sent by Aunt Sophia as a christening present. Virginia had carried it about in the bottom of a canvas trunk until an eventually literate Marietta had discovered it and been enchanted instantly. Now she made the hotel shrubbery, in bloom after the rains, the setting for an elaborate make-believe. With Sleeping Beauty to consult in matters of etiquette and style, she prepared the ball at Itep on the occasion of her marriage. She and Violet arranged pineapples and pawpaws in heaps on groaning tables and ordered beautiful clothes from Mrs. Vejay, the Hindu seamstress who lived above the Bicycle and Machinery Parts, Ltd., Inc. They drew up a guest list including a great many people, from Violet's grandmothers, who liked weddings better than anything, to Curtis, Lady Bilton's housekeeper, who, once she'd met her, would surely approve of Marietta and certainly wouldn't want to be left out. They hired the three-piece band Marietta had heard playing in the Norfolk in Nairobi (a wind-up gramophone would not do, she insisted), and with Violet in knee breeches and a kingfisher-blue silk coat and Marietta in taffeta and lace, they waltzed round the grove of Brazilian dogwood at the bottom of the shrubbery while Neville beamed with happiness and all the guests applauded.

But in her ordinary humdrum life, Marietta was cross and restless. She was tired of Dr. Vorster. She wanted to go to school. "I do, Mum," she insisted, trailing her mother across the lawn past the bougainvillea.

"Why? How? Where?" Virginia was irritable whenever a big, white, important-looking envelope came in the post, and there'd been two that morning. "Where are we going to find a school in Baluga, may I ask?" she said, and then, with a sigh, "All right, maybe something could be organized." At least it wouldn't hurt to ask around.

The following Saturday night in the Wayfarer bar she asked Hedley, the education officer, what he might suggest. "You could try the Quaker Mission at Keriki," he told her. "They've got a school up there. It was the first one in these parts, in fact. The missionary's a man called Tyson, an American. His wife's the school principal. She might be willing to teach your daughter after hours."

Although she thought the way they stood up to bare their souls at their meetings was pretty far-fetched, in other respects Virginia rather approved of Quakers. She'd found that Quaker servants were more reliable than most. More reliable than Catholics, oh God, yes! And the Pentecostals were the bottom of the heap.

On Monday afternoon Virginia went up to Keriki to talk to the Tysons. She drove due east along the escarpment with the coffee farms on one side and on the other, far below on the valley floor, the pale green of the sugar plantations. After thirteen miles she came to the Keriki market and then to the Friends' African Mission.

Virginia found William Tyson in his office. He wore a permanently discouraged expression. Eighteen years he'd been at Keriki, which for him was at least five years too long. Virginia made her request.

"I have a daughter, almost twelve. We've lived all over the place. She's had a correspondence course, and whatever else she knows, she's taught herself. Now she badly wants a change. Would your wife consider tutoring her?"

William Tyson pursed his lips. "I'm not sure what she'll say. She's in the classroom now, but she'll be through soon. Would you care to wait?"

At five o'clock Mrs. Tyson came into the office carrying an armload of books and papers. In contrast to her husband, she didn't seem at all discouraged. It never took much to start the Africans laughing at those who brought the Word among them, and Janet Tyson, being thin and childless, was an easy target. And yet she escaped mockery. Her unpretentiousness was disarming. "What brought you here, over that appalling road of ours?" she asked.

Virginia explained, and Mrs. Tyson shook her head. "Tutoring Europeans isn't something I do. Tell me, though, would you consider letting your daughter come to our school?"

"But it's only for the Africans."

"From what you've told me, Mrs. Hamilton, your Marietta's pretty much used to Africans. She should do just fine here."

When Virginia got back to the Wayfarer, Marietta was shelling peas in the kitchen.

"Well, Etta," Virginia said. "I've found you a school of sorts. Getting you there will be a chore, though."

"Is Violet coming too?"

"Violet? Can't you do anything without your little satellite?"

"But Violet wants to go to school too," Marietta said stubbornly.

Virginia turned to go. "Let's see how you get on first. If all goes well, then we might ask them about Violet."

"We will start at verse fourteen of the twenty-fifth chapter of the Book of Matthew," Mrs. Tyson announced. "The girls shall have their turn first and then we shall hear from the boys."

Marietta stood at the end of the front row. As of this morning she had a uniform at last. A blue cotton dress with a white collar and white cuffs. No shiny black shoes, though. She wore sandals. The other children in the class were barefoot. So far they'd had arithmetic, English, geography (monsoons in India), and history (the British defeat of the Germans in Kisii, South Nyanza, in 1914). Now they were having Bible study with the principal.

At the beginning of the day Mrs. Tyson had said, "Marietta, I'm putting you with the three Mattias sisters. They'll keep an eye on you." The twins' cotton dresses strained across their breasts; already they had the powerful shoulders and calves of women used to digging in the fields and carrying heavy loads. It was a marvel that their father hadn't removed them from the school and that they weren't already wives and mothers. They looked cheerful and contented, but their younger sister, a gangling child who appeared to be about Marietta's age, was taut and restless. As she recited the parable of the talents half a syllable before the others, she caught Mrs. Tyson's eye and held it fiercely. Marietta looked down at the ink-stained desk. She had never read the Bible and couldn't pretend she knew the verses.

"And now we have a few moments left for questions," Mrs. Tyson said as the recitations came to an end. She leaned lightly against the blackboard, her mild Midwestern face still reflecting an optimistic generosity after nearly two decades away from Indiana.

Keriki fathers would appear at the principal's office saying, "Take my child. He's big enough. Teach him how to read so that one day he may become a clerk in a government office and bring honor to his parents, his lineage, and his clan." But every father had a different notion of what was "big enough." In Standard Six some boys were slight and smooth-skinned children, and others were full-grown men. A boy with the beginnings of a beard raised his hand.

"What is it, Moses? What do you wish to ask?"

But Moses needed to scratch his head, not ask a question.

In the moment before the lunch bell rang from across the football field, the third Mattias sister rose to her feet. "What of these talents?" she challenged. "If a person should have talents and yet allow himself to be prevented from using them, is that not very wrong?"

"That *is* wrong, Catherine. We must always look for an opportunity to use what we've been given. We must not let ourselves be discouraged by things standing in our path. If we are sufficiently persistent, we will find a way." This, Janet Tyson's creed, had brought her from a hog farm near Bloomington to Keriki. In the eighteen years at Keriki she marveled at what had become of her, at her escape from the life of her sisters — an endless round, she thought, of baking apple pies, going to coffee klatches, hosing down hog pens, digging oneself out of snow drifts. The work at Keriki had demanded more of her each year, and she'd responded gladly. Her cross was that her husband no longer shared her gladness. She thought regretfully that though he was a good man, despite his calling he wasn't *friendly*.

Marietta was invited to eat her sandwiches in the Tysons' house. "This is nice," Mrs. Tyson said as they walked across the compound. "It gives us a chance to get to know each other." Mr. Tyson wouldn't be there. He'd gone down to a regional mission meeting in Kisumu.

"You and Catherine are going to get along just fine, I know it!" Mrs. Tyson exclaimed. "Like you, she insisted on coming to school. She wouldn't take no for an answer." She laughed. "I'll never forget the expression on her father's face, the day he brought her here. 'My daughter forced me to come,' he said. Before that I bet no one had ever forced the chief to do anything."

"Chief Mattias is her father?"

"Yes indeed. And Catherine couldn't have been a day over six when she made him bring her to me. *He* was in a state! 'I myself came to this school and learned how to read and count on an abacus and wash my hands and head and face. The education that they gave me here enabled me to become Registrar of Births and Deaths down in Baluga and eventually a chief. But women don't become chiefs! Their work is bearing children, digging, and obeying their husbands!' But Catherine hadn't given him a moment's peace for weeks. 'So here are three of my daughters,' he told me. 'One will learn and the other two will watch her.' And that's about how it's been. There's not been too much competition for her, but I hope all that will change, now you're here."

At lunchtime the next day Agnes Mattias said to Marietta, "Come with us, please. Our mother is waiting for you. Her homestead is not far away." She touched Marietta's hand. "Come."

They crossed the football field, Elizabeth and Agnes on either side and Marietta between them. Catherine walked behind them, reading *Little Women;* she'd borrowed it from Mrs. Tyson after school the day before.

On both sides of the path, round thatched huts stood in fields of maize. "These are the houses of our father's wives," Elizabeth explained. "Our mother's house is near the top of the hill." They came to a broad sweep of open ground; in the middle was an iron-roofed bungalow, painted dark red. A great many people crowded round the door.

"Our father has come from Uganda," Agnes said. "He returned early this morning, and now many wish to see him. But our mother is expecting us at home"

"Wait!" Catherine slammed her book shut. "First you should greet my father," she insisted, and tugged at Marietta's arm. "Those people are forever wanting his attention. They will not let him rest, even after his safari. Nevertheless, he will speak with us." The twins watched helplessly as Catherine led Marietta away. At the door the crowd parted to allow them through.

At the far end of his audience chamber Chief Mattias sat on an elaborately carved chair. Long ago he'd had a picture of the royal throne in Westminster Abbey copied by Ranjit Singh in Kisumu. The plush on the arms was rubbed away now and one or two of the knobs were missing from the back, but Mattias was regal nonetheless, elevated above his subjects, who squatted before him, waiting their turn. A youth in a ragged jacket had the chief's ear. Beside him hovered an old woman, his mother, clasping a chicken with bound legs. With its help, the young man hoped to find favor in the chief's sight. Its eyes snapped as it tried in vain to fly away. The youth spoke in a low voice, his gaze fixed somewhere between Mattias's sandals and his knees. His mother, two steps behind him, was bent at the same supplicating angle. Mattias leaned back, his eyes closed and his head resting on velvet stained with the sweat of many audiences.

But suddenly he was roused from the borders of sleep by the sight of Catherine and Marietta picking their way through the supplicants crouched on stools and haunches on the earthen floor. With one great hand he silenced the young man, grasped the arms of the throne, and pulled himself to his feet. Reaching for his staff, he stepped down from the dais.

"Who have you brought me?" he cried. "Who is this new friend?"

"Her name is Marietta. She started yesterday at the school."

"So you have come to learn with Mrs. Janet? You should listen well to her, just as my daughter does. Where are you from?"

"Baluga. My mother runs the Wayfarer Hotel."

"Is that so! Last year I wished to buy that place. I offered a very good price for it, but because your mother came I was refused and I was very disappointed." He thumped his staff on the floor, threw back his head, and roared with laughter. Marietta was awed by the bullet head, the huge shoulders. But why was he laughing? He hadn't seemed at all amused.

"I didn't know the Wayfarer had been for sale," she said.

"It was. It will be again, and next time I shall buy it. Meanwhile, tell your mother she should keep it very well. When I buy, I expect that place to be in excellent repair!" He took out a large red handkerchief and blew his nose. The rafters shook, the supplicants started. "Your mother has chosen your teacher wisely," he said. "May you do well with Mrs. Janet, unlike my sons. They don't care for books, only for pleasure. Dancing" — he jerked his hips a little — "things of that sort. But this one is different. She is very clever." He laid his arm across Catherine's shoulders. "This one reads far into the night. There have been times when I myself have turned that lamp out, or the stars would have gone from the sky and she not slept yet. Perhaps she already knows more than I knew when I became a chief." Catherine stood quietly beneath her father's arm. With her toe she slowly drew a line in the dusty earth of the floor, but then she glanced up and Marietta saw that she was smiling. "In my old age she is my greatest pleasure."

"Are you so old, Father?" Catherine teased, lacing her hand with his. "Does an old man take new wives? And does he keep them? You are not old!"

"Before the Christians came, I herded cattle where now you learn. Yes," he laughed back at her, "I am old. I need my daughter to read the newspaper to me. Those little letters, uneven and poorly printed, those are too small for me. You are so helpful to me, Catherine. Such a clever girl as you will be helpful also to her husband."

Abruptly Catherine let go of her father's hand. "Husband? What husband? How many times have I told you that I will never marry! I don't want to hear you speak of husbands ever again!" She scowled and turned away.

"Why must you leave me so soon? Please stay." He gestured to the dais at his feet. "You could sit here with your friend and eat with us when we have finished with these people," Mattias pleaded, but Catherine was unyielding. The chief studied his daughter's back a moment and then he drew himself up. "I was

50

gone for seven days and there are some who have been here waiting all that time," he told Marietta self-importantly. "Now I must
attend to them. I hope, Miss Marietta, that we shall soon see you
again."

As she emerged into the sunlight, the twins pounced on Marietta,
positioning themselves firmly on either side of her. "Our mother is
waiting," Elizabeth said plaintively.

Catherine tossed her head. "Are you afraid she'll beat you?" she
mocked, and went back into the bungalow.

"Why doesn't she come with us?" Marietta asked.

"Her mother is dead," Agnes replied. "Alone of all of his children
she lives with our father."

Though she drove Marietta up to Keriki in the morning, Virginia
was too busy at the end of the day to fetch her home. So Marietta
came back on her own. Sometimes she had to wait a long time for
a vehicle outside the mission gates and didn't reach the Wayfarer
until the sun had set.

"How was school today?" Virginia would ask, meeting Marietta
in the lobby, but she didn't stop to hear how it had been. She had
so much to do in the bar and in the dining room. Then the second
week after Marietta started at the mission Virginia went down to
Nairobi, and Marietta missed four days of school. When Virginia
came back she was short-tempered and distracted. The following
morning the pump broke and she had to go down early to Kisumu
to get the necessary part. Marietta missed another day of school.

At lunchtime that day Marietta went with Violet to the hut Violet shared with Justin, behind the stand of bamboo at the edge of
the hotel garden. They prepared porridge for Justin's midday meal.
From the hotel dining room Justin brought some sugar wrapped
in a piece of newspaper. He tipped the sugar carefully into an old
jam jar, then crumpled up the newspaper and threw it in the direction of the cooking fire. It landed at Marietta's feet. She picked
it up and smoothed it out over her knees.

It was the front page of yesterday's *East African Standard,* and
Neville Bilton stared at her from the lower part of the third column. Slowly she read: "Sir Neville Bilton of Itep, Trans-Nzoia, was
granted a divorce nisi today from his wife Virginia, currently of
Baluga, North Nyanza. At the hearing Sir Neville testified that
Lady Bilton, having treated him in a most cruel manner, deserted
him on December 4, 1957, since which time she has rejected all

attempts on his part for a reconciliation. Mr. Justice Parish granted the plaintiff a divorce and ordered the return of such jewelry as he had placed in the keeping of Lady Bilton at the time of their marriage."

The article gave some details about the families of the couple; Marietta read that Lady Bilton's first husband, Charles Hamilton, a geologist, was believed to have taken his own life at Songo, Lake Tanganyika, though the coroner's report said the cause of death was undetermined. Lady Bilton's father, Captain Harold Parkson, had attracted considerable attention in his time. Apart from his passions for hunting and polo, he was very fond of walking. Indeed, in 1903 — that is, the year *after* the Uganda railway had been completed — he walked from Mombasa to the Ruwenzori Mountains in four months and five days. He later settled as a cattle rancher north of Thomson's Falls. "Sir Neville Bilton's family, notably his uncle Gerald, was prominent in the founding of the colony —" But at this point the reader was directed to page four, which Marietta did not have.

"Did you see this, Justin?" Marietta waved the scrap of newspaper. "It's Bwana Bilton. It says, Turn to page four. Where's the rest of the paper?"

Justin glanced up. "What does it say about Bilton?"

Marietta read the article aloud. "What do they mean by divorce nisi?"

"That Bilton sent your mother away."

"But *we* left *him*."

"That's right," Justin said patiently. "And now he is sending your mother away for good."

"She didn't want to go back! I was the only one who wanted to go back!"

"Men always fear that their wives will come demanding part of their land."

"But my mother hated Itep. She'd never ask for any of it."

"Bilton can't be certain of your mother's character, so he asked the judge to protect him. He wants that land for the son he hopes to have by his new wife."

At suppertime Virginia came back from Kisumu and shut herself into her office. On the veranda Marietta heard the door slam. She went and placed her ear against it. Her mother was opening and shutting drawers. Slowly Marietta turned the handle and slipped inside, the page of the *East African Standard* in the pocket of her shorts. Her mother flopped into her chair. She looked at Marietta over the unfiled correspondence and unpaid bills.

"I got the part." She pushed her hair out of her eyes. "I waited six hours while they looked for it. I thought they'd tell me they'd have to send for it from Eldonia, but I was lucky. Rajpal says he'll work on the pump for as long as it takes to get it going again, so by tomorrow morning our patrons should have water for their baths. You might think from the way they carried on that none of them had ever come across a broken pump before, that they all live in a world of gushing pipes. Well, I know for a fact that that obese man Spaulding who was shouting at me across the dining room at breakfast this morning has lived for thirty years outside Busia in a shack with a latrine under a tree in the *shamba,* and the only bath he ever gets is in this hotel! He spends hours in it and the others bang on the door and come sniveling to me that he's hogging the facilities!" She burst into tears.

Marietta, who had never, through all their adventures, seen her mother cry, stared in disbelief. "What's wrong, Mum?"

"It's the *day* — the *heat* and *bloody* Mr. Spaulding — and Rajpal stealing me blind." She pulled her handbag towards her and extracted a handkerchief. The handbag toppled off the desk; its contents were spilled across the floor. When she ran to pick them up, Marietta saw the same newspaper cutting that she'd tucked into the pocket of her shorts.

"Justin wrapped his sugar in this!" She pulled out her own crumpled page and waved it in front of her mother.

"Christ!" Virginia said. "Whatever do you mean?"

"For his porridge. He brought it from the dining room. Then he dropped it on the ground and I noticed Neville's picture. Where did *you* see it?"

"Everywhere! I saw it in every shop in Kisumu. I saw it in the hotel lobby when I went in to have lunch, and later, when I went to the warehouse to pick up the part for the pump, the lake breeze lifted that page out of the gutter and wrapped it round my legs."

"Justin only brought page one," Marietta said, frowning. "At the bottom it says, Continued on page four. Have you got that, too? Who's Gerald? Do we know him?"

Virginia blew her nose. "I need a drink. I'll *die* without a drink. No, we don't know Gerald. He died of a stroke at Malindi in 1949."

"Why did your father walk from Mombasa to the Ruwenzori when he could have gone by train?"

Virginia shrugged. "He did lots of peculiar things. Some people say I take after him. I trust you won't."

Marietta read aloud, "'Lady Bilton's first husband was believed to have taken his own life while out prospecting.' What was he prospecting for?" she asked.

"Gold and diamonds, precious stones. He didn't find them, though. Not on that trip, anyway."

"Is that why he took his own life?"

"It says that he was believed to have taken it, not that he actually took it."

"You told me he just died. You should have told me the truth," Marietta exclaimed. Then she added, "Why did he want to kill himself? Did he say?"

"I wish you hadn't found that piece of paper. It'll only muddle you up. It's muddled *me* up, for heaven's sake!" Virginia sighed. "Your father went through a lot in the war. In fact, a good many people found the war a bit too much. When it was over they didn't know where they were or what they were meant to be doing. I felt that way myself, but I ended up where I'd started, in Africa. I belonged here. Also, I was going to have you, so I knew what I had to do. Things were simpler for me than for your father. He'd never lived in Africa before. He was an outsider, and I wasn't enough for him. I mean, I couldn't make Africa home for him."

"Is that something you die of, not having a home?"

"Maybe."

"Where's our home, then?"

Her mother looked at her in wonder. "You ask tricky questions, don't you?" Then she smiled. "We have each other."

"And Justin and Violet."

Her mother pushed back her chair. "Of course. Where we go, they go. Do you want a ginger beer with your supper? I'm starving."

After dinner was over and the dining room had been cleared and her mother was back in the office again doing the accounts, Marietta went to find Justin in his hut behind the bamboo. "Tell me," she said, "about my father."

"Who am I to tell you anything? You should ask the memsahb," Justin replied.

"She doesn't want to tell me, so will you? Why did he kill himself?"

"Perhaps he didn't, Mari."

"Tell me what happened," Marietta insisted. "Whatever you remember, tell me that."

"Why do you want to know about it, Mari? We forgot your father. It was better so," Justin said, and looked away.

"*You* forgot him," Marietta exclaimed. "I didn't. I never knew him! What he was like? What happened? Tell me!"

"Sit down, then," Justin said, frowning. He gave her a stool. Violet was perched, eyes round, on a broken chair in the corner. "It was before you were born. A long time ago," he said.

Her parents had hired him in Moshi, he said; they were beginning a long safari ending up in Mwanza, which was not very far from his home. It was two years since he'd been back there, so he was glad to be employed by Bwana Hamilton in the hope before long of getting to Galana and seeing Boremo and her child. But very soon he saw that the bwana and the memsahb weren't happy together. "He was a huge man, your father, and when he was angry he seemed huger. He was often angry as the time went on and he did not find the metals he was searching for. But the memsahb stayed very quiet. She was afraid of him, I think." Justin rubbed his hand over his shaved head. "I was afraid of him and the cook was also. He was a Sukuma man. We talked about running away and not waiting until we got to Mwanza. But one day we reached Songo and we set up camp a short distance from the town and there it was that I saw your mother was with child. Ruba women, with child for the first time, are very quiet but proud and happy. Your mother, on the other hand, was sad. The bwana told us we would spend fourteen days in Songo. Each day he would go out to the bush early, but I think he did nothing there. No searching. He was drinking most of the day.

"The memsahb began to walk to town each morning. I think she had a friend there. A policeman. She'd known him in some other place. In Nairobi, perhaps. She always came back by four o'clock, before the bwana. But one morning she packed a bag and told me to carry it, and together we walked to a certain house in the town. The memsahb said to me, 'I shall stay here now. I have written a letter. The bwana will find it later on.' Then she told me, 'Now you return to camp,' and left me and went inside.

"I was very afraid of the bwana's coming back, and when he

came I watched him fearfully as he read the letter your mother had left behind. But when he had finished it, he said nothing at all. He poured himself a glass of whiskey and sat down. He only drank a little. Soon he got up again. He was going to shoot ducks, he said. It was sunset, the time of day when the ducks came in over the water. Wait for the memsahb, he told me, and when she comes back, whatever has to be done to help her you will do. Promise me that! And afraid as I was of him, I agreed. Then he went out in his vehicle to drive to the lake shore. The wind had died, the air was very still. I heard the shot. There was only one. It was by that one he died.

"There was an investigation afterwards and when it was finished that policeman was transferred to another place, in the south. I can't remember where it was he went. But your mother did not go with him. A manager was needed for the Songo rest house. She made an application and was chosen and gave up her friend. 'I shall stay,' I told her, 'until your child is born.' She was quite alone. No parents, no sisters, no one to return to. That Sukuma man, the cook, had run away and she had nobody except myself. I thought, After the birth I shall go home to Galana. But when we were coming from the hospital, and it was I who held you, I remembered again what I had promised your father. I understood then that he'd left nothing of himself, no one to bear witness that he'd ever lived, but you. Yes, I would do what had to be done, I would take you and raise you until such time as you were old enough to honor him. There is nothing more terrible, Mari, than the rage of the spirits whose children do not honor them. They are merciless and unforgiving, they give us no peace!

"So you see, that is how things happened. When you were three months in the womb I made a promise to a stranger. Your father scarcely knew Swahili, and yet I accepted his child! But *you* are not a stranger, Mari. How could I pass my days without you now?" He shook his head and cracked his knuckles. "Each year I have gone home to Galana, and each year I have returned to care for you."

"Why did my father kill himself?" Marietta said.

"They could not prove he did so, Mari."

"What do *you* think?"

"Who am I to tell what goes on in the head of another?"

"What did my mother think?"

Justin sighed. "Your father's death has been her affliction. She suffers from it still. Perhaps she'll suffer always until the end of her life." He paused a moment and then went on, "If a woman is adulterous while carrying her husband's child, then her husband will die. This, Ruba people believe. And they say that ever after such a woman must run from one man to another." Again he cracked his knuckles. "So it has been, has it not, with her."

When Marietta arrived at school on Monday, Catherine was standing by the gate. "You didn't come last week. You had malaria?"

"My mother was in Nairobi so she couldn't drive me up. I'd have arrived too late if I'd taken a bus."

"Why did she go to Nairobi?"

Marietta stopped in the middle of the playground. "What business is it of yours?"

But Catherine wasn't put off at all. "Your mother is interesting," she said slowly. "I have heard that she has no husband and that you have no father."

"Who told you?"

"Ongeso. He is my father's cook. He knows everybody in Baluga."

Later in the morning, after English grammar and before Swahili, Catherine whispered, "At midday, will you come to my house again? I told Ongeso you would come and eat with us. He is expecting you," Catherine persisted.

Marietta sighed. She had brought a sandwich, a banana, and some biscuits. She had a book she wanted to read. But Catherine's hand lay over her own. "If you like, I will, then."

This time the shutters on the window of the red bungalow were closed. "My father has gone to Baluga," Catherine explained. "He won't be back again until tomorrow." She led Marietta round the house. Across a grassy space, in a smaller house, an old man was cooking over an open fire. Catherine pushed open the back door of the bungalow. "Have you seen the Queen?" she said suddenly.

"Of course not. I've never been to London."

"My father saw her at the coronation," Catherine said proudly as they came into a sitting room. A row of chairs with plastic seats stood against one wall. On the opposite wall hung a large photograph of Chief Mattias shaking hands with Queen Elizabeth. Beside it was another picture, not quite so large, of the chief with medals across his chest and an African woman in a brocade suit. She looked frightened. Mattias, on the other hand, looked perfectly delighted. "Both were in the *Standard*," Catherine said, "and my father had fifty copies made for his friends. Among others, he gave one to the DC and one also to the provincial commissioner. It hangs in his office. I myself have seen it there."

"Is that lady your mother?"

"No, that one is Matilda. She is my father's twelfth wife. He chose her to go with him because she knows English. She worked for a white family once, on the sugar plantations. She looked after their children. A boy and a girl. They were spoiled, she said. They would not share their food. My mother was the sixth wife." Catherine added, "She died when I was born."

"I'm sorry."

"Why? Am I an orphan? No! I have my father! I've always lived with him since my foster mother weaned me." She opened another door. "See, we have two rooms. One for him and one for me." She pointed at a great bedstead in the larger of the two rooms. "When I was young I shared that with him, but when I reached the age of circumcision my father said, 'You are no longer a child, henceforth you must sleep apart from me.'"

Ruba people said circumcision was barbaric, a senseless mutilation of the body, male and female. They sang rude songs about it, and Marietta, who had learned them from Violet, had all the Ruba prejudices, but she knew better than to air them now.

Catherine went on, "For seven days I wept and then my father told me 'Come,' and together we went down to Kisumu, to the market, and there he bought for me a small bed of my own. We brought it back and placed it in the second room and now we sleep apart. But not so very far apart. The door stands open between us." She sighed. "When he travels, and he travels frequently, I miss him very much. This is too large a house for me alone."

"Then why don't you stay with Agnes's and Elizabeth's mother?"

Catherine tossed her head. "It's better to stay alone than to listen to the chatter of those girls! They talk about this boy they've seen in the market, or that one in Standard Eight! Come, let us go now to Ongeso. He has prepared porridge."

Ongeso was bent and grizzled. He wore his master's cast-off shirt, with the sleeves rolled up past the elbows, and a pair of tattered shorts.

"After myself, Ongeso is my father's greatest friend," Catherine said. "My father does not trust his wives. He will not eat their food lest they poison him. For all of the time of his chieftaincy he has eaten only what Ongeso prepares. And even that Ongeso must taste. Will you take porridge now?" She added, "It's good. No harm will come of it. Ongeso has already tasted it!"

On the Friday of Marietta's third week at school, Mr. Tyson organized an athletics competition for Standards Six, Seven, and Eight. Although Marietta had never taken part in anything so formal as an athletics competition with starting lines and finishing lines, in every place they'd lived together she and Violet had had an obstacle course, over veranda balustrades and laundry baskets, around fish ponds, through rock gardens and shrubberies, and once, briefly, across Neville's rose beds, one, two, three, four, five, the whole length of the terrace at Itep, down to the south wall and back. They'd never known or cared how fast they ran. With its flags and measuring tapes and stopwatches and whistles, Mr. Tyson's competition seemed extremely serious.

Catherine won the high jump and Marietta the long jump as well as the hundred-yard dash. Mr. Tyson came up to congratulate Marietta afterwards. She'd broken the long jump record, he said. "You're going to be a real asset to our school," he added, smiling broadly. (He very rarely smiled.) Catherine scowled beside her.

When school was over, Marietta went out to the road to catch a bus down to Baluga. "One just left," an Indian shopkeeper told her. "You may wait here for the next." He brought a chair for her out to the veranda, and she took a book out of her satchel and began to read.

"What is that?" Marietta looked up and saw Catherine standing there.

"*Anne of Green Gables.* Mrs. Tyson lent it to me."

"Ah, so she has become your friend also."

Marietta shrugged. "She's my teacher. I've never had a teacher before."

"Why not?"

"Because we've usually lived in places where there weren't any, or if there were, my mother didn't think they'd do."

"Ongeso says your mother is very different from Mrs. Tyson," Catherine remarked in Keriki. "Mrs. Tyson is helpful both to her husband and to all the rest of us. She is always thinking of other people. But Ongeso says it is her own pleasure that your mother thinks about."

Marietta looked down at the book in her hands. She felt dizzy, and around her heart were little prickles that she recognized as fear.

Catherine, still rooted beside her, reached out and touched Marietta's bright hair. It was shoulder length, cut abruptly by Justin with the kitchen scissors just the other day. African children often touched her hair, but they were always very young, incredulous, ignorant. A girl whose father had attended the coronation of the Queen certainly ought to know better. "It is wonderful," Catherine murmured, "how this grows so straight and soft, and how it shines." And then she aded, urgently, "Is your mother's hair as beautiful as yours? All over Keriki people speak of her, and yet I've never seen her. I wish to, though. Ongeso told me," she went on, her voice rising, "that your mother has a boundless appetite. She is impossible to satisfy."

Anne of Green Gables fell to the floor. Marietta reached for it, but her hand grasped vainly. She felt as if a great, cold lump had lodged in the middle of her chest. "The cover's torn," she said wildly. "Whatever shall I tell Mrs. Tyson now!"

"Your mother has very many friends, and once they have known her," Catherine said clearly, "they are spoiled for other women. They cannot marry and have children of their own. Your mother is a wanderer and every man she loves becomes a wanderer too."

Marietta seized her satchel and jumped up. "Why do you believe that old bush man?" Her face was scarlet; the lump in her chest had dissolved abruptly into fire. "Is that why you followed me here, to tell me the gossip and lies of a slave?" She turned and ran away down the road.

At dinner that evening, Marietta took a couple of bites of lamb stew and pushed her plate away.

"Not hungry?" Virginia frowned. "As a matter of fact, I'm not either. If it isn't one thing, it's another." At their table for two Virginia faced out into the hotel dining room. On a Friday evening it was almost full. People liked to spend their weekends at Baluga. There was the sports club for golf and tennis and the Wayfarer for everything else. On weekend nights Virginia wore low-cut dresses and provided style, a certain enigmatic drama, until long after the bar closed at twelve. "As if this last fortnight hasn't been enough,

60

now the Land-Rover's on the blink. This morning a lorry edged me off into the ditch and bent the back axle. They're going to have to tow the Land-Rover to Kisumu and keep it there at least a week. I don't know about getting to school, Etta. When I agreed to drive you up each day, I didn't realize how hard the road would be on the Land-Rover, or how much time the trip would take. We're going to have to think of another plan."

Two young men came into the dining room and stopped to talk to Virginia; she was transformed before Marietta's eyes into a gay and laughing creature, one whom divorces, generators, and bent back axles couldn't faze. When they'd gone, Virginia said, "You like Mrs. Tyson, don't you, Etta? Missionaries tend to be so very grim and holy, especially the Americans, but she doesn't seem like that at all. I thought of asking her if you could board with her."

"Don't bother, Mum," said Marietta. "I want to go back to Dr. Vorster."

"Why in the world! I thought you liked that school."

"All that reciting and reading aloud and queuing up! It's so boring and stupid. That school's not worth the trouble of getting there."

So Marietta went back to Dr. Vorster.

4

Baluga

In Baluga you could get a fistful of roasted groundnuts for two cents from a woman who sat in front of a shop that sold dress material and nylon shirts from China. In good weather she sat in the street; when it rained she moved under the veranda. This morning the sun was shining. Business was brisk, and she kept having to put down the sweater she was knitting of brilliant blue wool in order to attend to her customers. She sometimes gave you extra for your money, but her generosity depended on her mood, which depended on how she was getting along with her sister-in-law. They both sold groundnuts in twists of paper, in front of shops a hundred yards apart. Besides being business competitors, they were competitors for everything else. This morning, however, she seemed cheerful and good for a bonus if you listened first to her stories. Marietta and Violet stood with their backs to the market-day crowd, shifting from foot to foot. Each was thinking, I've heard this one about her youngest daughter at least a dozen times, so let's settle for an even two cents' worth, when a Land-Rover stopped in the street behind them.

"It's a white man," the woman remarked. "Perhaps he wants to buy."

The white man was Neville Bilton. He bought himself and the children five cents' worth each, and they all climbed into his Land-Rover and drove down the town to the Wayfarer.

Marietta hadn't seen or heard from Neville since he'd pulled her out of his closet at Itep, but for eighteen months he'd played the central role in all her daydreams. They'd traveled the world to-gether, climbed mountains, sailed oceans (by raft, of course). Now, this unexpected encounter with the real Neville stunned her into silence. She sat close up against Violet with a foot and a half of seat between herself and Neville and stared out the window on Violet's side. She noticed that Mrs. Vejay was keeping a cock trussed up in a basket on her balcony and the lunatic who sat in front of the Baptist bookstore was wearing sandals. He must have gone into a shop and taken them, and the owner had been too scared of his ferocious frown to interfere. Once he'd come to the Wayfarer and stood at the kitchen door, his hair in red clumps around his head. The cook had fled, but Justin had given him a chipped bowl with a crack down one side, which wasn't good for puddings anymore. The lunatic had carried it happily away, and for two days he'd worn it as a hat. Then he'd left it on the doorstep of the Catholic church. This morning he looked delighted with his sandals, but by the next market day he'd be going barefoot again.

"I was afraid you'd gone off on safari somewhere and I'd miss you," Neville said lightly, slowing behind a herd of goats being driven to the Tuesday market. They crowded one upon another as an old man in an ancient raincoat whacked them with his stick in an effort to clear the road for the *mzungu*.

"I don't go on safari. I always stay at home."

"In that case I could drop in any time I wanted, couldn't I?"

Marietta flushed. "Obviously you haven't wanted to, or you'd have come before. I'd even thought you died, only no one'd told me. I'm often not told about things," she added bitterly.

"Not dead," Neville said evenly, "gone abroad. To Canada."

"You might have sent a postcard!"

"I didn't know if you'd have welcomed it."

"Why wouldn't I have welcomed it?"

Neville shrugged. "We parted under a cloud, as I remember. I was afraid that cloud still hung."

"*We* parted friends," Marietta replied heatedly. "It was only you and Mum who didn't." And she added, before he could say any-thing, "Why on earth did you go to Canada? Didn't you get frostbite?"

"I went for a change, and it's not as cold as all that, provided you wear the proper clothes. But now I'm very happy to be home again. How are you two?"

63

"Violet and me? We're okay. If you mean Mummy as well, you'd better ask *her*. Violet and I like Baluga a lot. It's cooler than Runga and warmer than Itep and the garden's beautiful. Justin's happy too," she went on very fast, "because we're much closer to Galana Island than we've ever been before. In fact, on clear days you can even see it from the flagpole at the top of the town. By land it's still a long way off, but over the lake, as the crow flies, Mum says it's only twenty miles. Justin likes the garden too," she added. "Mum let him have a little *shamba* and he grows his own maize. In Runga he didn't have a *shamba*. There wasn't enough room."

They were turning in at the Wayfarer. At midmorning the gravel was empty of cars. Last night's guests had departed and the lunchtime patrons hadn't yet arrived. Marietta saw that the hotel Land-Rover was gone.

"Mum's in Kisumu, probably."

Violet nodded. "It was for the water heater. She'll be away all day."

"That's too bad," Neville said with a little laugh. "I'd been very much hoping to see her." Marietta stole a glance at him. He sounds so relieved that she's not here; maybe he's worried that Mum wouldn't want to see *him*, Marietta thought. "Perhaps you girls could show me about. I'd really like to see the place if you've got time."

Marietta was silent as she led the way through the garden. "Why the hurry?" Neville called after her. They reached the grove of Brazilian dogwood where Marietta and Violet — and Neville too, of course — had attended so many wedding balls. "What a pretty place!" Neville exclaimed. The trees were laden with creamy, star-shaped flowers and the grass was strewn with petals. Marietta looked sideways at Violet and the two burst into giggles. "What's so amusing?" Neville asked, as Marietta clapped a hand over her mouth to keep in her laughter.

"You've seen everything now," she said, looking straight at Neville for the first time since he'd come upon her and Violet in the town. He'd got pale in Canada. She'd seen that happen before to people who went to the U.K. The bank manager and his wife, for instance. They'd come back from leave a few weeks ago, looking as if the rest hadn't done them any good at all. Otherwise he seemed much the same. What's he going to do now? she thought. Has he still got room for me?

"I believe I came here once," Neville said softly, "when I was a kid. My father wanted ideas for the garden at Itep. I had to walk round with him and Old Muir, the owner. My father looked at every shrub and tree and asked the names of those he didn't recognize and wrote them down in a notebook with hard black covers. And I was bored to death. I kept on asking for a drink. I didn't have enough imagination. I couldn't see how lovely Old Muir's garden would eventually become. I think I must have been a rather cross and selfish little boy. You two wouldn't have given me the time of day."

"Oh, we're often cross and selfish," Marietta said offhandedly. "And you're right. We don't care much for boys."

"You'll change your mind, given a year or two," Neville said. "By the way, don't you think it's time *we* had something to drink after those nuts? They make one fearfully thirsty."

Neville asked Marietta to join him for lunch in the dining room, but she muttered something about having to eat with Violet, who of course wasn't allowed in the dining room, and ran off to the boys' quarters. So Neville had a table all to himself. The fact was, though, that Marietta wasn't ready for Neville's undivided attention, not yet.

She came out to the driveway just as he was leaving. He told her he was hoping to get to Itep that night and he had a long way still to go. "Thank you for having me," he said gravely as he shook Marietta's hand. He didn't offer to kiss her.

"Thank you for coming," Marietta replied, just as gravely. Then suddenly she asked, as an afterthought, "What should I tell Mum?"

"Give her my love and say that I'm sorry I missed her. And I'll come back soon, now the ice is broken."

The next time Neville came to Baluga it was the middle of the afternoon and Virginia was behind the bar, taking stock. He walked in, his floppy safari hat in his hand, with Marietta close behind him.

"Are we disturbing you?" he said.

Virginia narrowed her eyes, seeking to conceal her discomfort with the excuse of the afternoon glare. "Lord, no!" Wiping her hands on her skirt, she stood awkwardly on one side of the bar, Neville on the other, beyond the extra protection of the bar stools.

"May I greet you?" He took her hand across the stained wooden surface and he kissed it.

65

"You found me at my least favorite chore," Virginia said. "The drink goes awfully fast. I have to check each day. Sometimes twice a day. I can't trust my barman. He promises he's done it, but usually he hasn't." She spoke too rapidly. "What can I get you?" She inclined her head towards the bottles on the shelves behind her.

"I see you're doing well here. You must be very pleased."

"If I've done anything, it's by courtesy of you," Virginia said, shrugging. "Will you have a beer?"

He edged onto a stool. "By courtesy of me? What does that mean?"

"I'm a partner this time, Neville. Dick Muir took me in. I've come up a step from the Runga days. I'm no longer an employee, I'm an investor. Of your cash, of course. You set me up. I used my severance pay, the money from my settlement, to do this." She handed his beer mug to him and poured one for herself. "Shall we drink to our separate fortunes?" They touched glasses.

Neville, watching her over the rim of his mug, thought, Yes, this is a long way from Runga. He remembered, with only a little pain, Virginia's pleasure in Runga. Her pleasure in him, and what he did for her. Undoubtedly she'd forgotten.

"Well," he said mildly. "You might have blown it all in Monte Carlo. Others have, people you and I both know. But instead you put it into the development of an African colony."

"Oh, come on, Neville! I was worried about eating, that's all! Etta," Virginia said sharply, "can't you find something else to do? Neville and I are having a talk." She looked at Neville. "Well, we are, aren't we?"

Marietta slipped out of the bar onto the veranda. But she didn't go far. She wanted to stay as close as possible.

"You won't take any credit, then?" Neville took a long swallow of beer. "I'm dry! I was on the road by seven." He went on quietly, "You forget that I've had experience in throwing money away. At least with you I knew I was finished, but with Clarissa I was far too tenacious. Three times I went to California to plead my cause. Poor fool that I was, I couldn't give up, and when I did, eventually, it cost me an arm and a leg. The American courts have a way of making one out to be a brute, whatever the facts might be. Clarissa behaved abominably, but that didn't help my case. She's been living in considerable comfort ever since. She hasn't used her severance pay, as you gracefully call it, for the benefit of anyone but herself. But look at you! Two years ago we stopped in, do you remember, and we were the only people in this place. It was moribund. But with just two thousand quid you've turned it on its head. You'll be running the Norfolk next!"

Virginia traced a figure eight on the surface of the bar. "I always think I'd have been a first-rate housekeeper, but a rather special one, mind you — to a duke, say. I'd have whipped about from hunting lodge to hunting lodge, cleaning out the pantries and bullying the servants, pitying his duchess, poor dull thing, being taken care of."

"I can imagine."

For a moment they were silent; then Virginia observed, "I heard you went to Canada."

"Yes. There's a mining company in Alberta I wanted to look into. Though that was only an excuse. I needed to get away from here. From you, specifically." He smiled slightly. "I did a bit of fishing on the west coast, and this and that. I stayed almost eight months. I'm thinking about going there for good."

"And selling Itep?"

"I dare say. There's not much future here for me. Besides, I don't fancy being at Itep alone."

"Come on, Neville," Virginia teased. "You should get married again and fill those rooms up with children. Itep's a child's dream, you know. Etta loved it."

"Two marriages in Africa are enough," Neville replied quietly, "and besides, it's absurd for me to go on living as I have. In my youth I thought, I'll do what I like, when I like, and wherever I like. No one's going to stop me. Well, no one *is* stopping me. I've simply had enough of Africa. I've decided to sell Itep to one of those African settlement schemes."

"You aren't saying this just to impress me, are you?" Virginia said uneasily. "It's too late to impress me."

"I long ago gave up hope of that, my dear." Neville smiled. "I wonder what *would* impress you? I suppose that's what I found so fascinating about you. You couldn't be trapped or bought or beguiled."

"Are you sorry for yourself? I don't believe it." Virginia shook her head. "You're well rid of me. Surely you know that!"

"Certainly I *was* sorry for myself. Seeing you drive off into the world, the four of you in my dented Land-Rover, of course I wished there'd been a place for me. The house was deadly after you left. The rains were terrific that year. Sometimes it rained all day long and the mist was low over the mountain, all around the house. Once I didn't see further than the fence at the end of the lawn for a week. In the library there were mushrooms growing on the cushions, the ones you had re-covered on the window seats. I almost came after you, though God knows what *that* would have accomplished!" He grinned. "Anyway, I was saved from such insanity. The rains eased off, the sun started showing itself. I went about my business, just as you, so I heard, were going about yours."

Virginia grimaced. "Why on earth didn't we just have a fling and leave it at that?"

Neville smiled faintly. "We hoped we might be different, after all, from how we actually are. But I'm a plodder. I need a predictable order. You might think Canada a daring idea, but it's not. It merely seems, in an uncertain world, to offer me the best chances for predictability. I'll settle down and be an eccentric, someone to tell stories about. But you, you've said it yourself, you hate to be protected." He laughed. "At least we've realized how stubborn we are!"

Virginia touched his arm. "I'm so glad to see you. I was dreading the day you'd show up. I've felt despicable. You should know that. I *knew* I should have stayed in Runga. I knew it at the time and I simply pretended otherwise and went right on with the make-believe. It was all my fault. What a disruption!"

"It was *our* make-believe. Not just yours. Mine too. I'm equally responsible. And whatever we did was no tragedy. We merely acted out of character. That's humiliating, perhaps, but far from tragic. Can I have another beer?"

Virginia opened a second bottle of Heineken.

"I should have warned you I was coming today," Neville said, "but I didn't want to make an event out of it. I told myself, if I missed you today there'd always be another time. All the same, I'd have felt terribly let down if you'd been out. One builds up a certain steam." He smiled. "I had the bizarre idea that if I came here at lunchtime and went into the dining room, along with the rest, and you came past my table, you'd refuse to recognize me. Last night I actually dreamed it. When I woke up I had to convince myself that in reality you were a reasonable woman who behaved in a civilized fashion on most occasions."

68

"But about the divorce I wasn't civilized! I wouldn't see you alone; I wouldn't even speak to you, except about the Land-Rover and the pearl necklace. The newspaper account said I rejected all your efforts at reconciliation, but the fact was there weren't any. I didn't give you an opportunity to make any. You see, I was terrified that if I gave you the chance, you'd ignore it because you didn't *want* a reconciliation. I didn't either, in the end, but I had hankerings that I didn't dare have you expose. That's why the twice we saw each other in Nairobi before the divorce, I behaved as if I hardly knew who you were. But I'm over my hankerings now and I'd recognize you anywhere!" She laughed and shook her hair back from her face. "Christ, I need another drink. Gin this time." She poured a gin and tonic and cut herself a slice of lime. "Well, what shall we drink to?"

"Your untrammeled life?"

Virginia leaned back against the counter behind the bar. "It's hardly an untrammeled life. Anyone less romantic than you would see how very ordinary it is. I have few alternatives, which suits me, since I'm not good at making choices. I do what I have to do."

"Incidentally, Marietta appears to be thriving."

"Yes, doesn't she! Daphne gets after me about school, which I think is cute since she scarcely ever saw the inside of one herself. Last year we tried Etta in a mission school, but it didn't work. I had to drive her every morning. The road was dreadful. It wrecked the Land-Rover. So I took her out. She didn't mind. She said she was bored with reading out loud and reciting from the Bible. She went back to her correspondence course and she hasn't complained. But Daphne insists schools aren't just for learning. They're for socializing you. What exactly she means by that isn't clear. Anyway," Virginia added, yawning, "it's out of the question. I can't afford it. She won't be the first *mzungu* in East Africa to stay home. There were plenty in my day, and I bet you'd find a few even now."

Neville said slowly, "How about my sending her? My paying. We talked about it at one time."

"You mean *you* did!" Virginia grinned. "It wasn't my idea. And I had the same objections then, too. Those schools are horribly pretentious, though about what, God only knows. There's nothing special about those kids except that they're white in a black country. By the time they leave they might have acquired a bit of veneer.

They've squashed their feet into high-heeled shoes they probably can't afford, and they've learned to set their hair. But they aren't any less bush underneath than when they arrived. They can't even earn their living, either. To do that they have to go to typing school so they can get a job in some firm that has to hire them, however incompetent they are, because only white girls type. Marietta could learn from a teach-yourself book. In fact, she already types much better than I can. She uses two fingers, but so what!" Virginia sighed. "I don't want to be ungracious, but I couldn't accept. For lots of reasons."

"But you *are* being ungracious. Incidentally, I'm not offering to do this as a way of getting you back into my clutches. This would be for her sake, not yours or mine. She has several of your admirable qualities, my dear, but she's rather easier to approach. We agree our marriage was an aberration. I should have been just another in your succession of admirers, but since we actually married, technically Marietta was my stepdaughter, at least for a while. This leaves me with a sense of obligation to her. If you should change your mind, you can always find me through my bank in London. I'd be delighted to help. In fact, nothing would please me more."

As Neville came out of the bar, Marietta was instantly beside him. "You're leaving. Going to Canada." She grasped his hand. "Take me too, Neville! I'd be useful. I can cook and clean. I do know how."

Close behind them, Virginia laughed. "Are both of you abandoning ship? What is it about Africa these days that everyone wants to leave it? You wouldn't find *me* going to Canada, not even if they paid me! I'm staying here, and Etta, so are you, until you're old enough to make your mind up sensibly. The grass always looks greener on the other side, but once you're over there, it's usually just as patchy as it was at home. Better the grass you know than the grass you don't, I say!"

At the end of June, Daphne Dawson telephoned. "Peter's mother's died," she announced. "He's had to go to England to pay the death duties. Can I come up? I've never seen you on your own turf, Virginia; I mean on turf which actually belongs to you. I've got to see you in action."

Daphne arrived at teatime on Tuesday. She swept through the

70

lobby of the Wayfarer in a cloud of Chanel No. 5, which she kept in the glove compartment of her Land-Rover. She wore khaki slacks, a purple shirt with eyeshadow to match, and a great many gold bracelets and a knob of a ring set with turquoise on the third finger of her right hand. She wore earrings, too, but they were hidden by her dark brown curly hair, which by now should probably have been a little gray, only she took measures to prevent that. Marietta found Aunt Daphne fascinating.

Virginia told Justin to bring a tray to the cottage. Marietta followed with the scones.

"You're looking so well, Virginia! By the way, guess who came to see me? Neville, of course! Since Cambridge he's been Peter's buddy, really, not mine. I told him on the phone, Peter's not here, he's had to go to London, and so on, thinking Neville might back out. He said that was too bad, but he wanted to see me anyway. He appeared looking a bit woeful, and said straight away he'd stopped in here and seen you, Virginia. We sat in the gazebo, drinking gin, and I waited for him to tell me how he missed you and how wonderful you were. Well, he talked about you all right, about the alterations you'd made in his house and how they looked better than ever, now he was back from his trip. But I tell you, he could've been talking about a guest who'd given him advice and then stayed long enough to see her suggestions put into effect. After a bit I said, 'Do you miss Virginia, actually?' and he said, 'I don't believe I do. It was tiring living with someone so intransigently opposed to one. She didn't approve of me, you see.' He got rather quiet then, so I thought, Maybe he's after *me*, how incestuous! Well, it would be rather, don't you think? The sun began to go down. It was really quite romantic, or it would have been. As it turned out, romance wasn't at all what Neville had in mind. He suddenly said, 'Tell me about Marietta!' And I said, 'Oh, God, Neville, I was there at the birth,' and he said, 'Then tell me about it.'"

"*That* old story!" Virginia grimaced. "He wanted to hear that one?"

"So do I," Marietta said. "Mum's never told me, so will you?"

"How old are you?"

"You should know, since you were there when I was born."

"True." Daphne's eyes narrowed. "Let me see. It was August, I think. The first August after the war. So that makes you almost thirteen. I suppose you're old enough to hear the saga."

"It's okay with me," Virginia said, "but I'm going to talk to the cook," and she went out across the garden to the hotel.

Until Neville asked her, Daphne hadn't thought about it in years. In fact, being childless herself, and destined, it seemed, to remain so, she'd chosen not to think about the birth of her friend's daughter. But Neville was determined.

When Virginia was nine months pregnant and five and a half months a widow, Daphne arrived at the Songo rest house on the shore of Lake Tanganyika. She came in a jeep with a driver, a baby's bath, two dozen nappies, a bottle of Cutty Sark, and three cartons of Benson and Hedges cigarettes. She'd sent a telegram announcing her arrival, but the telegram never reached Songo.

"Seeing that you couldn't leave this place and come up to Nairobi for the couple of months it takes to have a baby decently, Peter and I decided there wasn't anything else to be done but for me to come down to be with you. I wouldn't guarantee knowing one end of a baby from another," she said, laughing, "but I do know *you*." As Daphne jumped out of the jeep, Virginia put her hands over her face and burst into tears. "What kind of welcome is that!" Daphne kissed her. "Look, it's eleven minutes past six, the sun's sinking into the lake. Isn't it the cocktail hour?" Grabbing the Cutty Sark, she made off to the veranda. Virginia wiped her eyes with the back of her hand and followed her friend, who, despite her mud-streaked shirt and trousers and hair tangled by hours of riding in an open vehicle, appeared quite unfazed after a week's journey over rainy-season roads down from Nairobi.

Ten days later Virginia went into labor in the middle of the night. Daphne, who slept on the other side of the partition dividing the manager's bungalow in two, heard the bed creak loudly and then Virginia bumping into a chair.

"What's up?" Daphne called over the partition.

"The bed's all wet. My water's broken. Isn't that what happens first?"

Outside it was sluicing rain. The night watchman, huddled under the front porch of the main building, was sent to awaken Daphne's driver. "I bet he's drunk," Daphne said. After an eternity, the watchman returned, shaking his head. The driver could not be roused. "I knew it!" Daphne said. "I'm going to have to drive you to the mission myself." She laughed. "I wish you could see what you look like, Virginia!"

72

"You aren't so glamorous either," Virginia retorted. Daphne had set her lamp on the top of the porch and the two women stood in its flickering light, their hair plastered to their heads, their cotton dresses clinging round their legs. Virginia's dress rose high in front, over her stomach.

"Well, at least it doesn't show my leaking like this," she said. "I can't tell if it's me or the rain."

"Do you hurt?"

"No, actually. I don't feel a thing."

Daphne got the jeep out and they lurched out of the rest house compound and off up the shore road. Though he'd failed to rouse the driver, the night watchman had awakened Justin. Virginia would have preferred to have him come with them, but he had to be left in charge. When the jeep got stuck, then, in the mud at the turnoff to the mission, the two women were unable to free it by themselves. It was still raining hard and pitch dark. "I hope you know the way," Daphne said, switching off the jeep's headlights. She extracted a flashlight from under her seat. "Let's go, frontier lady. How far is it from here?"

"Four miles, maybe. It shouldn't be more."

"It had better not be. How are the pains?"

"I'm not having any. Perhaps it's a false alarm."

"Heaven forbid! I'm not used to walking through the bush in the middle of the night. It's definitely an unwise thing to do. I only do it for special events."

By the time they reached the mission the sky had cleared and the east was growing pale. In the homesteads on either side of the road people were beginning to stir in the still dawn after the night's heavy rain. Wood smoke from cooking fires rose straight above the thatch. On their way up the rutted road the women slipped many times. A child peering out through a gap in the hedge caught sight of them as they passed, their clothing mud-stained, their hair in rats' tails round their faces. He stared at the two white women in terror and scuttled away to the safety of his mother's kitchen. At the mission, the African novice, nodding behind the front desk inside the clinic building, gasped awake as Virginia and Daphne came in.

"Don't be afraid," Daphne told her in Swahili, "nobody's dying. But my friend needs to lie down."

In fact, Virginia had no labor pains at all until she had bathed and was safely on a bed in a little room at the end of the maternity ward. "Thank God *some*thing's happening," she giggled to Daphne, who sat on the edge of the bed. "I was scared to death it was a false alarm. I've been more scared of you, actually, than of labor. You're always so exacting, Daphne. For you, one must perform."

"Oh, nonsense! You're the one who performs, my dear. I merely understudy."

After that Virginia was in labor for three days. The baby was upside down and should properly have been delivered by Caesarean. But Sister Maria-Theresa was a midwife, not an obstetrician. The nearest obstetrician was two hundred miles away by *murram* road, which, after the most recent rain, was probably washed out. For the second half of the third day that Virginia was in labor, Daphne, sitting and standing by the bed, watching her friend's torment, made up her mind a dozen times to take her regardless, to try to make it up to Ibithi. But a dozen times she changed her mind, and eventually Sister Maria-Theresa said, "The road could kill her. She must stay here and we will do whatever we can." Her face was pink and soft and round beneath her white cap; her hands, hard and veined, laboring hands, extending from her sleeves, looked as if they belonged to someone else. "You should go back to the rest house to sleep," she added kindly. "This is an ordeal for you as well as her."

But Daphne stayed at the mission. At times she went out into the veranda to sit on the steps with the Africans who, like herself, were waiting for their relatives to live or die. They were shy of her at first as she sat smoking cigarette after cigarette among them, poor country people. But when a boy came to the veranda with sugar cane for sale, Daphne threw away her cigarette and bought a stick from him. She sat yanking at it with her teeth, pulling away the outer strips to get at the sweet center. A gnarled man beside her watched her tearing and spitting at her cane. "You are strong. Your teeth are strong. The cane was good, too, in your father's place?"

Daphne smiled at him, grateful to be recognized, one vigilant by another. "In my father's place there was no sugar cane."

"What did you eat, then, as children, in the afternoons before your mother cooked?" a woman asked.

They engaged Daphne eagerly. They knew about babies coming upside down, and one of the waiting women had herself survived the experience with the aid of Sister Maria-Theresa. "When you

74

take your sister home to her husband," she asked, "will he not keep her in the house for sixty days, as we do when the child comes by his feet?"

Virginia's child was born at dawn on the fourth day. The midwife put her hand into the birth canal and pulled the baby out. Daphne, watching this final violation, was convinced that both child and mother were dead, overcome by perverse impediments to what was meant to be a natural process. Virginia showed no visible signs of life, and the baby, a girl, emerged limp, bloodied, and silent. But within seconds she was shrieking. Sister Maria-Theresa, wiping her forehead with her arm, smiled. "A miracle, truly a miracle!" Daphne watched the yelling baby being washed in a tin bowl on a table beside the bed, and thought, Peter would like a daughter. He'll be glad.

"Your friend is a strong young woman," Sister Maria-Theresa said as she sponged the child.

It was only then that Daphne understood Virginia wasn't dead. This being the case, her child did not need to be adopted after all, and the Dawsons, accordingly, became Marietta's godparents. Much later, when Marietta was old enough to walk to the font and vociferously resist the baptismal water, Daphne insisted upon a christening in the Katari parish church. "I brought her into this world, didn't I? I want to set her right for the next. At least let me put her name down for it."

Daphne thought she knew what the Africans needed children for: children grounded you, dated you, established you. And because she had seen Marietta being born, Daphne fancied that the child might ground *her* as well as Virginia. Having brought Marietta into the world, so to speak, she'd taken an interest in seeing what became of her, how she grew up. But as Daphne now admitted, "I don't think I've been that attentive, really, do you? I said so to Neville, too. I told him, Peter's the one who got down and played lions and tigers on the floor. It's a pity he's not here. He could've answered all your questions." She lifted the lid of the teapot. "Damn," she said, "no tea left. Never mind." She looked at Marietta. "You know, it was touching to see how fond Neville is of you. He seems to have got over your mother, but he's still devoted to you."

5

Itep

He wants to take you on a trip, Etta," Virginia said. "The letter was in the post this morning. I stuck it somewhere and now I don't remember where."

"You mean Neville?"

"Who else but his lordship?"

"He's not a lord, he's a baronet."

"You know perfectly well what I mean. He has lordly ways. He follows his whim, and his current whim is to take you on safari."

"Where to? The Ruwenzori? Ethiopia? The Victoria Falls?"

"Nothing like that. Haven't you noticed, Neville's turning plain and simple. He's giving up his castle, he's going to live an unpretentious life. And take unpretentious safaris. He proposes to take you camping for a week above the tree line on Mount Elgon — that is, in his own back yard. Before he gives it away to the Africans."

"You'll let me go, of course."

Virginia wrinkled her nose. "You really want to?"

"Yes." She'd be happy to go to the Okay Teahouse in Baluga if Neville asked her. Or to the end of the earth.

"It's cold up there," Virginia persisted. "You don't like the cold. You're not used to it."

"I'll wear two sweaters and trousers and thick socks. I'll be fine."

"You might find it boring. There's nothing much to do at eleven thousand feet but scrounge for firewood and boil water for tea."

"Being with Neville's never boring. We'll find plenty to do."

Virginia stared distractedly at Marietta. After a moment she said, "I suppose you'll be all right so long as Justin's with you."

"Justin! Did Neville invite Justin?"

"One doesn't *invite* servants. One assumes they'll come along."

"If he wanted Justin, he'd have said so in the letter. Where *is* the letter? If it's about *me*, I want to see it!"

They looked through every drawer in the office desk and all along the bookshelves. Eventually Marietta found it in the bar, wedged between the Dewar's and the Teachers Highland Cream. The writing paper was eggshell blue and the address was printed in raised black letters: Itep, PO Box 12, Kitale, Kenya. Sir George had taken Box 12 in 1913 and immediately sent off to Asprey's to have his writing paper printed. He'd ordered fifty boxes. He was expecting to stay in Africa a while.

Neville's writing was in black ink, to go with the letterhead. "My dear Virginia, I'm going to ask you a great favor. With only five weeks left until . . . I tried to telephone but of course the line was out of order, so rather than wait, I'm committing myself to the Royal Mail . . . Would the seventh be convenient? I'll be driving up from Nairobi. Long ago I promised to show her the crater and this looks like my last chance."

"Justin would hate it," Marietta said. "He's never liked mountains."

"He'd go up one if I asked him to."

"He doesn't like tents, either. He likes walls and a roof and a door you can lock. Why *should* you ask him?"

"You've never been off on your own before."

"I won't be on my own, I'll be with Neville, and Neville knows Mount Elgon like the back of his hand. He was born there!"

"I still think Justin should go with you."

"What for, as my ayah?"

When she heard about the expedition Violet cleared her throat and spat. Her aim was perfect. Her spit landed an inch from Marietta's right foot.

Marietta snorted. "What have *you* got against him, may I ask?"

"You change when he comes, Mari. You don't hear what we say, Justin and I. You don't notice us. You only listen to him, and after he goes it's so long before you become yourself again. We ask ourselves, What has become of the girl we knew?"

Justin's objections, freely given in the laundry, while he was doing the Monday wash, were practical. "What will you eat? When did the bwana learn to cook?"

"He didn't," Marietta said, "but I did. I'll do the cooking."

"There are smugglers up there," Justin went on stubbornly, "crossing from Uganda. That's how they evade the policemen on the border, by going over the mountain, almost to the summit and down into Kenya, through the forest. What if they see you and you see them? They'll kill you."

"No, they won't, Justin. They'll think Bwana Bilton's a policeman and they'll run away."

Justin sighed despairingly. He didn't like the idea of this safari at all.

Neville arrived about two. He'd left Nairobi before dawn, raced to Eldonia, and then on the Kericho road got a puncture. He'd changed the wheel and in the process covered himself with mud.

"Not quite as impeccable as usual," Virginia said. "D'you want to use our shower and get on some clean clothes?"

"Can't spare the time, but thanks anyway. Our guests are due at seven-thirty. We should get on. I hope you packed a party dress, Marietta," he added as he picked up her duffel bag.

"I thought you were going camping," Virginia said.

"We are, but following the party. The party's tonight. We go up the mountain in the morning."

"Is this the last bash?"

"That's the general idea."

"Etta's almost grown out of the dress Daphne gave her for her last birthday."

"I'll have to bring it," Marietta said gruffly, "even if it doesn't fit. I haven't got another."

Virginia kissed her forehead. Justin shook her hand. Violet's nostrils flared with disapproval. Neville opened the door for her. "It's a bit of a mess, please forgive me." Then he got into the driver's seat and they were off.

"Are there lots of people coming to your party?"

"You'll see," Neville replied.

"I hardly ever go to parties," said Marietta stiffly.

Neville chuckled. "Living at the Wayfarer's a constant party, isn't it?"

"That might be your impression, but it certainly isn't mine!"

78

After a moment she asked, "Are you going to have dancing?" Aunt Daphne always had dancing at her parties, and since those were the only ones Marietta had attended, they provided the ground rules.

"If we want. We can do whatever we like."

Then couldn't we cancel your stupid party, Marietta wanted to say, but she didn't. As they bounced northward through the reserves with their patchwork quilt of maize and coffee and pasture and climbed higher into open Settler country, her disappointment over having to share Neville with strangers receded. It was only for tonight. In the morning they'd be leaving, they'd be going to the top of the world, with the two hemispherical tents with inch-wide zippers, the aluminum pots, the collapsible cups, and the goose-down sleeping bags that Neville had ordered from a Canadian sporting goods catalogue and had shipped airmail to Nairobi, just in time. He'd picked them up the day before yesterday, and there they all were in the back of the Land-Rover, still in their cardboard boxes. Neville and Marietta were going to be dropped with their packs at the end of the lumber road and then they'd be on their own. They'd only take what they could carry — hence the new equipment, lightest weight. The tents weighed less than four pounds each! Neville told her that he'd never been on such an expedition before, two people, without a single porter. He'd never been able to think of anyone whose undiluted company he could take for a whole week.

Hot with happiness, Marietta laughed.

"What's so funny?"

"Them — the opposition. Mummy, Justin, and Violet. Did you see the looks on their faces? They were like a row of old crows perched on the wall round the Baluga rubbish dump." And having lain awake most of the previous night in trepidation, she fell asleep.

When she awoke it was evening, and there on a spur above them stood Itep, with its tower from which you viewed the heavens and its castellated parapet. She hadn't been there since the day of the decampment two years — half a lifetime — ago, but she hadn't forgotten the way the shadows fell at sunset in the courtyard, or the softness of the moss on the balustrade round the white and purple garden her mother had planted before fleeing. She remembered exactly the view from every mullioned window, how from April to December the countryside had turned from brown to green to gold to brown again, how the bark of the trees that she and Violet climbed felt against her hands and arms and the insides of her knees.

"Welcome, Marietta!" Neville took his left hand off the gear shift, reached out for her hand, and brought it to his lips and kissed it. "I'd been hoping you'd find your way back somehow."

They spurted over the cattle grid and up the farm road, edged by laborers heading home at the end of the day. They reached the house as the first stars came out above the mountains. Festus and Owangi, Neville's butler and cook, were on the front steps to greet them. "How was the safari, bwana? How Mari has grown!"

On the bed in her old room was a doll Neville had given her during his courtship of her mother, and as she opened the closet door she spotted the green sweater that he'd brought to searing Runga with the chill of Mount Elgon in mind. Virginia hadn't thought too much about belongings, either hers or Marietta's, when she was escaping from Neville. Marietta smiled as she went into the bathroom to turn on the water. It was different at Itep without the restless Virginia. It was even better.

After her bath she put on the blue taffeta dress she'd just about grown out of — under the arms it was tightish, and it barely covered her knees — and went down to cocktails. Neville, in his dinner jacket, was sitting in the library, in front of the fire. He'd aged since the debacle with Virginia. His hair was gray now and his eyes weren't quite the deep emerald they used to be. But to Marietta he seemed more reflective, wiser, more distinguished.

"Where are all the others?"

"There aren't any others," Neville said.

"You mean you canceled the party?"

"No, not at all. Will you have cider or ginger beer?"

"You told me half past seven. Did you tell them eight?"

"I never told them anything. Our smart party is just for you and me. I've given so many parties here out of obligation. They always turned out more elaborate than I'd intended, too, and in the end they were never that much fun. So I said to myself, All right, I'll give one last party before everything gets packed up and sent away. And this time, no paying back old invitations to people I don't really care for, I'll keep the guest list to a minimum. I'll only invite people I know I'm going to miss. But when I sat down with a pencil and paper and gave the matter some thought, I realized there were only three such people — my cook and my butler and you, Marietta. Since Owangi and Festus were here already, that left only you to invite. I hope you're not very disappointed. You were expecting a glamorous occasion, I know."

"I was," said Marietta, "but I'm very glad to do without."

After she'd finished her ginger beer and Neville his martini, Festus announced dinner. "Shall we go in now?" Neville said, smiling. The dining room was all lit up. There were candelabra with three candles in each and roses arranged in silver bowls down the length of the table, which seated sixteen, but all except two of the chairs were back against the walls. Neville and Marietta sat at the center, facing each other. Marietta's back was to the fireplace and Neville's to the windows. As he waited for Festus to serve the sorrel soup, he watched Marietta unfold her napkin and smooth it across her knees. When she looked up he said softly, "It suits you."

"You don't think it's an awful color? It was Aunt Daphne's choice, not mine. She got it in London, so it couldn't be exchanged. And anyway, because it was a present, I couldn't say I really didn't like it."

"I didn't mean your dress," Neville said, "although I think that suits you, too. I've always admired Daphne's taste in everything but her boyfriends. What I meant was, you fit in here, Marietta. There haven't been many who have. The idea of the house was so long with me, it was so familiar, so much a part of me, that when it became reality — a place to live, not just to imagine — it came as a surprise when other people took such great exception to it."

After the soup was served he went on slowly, "I'd been planning it ever since my aunt Janet took me to France when I was a year or two older than you. One afternoon in Languedoc we drove round a river bend after a rainstorm, and there on the cliff was the castle, held in a shaft of light. It was like a painting by El Greco — against turbulence and darkness an illuminated miracle occurs. I told Aunt Janet we had to see it, so we drove up and found the caretaker or the bailiff, whatever he was. The owners were some terrific aristocrats who lived in Paris and never came near the place if they could help it. But the bailiff let us poke around and I made a few sketches, and then Aunt Janet dragged me off; we had to meet my uncle in some hotel or other. That was how it started, this notion of a castle. I went back once before the war. By that time I'd read up on it. Château de Saint Guillaume de Pont du Boeuf was its name and it was rather celebrated, being early Romanesque with Moorish as well as Norman details. A hodgepodge, which I found entrancing. You could say it became an obsession. During the war I whiled away untold dreary hours at Aldershot and Camberley and many other forgettable places imagining the doors and windows, the terraces, the parapet, and of course the tower. But when I went back in 1946 it was a blackened ruin, derelict. They'd had a fire and the owners had died and the place now belonged to a local builder who used the stables to store pipes and planks. So then I decided, There's nothing to stop me, I won't be offending any ancient family if I copy their castle at Itep. And that is what I did, as soon as my father handed the farm over.

"But unfortunately" — he smiled wryly — "I ran into so much disapproval, especially from my wives. I suppose it's a mistake to expect people to share one's obsessions. It should be enough just to pursue them on one's own. But I took a long time learning that. The truth is, when I look back over the last ten years I can remember only one point at which I felt my pleasure in this place was shared, and that was when you lived here, Marietta."

After sorrel soup they had trout, Châteaubriand, asparagus, Camembert, and crêpes suzette. With the crêpes Neville opened a bottle of champagne, King '49, the year Itep had been finished. He called Owangi from the kitchen and gave him and Festus glasses too, and they drank to the time they'd spent together and to the future, when they would be apart.

PART II

1961

6

Baluga

The clouds towered into the sky, billowing white fortresses with dark underbellies. The trees were listless in the heat. Later the lightning and thunder would come, and in the sudden wind the trees would spring alive, tossing their blossoms over the grass, while the rain swept across the hills in dense gray sheets. But now it was the quiet time after lunch. The servants had gone to their quarters. Only Osoro the *askari* nodded on his watchman's stool by the front door, his fez slipping over his eyes.

Marietta, barefoot, in an old cotton sundress, walked slowly down the veranda that ran along the garden side of the hotel. She usually spent the afternoon in her room, working on her stories. Last Christmas a young man had offered twelve cows for Violet; Justin had accepted, and Violet had gone home for good. She was a married woman now. Marietta had written so many stories since then; she illustrated each one carefully. Some she sent to Violet at Galana, some to Neville in Alberta, and some she kept. One or two of these Virginia had read.

"Why d'you always write about Africans?" she'd said, frowning.

"Because apart from you and me, they're the people I know best," Marietta had replied. "If I wrote about anybody else, I wouldn't get them right."

But her notebook was shut up in the chest of drawers in her room in the cottage that she shared with her mother. There was a three-foot gap between the top of the partition wall and the high, thatched roof. This was for ventilation, but the design precluded privacy, and Marietta knew that on her side of the wall Virginia was in bed with a man. In an hour it would be time for tea, and Virginia would leave the cottage in the garden to organize the servants. Then Marietta would be able to slip into her room and get on with her writing. Clearly Virginia and this man had it in mind to spend the afternoon together; in the bar, before lunch, he hadn't been able to take his eyes off Virginia; he'd stood too close to her, hands in his pockets as if to stop himself from stroking her then and there, in front of the bank manager and the assistant district commissioner. As for Virginia, she'd tossed her head and run her hands through her hair continually. And laughed often, as if anticipating pleasure.

It had been silly not to think ahead, but Virginia's gaiety always confused Marietta. She preferred to escape from it, and so after lunch she'd been willingly distracted by an accident in the road outside. An Indian swerving to avoid a goat had run into the stone wall at the edge of the hotel compound. There had followed a tremendous *shauri* between the Indian, who was young and very angry, and the owner of the goat, who was old and even angrier. Everyone had taken sides. By the time that was over and Marietta had run back across the lawn to the cottage, her mother's door was shut. As she'd stopped on the front steps, she'd heard the bed creak.

She and her mother had an arrangement. They hadn't actually discussed it, but it was just as binding as if they had. Virginia brought her men friends in during the afternoon, never at night. When Violet had still been at Baluga, Marietta hadn't used her room much in the daytime anyway — there'd been such a lot to see and do elsewhere. It was only since Violet left in December that Marietta needed four walls and a door, a place in which to construct a world of her own. The last time she'd seen Neville, on the Mount Elgon safari, he had told her this was essential. They were making their way to the highest part of the crater on the Kenya side, with Neville climbing steadily hand over hand and Marietta, less expert, scrambling up behind him. When they reached the top, below them lay the sweep of the Rift, shimmering in the February sun.

"You can't see Mount Kenya at all," Marietta said, disappointed. "It's completely hidden by the heat haze."

"One imagines it perfectly, though," said Neville.

"That's not the same."

"Not the same, no. In my opinion, better. It's entirely blanketed in snow."

"How do you know?"

Neville smiled. "The fact is," he said, "I've never seen it blanketed in snow, because it never is. A frosting round the top is the snowiest it ever gets and at this time of year it has hardly any at all, given that this is the driest part of the dry season. But since we can't see it, we can imagine it exactly as we please. Why be constrained by how things are, Marietta? One's concept not of how the world *is*, but of how it *might* be, is what's sustaining."

"What's so wrong with the world as it is?" She'd hardly begun to know it. Apart from a few lakes and tired towns, one castle, the odd mountain, she'd seen the Kenya Coast three times, and that was that. She'd never been to London, let alone Languedoc.

"I'm not saying anything's *so* wrong with the world," Neville said, "but rather that one's imagination can so much improve it. Then one has it in one's head, it's safe, it can't be taken away, the way the real world can."

"Can it?"

"Of course! It's happened to me regularly."

"Who took it from you?"

Neville frowned. "Let me see . . . Well, the first time I suppose it was my parents. I suppose it generally *is* one's parents, the first time. No doubt they sincerely believe they have one's interest at heart. They're doing whatever it is for one's sake, not for theirs."

"Doing what, for instance?"

"Forcibly removing one from A to B — from Africa to England, in my case. I was eight at the time."

"But you adore England, Neville!"

"Not when I was eight, I didn't. I hardly had a notion about what England was. You're right, of course eventually I did love England, but that took many years. At the beginning I didn't want to be there in the least. I wanted to be home in Africa, but Africa had vanished without a trace, other than a few traces that had stayed with me in my head. At eight that tends to be quite an odd assortment. A particular butterfly on a windowsill — this one was white with four green dots on the tip of each wing — and the smell of wood smoke, damp and strong, so different from the dry oak of English winter drawing room fires. Boys always remember their dogs, of course. Mine was a bull mastiff called H. Morton Stanley. He had great sad, wet eyes, and he snored at night and had soft folds of skin on his neck. And he was desperately attached to *me*. I'd lie in my boarding school bed at night and talk to Stanley by the hour." Neville smiled. "His conversation was so utterly absorbing that every dog I've had since has been a letdown. I tried lots, hoping for another Stanley, but in the end I saw, obviously, that I'd never find him, and I gave up."

It had taken a long time to explore the world of his imagination, Neville said. He'd been very cautious to begin with. He'd had glimpses of what might be there, but he hadn't quite had the courage to rush ahead. Then bit by bit he became more daring, and the further he went, the more there was to see. He didn't expect to see the whole of it ever because new territories were always opening up.

"Are there any *people* in your world?" Marietta asked.

"Only a few. You see, I don't know that many who deserve to be included." Neville chuckled.

"Do I know any of them?"

"You know one who used to."

"Who?"

"Your mother. But one look was enough for her. She didn't care for what she saw, so she drove off. Fortunately she didn't take you with her."

"She *did*, though!"

"No, she didn't. That's the great charm of having one's own world — one can change things from how they are to how they ought to be. By no means everybody has the knack, but I've no doubt that you're one of the lucky ones, Marietta. If *you* see that at midnight the sun's high in the sky, don't let anyone convince you it's not so!"

She was one of the lucky ones, he'd said. On an empty afternoon following Violet's departure, she'd bought a book with purple cardboard covers in the *dukas* and set to work. It turned out that her world was very different from Neville's. There were no dogs or butterflies in it, and smells weren't featured either. No, *her* world was full of people, people like Rose Achola, a Luo girl who lived on the shore of Lake Victoria. She was sixteen, her breasts were full, and she'd fallen in love with a boy called Tobias. But Tobias was poor; he couldn't afford to pay the price that Rose's father demanded, so against her will she was married to a rich old deaf, foul-smelling man with six wives already. But on the wedding night, while Rose lay pining for her lover, a buffalo came and knocked down the house. In the confusion Rose escaped. She ran through the bush until she reached Tobias's homestead. She wriggled through the euphorbia hedge without a single scratch because the thorns had suddenly grown soft to let her pass. Her family realized that the destruction of the rich man's hut had been an omen from the ancestors, which they interpreted as meaning that the marriage ought to be abandoned. So love triumphed over avarice, and the young people were permitted to remain together. In time they were blessed with a son.

Rose Achola was willful and determined, but in a decorous way that endeared her to her elders and put them off their guard. They didn't know what they were dealing with until too late; and this gentle, courteous maiden adroitly — ah so smoothly! — got things her own way. In many respects the young girl she wrote about reminded Marietta of Violet.

Now Marietta flopped into a cushioned chair and propped her feet up on the railing of the veranda. The lawn sloped down the hill to a high hedge, and beyond the hedge to the river where she'd swum, as a child, with Violet. She didn't think of herself as a child anymore. She didn't know exactly where she stood. Both girls had been perfectly aware that eventually it would happen, but when it did, when Violet went off to her husband, a man she'd seen only once, Marietta was horribly confused. Not only did she miss Violet (and expected to miss her forever), she felt that she, too, should do as her friend had done: she should plunge into living with a man.

Violet had claimed reluctance, but Marietta, knowing Violet very well, had detected excitement not far below the surface. When Violet had said good-bye, she'd wept, but Marietta had believed her tears were for form's sake. Now at night Violet was warming a man named Daniel, while Marietta, who'd shared a bed with her for as long as she could remember, slept alone. As children they had promised one another that they'd never be parted, that they'd marry the same man. Whoever wanted one could only have her if he took the other also. Ruba people often married sisters, after all. But it turned out that they weren't really sisters, and one of them wasn't even Ruba. That one had been left with the burden of sorrow while the other had escaped into womanhood. Violet had been a child, and then, overnight, she had become a wife. She'd confided in a recent letter that in September, just three months from now, she expected to become a mother. For her it had all been miraculously simple.

At times when Marietta was certain her mother was busy in the hotel, she examined herself, naked, in the mirror. Virginia, she was convinced, still thought of her as a child. It was simpler to see her that way. Marietta groaned inwardly. She felt sometimes that if she had to go on like this, treading quietly round the edges of her mother's life, she might find herself taking off her clothes one hot noontime and running naked through the Baluga market, as Josefina, the watchman's daughter, had done in January until five strong men caught her and locked her up in the police station.

Of course Violet's sixteen, two years older than I am, Marietta told herself, and Justin had been considering offers for quite a while before he accepted Daniel's. I've got a little time yet. Besides, whom do I want? Not one of those schoolboy soldiers she'd danced with at the Katari Club on gala nights when she was staying with the Dawsons. They had hot hands and scarlet faces and when they got drunk they dashed outside and vomited into the agapanthus lilies. She didn't fancy Nigel Baker-Lyle much either, though he liked *her* enough to send her a Saint Valentine's Day card. He hadn't signed it, but she knew by the postmark that it came from him. He'd gone to England last September to the Cirencester Agricultural College. He'd be home soon for the summer, and no doubt he'd drop in at the Wayfarer and bore her to death about racehorses — betting and the money to be won if you watched the form closely.

In fact she liked Benjamin, the newest houseboy, better than anyone else. He was extremely handsome and the star of the Baluga soccer team. Whenever there was a home match she went to watch him play, barefoot and without a shirt. And he was a terrific dancer, too. They'd danced together in the laundry often, to Jamaican music on the radio.

Virginia had been down on Benjamin from the beginning. She hadn't wanted to hire him because she already had a head cook, an assistant cook, a bartender, four houseboys (who, after a great deal of effort on her part, were reasonably efficient), a laundryman, four gardeners, and a watchman, not to mention Justin, who looked after her and Marietta. Virginia was pleased with her staff and she didn't want to bother to train anyone new. But she'd had to hire Benjamin, like it or not, because he was one of the forty-four sons of Chief Mattias. The colonial authorities cherished Mattias. In return for a free hand he kept the Pax Britannica in Keriki Location at minimal expense to the Crown. Seven clans lived there, and anyone who could keep their ancient antagonisms in check was worth cherishing. In February Mattias came to the Wayfarer in his green Chevrolet and marched in with Benjamin, and Virginia, before she knew it, had agreed to hire the boy at forty shillings a month plus two uniforms and a pair of shoes. His business satisfactorily concluded, the chief drove away; Virginia was left with the task of teaching his son a trade. When Benjamin established a pattern of incapacity owing to inebriation at the end of each month, Virginia's hands were tied. Given the clout of the young man's father, she was obliged to hold her peace, at least in public, although in private she complained about him freely. The spiv, she called him. "The last thing he's interested in is *working*. All he cares about is having a good time."

That, of course, was just what Marietta liked about him. It was strange to think that he was Catherine Mattias's brother. Half-brother, rather. He wasn't a bit like her. She didn't know what had become of Catherine; Marietta secretly hoped she'd been married off to some determined man who'd cut her down to size. Marietta could have asked Benjamin, but why bother? She wasn't at all interested. Benjamin, of course, was quite another matter; she was very much interested in *him*. Unfortunately he had a girl already, who spent almost every night with him in the boys' quarters.

With Benjamin taken, she'd have to bide her time and wait and see who else came her way. Meanwhile, when she walked across the garden or down the veranda, excitement (which she'd caught like a disease from Violet) tugged at her and made it difficult to move normally; she was certain people noticed and guessed correctly what was going on.

She dozed in the heat of the afternoon, and when she awoke the man who had spent the afternoon with her mother was crossing the lawn. She tried to feign sleep but she had pins and needles in one leg. She jumped up. "What's the matter?" the man asked, coming onto the veranda.

"Pins and needles." She grimaced.

"Stretch," he said, "and you'll feel better. By the way, I'm Geoffrey Lucas. We met in March a year ago. You've grown up a lot since then." He seemed eager to please. He had curly reddish hair and light eyes.

Marietta flexed her leg. "I remember all about you," Lucas added, looking down at her intently. "The East African safari weekend — you were taking food to the drivers down at the gate. You kept running up and back with empty thermoses, getting them filled. But then a car whipped up and the driver didn't see you in time. His brakes were wet and he couldn't stop. I grabbed you. Surely you haven't forgotten *that!*"

Marietta shuddered. "Afterwards I was sick."

"You were damned lucky! That car missed you by a whisker. Actually, I strained my shoulder when I yanked you off the road. Couldn't play tennis or golf for a couple of weeks. A small price, though, to pay for a young woman's life!" He pretended to take his hat off to her. "Well, now I've recovered and you're quite grown up, how about tea? I see those fellows are setting things up for us." One servant was draping a cloth over a long table, and another appeared with a heavy tray of china.

Marietta had intended to take what she wanted and carry it off to her room, but Lucas made her sit down again with him. When Virginia came from the garden he beckoned her over. "We were reminiscing about how we first met," he said. "I told Marietta I didn't recognize her. She's shot up and turned into a beauty. I didn't tell her that, actually, but with your permission, Virginia, I do so now."

As her mother sat down with them, Marietta thought, So many men like her, but she keeps herself to herself. Men don't realize that, at least not right away. Lucas doesn't realize it.

"Everyone tells me Etta's got so tall," Virginia murmured, signaling a waiter to bring another cup of tea. Marietta wondered, Had the afternoon with Lucas been a pleasure? Behind appearances, Virginia wasn't often pleased.

Lucas was full of himself, talking about people Marietta didn't know. Virginia nodded every now and then so he would think she was listening, when, in fact, as Marietta knew, she hardly heard a word. Lucas said, "Don't you remember last January Bennington told us he was leaving?" Bennington hadn't been to the Wayfarer, which meant Virginia and Lucas must have been with him, whoever he was, somewhere else last January. Virginia had a life, a patchy, pieced-together life, that Marietta heard about only by accident. Lucas belonged to that life. She wished he hadn't come, that he'd stayed away and not impinged upon them. She stood up.

"I'm going to do my work," she said, leaving her half-empty cup on the table.

Lucas, in mid-anecdote, smiled indulgently. "That sounds important."

"It is. To me."

"Won't you explain?"

"It's just her correspondence course." Virginia gestured with her hand, allowing Marietta to escape.

At dinner that night the dining room was almost full. Virginia had on her new dress; it was red with a deep neckline. She'd brought it up from Nairobi after her last trip. The material clung over her breasts and flowed away from her hips. Even Justin, passing her in the garden before dinner, was moved to remark, "Very beautiful." Marietta sat through the meal aware of the attention her mother attracted in a crowd almost entirely male. As soon as she'd finished her apple tart she slipped off to the cottage.

By eight o'clock on a June evening it was chilly in Baluga. Marietta wanted a fire. She carried some logs in from the woodpile on the porch and took her lamp into her mother's room to look for matches and a newspaper for kindling. Benjamin hadn't tidied the room yet. It was his job, but he did their cottage last, after he'd finished the guest rooms. The top bedsheet had been pulled away and lay across the floor, and the pillows were scattered about. The matches were by the bed, next to an ashtray full of cigarette butts. Some of them had lipstick on them, others did not. Marietta found a week-old *Standard* under a chair. As she passed the dressing table on her way out, she saw the top was off the perfume bottle and she dabbed herself liberally behind the ears and at the temples. In a film she'd seen once in the Baluga Club, Ava Gardner had dabbed perfume on her temples before going out to dance with the ambassador under Spanish stars. Marietta looked at herself in the mirror. The lamp illuminated her neck and the lower half of her face. Her forehead and hair were dim. She narrowed her eyes and breathed in deeply. Would she be beautiful? Was she beautiful already? But for whom? Maybe she'd go on forever at Baluga until she shriveled up. How Violet would pity her! How simple things had been for

Violet! In the course of time a man had come, claimed her, carried her off.

Marietta put the top back on the perfume bottle, gathered up the matches and newpaper, and went with her lamp through the bathroom into her own room. Once the fire was lit she undressed and put on an old robe of her mother's. Today, the thirtieth of June, was payday, and Benjamin had received his forty shillings at noon. Marietta didn't remember seeing him at tea or dinner. Undoubtedly he was in some bar in town with his Kikuyu sweetheart, drunk out of his mind. Judging by May's performance, he wouldn't be seen again till the middle of next week.

Marietta was reading in front of her fire when she heard the cottage door open. So Benjamin had come after all! He crossed the sitting room and entered her room without knocking. He's plastered, Marietta thought drowsily, otherwise he'd have knocked. Anyway, she was pleased he'd come and not gone straight off with his girl. Felicitas, her name was. Joy, happiness. Of course they had a wonderful time together, those two. Everyone had somebody. Except for her.

"You're still awake."

Marietta jumped. Geoffrey Lucas stood above her, his hands in the pockets of his bush shorts. She saw the fair, curling hair on his thighs. She scrambled to her feet. "I thought it was one of the boys."

Lucas put his hand on her shoulder. "Don't move. You looked so comfortable."

She sat down again by the hearth. "My mother's not here," she said stolidly.

"She's in the bar. There's quite a crowd there. Someone's playing the piano and they're dancing. Your mother's the belle of the ball." He squatted down near her. "I knew you'd be here. I thought I'd stop in. D'you mind?"

Mairetta looked into the fire. Lucas was a little behind her, filling the room. Beyond was the sitting room and then the dark garden. The cottage was set apart from the rest of the hotel.

"Won't you look at me?"

Marietta turned to him. "What d'you want?"

"Do you realize how pretty you are?"

She pushed her hair away from her face. She wanted to hear that, of course. "Did you come just to say that?"

94

"Oh, you mean it's something men tell you every day?" He laughed. "I'm another in the line. Like mother, like daughter."

"I'm *not* like my mother," she said passionately.

"I didn't mean to offend you, or her." Lucas sat on the floor beside her. "You're both lovely women. That's all I meant. It was a compliment."

"I'm not like my mother," Marietta said again, quietly this time. "She doesn't listen to people and I do."

"Her elusiveness is part of your mother's charm," Lucas said. "When I first came out here I heard that she carried the torch in the bush. And when I finally met her I wasn't disappointed. It's a pity you've decided not to be like her. You'll be doing yourself and others out of a lot of fun."

Marietta didn't think of her mother as fun. But there were two sides to her. When Marietta sat opposite her at meals she could see what strangers saw. The flashiness. She supposed that was what Lucas called fun. It was for the public. The other side was what she knew much better. Neville knew that side better, too. The last night of all, up on Mount Elgon, when she and Neville were sitting by the fire, he'd been talking about his childhood. He told her that growing up as he had, neither here nor there, had made him different. At one time he'd tried to be like other English people, but it hadn't worked; he was like a dog with some odd strain in him. He believed Virginia was that way as well, and Marietta should be warned: she might find she was too. Marietta hadn't really understood what Neville meant, but she hadn't forgotten it. And now she found herself looking at her mother differently. The odd strain Neville had talked about made Virginia smoke a great many cigarettes and stare across the valley beyond Baluga, in a thick, distracted silence.

"No," Marietta said, smiling at Lucas, "you're wrong. I *do* want to have fun."

"I'd hoped so." He leaned forward and brushed a strand of hair away from her face. "You're going to be prettier than your mother," he said. He pulled her towards him. "Has anyone done this with you before?" Against his shirt, Marietta shook her head. "Then I'm a lucky man."

Virginia was waiting until the bar emptied. Tim McCormick, who worked for Barclay's Bank, was still at the piano as she collected

95

the glasses. Outside rain began to splatter against the window. "These foolish things," Tim played softly, "remind me of you."

"Bed," Virginia said, coming to the piano, "at least for me. I have to get up in the morning."

Tim pushed back the piano stool and stood up. "Where's my invitation? I've waited long enough."

"No invitation, Tim. I'm a working woman."

Edward, the bar boy, turned down the lamps, raised the wooden flap of the bar, and came out. Virginia bade him good-night.

McCormick shook his head sadly. "You're harsh to those who love you." He kissed her forehead and picked up his jacket to go off to bed. At the door he turned, supporting himself against the doorpost. "For God's sake, Virginia, burn that dress. You're not being fair to man or beast."

Virginia blew a kiss to him. "Good night, Tim, sleep well."

McCormick put his jacket over his head. "It's wet as the dickens," he called back and went out into the night.

Virginia went onto the veranda where the *askari*, Osoro, lay dozing in his army surplus overcoat. The rain was coming down hard. She didn't want to spoil her Italian sandals, red mock alligator, to match her new dress. In her office she kept a pair of rubber boots and a mackintosh cape. She passed Osoro, who awakened with a start and pretended he'd been awake all the time. In the office Virginia felt around behind her chair until she found her boots; she slipped off her sandals and put on the boots. Then she pulled down the poncho from a hook on the wall, took her flashlight, and went out into the rain.

Round the bougainvillea she came into line with the cottage, far down the path at the end of the garden. The cottage was dark. Usually Benjamin set a lamp on a table by the sitting room window; tonight, obviously, he hadn't. Virginia cursed him silently. Tomorrow was a Saturday, a party was expected from Kisumu; she'd have to get one of the other boys to do Benjamin's work. She thought of him privately as the crown prince and prayed that his father would soon find him an alternative career, one in which he wasn't expected to work the first three days of the month. In the morning, of course, there would be complaints from those same men who'd just been competing to dance with her. They wanted her to provide them with life, lake perch, excitement, Baked Alaska, everything that wives couldn't or didn't, in one complete package. If their beds weren't turned down, though, they felt neglected, uncared for. Auntie didn't love them as they deserved to be loved.

She went into the cottage. Marietta's door was slightly ajar and through it she saw the flicker of a dying fire. Marietta must be fast asleep; it was past midnight. In her own room Virginia put on her nightdress and turned to the unmade bed. At points during the evening she'd wondered where Geoffrey was. She'd expected to see him after dinner, but he was an odd character, afraid of compromising her on her own turf. She picked up the pillows, plumped them, and hurriedly remade the bed. He'd been so careful at teatime to include Marietta. It was rather quaint of him to be gallant, and protective of Virginia's reputation, when she herself didn't care about her reputation. She was a woman alone. She'd explained that to him in Nairobi. "I'm by myself," she'd told him. "I have friends but I like being alone."

He hadn't believed her, though. He was thinking of Gillian, his wife in England, whom he'd left. *She* hated being alone. It was essential for Geoffrey to think that all women were like that, and that all men wanted to be free, regardless of the evidence. In the afternoon, in her bed, he'd told her how he wanted to lease an island off the coast and start a fish nursery. He'd ship oysters by air to Covent Garden. They'd grow by themselves, quietly, in their oyster beds. He'd have all the time in the world to snorkel and sail and make love. "Would you like that life, Virginia?" He was touching her breasts, wanting her again.

"I know I wouldn't," she'd said. "I don't like the sea."

He'd taken his hand away then and said fussily, "It's hot. Don't you have any ice here? Must one trek to the bar?"

"Oh, Geoffrey," she'd laughed, "I said I didn't like the *sea*. Don't take it personally."

But the fact was, he'd been hurt that she hadn't jumped at the idea of going off with him, that she hadn't jumped into his daydream. It had taken some guile on her part to bring him out of his sulk. Of course he'd never lease that island. By the time he got his divorce he'd have found himself another Gillian. Sexual adventuring wasn't really his cup of tea. The sex was fine. It was the adventuring that before too long would scare him. He needed to let himself be bound.

Virginia watched herself in the mirror as she brushed her hair.

It fluffed out in the lamplight. In her youth it had been almost white, but her youth was definitely a thing of the past, she told herself. It was a wonder that young men still wanted to carry her off to tropical islands. She was in her prime, had been for some years, with still some more to come, but looks were terribly deceptive. Somehow she'd never had the feelings to match her looks. Her friend before Geoffrey had put his finger on it. He'd said, "You look like a peach, soft and warm. But you can't *behave* like one." He'd been very angry. Virginia had laughed. "What's a peach supposed to feel like?" Life would probably be easier once she was past her prime. No more men to be angry with her.

In the bathroom between her room and Marietta's a lizard scrambled up the wall and into the thatch. Virginia splashed cold water against her face and neck. She was very tired. The end of the month was always exhausting. Before she went to bed she'd better make sure Marietta's fire was all right; there used to be a fire guard in there, but last week Benjamin had taken it away to a guest room. Sleepily she opened the connecting door and went into her daughter's room. The fire had burned down very low. She took the poker and pushed the logs back, away from the hearth, and in doing so she rekindled a flame. The room was suddenly illuminated. It wouldn't last, though, and the logs were far enough back into the fireplace to be safe.

Virginia turned into the room. In the firelight she saw Marietta, and next to her, in the narrow single bed, Geoffrey Lucas fast asleep, his arm under Marietta's head. His clothes were on the floor. Automatically Virginia bent and picked them up. She shook out his trousers and draped them over a chair, and then hung his shirt over the trousers. But as she stopped beside the bed to look at the two of them she was suddenly, astonishingly, engulfed by rage. She grasped at the tops of her own thighs to stop herself from pulling Geoffrey off the bed, from beating his head upon the cold tile floor. She hated him for violating her child, for dragging Marietta into what ought to have remained an inconsequential part of her mother's life. But she hated herself still more for her own refusal, out of fear for herself, fear of loneliness, of being ultimately, intolerably bereft, to see what Marietta had become, and for not protecting her accordingly.

Marietta stirred in her sleep and turned her head towards the hearth. Her mother saw then that she wasn't a child.

Virginia went back through the bathroom into her own room, closing the door softly behind her. She lit a cigarette and lay down on her own bed. She smoked a second cigarette and then a third, adding to the afternoon's accumulation in the ashtray. While she was smoking her fourth she heard Geoffrey Lucas leave her daughter's room, cross the sitting room, and let himself out into the night. The rain had stopped. He had a moon to light his way across the garden.

7

The Mountain School, Tintinet

In the third week of July, in her office on a Friday morning, Virginia announced that Marietta simply couldn't go on at the Wayfarer. "I've been in touch with Neville," she said. "We think, or rather Neville has thought for a long time and now I see he's right, you should go to boarding school."

Virginia had done her hair in a chignon that day. *She* called it a chignon. Marietta called it a bun. She'd been putting it up like that rather often of late. It must be a sign, Marietta thought, that she was setting her mind to something. Marietta was used to her mother not quite looking at her when she spoke, as if there was an invisible rock between them that Virginia saw, though Marietta couldn't. But now, standing squarely on the other side of the typewriter, with her hair scraped back, Virginia looked right over the rock.

Marietta had been typing, with two fingers of each hand, a letter to Neville in Jasper, Alberta. He was building a house there, on a mountainside. It had a view, he'd written, over lakes and forests, and the birds were very interesting. The butterflies were disappointing, though. And Marietta was writing to him, as she did every fortnight, about the books he had sent to her, six at a time, from Foyle's in the Charing Cross Road. Today she was giving him her reflections on *War and Peace.* Since she had many, the letter was already several pages long, which was tiring with only four fingers. And just as she was busiest with Natasha (who had instantly brought to mind that old make-believe of the wedding ball in the dogwoods; how silly it seemed now, with Violet married and about to have a child), her mother positioned herself across the desk and made her announcement about boarding school.

"Neville wanted us to do this years ago," Virginia said, sitting abruptly on a case of Lux soap powder. "It isn't too late, is it? Surely with all those books you read you can't be all that much behind."

Marietta turned the black ribbon to red and punched a line of X's across her page. "Why," she said sharply, "if you didn't listen to Neville then, have you decided to now?" She swung one foot back and forth in the kneehole of the desk, thumping the wood.

Virginia looked down at her hands. "I've been putting off the day to suit myself," she said sorrowfully. "The same way my mother did with me. I swore I wouldn't, but I have."

Her mother, she said, had made the same excuse on their farm a hundred miles from anywhere. Poverty. They'd been terribly hard up. Meat and hides in those prewar years hardly fetched anything at all. "We should send Virginia to England," her mother would say wistfully. "But there isn't the money to send her." Had there been, Virginia doubted she'd have gone because her mother couldn't bear to be left alone with her father.

"He was utterly grim and cold," Virginia said. "He wasn't interested in human beings, only in getting what he wanted from the bush, and at that he wasn't much of a success." She stared past Marietta, her eyes wide. "Twice a week in the dry season I rode twelve miles down the valley for lessons with a Presbyterian lady missionary. Her skin was dry and flaky, and she sang hymns under her breath, which smelled horribly. Of disappointment, I believe. She made very few converts among the Samburu herdsmen round our place.

"Each year we began with Calvin and the Reformation. For fun we recited Robert Burns and *Paradise Lost*. She taught me French in order to read Molière — I couldn't speak a word, though — and a little bit of Latin. So when the war in Europe broke out and I had an airtight reason for leaving at last, I wasn't what you'd call ready for the world." She shook her head. "I'd done my time but Mother couldn't bear to see me go. For days she cried and wouldn't eat and couldn't sleep. I honestly thought she'd die of my leaving. But I was determined to leave. If I stayed, *I'd* die; I knew that perfectly well. It didn't matter to my father what I did. Stay or go. It was all the same to him.

"I went down to Nairobi and joined up as a nurse. I was afraid

101

of my own shadow. If I was told to do something, I never stopped
to ask why, I went ahead and did it. They could have said, 'Stand
on your head on Government House lawn,' and I'd have done that,
too. But then, I'd have done anything rather than go back home to
suffocate on that plain." She frowned over Marietta's shoulder into
the garden, where the birds were busy on the grass. "At home the
mountains changed color in the distance, according to the time of
day and the time of year. Sometimes they were purple, sometimes
gray or brown or green. But my parents didn't change. I used to
hope that one day Father would find me interesting. He never did."
She smiled grimly. "And Mother found me *too* interesting. If I lived
and breathed, then she could too. She wouldn't do it just for her
own sake." Virginia stopped. Her shoulders drooped. "Why am I
telling you this?"

Marietta leaned back in her chair. Her mother was courting her,
she knew, and she didn't wish to be won. She frowned. "You're
explaining why you want to send me away from Baluga before I'm
ruined."

"Did I say that?"

"No. It's what you meant, though."

"Don't you see, I want you to be better off than I was," Virginia
cried. "At eighteen I was entirely ignorant! I'd read a few novels
and listened for twelve years to a spinster missionary in gray lisle
stockings and tennis shoes, whose mind wasn't on this world anyway. Of course," she said, sighing, "there was Aunt Sophia. She
came out from England once to spend the winter. She'd just got
married, and she brought her husband, Jock. I'd go into the guest
cottage when they were out riding and look at her things, and daydream about a life in which I wore underclothes like hers, with
shell-stitched edging. Sophia gave me a whiff of the outside world.
Only a whiff, though. When I left home I felt exactly as if I'd been
told to take a car and drive it and I wasn't even sure where the
ignition was!" She laced and unlaced her fingers. Marietta noticed
for the first time that there were little lines at the corners of her
mother's eyes.

Virginia smiled quickly. "Thank God, in Alexandria I ran into
Daphne. She'd grown up in Cape Town, which might as well have
been Paris to me, coming as I did from the plains beyond Thomson's Falls. Daphne saw instantly how green I was but she didn't
despise me for that, and once we'd latched onto one another we

had adventures which would have struck that Presbyterian lady dead in her tracks, and I don't mean changing bedpans. We did that, too, of course, and though it was odious, you got used to it, and sometimes," Virginia added, laughing, "you changed the bedpans of delightful people. Daphne used to say how much clearer an idea of a man you got that way than if you had a drink with him in the Officers Club . . ." Her voice trailed off.

Marietta saw that a lock of hair had escaped from the chignon. Perhaps her mother was losing her determination. Perhaps the boarding school idea had been forgotten. But Virginia felt the straying hair against her neck, scooped it up, and pinned it back where it belonged.

"I used to tell myself that I was having a good war," she said quietly. "What nonsense! In fact, I felt like a feather, a leaf — weightless, being blown about." Her voice cracked. "And it wasn't because of the war. If it had been peacetime, I'd have felt just the same. I didn't know what other people expected of me, or what I should expect of them. If they treated me well, fine. If they treated me badly, I didn't catch on until too late. And even if I had caught on, I couldn't have stopped them. Etta, you can't grow up to be like that!"

"I'm not a leaf or a feather. I can take care of myself!" Marietta stood up, her two thick braids swinging behind her shoulders.

Virginia stood also, across the desk from her daughter. "Can you, though? What's up with you and Benjamin?"

Marietta flushed. "Nothing in particular."

"Really? I saw you in the laundry yesterday. I wouldn't call what you were doing with him nothing in particular!"

"We were dancing," Marietta muttered. "Why shouldn't we? We often do. He's fun."

"I'd seen you making eyes at him before," Virginia said. "I'd thought, Can't be, she's got more sense. But obviously you haven't."

"Supposing I do like him, what's wrong with that?"

"First, he's a servant; second, he's a drunkard; third, he hasn't a brain in his head!"

"And fourth, he's black. But you don't have to worry," Marietta said coldly, "he's got a girl already. A Kikuyu with crooked teeth."

"What about Geoffrey Lucas, then! You can't say you took care of yourself that time, can you!"

Marietta sat abruptly. "What did Lucas say?"

Virginia came round the side of the desk and reached out to touch her daughter. Then, awed by her stillness, she let her hand drop. "I'm so sorry, Etta." Beyond the closed door they heard the cook shout at one of the houseboys and then a crash as a stack of plates fell to the floor. In the garden a crow cawed and flapped its wings, wheeling over the grass in the sunlight. "I came into your room to see to your fire and he was with you," Virginia said. A dread rose in her, a sense of losing something all over again. "Etta, why do such things happen?"

Marietta swiveled slowly away from her mother and round again to face her. "I wanted to see why you liked him. You do, don't you?"

"Like him?"

"You must, or you wouldn't have let him come."

"I couldn't stop him. A hotel is a public place."

"Maybe, but you didn't have to go to bed with him, not unless you liked him. *Do* you like Geoffrey?"

"I believe I hate him," Virginia said.

"I don't know him well enough to tell if I like him or not," Marietta said evenly. She swiveled her chair round again. "Well" — she caught at the edge of the desk to stop herself — "now I see why you wanted to send me away. You should have said so in the first place."

Virginia swerved the Land-Rover onto the grass, out of the path of a bus barreling round the corner through the black-wattle trees. Inside there were three people to a seat; poultry baskets were roped to the roof. Chickens squawked and scrambled as the bus sped by, and the young Indian driver flashed brilliant teeth at Virginia, in defiance, she knew, not gratitude. In the back Justin cried out, "I know that madman! He struck his teacher in the Hindu College and was sent away forever."

"You've always got a story, haven't you?" Virginia said in English. With Justin she used English or Swahili, depending on whether she felt more like a memsahb or more like a person.

"What I tell you is the truth," Justin said calmly. He was in the best of spirits. That morning he'd received a letter; it protruded now from the pocket of the blue-striped shirt that Neville had presented to him before leaving for Canada. The letter announced the birth of Justin's first grandchild. Last Sunday Violet had produced a son.

Marietta had been sorting her things in her room when Justin burst in with his news. In his excitement his face seemed more densely wrinkled than ever. Marietta shook his hand. "Now you're a grandfather! You must carry a stick and wear a hat. A black felt one, that's what the most respected elders wear!"

She was glad, she truly was, that Violet had had her child safely, that the child was a son, that Justin was so extraordinarily delighted with this achievement, which he thought of as his own as much as Violet's. But it was wickedly unfair, she thought, that the news, so long awaited, should come today of all days, when she, Marietta, was packing her trunk in preparation for becoming, not a wife and mother, but a Third Former in the Mountain School for Girls.

They were climbing steadily now. On either side tea plantations stretched almost as far as the eye could see, and here and there in the midst of them were laborers with great baskets on their backs, picking the daily harvest of bright leaves. The air was oppressive with the smell of tea. Marietta watched the laborers moving slowly, waist-high in the dense green. She smoothed her skirt over her knees. Her uniform — four blue-checked cotton dresses with white collars, four blouses, and four pairs of athletic shorts — had been made for her by Mrs. Vejay. At the fittings Mrs. Vejay made it clear that Memsahb Hamilton was indeed fortunate to have her daughter attended to; she was overburdened. So many girls were requiring uniforms at once.

A horn sounded urgently, and in the mirror Virginia saw a large green car grinding up the hill behind them.

"Someone's in the dickens of a hurry." She swung to the side to let the other car go by and saw that it was driven by Chief Mattias. Beside him sat a white woman. As he passed, the chief raised his hand in greeting and the woman waved too. Two heads bobbed in the rear window.

"The father of Benjamin," Justin said, grinning. "He has abducted the wife of the missionary at Keriki!"

"Mrs. Tyson? I wonder where he's off to with her, the old rascal. I'd really like a word with him about his precious son. That young man doesn't listen to a thing I say!"

"It's his girl," Justin said. "The Kikuyu with crooked teeth. It is because of her that he doesn't listen. He is all the time thinking about her!"

They were at the edge of the tea plantations now, and despite the sun, the air was crisp and cool. Ahead of them lay the town of Tintinet. It looked much like Baluga, with lines of Indian shops and a park and a flagpole and a fountain, run dry. As she passed the market Virginia slowed to navigate her way through donkeys scampering on light hoofs down the middle of the road.

"Baluga!" a boy shouted, reading the name on the door of the Land-Rover. "Ba-lu-ga!" He grasped the tailgate as if to jump up and ride with them. Virginia, out beyond the donkeys now, picked up speed again, and the boy faltered and fell back.

The jacaranda trees that lined the road in an attempt to give the town a modicum of grace came to an end, and a signboard announced that they had reached the Mountain School for Girls, Miss Jellicoe, headmistress. Seeing herself in the mirror in her uniform, Marietta thought, Benjamin's girl is so gay and certain of herself. No wonder Benjamin prefers her to me.

They turned off the road onto the loose gray stones of the drive. Passing a stand of conifers, they found themselves in front of a brick mansion with a red, tiled roof and many chimneys. Parked in the driveway were Land-Rovers and jeeps, a Mercedes or two, several horse trailers (one with a tail cascading out of the back), and, last of all, Chief Mattias's Chevrolet. Against its rusting radiator leaned Ongeso, Chief Mattias's cook. Mrs. Tyson, the chief, and an African girl in a blue-checked dress with a white collar, white socks, and black shoes were approaching the front door.

"Good God!" Virginia exclaimed. "That must be our Benjamin's sister! I had no idea this was a *mixed* school," she added as she drove the Land-Rover up next to the Chevrolet. "In her letter Miss Jellicoe never said a word about its being mixed. That poor little girl! But if she takes after her father rather than her brother, she'll do okay. Nothing'll ever stop that old boy."

"What are we sitting here for?" Marietta said angrily. "We didn't drive five hours just to sit." She wrenched the door open and jumped out.

Virginia stared at the fan-shaped mark that the wipers had made on the windshield. She sighed. Marietta was so different these days; nothing pleased her. Virginia marveled at how long she had resisted Neville's offer. She should have snapped it up years ago, of course. She dropped the car keys into her handbag. "Justin, you stay here. You can bring the trunk in later when we're ready."

106

"No, Justin's coming with us," said Marietta loudly. "He's the one to tell Miss What's-Her-Name about me. *He* knows I shouldn't be forced to eat tomatoes or my eyes swell up, and he remembers every single mark I've got from Dr. Vorster since I was eight, whereas *you* hardly ever bothered to check if I'd finished the assignments! I'll ask that old man to keep an eye on the Land-Rover," she said, and she went up to Ongeso. "Can you watch our vehicle?" But Ongeso was hard of hearing. She touched his shoulder and he spun around in terror. Then, seeing not a phantom but a European girl in a dress like the one his master's daughter had put on today for the first time, he recovered himself. Marietta repeated her request, adding, "I've seen you in the chief's homestead — I'm from Keriki too. Have you forgotten?"

At the top of the front steps Virginia was greeted effusively by a woman in brown slacks. Behind her trailed a husband and two daughters.

"We'd no idea your girl was coming to the Mountain!" the woman cried. "We saw Daphne at the Halseys' last Sunday for drinks, and she didn't say a thing!"

"Marietta's fifteen — she couldn't stay in the reserves forever. Etta, love, say how d'you do to Mr. and Mrs. Fullerton."

"And Rosemary and Philippa. It's Philippa's first term," Mrs. Fullerton added, *sotto voce*, "and she does seem to mind so!" Philippa stood apart, damp-faced. "Poor Rosie was the same way as her sister to start with, though she's very happy now. It's a happy school, you know, or it *was*." She raised one eyebrow and glanced back a hundred feet to the wide doorway framing Chief Mattias, his daughter, and Mrs. Tyson. "This is quite a surprise, I must say," she whispered loudly. "Miss Jellicoe told us the Minister of Education insisted. He's making all the schools do it, even the Prince of Wales! Boy says now he remembers seeing something in the paper about a scholarship scheme, but he couldn't make out whether it was for this September or next. Isn't that right, Boy?"

Mr. Fullerton struggled to speak. "S-s-susan was at the Coast with the ch-ch-children. It s-s-slipped my mind. It was a s-s-small paragraph, on the back p-p-page."

"So I knew nothing about it," Mrs. Fullerton concluded, "until I ran into Miss Jellicoe in the corridor fifteen minutes ago! She was good enough to draw me aside, to warn me, so to speak, and just in time, because as soon as we'd got the girls settled and were on our way out to say our good-byes, we practically bumped into them in the front hall."

"We know them," Marietta said distinctly. "That's Chief Mattias. One of his sons works for us."

Mrs. Fullerton brightened. "Oh, so perhaps you can vouch for his sister! Poor Rosie has to share a room with her."

"The father is very big in our part of the world," Virginia remarked.

"I must say, he looks most awfully like an elephant!" Mrs. Fullerton giggled. "Well, we should be on our way. Boy's retriever is about to drop a litter. The vet says to expect nine this time. Last year there were four plus one she lay on, and Bill McKenzie — he's the vet, wonderful with dogs, though we've had good luck with him and our horses, too — well, Bill says they often have double the number the second time. She was nesting this morning when we left. I only hope we aren't too late. The servants would be useless, in the event." Spreading out her arms, she swept her family down the steps and got on with the business of parting.

"Can I help you?" a girl asked as Virginia came into the entrance hall with Justin and Marietta behind her. "Where d'you want to go?"

They passed a dining hall hung with heraldic motifs and with rows of silver cups on shelves, and a sitting room with glass doors opening onto a croquet lawn. Girls swept by them, whispering and laughing and calling out to one another. Justin rolled his eyes. "How beautiful they are! Such fine young women. They should be with their husbands, not idling here!" Finally they reached a room with five iron beds in it. "The owner of this place is surely very rich," Justin murmured. "In the Kisumu market you pay sixty shillings for a single bed." Marietta, regarding the records, hockey sticks, and hair curlers littered about the room, wondered, What are people like who own such things?

"How are you?" a great voice roared behind them, and suddenly Chief Mattias, his khaki solar topi under one arm, his medals pinned to his chest, was vigorously pumping Virginia's hand. "Have we both come here for the same purpose, for the education of our daughters, that they may be leaders in the new Kenya?" He thumped his staff on the floor and roared with laughter.

Marietta a leader? Virginia wanted her out of the way of indolent waiters and self-indulgent hotel guests. She hadn't thought much beyond that.

"My friend Mrs. Janet assures me this is the best school of all!" he boomed.

"Certainly one of the best," Mrs. Tyson chimed in. For the occasion she was wearing a yellow dress with pin-tucks down the front and white gloves.

"It was Mrs. Janet who insisted on a transfer," Chief Mattias cried. "My daughter was at Alliance High School. Very good, I thought. She is doing well. She is top of Form Two. But Mrs. Janet said, 'Alliance is only for Africans. Those European schools are better. They have laboratories and libraries and very clever teachers from Oxford and Cambridge.' Like a young child, I did just as she told me. She took my hand and led me here!" He laughed, delighted with himself and with his choice of counsel, of school, of strategy. "It is rare that I consult a woman. Two only. My mother and my daughter, and now a third, this lady here."

Mrs. Tyson said gently, "We didn't have a great deal of time to make the arrangements. Am I glad to see you, Marietta!" She smiled at her. "I know you'll keep an eye on Catherine for us."

Catherine, standing next to Mrs. Tyson, had her hands clasped behind her back. She'd grown much taller and seemed even darker than before. Her features were eerily like Benjamin's, but his expression was cheerful, easygoing, hers guarded and stern. As she glanced at Marietta her eyes flickered. Perhaps she's afraid, Marietta thought. Perhaps she wants to run off, back to Ongeso and the green car, back to Keriki. Is that why she's so stiff?

"I know your girl," Chief Mattias boomed. "My daughter brought her long ago to greet me."

"Funny," Virginia said. "I don't remember hearing about that."

"Oh, I told you all right," Marietta said, "but you didn't take it in. We were in the same class up at Keriki, she and I. We went to her father's house one day at lunchtime."

Mrs. Tyson shook her head sadly. "Such a pity you couldn't stay on with us, Marietta," she said.

"Where's your friend," Chief Mattias asked loudly, "the one I've seen you with in town? Why is she not also here? It would be fine to have three from Keriki. Two is not enough!"

"She married," Marietta replied.

"Is that so? Well," he breathed out at length, "not all should marry." He bowed to Virginia. "I have my daughter's boxes to fetch," he said as he turned away.

"We'd better bring yours in too, Etta," Virginia said.

"Justin and I'll get it."

Outside Justin sighed deeply. "Now that both my girls are gone, who shall I chatter with? Who'll keep me company?"

Marietta's eyes pricked with tears. "Don't you dare, Justin! You, a grandfather! You should be quiet and proud. Don't let me hear you talk that way!"

Miss Jellicoe hadn't been happy about the new developments. Of course, the moment Kenyatta had been let out of jail to become prime minister one knew it wouldn't be long before the government started interfering with the European schools. She'd hoped for a postponement, though — enough time for the people whose daughters she had charge of to become, if not enthusiastic, at least resigned to the idea of integration. But the Ministry had insisted on starting right away. The first African girl was to be admitted in September, and in January two more, and so on. The goal was equality of numbers in three years. In three years, Miss Jellicoe intended to be back in the U.K. She already had her scouts out for a position — on the south coast, preferably, for the better climate. She'd done her time in the colonies: thirteen years in East Africa, eight in Darjeeling, four in Kuala Lumpur. Overseeing the transition was one thing, but she wasn't the type to stay on.

She'd been due for home leave, too, this year; but instead of going to Stratford and the Trossacks, she'd had to spend her August interviewing African applicants. Of the original twelve, she'd quickly narrowed it down to three: a half-English, half-Kikuyu girl who'd spent most of her life in London; the daughter of a two-term member of the old Legislative Council; and Catherine Mattias. Eventually she'd chosen Catherine. Apart from being the brightest, Catherine struck one as the most African of the three, and these scholarships were for Africans, after all. Not for girls who were almost European. Miss Jellicoe hadn't sent a circular announcing the new developments. That, she decided after much debate, would only make the Mountain parents unnecessarily upset. Better to slip Catherine in, and play things by ear from there.

"Dear Neville," Marietta wrote. "So you got your way and here I am, imprisoned in a boarding school, waiting to be socialized! It's a pretty odd place, I must say. We're surrounded by a high hibiscus hedge, flowering furiously. On this side of it there's a croquet lawn,

110

a hockey field, and statues of the Muses, donated by Lady Some-body who had them brought from Sussex to her garden at Tigoni (there's a plaque). On the other side are banana groves and maize plots and round thatched huts. From the croquet lawn you can hear the people talking and smell the smoke of their fires. Two worlds, English (presumably — is England really so orderly and bare?) and African, within a few feet of one another.

"The headmistress comes from Devon. Her father was a rural dean. (Long dead, though. Now Mother lives with her in her bun-galow on the school grounds.) Besides her there's an assistant headmistress who wears her hair in plaits, wound on each side of her head like earphones. (She was born in Halifax.) Numerous teachers, all female with one exception (the art master), and sixty-eight girls in various shapes and sizes, all white, again, with one exception. Her name is Catherine and she's from Keriki, too. Nat-urally we've been put in next-door beds.

"Apart from Catherine I'm sharing a room with Joanna Bellows from North Kinangop and Nancy Ashford from Thomson's Falls. They're both farmers' daughters. Big and quite laborious. Joanna knits, Nancy keeps scrapbooks about the Royal Family! The fifth girl's called Rosemary Fullerton. Her parents are moving to Salis-bury, Southern Rhodesia. The moment they find a buyer for their coffee plantation in Limuru, they'll be off. They're not waiting for Uhuru, thank you! To people like them, Africans are just servants, laborers, and Mau Mau fighters. The fact that they also happen to be human beings has somehow escaped the Fullertons' attention. As you might imagine, Rosemary's not thrilled to be stuck with Catherine, and I'm sure there are lots more like her in this school. I wouldn't want to be in Catherine's shoes, not for anything!"

Rosemary Fullerton sat cross-legged on her bed, painting her nails vermilion. There was half an hour left until Sunday evening chapel, time for the polish to dry and be scrutinized and removed again. Marietta was drawing an old man gutting a fish. Joanna was finishing a pale blue sleeve and Nancy was pasting pictures of an infant Prince Andrew into her scrapbook. Catherine was lying on her side with her back to the room, reading.

Rosemary blew on her nails and held them out to get the full effect. She was a thin-faced girl with pale lashes and scuffed el-bows. Her mother often told her, "Any day, darling, you're bound to blossom." But Rosemary would be sixteen in November and there was still no hint of blossom.

"Catherine," she said, squinting at her outstretched hand, "there's something I've been dying to ask you."

Catherine didn't look round.

Rosemary said quickly, "I wish you wouldn't turn your back on us! It's awfully rude. Didn't they teach you *any* manners at that school you went to? I suppose not. They had their hands full getting you to eat with a knife and fork!"

Catherine put her book aside and sat up. "What is it you wish to ask?" she said.

"That's better," Rosemary said. "It's nice to see your face, especially since my question's rather personal." She giggled. "One could have asked the girl at home who does the ironing, but one never quite dared. With you it's different, though. I mean, we do live together, don't we?" She frowned at her nails. "D'you really like this color? Or do you think it's rather dark?"

"Is *that* your personal question?"

Rosemary looked up. "No, as a matter of fact." She paused for an instant, then with a crooked smile she said, "You've been circumcised, I take it."

Catherine nodded. "Of course."

"Do they really cut everything off and leave a little hole?"

"There has been much written about those things," Catherine replied quietly.

"I don't happen to have read them."

"Then you should. The library here is very good. You will find many books there about the customs of our people."

"But I don't want to *read* about it. I want to *hear* about it from someone who's been through it."

"Then ask the girl who irons your clothes," Catherine answered, picking up her book again.

"Why be so secretive?" Rosemary said. "I'd have thought" — her voice rose — "you'd jump at the chance to educate us. I mean, isn't it your job to teach us what we ought to know about your customs?"

"Your ignorance is your responsibility, not mine," Catherine said flatly, lying down again.

"Perhaps you're right," Rosemary conceded. "But the fact is, reading about circumcision wouldn't be the same as seeing exactly what was done." She laughed. "Reading about the sex organs in a biology book and looking at those diagrams doesn't faintly resemble having sex."

"You mean you've had it?" exclaimed Joanna, her knitting needle in midair. "When? Where?"

"I think," Rosemary said loudly, "it would be rather educational for all of us if you let us have a look." She jumped off her bed and ran to bolt the door. "There," she said, "no one will come in. We're completely private and we shan't breathe a word to anyone. You can count on that. She can, can't she?" Rosemary added, looking at Nancy. "This is between us and Catherine. Right?"

Nancy flushed. "Couldn't we just imagine what they did to her? Do we have to look?"

"*I* couldn't imagine," Rosemary replied. "I'm not imaginative enough!"

Joanna said eagerly, "They do it in December on our farm. When I was small I once went down to watch, but our cook spotted me and sent me packing." She added, grinning, "I'd rather like to see."

"What about you, Marietta?" Rosemary said. "Or do they do it to everyone where you come from, whites as well as blacks?"

Marietta said nothing. The old man's hand was giving her trouble; it looked more like a cabbage than a hand. Rosemary's not serious, she said to herself. She's bored. She's simply passing the time. But then Rosemary said, "You can choose, Catherine. Either you show us of your own accord or we'll make you. It's four of us against one of you. I'll count to ten. Are you ready?"

Catherine's eyes narrowed. Otherwise she gave no sign of having heard. Slowly and deliberately she turned a page.

"One, two . . ."

In a flash Marietta remembered another time and another place. "Your mother is a wanderer and a lover of men. And once she has loved them, they are spoiled. Never again will they be satisfied." It's her turn now, Marietta thought, her heart pounding.

"Six," Rosemary said. "Seven . . . Don't forget, it's four against one. Eight, nine . . ." Nancy and Joanna slipped off their beds to join her. "Ten! Okay, now let's see what's what!" Rosemary threw herself on Catherine. "Grab her arms, you two, Marietta and I will get her pants off!" But Marietta stayed where she was, eyes riveted to her drawing.

For an instant Catherine lay inert. Then she sprang to defend herself. She threw off Nancy and Joanna, who stumbled back, mortified, suddenly, at having let themselves be drawn into such a thing. Alone, Rosemary was no match for a girl who had weeded maize and carried water from the river almost since she learned to walk. Catherine seized Rosemary by the wrists and forced her backwards across the room.

"As you see, I am ever so much stronger than you are," Catherine said coldly. "You must swear never to behave like a barbarian again. For that is what you are, one who has no respect and so deserves none in return. Or else I will take you like this, before your friends, to Miss Jellicoe. There you will tell her of the shameful thing you had in mind to do. And you will tell her, also, that after living all your life in Africa, you know nothing about Africans except that they can iron your clothes and cook your food and provide you with a chance for making cruel and stupid jokes. It is your turn to choose. Which do you prefer, Rosemary, to appear ridiculous before your classmates or to swear that in the future you will treat those with whom you are not familiar with the same restraint and courtesy that you treat your friends?"

"I didn't mean it," Rosemary gasped, her head pressed painfully against a hook on the back of the door. "I was teasing. I wouldn't have gone through with it!"

"Yes," Catherine said gravely, "yes, you would, for you were very serious. Were I not stronger than you, you would have finished what you had begun. So which do you choose, Rosemary?" Catherine paused, then looked round at Marietta. "She must be Tugen, or perhaps a Pokot, a wild bush woman who somehow slipped through the door of this fine place when nobody was watching!" She went on in Keriki, "So therefore it is our responsibility to civilize her, to show her how to live in peace with her neighbors, offending neither the living nor the dead. Should she not swear, Marietta, never to behave like a barbarian again?"

"Speak English, can't you? Since the rest of us didn't have the privilege of growing up in the reserves, we don't understand the language," Rosemary muttered.

"I was consulting Marietta about the oath that you should take," Catherine replied, "and a second question is where it should be taken — this evening during chapel, or tonight, on the terrace, under the new moon?"

"Whatever you want, I'll swear it," said Rosemary.

114

8

The Hotel Simba

The school was closing for the Christmas holidays. Catherine and Marietta sat on their trunks at the bottom of the front steps, waiting to be fetched. They were the only two students left. It seemed that everyone else had gone to the Coast to swim and sail and dance and swelter on the beaches. Rosemary Fullerton, for instance, was going to Lourenço Marques. Her mother's uncle had a cashew nut plantation on the Indian Ocean. She'd gone there last Christmas, and two Portuguese boys had fought a duel over her, so she said. Marietta knew this was a lie. Rosemary had a laugh like a donkey and a most unpleasant personality. No two boys anywhere on earth would take up arms because of her!

Marietta scowled to herself at the prospect of *her* Christmas: the paper chains in the Wayfarer bar and the casuarina pine near the front door, decorated by her and Violet with blocks of wood, painted red and white and yellow, and with colored lights, fewer each year, as the bulbs gave out and weren't replaced. But this year Violet wouldn't be there. She'd left early in the morning last Christmas Eve, having climbed onto the hotel roof the night before in order to tie a silver-paper-coated star to the top of the pine tree. (Marietta was afraid of heights.) Now Violet was nursing her son — a very huge boy, she wrote, resembling his father exactly. Wouldn't Marietta come to greet him? She could take the bus to Homa Bay, and a boat from there. Marietta, dreading the forced hilarity in the lounge, the desolation of a public place, had resolved to tell her mother that very afternoon that she intended to accept Violet's invitation. She'd saved her birthday money and she'd use it for the journey and the necessary gifts.

The fact was, though, she wanted to get away from her mother even more than from the Wayfarer. Virginia, who used to look around and past and over her, scarcely seeing her at all, now watched her closely, as if quite suddenly, after fifteen years, she'd realized for the first time she was there. After the half-term holiday, back at school again, from three days of Virginia's scrutiny, Marietta had written to Neville, "My mother's trying to get inside my head. I hate it! If anyone ever tried that with you, how did you stop them?" Two weeks later she'd received her answer. "At your age I was in England and my parents were in Africa. Your news rather surprises me; this attentiveness on the part of your mother is a side of her I didn't see. I would guess it's a result of your going away. That must take some getting used to, since she's the one who's left behind, plugging away at her old life in Baluga while you begin a new one on your own. She's wondering what you're turning into. I have to say that I am too!"

Virginia's paying attention had begun with Geoffrey Lucas. Virginia wouldn't have told Neville about that, though. For one thing, Virginia was a rotten letter writer. She'd peck away at the typewriter, putting down the barest facts; then she'd pop her single sheet of paper in an envelope and that was that. Not for her the working-out of thoughts and paragraphs, the pleasure of crowding it all in, and afterwards of imagining how it would be read. For another, Neville and Virginia weren't·friends; they were only a man and a woman who had somehow married one another in a misguided moment and then realized they weren't suited. Daphne Dawson was Virginia's only real friend. Virginia might have confided in Daphne, but in Neville, no.

Marietta hadn't told Neville about Lucas, either. She only wrote to Neville about what mattered, and Lucas didn't. She didn't remember his face, his voice, how he had touched her. She had no affection for him, no remorse. There had come a time when a change was needed. After an hour with Lucas — no, surely it must have been more than that — after some churning of bedclothes, some intertwining of limbs, the future had opened up. Though she no longer remembered his face, she was grateful to Lucas, because his coming had marked a new beginning.

116

The Mountain School for Girls hadn't turned out so badly after all. There was a lot of praying in the chapel and reading of the Bible before bed, and gossip, and competition over clothes and over whether you spent August in Scotland or in France. But Marietta quickly learned that you watched what went on and dealt with it with a bit of yourself, keeping the rest in reserve.

Meanwhile, there were definite compensations, the most important one being Mr. Parker, who taught art. He had a thick black beard and a wooden leg and he clumped about like a pirate. He'd been bitten by a snake in the Mara and they'd had to amputate on the spot, above the knee, without an anesthetic. (He'd been a game warden before becoming an art master.) Marietta spent every available moment in his studio. She was learning to work with clay and to use oils, too. Four weeks away from all of that would seem endless.

Marietta sighed and stood up. Where *was* Virginia? It was far too hot to sit out in the sun any longer. "Wouldn't you be more comfortable up on the terrace, in the shade?" she said to Catherine, who sat reading a few yards away. But Catherine didn't answer; she was too engrossed in her book. She read perpetually. She read as she walked through the corriors. If the prefects hadn't stopped her, she'd have read through meals as well. When they went into Tintinet on Saturdays, she always bought two flashlight batteries. Two saw her through a week of reading under the blanket after lights-out. Between the covers of a book she was immune to the petty cruelties of the other girls.

That morning in the school assembly Catherine had been presented with the Third Form essay prize, a leather-bound edition of the plays of William Shakespeare. Now she was absorbed with Portia, and the compelling notion that she, too, might become a judge one day, the first woman judge on the High Court of East Africa.

Miss Jellicoe was crossing the terrace with her dachshund at her heels. "Still here!" she exclaimed. "It's almost half past two."

"My mother's Land-Rover must have broken down," Marietta said. "It very often does."

Catherine closed her book. "When my father is delayed," she said gravely, "it is because he has so very many responsibilities, not because he has forgotten."

"I'm sure that's so," said Miss Jellicoe mildly. "Had we known your parents were going to be late, we'd have given you a picnic lunch. As it is, the kitchen's closed for the holidays. I'll tell you what," she said, brightening, "why don't you come to my house and my cook will cut you some sandwiches."

Catherine bowed slightly. "Madam," she said, "I am not in need of any sandwiches. My father will provide for me."

"As you wish, my dear." Miss Jellicoe turned away. "Come along then, Marietta."

As she walked up her own path Miss Jellicoe reflected wryly, and not for the first time, that during her tenure at the Mountain School she'd had charge, among others, of the daughters of a German prince, two peers of the Realm, and a duke, but none of them had come up to Catherine in terms of self-possession. Her equanimity in the face of provocation had unnerved her classmates. She'd made them feel that they, not she, had been tried and found wanting, and soon they'd left her alone. In a way, Miss Jellicoe admitted, this forced experiment in integration had been a success. Or at least not a failure.

Marietta returned with a cheese sandwich and three gingersnaps in a brown paper bag just as a large brown car was pulling up at the steps. Chief Mattias poked his head out, then his staff. Flinging the door wide, he arose to his full height and declared, "This vehicle has worms in its stomach." He had exchanged his old car, he announced, for a new one, ordered months ago; it had arrived just in time for today's safari. "That old one, I knew it so well, as if it were my hand, my arm. It played no tricks upon me. But this stranger, below Mau Summit, it stopped. *Kaputi!* It could not creep another foot. My man here" — he pointed back to Ongeso, crouched in the corner of the plastic-covered seat — "he squatted at the roadside to lament. *Bobee!* But I pulled him up. I told him, did I not pay fifty thousand shillings? Surely there is life there still! And I leaned upon the front and shook it." Mattias, demonstrating, made the car shudder on its wheels. "And thus it came alive!

"Greetings! How are you, Miss Marietta? Are you well, does your head spin with so much information?" Then, turning to his daughter, he said softly in Keriki, "And how are you, my dearest child?" For a moment he held her face between his two great hands. "Can you know how empty my house has been without you? No, better that you know nothing of it!" And releasing her, he cried, "Let us be off immediately, lest this worm-infested vehicle dares to die again!"

118

With his staff he prodded his daughter's clutter of belongings. "Aye, old man, Ongeso, take these things. And that," he said, pointing at Marietta's trunk, "is yours? You are to come with us also. I met your mother in the bank on Tuesday. I told her, 'I am going to recover my daughter,' and she replied that by fetching you home, too, I would help her exceedingly."

Marietta nodded. "This time of year is busy for my mother." She smiled, picturing Benjamin's astonishment as she emerged from his father's brand-new car. "Thank you. This is very kind of you."

While Ongeso stowed away the luggage, Catherine and Marietta settled themselves in the back seat. "If this vehicle plays tricks with us, then we shall outwit it," Mattias declared, tapping his forehead vigorously with his index finger. The engine roared into life, and he swung the car round with a spluttering of gravel. Miss Jellicoe appeared at that moment on the path from her bungalow, and Mattias waved to her, calling out, "A happy New Year to you, madam!" as they sped away down the drive, through the stone gateway, and off into the world.

The new brown car died on a long smooth stretch of road in the bottom of the Rift. But ten minutes later, after Mattias had shaken the front of the car and the girls and Ongeso had shaken the back, the engine burst into life again, and they all jumped in and drove noisily on, scattering a troop of baboons that had sprung across the ditch to watch.

The chief talked constantly, jumping from one subject to another in English and Swahili, in deference to Marietta. But Catherine always answered him in Keriki. She spoke very rapidly, running her words together. Marietta, whose grasp of Keriki was fairly good, could not follow what she said. Catherine sat in her corner of the wide back seat; she had scarcely spoken to Marietta since they left the school. Marietta thought, She was expecting her father's exclusive attention and instead she's having to put up with me all the way back to Baluga. I've slept in the next bed, I've sat at the next desk, I've been her partner every Friday night in ballroom dancing class because no one else would dance with her, no one else was willing to be that close. I've walked with her every single Saturday to buy batteries in Pujwani's general store in Tintinet, I've been her croquet partner, I've tested her on Latin verbs, I've practiced backhands and serves and volleys with her because she and I are always left till last. No, not once have I been cruel to her.

But I haven't gone out of my way to be kind to her, either. She's so self-contained. A friend isn't anything she needs or misses.

They climbed through the pine forests in a sudden rainstorm; then they drove down again into the darkened plain, where for a second time the car shuddered and coughed its way into silence. When neither their shakings nor the efforts of a passing lorry driver had any effect, Ongeso was left to defend the Chevy with his life and a panga, which he pulled out from under the front seat, and the rest of the party clambered into the lorry and set off to find a mechanic in the next town.

But the next town was only a crossroads, and the Ismaili proprietor of the petrol station wouldn't forsake his evening mosque. And the owner of the only taxi in that crossroads town was sprawled head over hands across a table in the Hotel Simba, next to the petrol station. Behind the Hotel Simba, however, were five small rooms that the proprietor rented by the day to prostitutes. The chief decided to rent two of these rooms, one for himself and one for the girls. Next morning, as soon as the mechanic was finished with his pieties, they would take him back to Ongeso and the Chevrolet.

While Catherine and Marietta hung by the door, Mattias towered in the lamplight making terms with the hotel keeper, who sported a baseball cap and, despite the hour and the blackness of the night, a pair of sunglasses. The hotel keeper agreed eventually to oust two of his stable of five as soon as their current customers were satisfied. It was understandable, of course, why these woman couldn't be driven out at once, for they had contracted for their rooms and paid sums in advance; and indeed, they were his friends. Whether his business flourished or failed depended on their willingness to use his property, rather than hurrying on to larger towns. Mattias took out a banknote and handed it over before the eyes of a dozen patrons. Slipping the money into his pocket, the proprietor went off through the back to thump on the doors of the two most worn "travelers," the two whose indignation he could most easily afford. In a few moments he was back. All had been arranged, he told them, smiling, and while they waited, would the chief prefer Tusker or Heineken?

Room was made for Catherine and Marietta on a bench against the wall.

"I'm sorry," Mattias said to Marietta as she squeezed past him. "I'm sorry that we must sleep amongst Luos."

120

Above the bar hung colored photographs of the Queen, the Order of the Garter across her breast, and of the Governor, hand on sword, plumed hat tucked beneath one stiff arm. Of the two, Marietta preferred the Queen. Though reserved, she had a suggestion of warmth, as if she would acknowledge an ordinary person, should she stumble over one. But the Governor had no conception of the ordinary person. His light blue eyes bore down upon Marietta on the bench opposite. What are you doing in a place like this? he seemed to be asking. What has befallen white supremacy?

No doubt Virginia was at that moment pacing the corridor at the Wayfarer, from the office to the front desk and back again, but there was no way of getting in touch with her, no telephone at these crossroads in the midst of the sugar plantations. And supper, Marietta thought, would surely be more interesting here than at their usual table by the door in the hotel dining room, pretending they were private when they were in full public view. Of late she'd come to resent the hypocrisy of the hotel guests who watched you while pretending to ignore you as they ate their tapioca pudding and stewed Victoria plums. In the Hotel Simba, on the other hand, the patrons made no attempt to hide their curiosity. Apart from the man who slept head on hands, all watched the chief and his daughter and the European girl with the closest possible attention.

Mattias was already on the move. He had identified a man in a polka-dotted tie (askew now, after six bottles of beer, lined up empty before him) as a trader from Eldoret who owed him one hundred and ninety-four shillings, the balance on a sale of flour from six months back. The chief settled his great bulk upon a stool — upon the seat, rather, of a chair that had lost its back in some forgotten brawl — and, grasping the beer the proprietor brought him, proceeded to the business of his debt. The trader, less than alert after several hours of drinking, was defenseless in the face of Mattias's attack, which came punctuated with puns, metaphors, and roars of laughter. By the time Mattias was on his second bottle of beer, he had his money, three notes and a cotton bag full of shillings, secure in the inside pocket of his coat.

A servant brought two orange sodas, slapped them onto the table in front of Catherine and Marietta, and snapped off the caps. He ran back to fetch two streaked glasses. Catherine poured a soda and offered it to Marietta. "This is for you," she said in English. "Surely you are thirsty. Drink, please!" Now that Marietta was her father's responsibility for the night, Catherine was obliged to be more gracious. "And what will you take to eat, Marietta? Though this is a poor place, still they can cook for us." She called the proprietor over, telling him to grill meat and to prepare rice for the two of them, *ugali* for her father. Mattias, engaged still in extortion, glanced at Catherine, nodded approvingly as she ordered, and turned back to business.

The displaced prostitutes emerged. They were both Somali women; one was swathed in pink, the other in orange gauze. Their clients, too, appeared, settling pants on hips, thrusting back shoulders, just as the servant brought in the supper. Mattias fell upon his food and proceeded, between fingerfuls of *ugali* and singed goat's meat, to entertain the hotel patrons, the Somali ladies, and, when they came out to exchange partners, their "sisters," too. Finally, having cleaned off the bottom of his flowered tin plate, he stood up and announced that the time had come for sleep. He shook hands with every man and woman in the room, stopping at length before the youngest prostitute, a plump Kamba girl in a tight black skirt, her hair elaborately plaited. But in the end, out of respect, perhaps, for Marietta, he left her for the pleasure of the regular patrons.

The proprietor took up a lamp and led them out past a row of padlocked doors to the end of the building. There two doors stood ajar. He took Mattias into the farther room, and, returning, led the girls into the other. In it were a crude table and a plank bed on which was laid a mattress covered in gray and white ticking. The window in the rear wall was bolted and the room smelled densely of perfume and stale bodies. Taking the stub of a candle from his pocket, the man lit it at his lamp and balanced it in a saucer on the table. He turned to go.

"Are there no blankets?" Catherine said sharply. "My father told you to bring blankets."

The man shrugged. "The sum your father paid was for the bed alone."

Catherine said firmly, "We cannot lie just as those women lie, on the same filthy mattress!" In the end room the bed creaked as Mattias, less fastidious, lay down. The proprietor reset his baseball cap and grasped the door latch, as if to leave. But Catherine was too quick for him. She jumped forward, slamming the door shut. Leaning against it she called out to her father, "This man refuses to bring us blankets!"

122

On the other side of the wall the bed creaked again. "What is that? Wait, I am coming. Let me find my shoes."

But the proprietor, accepting defeat, said loudly, "She is very impatient. She did not give me time." Out he went, and a moment later the servant came down the veranda with a blanket and a large red tablecloth.

By the flickering light of the candle stub, Marietta and Catherine covered the mattress with the red cloth. The blanket they rolled up as a pillow. Marietta stood on tiptoe to open the shutter, but Catherine stopped her. "Don't!"

"But it's stifling in here and it stinks."

Catherine took off her shoes and lay down in her school dress. She put her hands behind her head and there were two dark patches under her armpits. "It's wiser not to sleep at all than to leave an open window."

"What have we got that anyone would steal?"

"Nothing," Catherine said, "but still they would steal it."

Marietta blew out the candle. "Poor Ongeso," she remarked in the sudden darkness. "I'd hate to be in that car alone."

"He's safe enough. The hyenas won't climb into the vehicle. Town is much more dangerous. Here, it is people you must fear, not hyenas."

Marietta lay down in her cotton slip, her head on the rolled-up blanket next to Catherine's. She remembered nights spent with Violet in servants' quarters up and down the center of Africa, whenever Virginia, desperate for life of a sort not to be found in remote little towns, took off alone for a week, leaving her daughter to do as she pleased. But Catherine moved away at once, setting herself carefully apart.

"There's not much room, is there," Marietta said. "Still," she added, "two people were perfectly happy on this bed just a little while ago. Isn't the mattress still warm, or is that my imagination?"

At the end of the veranda the door of the bar opened, and a gust of voices and laughter swept out. As it shut again, footsteps came towards them and someone fiddled with a padlock. Then the door of the room next to theirs slammed upon a man in need and a girl, the youngest and prettiest prostitute, whom Chief Mattias had admired and denied himself. Though the customer was drunk, he had a degree of energy that took him from ten-thirty to twenty minutes to twelve, by Marietta's watch, to exhaust. Even then he demanded more, but appetite had outstripped capacity, and so, by mocking him, the girl got him up and dressed and out again. At twelve-thirty she was back with another man.

Through all this Mattias slept. His snores rent the night in perfect syncopation with the rhythm of the couple on the plank bed two doors down. From her deep, slow breathing, it appeared that Catherine also was asleep. But of course, Marietta reflected, nothing unnerved her, neither cruelty nor ostracism, so why should other people's sex? As the sole witness, Marietta was nauseated at first, then suddenly, cravingly, excited. She tried to block out these night noises by clenching the muscles in her ears to make a sound like the roaring of the ocean. But her muscles soon tired. And she didn't dare betray her state of mind and body by blocking her ears with her fingers, in case Catherine should wake up and see her. As the girl next door cried out for mercy or for pleasure, who knew which, Marietta sat up.

"God," she remarked into the darkness, "will this go on all night?"

Catherine raised herself on one elbow. "Soon they will finish."

Marietta frowned down at her. "Will they? The men wear themselves out but she goes on and on."

"They'll stop. It's the middle of the month, you see," Catherine said matter-of-factly. "Few men have money left. And those who had some earlier this evening have spent it by now."

Marietta lay down again, her hands behind her head. "Tell me, have you been here before? You seem to know the ropes."

"Not to this very place, no. But often when my father travels I go with him. I help him choose a woman, and we take her to Keriki with us in the car. Then she stays with us for some time and keeps me company, too, as well as my father." In the darkness, Catherine smiled. "Usually there are only two of us. Ongeso is with us, of course, but he's becoming old and blind and evil-tempered. So now and then, it is nice to have a third in our house. For a little while," she went on quickly, "I pretend that such a woman is my mother. I lost my mother, you see."

"I know that," Marietta said. "I haven't forgotten."

"I find these women interesting, the way they walk and talk and smile and dress. They belong nowhere. They have nothing, nobody. And still they can be gay. They laugh, despite their sorrows. And that is something wonderful, I think." She went on eagerly, "So-

124

malis are the prettiest and Kambas are the gayest. But Ugandans are both pretty and gay. My father prefers them above all others. He says they know best how to please men. In September we met one in Kitale and brought her home. My father liked her so much I thought that he might marry her. But when I went back at the half-term holiday she was gone. Ongeso told me that, having stolen a radio and sixty shillings, she'd run away. I was sorry not to see her anymore. I think she liked me, not just my father. She had pretty clothes, too. I wanted blouses like hers," Catherine said, frowning in the darkness, "but I received only a school uniform."

"Did Mrs. Vejay make yours, too?"

"Of course." Catherine stretched, pointing her toes out beyond the end of the mattress. "She does not like to sew for Africans. When I was measured for these dresses she hissed through her teeth. But she did not refuse, because my father owns the building that she lives in."

"She hissed at me as well," Marietta said, laughing. "My mother says it's the change of life, making her bad-tempered."

Next door there was a crash as the man fell off the bed. In a fury he scrambled to his feet. The girl screamed as he struck her, but after a moment's tussle, she, being sober, gained the upper hand, thrust open the door, and pushed him out into the yard. He lay there cursing for a while; then, with one last obscenity, he stumbled to his feet and groped his way back to the bar. Hearing him leave, the girl went out to the latrine. In a few minutes she returned alone and bolted her door. Soon she was snoring as loudly as Mattias.

Marietta listened to the snores and to the lizards scrambling up the walls and through the rafters. "Why does your father like Ugandans, did you say?"

"Because they're soft," Catherine replied sleepily. "Kenyan women are too quarrelsome. They're always jealous, so my father says. However" — she snuggled down into her side of the pillow — "though that one we brought from Kitale pleased him, in the end she took his money like the rest. And the radio, in fact, was mine," she added, yawning again. "Let us sleep now, Marietta. Soon we must go to save that old man from the hyenas."

"I shouldn't have asked him," Virginia said, turning toward the hotel as Mattias drove away. "I should've known better. You must have had an awful time! I thought you'd crashed, of course. I

125

hardly slept all night! The old brute came at me in the bank. You know how he is, like a tank. And it did seem to make sense at the time. I mean, what was the point of us both driving all that way?"

Osoro and Justin went ahead with Marietta's trunk through the garden to the cottage. Behind them Virginia carried an armful of racquets and rubber boots, and in the rear came Marietta with the cardboard case in which she kept her drawing pads, crayons, pens, and India ink. It was ten minutes to two, and the driveway was full of cars.

"The Hotel Simba's a lot cozier than this place," Marietta remarked.

"I can imagine! Did you catch fleas?"

"Probably. But you can catch them here, too. I found the evening rather interesting, in fact."

Virginia hurried past the bougainvillea. She had to get back to the dining room as soon as possible. Fridays were always busy, especially before Christmas, and Benjamin, dazzling in white jacket and scarlet cummerbund as he cut the apple tart and spooned out the mousse, needed supervison. If Benjamin was left to his own devices, tart and mousse would slip past plates and onto the floor. In the cottage she dumped her armload onto the sofa. "I suppose you and that child are best friends now."

"You mean me and Catherine?" Marietta laid her case carefully on the table. She went over the case of butterflies that she and Neville had caught and set at Itep. With the tips of her fingers she touched a gourd, a present from Peter Dawson, who'd got it for her from a Turkana fisherman when she was nine. She'd cradled it in her lap all the way from Nairobi to Runga and set it in the middle of the table in their sitting room. Here in Baluga it sat on the mantelpiece, bearing a fine mushroomy covering that bloomed or shriveled according to the season and the level of humidity.

She turned and flopped into a chair. "Catherine doesn't need a best friend," she said. "She's got her father."

"Oh, really? The chief doesn't take much interest in Benjamin, so far as I can see."

Marietta rolled her shoulders, first one, then the other. She was stiff from sharing the narrow bed and squatting in the back of the mechanic's jeep. They had driven out at sunrise and towed the car back to the petrol station. "From the way she talks you'd never know she had a hundred brothers and sisters. You'd think there were just the two of them, her and her papa."

At four o'clock Virginia brought a tray across the garden and set it down in the sitting room.

"Things have been frantic here," she said, laying out the cups and saucers, "and the phone's being dead hasn't helped. We need dozens of things from Eldonia, but I haven't had a moment to go down to get them. Thank God I got through to Kassim an hour ago, and he promised to send my order up. It's due tomorrow morning. I'm just keeping my fingers crossed."

Marietta said loudly, "Violet has asked me to come and greet her baby. I haven't seen her since she left here. I was hoping, since you've got so much to do, to go to Galana over Christmas. If I weren't here that would be one less person for you to worry about."

"You can't go." Virginia frowned. "You and I are going to Katari. I didn't write about it because I wanted it to be a surprise."

"You can't shut the Wayfarer and go off, not at Christmas time! There must be scores of people booked to come. There always are."

But Virginia explained that she had found a young couple, Jean and Ian Macdonald, to look after things at the Wayfarer. They'd come out from England to the tea estates, but after a year they'd got fed up with tea. They wanted to try the hotel business and were eager to fill in for Virginia while she was away. "You know, Etta," said Virginia, "I haven't had a holiday at Christmas since before you were born!"

"And what did you do that time? Whoop it up in Alexandria with Daphne?" Marietta wasn't pleased to be going to Katari. It didn't suit her at all.

"No. I was in Moshi, with your father, as a matter of fact. Four days before Christmas he announced we were going up Kiliman-jaro. I'd been looking forward to goose and Christmas pudding, the first after the war. But I was a new bride and my only aim was to please my husband. So off we went." She stopped.

"You never told me you climbed Kili!" Marietta exclaimed.

"Only tried to climb it, as things turned out. At fourteen thou-sand feet on the button I felt extremely ill." Virginia was silent for a moment, running one finger round the rim of her cup. "But I trudged on up, to just below the crater, where I was sicker than any dog has ever been and had to be left behind with a Chagga porter, while your father went the last leg without me." She smiled, faintly. "He took photographs at the top, but he forgot to take the film out of the camera, and by the time I did, the pictures were spoiled. Hundreds of people have tramped up since then, of course — ten-year-olds and cripples and blind Boy Scouts; it's nothing special nowadays. But it was still an adventure then. I've always been sorry I didn't make it. The porter who stayed behind with me had teeth filed to a point; I thought maybe he'd eat me if your father left me with him overnight. But Charlie came back in the nick of time, just as the sun was setting. I wouldn't have made much of a meal anyway," she added. "I was really horribly ill. And even after we came down off the mountain I didn't get better for a week. It wasn't the altitude after all, you see. It was morning sickness. All-day sickness, rather. I was expecting you and hadn't had the wit to realize it."

"Why didn't he wait until Boxing Day to go? Didn't it matter to him that you wanted a proper Christmas?"

"I didn't dare tell him."

"I don't believe it! You always tell people exactly what you want."

"I was different in those days. You've never known anyone like your father, Etta, and I hope to God you won't!" She took a cigarette out of her pocket and tapped it on the back of her hand.

Marietta said quickly, "Whenever I've asked about him, you've shut me up. Justin told me he drank too much and he was very huge, and whenever I see Chief Mattias I think, Was my father like *him?*" She went on, "Did he have parents or a home? Have I got cousins somewhere? Why am I allergic to tomatoes? You're not. Could he draw? Was he glad you were going to have me? I want to know what he was like, Mum!"

Virginia snapped her lighter into flame and lit her cigarette. After a puff or two she laughed suddenly. "He strode across the world in ten-league boots, that's how I saw him in the beginning. He was dazzlingly handsome and wonderfully wild." She stopped. "Oh, Etta, d'you know how many years ago he was?"

"Why would somebody so wonderful drag you up Kilimanjaro if you didn't want to go?"

"I didn't tell him how I felt about it."

"Why not?"

Virginia stubbed out her cigarette and stood up.

"Where are you going?" Marietta cried. "Don't go. You can't!"

"It doesn't bear thinking about."

"I believe you," Marietta said, quietly. "All the same . . ."

Virginia sat down and dug deep in her pocket for another cigarette. "His mother died having him. As for his father, I doubt they were ever married. Hamilton was definitely his mother's name. He was brought up by a maiden aunt in Uppingham, which is somewhere in the Midlands. He hated Uppingham; he left the minute he was able to. He only said two things about his aunt — she was a Christian Scientist and she kept Pekingese dogs. Oh, and her name was Betty Hamilton. By the time I met him, which was in April 1945 in Egypt, she was dead.

"I met your father at a party and fell in love with him on sight." Virginia lit her cigarette. "Daphne, watching my infatuation, was suspicious. I hadn't been one for falling in love, you see, just for having a good time. 'I know there's something botched about him,' she said, 'I'm going to do a little check.' And sure enough she discovered he'd been in a Home in Sussex the summer before the war, and back again for several months in 1942. 'I wouldn't touch him with a ten-foot pole,' Daphne said. 'I'm telling you, Virginia, he's had very bad times and who's to say he won't again.' 'With me he won't,' I said. 'That kind of thing, whatever it was, isn't going to happen again. I'll stop it!' 'All right,' she said, 'but I'm not coming to the wedding.' And she didn't, but plenty of other people were perfectly delighted to come to Shepherd's Hotel in Cairo and celebrate. We did a conga on the balustrade along the Nile and two of the guests fell in. And after that, since the war was over, we came down south, back here. I told him straight, 'I can't live anywhere else but Africa. I'm glad to have seen some other places, the war's been fun, but war isn't ordinary living. That, for me at least, has got to be done in Africa. One can do what one wants here; other people might disapprove but they'd never interfere.' Charlie liked that idea. He didn't care for being hemmed in, either.

"Of course, meanwhile, Daphne had come south, too, and married Peter, but I didn't see her again until she arrived in Songo, the week before you were born. She'd discovered I was going to have a baby, so she came. She's told you *that* story. Daphne's always been such a good friend . . ." Her voice trailed off.

"Wasn't my father your friend, too?" Marietta said.

"Friend!" Virginia threw back her head. "Oh, Etta, no! He *hated* me."

"Then why did he marry you?"

"He didn't hate me at first, don't you see? No, of course you don't see." She stubbed out her second cigarette. "How could you? At first I was the sun and the moon. The world had always been in darkness, he said, until I flooded it with light. That's the way he talked. He'd been lonely, desolate, dead, he said, until Virginia Parkson, from the plains beyond Thomson's Falls, miraculously appeared. I didn't believe him. How could someone so charismatic — that's exactly the right word for him — ever feel lonely or desolate? When we got married there were hundreds of guests at the wedding, not my friends, his. People flocked to him. He had an extraordinary charm. A kind of magic.

"He'd been in South America before the war. Brazil, Peru, Venezuela. He liked it there, but right away he didn't like Africa." Virginia bit her lip. "Well, anyway, he got a job with the Department of Mines. In three months he was fed up with that. He was going out on his own, he said. He couldn't stand red tape. He didn't sleep much, and he didn't eat, either, and yet you never saw anyone with so much energy! That time we came down off Kili he met some people in a bar. They were going up the mountain the next day. There were some lava formations he'd forgotten to look at in the crater, he said, so he decided to go straight back up again and take a look. He would have, too, only I was so sick that the wife of the hotel manager twisted his arm and got him to stay back. She drove me to the doctor. 'You can't go on like this,' she said. Her name was Mary Summersby. She was a very cheery, decent sort and she made it her business to see to me, since Charlie wouldn't. Perhaps he'd guessed already what was up.

"Anyway, when I came back with my news, he was drinking a whiskey and soda in our cottage. He said, 'That chap'll have to get rid of it. We haven't got time to go to Dar.' We were leaving at the end of the week on a long safari through the western part of the country.

"'You don't want this child?' I said. I couldn't believe my ears.

"'No,' he said, 'I don't, so you'll have to choose.'"

Marietta broke a biscuit into halves and then into quarters. She arranged them, edges pointing inward, in the center of her plate. She glanced up at her mother. With her hair lightened by the lowering sun, Virginia looked like a girl, not much older than Marietta.

"Choose between me and him?"

"That's right."

"Couldn't you have both? Other women do."

"He only wanted me," Virginia said. "Once I had a child, I'd abandon him, he said. I told him no, that wasn't true, and I wouldn't go back to that doctor in Moshi. I set off south with him to Morogoro and then west to the lake, but from the day I knew I was going to have you he never touched me. He cut me off."

"He made the choice for you."

"Yes." Virginia was silent for a moment. Then she shook her head. "No. He wanted me to prove that his world wasn't desolate. He wanted me to save him from his furies, whatever they were. But I wasn't up to it. I didn't have the stamina to ride out the storm. I lost my nerve. I ran away."

"Where did you go?"

"Does it make any difference? I went. I didn't have the guts to stay."

"Did he know where you'd gone?"

"He knew."

"He could have come after you."

"But he didn't."

"*He* was the one who didn't have the stamina, it seems to me," said Marietta.

Virginia didn't speak. She lit a cigarette. After a moment Marietta asked, "Did you miss him?"

Virginia blew a chain of smoke rings that rose above the sunbeams into the dimness near the thatch. "Miss him? That's hardly the word. I was consumed by him! There wasn't much left of me afterwards. Just a few cells here and there." She smiled. "Fortunately, after a very long time the rest did grow back. As you said about last night's adventure with the chief, it was interesting. Knocking about, seeing the underside, can be *very* interesting. And besides, you're so busy surviving, you're never bored." She stood up. "I'm sorry about Galana, but I very much want you to come down to Daphne's with me. I'm sure you'll be able to fit in Violet later on."

The following morning Justin showed Mrs. Tyson to the cottage. She had come, she explained, to invite Marietta up to Keriki for supper. If Marietta could get herself up there, then Mr. Tyson would drive her home again afterwards. And Catherine would join them, of course. Mrs. Tyson, crisp on this hot dry-season day, stood in the sitting room regarding Marietta, who was not yet dressed.

"Won't you sit down? Would you like a cold drink?"

"That would be nice."

Marietta looked at her bare feet. "I'm relaxing, as you see. At school we have to get up so early."

"I perfectly understand." Mrs. Tyson sat on the edge of a straight-backed chair. She leaned forward a little. "Did you enjoy yourself at school?"

Marietta sat opposite her, on the sofa. "On the whole I did. How about Catherine?" she added politely, thinking, That's what she's come to talk about, after all.

"She wouldn't use the word enjoy, I don't believe. She might say instead" — Mrs. Tyson smiled — "that they did not make her waste her time. However, her father is delighted that she won that prize. The very day she got home he brought it down to the mission to show it off to me. He came to the back door because he'd seen me through the window, washing lettuce at the sink in the kitchen. He walked straight in, not bothering to knock." Mrs. Tyson crossed her legs neatly. "Of course, Catherine would never have mentioned winning it, which is the other reason why I presumed to come to see you this morning. You see, she doesn't talk about herself much, and I wondered how she did with the other girls. It's an unusual situation, and I tend to worry about her," she finished, in a rush.

"You don't need to."

"No?"

"They were pretty unkind to begin with, but Catherine can take care of herself. When they didn't get the rise out of her they were hoping for, they left her alone."

"Am I glad to hear that!" Mrs. Tyson exclaimed. "I took quite a gamble. In fact, with Catherine I've been taking gambles ever since she came to Standard One. It's not that I ever had doubts about *her*, mind you. No, it's her father who presented the problem." Mrs. Tyson smiled. "He started talking about marrying her off in Standard Six. By Standard Eight he was very serious. He told me all about a marriage he'd arranged. He stood to get three thousand shillings, thirteen cows, and a bull, he said. But when the boy came with his parents to fetch her, Catherine ran away. The chief was beside himself at first! But after a while he calmed down and agreed that the boy could marry one of his other daughters instead. 'Let her go to school,' he said. 'Let her read there and teach others what she's learned!' As for the young man, he married one of her half-sisters last Christmas, and the following day in my living room, Catherine said to me, cool as a cucumber, 'My sister's husband's place has too many mosquitoes, and if you have malaria, how can you read? I could not be happy there.'

"So Catherine went to Alliance High School," Mrs. Tyson went on, "and settled down just fine. But last July we saw the Ministry of Education circular about the scholarships. My husband was disgusted with the whole idea. 'It's like sending lambs to the slaughter,' he said. 'How many Africans have ever spoken to Europeans their own age before? And suddenly they're expected to eat and sleep with racists!' But I didn't listen. I knew Catherine would manage." Mrs. Tyson smiled as she sipped her lemonade. "She's always been exceptional. Of course, her mother was the only one of all the chief's wives who wasn't a Keriki."

"Where did she come from, then?"

"Mombasa. They used to sing songs about her. Ballads, I guess we'd call them. You think it's finished and then there are twenty verses more. I bet there are some up at Keriki who could sing them still. Oh, yes, I remember seeing her! She was certainly different from her co-wives. That's exactly why Chief Mattias married her, of course." Mrs. Tyson laughed. "I guess you must have heard of his exploits. Everyone has. There were plenty of songs about him as well as her, and with all the details, too!"

From the day he attained his chieftaincy, Mattias, the erstwhile pious mission boy, fully exploited the privileges of power, especially the sexual privileges, and while the colonial officials in Baluga were vicariously excited by his excesses, despairing parents throughout the district vainly attempted to protect their daughters. But then, abruptly, in the sixteenth year of his chieftaincy, Mattias became impotent. He sat powerless and alone, drinking his Hennessy brandy, while young men, his classificatory sons, slipped by the red bungalow to offer solace to his wives. Deprived not only of ejaculation but of procreation, too, he had no future. He might as well have been dead.

Mattias spent months in consultation with practitioners of various sorts, seeking an antidote to the pernicious magic that had sapped his strength. But nothing worked. He hid himself, neglecting his fiefdom. The hut taxes went unpaid; the Nandi raided with impunity. Eventually, when the long rains came to an end, he set off with Ongeso by train to Mombasa, where the most celebrated wizards and healers were to be found.

In two months he was home again. He came by lorry from Baluga, driving along the edge of the escarpment in the late afternoon. At Keriki he descended, and from the way he glared at them and stamped like a bull in the dust, the loiterers by the mission gates knew immediately he had been cured. Behind him came Ongeso, who had tasted his master's food all the way to the Coast and back and had suffered — for the first time in his servitude — repeated bouts of diarrhea, though Mattias hadn't suffered once from the strange food. Last, a slim, dark girl clambered over the side of the lorry. Instead of the wide-skirted cotton dress and bandanna of an upcountry woman who spent her days digging in the sun, this woman wore a cloth tied above her breast and another draped over her head. In her flowing wrappers she looked like the Indian princess on the billboard outside the Gujarati cinema in Baluga. Bracelets jangled on her narrow arms.

Fatima was a city woman. Her grateful father, relieved of an affliction, had given her at age six in lieu of payment to the magician who had cured him. She had grown up in this thick-walled Arab house looking out across Mombasa harbor to the reef. In the household were other children like herself, left by former patients without means of paying for their treatment, but she was the prettiest and the quickest. When she was still young her master began to train her as his assistant. First she learned how to grind and mix the ingredients for the elixirs that the impotent and barren came in search of from as far away as Nyasaland or the Sudan — men and women journeying in panic across Africa, mindless of thieves and pestilence and even a world war. But as she grew older, this girl, who now had no family, no father to conclude a proper marriage for her, began to help her master's patients in more practical ways. At this she was wonderfully talented.

After seven days of thrice-daily dosages (Ongeso was not permitted to taste them first), Mattias was pronounced ready for Fatima's "treatments." These were immediately effective, and in his joy, relief, and gratitude Mattias offered fourteen head of cattle for her. Having no use for cattle, her master bargained hard. Could he give her to an infidel? Ten years he had invested in the training of Fatima and she was only just beginning to reward his time and trouble. As for the girl herself, at first she had doubts. Mattias spoke such poor Swahili, and though he told her he was rich, that he had coffee farms, power mills, three lorries, these things meant little to her; she'd never seen coffee growing, or ridden in a lorry. He told her also that white men came to his compound and drank his brandy. This she knew was a lie. But in the end her master and Mattias came to an agreement. Mattias extracted two thousand shillings in one-hundred-shilling notes from the inside pocket of his shirt and took the Muslim name of Hassan — a name he'd forget, of course, once the traïn left Kiliguni. The deal was done, then, whether Fatima agreed or not. But she wasn't above being persuaded. Mattias's craving for her gave her a sense of power, and this she found was enjoyable. So she parted from her master and his household and walked behind Ongeso through the thronging streets to the railway station.

They broke their journey in two places for Mattias to reassure himself of the cure, and by the time they reached Keriki, six hundred miles from the sea, Mattias was ready to put behind him the months of laxness that had preceded his pilgrimage. He fell upon delinquent taxpayers, hauled them into court, and bullied from them what they owed the Crown. With his band of thugs he scoured the hills, chasing up laborers to mend the roads and clear the drainage ditches. He attended to his wives, as before, by rotation, one each evening, but at midnight he came back to his own house to the big iron bed and his elixir, Fatima. Ongeso was put outside as garden boy, and Fatima, upon whom Mattias's second lease on life depended, cooked his food. He began to take rice in the coastal manner, though his stomach ached for *ugali*, and across the hills of Keriki, people sang a new song about the love of a chief for a wanderer. They didn't dare sing it in front of Mattias, but one day in a bar in town he heard snatches of it. At home he made Ongeso sing it for him, and, roaring with delight, had Ongeso sing it again. Then they sang it together.

But Fatima never went into the homestead of her co-wives or of the wives of her husband's sons. She left the bungalow only to buy salt and matches and to look at the fabrics for sale in the Indian shops across the road from the mission gate. For these forays she wore a pink cardigan against the chilly mornings of the Highlands.

As she walked like a queen across the market, the women selling cabbages and onions beyond the Quaker meeting house watched her like hawks. They waited to see if the body of the stranger, the wanderer, the pleasure of men, would thicken. Or was her womb spoiled already, rotted away? After twelve months, when they saw she was with child, the whole of Keriki knew it before sunset.

"When Fatima's labor began, none of her co-wives would come to help," Mrs. Tyson said. "They hated her, you see, because she was so much the favorite. So Ongeso had to fetch the chief's old mother. She must've been nearly ninety by then. In her time she'd delivered scores of children, but this child, she told me, was the most stubborn of them all. Four days it took, and at the moment of the child's first cry, Fatima died.

"They say the chief's grief was terrible to see. He shut himself up in his bungalow and only Ongeso was permitted to go near him. But one day, a whole year after Fatima's death, he went to the house of his daughter's foster mother and picked the baby up and carried her off. And until she went to Alliance, that's where Catherine stayed, in the bungalow with him."

Marietta said quietly, "They called her mother the wanderer?"

Mrs. Tyson nodded. "It's the word Keriki people use for, well, a prostitute, I guess."

"Once Catherine called my —" Marietta stopped.

"What was that?"

"Nothing."

Mrs. Tyson gazed at Marietta. "She called your mother a wanderer?"

Marietta looked up into the kind eyes. "She watched me all the time. She followed me constantly. She wouldn't leave me alone!"

Mrs. Tyson sighed. "She didn't intend to be cruel, I don't believe."

"No?" Marietta smiled wryly. "Well, I found all that attention very unpleasant. The truth is, in those days Catherine terrified me!" She added, "Thank you for your invitation, but we're off to Nairobi for Christmas, so I'm afraid I can't come."

As she watched Mrs. Tyson walk away across the garden, Marietta suddenly thought, I've been hoping for another Violet. Isn't that it? But Catherine isn't Violet. Violet's gone for good. I can't replace her.

136

9

Katari

Virginia and Marietta packed up the Land-Rover, waved to Justin and the Macdonalds, and jolted off up the main street of Baluga. At ten o'clock Virginia stopped to get water for the engine at the petrol station next to the Hotel Simba. The proprietor, baseball cap turned back to front, was stacking crates of empty beer bottles at the door. As he rattled the crates and bantered with the servant, the young Kamba prostitute emerged into the midmorning sun. She wore a black brassiere and a cloth tied beneath her armpits. She stretched, scratched her scalp between the ridges of her braids, yawned, and stared without any sign of recognition at Marietta. All white girls looked alike to her. A man who was leaning against the door of the garage, closed for the holiday, greeted the Kamba girl, and she sauntered across to talk to him as Virginia started up the engine and drove away.

In Eldonia Virginia turned off the main road into town. Though the streets were deserted, in front of the Red Lion there were half a dozen vehicles baking in the afternoon sun. "I have to use the lavatory," she said, "how about you? And we could have a bite to eat."

In the lounge on her way to the lavatory, Virginia ordered egg sandwiches. Marietta wandered over to a rack displaying newspapers and magazines, next to the front desk. There was the usual collection of farming periodicals, a week-old *Time*, some English women's magazines, and an October issue of *Country Life*, come sea mail. Marietta took it out of the rack to look at the house advertisements. She always liked to look at Wiltshire, where the fabled Aunt Sophia lived in a house by the name of Folly Court, which you approached between two rows of stone mushrooms. Every year they received a Christmas card with a sketch of this house on the front, ringed with mistletoe.

A young man with dark hair ran up the steps into the hotel lounge. He searched among the people waiting for their tea and came over to the desk. He said urgently to the receptionist, "Did anyone come in asking for me?"

"What's the name?" the girl said sulkily. She must be cross, Marietta thought, about having to work on a holiday, instead of being at the club with everyone else.

"Jonathan Sudbury."

"This is for you, then," the girl said, handing him a telegram. "They're not coming," she added malevolently.

The young man frowned. Over her magazine he caught Marietta's eye. "What would *you* do?"

"They're not coming at all?"

"They were meant to arrive today, and now they won't come till next week at the earliest. But meanwhile, what can I do with the people who're here already?"

"Are you taking them somewhere else?"

"To Mount Elgon, actually." He leaned one arm along the reception desk. Behind it, the girl had gone back to her ledger.

"We used to live there," Marietta said. "At Itep."

"Really?" He looked at her curiously. He had violet eyes. Marietta thought, I've never seen eyes that color before. "I didn't know Neville Bilton had a daughter."

"Stepdaughter. I mean, I was. Not anymore. We live in Baluga now, at the Wayfarer Hotel. My mother runs it; Neville's gone to Canada."

"If you live in a hotel, maybe you could give me some advice. You look like a tactful person. How do you deal tactfully with guests who behave very badly? We have a couple at our place now. They've been drunk for five days."

"You could lock up the drink."

"If I did that, they'd probably break the door down. One of them wrestled for Yale."

"You could tell them to go home."

"They each deposited five thousand dollars in advance in the

Chase Manhattan Bank in New York for the pleasure of going on safari with me. For that, I more or less have to bear with them."

"Of course you don't! You just have to have the courage of your convictions. Tell them you're not leaving the house unless they stop. Look them straight in the eye."

"You must've had a lot of practice. I shan't sound half as convincing as you."

Virginia was walking across the lounge towards them. Her hair was brushed and she had blue on her eyelids. People paused, cups halfway to their lips, to watch her as she passed. She's become her other self now, Marietta thought. And you have to look at her, whether you want to or not.

Virginia smiled up at the young man. "How d'you do?"

They shook hands. "I'm Jonathan Sudbury. Lady Bilton?"

"Goodness, no!" Virginia said gaily. "Not for ages. Virginia Hamilton. I see you and Marietta have already met." In the lavatory Virginia had taken off her bush jacket. Underneath she was wearing a pink silk blouse, tucked into khaki slacks. It was evident that she did not wear a brassiere.

Marietta, in her cotton sundress, green and yellow once but faded now by the sun and Justin's merciless poundings in the laundry sink at the Wayfarer, looked away to the table on which the waiter was arranging plates and knives. She said quickly, "Shouldn't we eat those sandwiches, before the bread curls up?"

"Won't you join us, Jonathan?"

"I wish I could, but I have to get home. I'm leaving on safari in the morning. That is, I intended to. Two people have already arrived and the other two were meant to come up this afternoon. But they're delayed." He waved the telegram. "So I have to decide whether to go on, or wait down here for the others. We're due above Kitale tomorrow evening."

Marietta thought, He was talking to me. Now he's talking to her. It doesn't matter that she's twice his age. She's a good listener. She always is, so long as it's a man.

"The other two got in several days ago. They've been drinking ever since they left New York, and if we wait any longer, they won't be able to tell a boulder from a buffalo. When people get in that sort of state, just living with them is a very risky business. They got up at nine this morning and by eleven o'clock they'd put away a fifth of whiskey between them. Thank God, their guns are locked in the gunroom and my father's got the only key. So for the moment we're reasonably safe."

"I'd think you'd be mad to wait for the others," Virginia said gravely. "Couldn't you go on without them and have them drive up to join you when they eventually arrive? In fact, they mightn't come at all. The telegram doesn't say what's delaying them, I don't suppose. They might have crashed in the stock market, and you don't recoup from that in a week!"

"You're right," said Jonathan, nodding. "It would be insane of me to wait. You see" — he colored — "I haven't been doing this long. In fact, this is only my third safari, and I'm not very good at changes of plan. I hate telegrams, for instance."

"Well, who doesn't? But we shouldn't keep you. You must have plenty to do if you're off in the morning. The very best of luck," Virginia added, smiling.

"What a pleasant boy!" she said as Jonathan ran off. "My father had a chum called Philip Sudbury. Ages ago, when he came out the first time, before he married and came out again for good with Mother and me. We had a large brown photograph of him and Father standing on the carcass of an elephant. That must have been this boy's grandfather. I remember hearing that he'd settled near Eldonia, at a place called Olgolulu. Interesting the family's still there. So many have left, after all."

"He liked you, didn't he?" Marietta bit fiercely into her sandwich.

"He seemed awfully put out, poor boy. The prospect of living in a tent with two drunks for a month must be very trying. At least in a hotel you can keep a little distance."

"Where did you get that blouse?" Marietta said suddenly. Her face was hot; she felt peculiar dampness round her eyes, as if they too were sweating.

"From Daphne, of course. One of her castoffs. If you mean where did she buy it, I don't know." Virginia offered the back of her neck to her daughter. "What does it say on the label?"

"It doesn't matter."

"Oh, do look. I never pay attention to labels, but since you asked."

Reluctantly, Marietta wiped her hands on her napkin and turned down the collar of her mother's blouse. "Hermès, Paris."

Virginia turned away again. "She must've bought it last spring when she and Peter were in France. But she never wore it. She gave it to me brand-new. She said it made her look flat-chested. She gave me some other things as well, things she'd bought on that trip and later decided against. A bathing suit and what she called a peignoir, which is an elaborate sort of dressing gown that women who have oodles of time on their hands wear to drink coffee and paint their fingernails. The blouse is the only thing I've worn so far, seeing that there's no pool at Baluga, and not much time for a peignoir, either."

"Why d'you accept things you won't ever wear?"

Virginia glanced at her daughter's glowering face. There she goes again. Daphne tells me it's a phase, but how should Daphne know? She's never had a fifteen-year-old-daughter! This phase, as she calls it, might be permanent. For ever and ever. She shrugged. "It would've been rude, I thought, to say, 'I'll take the blouse because it'll be useful, but not the other things. You must've forgotten that, unlike you, Daphne, I don't go to the Katari Club, and my mornings are spent on the run.' Anyway," she added cheerfully, "one day I might find the time to loll about. Peignoirs don't go out of style. They're always pretty much the same."

"If you ever do wear it, I hope it'll be in private, so nobody sees you've got nothing on underneath!" Marietta said furiously.

"Etta, what's the matter with you? We're on holiday. How often do we get a holiday? Don't spoil it, please!"

"Dear Neville," Marietta wrote. "I've got the most amazing thing to tell you.

"We're at Daphne's for Christmas. Mum's never left the hotel over a holiday before. We got down here last night. We'd been going since seven in the morning and when we arrived I was dead tired and longing for bed, but there at the front door were Daphne in an evening dress and Peter in black tie, and all the lights were on and the lion skins picked up off the floor and spruce boughs draped over the banisters. Daphne said they were having their Christmas party, and it was starting in half an hour. It sounded like fun, I said, but really, I preferred to go to bed, because I'd had a long, hard day. I'd get something from the kitchen and eat it on a tray upstairs. But Daphne swooped upon me (you know how she swoops?) in chiffon (peacock blue). She said, 'You haven't seen your present yet!' She took me to her sitting room, and there, behind the door, was this party dress she'd had made for me. It was awfully pretty, I do have to say. White piqué (which is bumpy cotton), embroidered round the neck and hem in pink. I've never had anything so pretty in my life. Of course, I'd been thinking I'd better go to bed because I had nothing to wear.

"First they had cocktails, and a young man called Nigel played cocktail music. Nigel is someone Daphne met in England last summer. He's her latest, and he's staying with them for the winter. He's useful to have as a house guest because he plays the piano so awfully well. He can play anything. Say you don't even know the title, only a bit of the tune. If you hum a little, he'll catch on. To look at, he's what Mum would call smooth. He plasters his hair down with rather smelly hair oil and he's interested in himself more than anything, I should say; but during cocktails he let me hang around and suggest tunes. And I can see how Daphne might fancy him. He's a sort of musical decoration.

"Then there was the supper. We sat at tables borrowed from the Katari Club. It was a bit of a squash in the dining room and rather hot, and so much food. They'd been cooking for a week and borrowing shelves in fridges all over Katari. I sat next to Nigel. He was the only person there who was more or less my generation, which was why Daphne put us together. But he's not very talkative, and I'm not either, by and large; and on the other side was General Llewellyn. He's large and red and deaf in one ear, and that ear was on my side. I got fuller and fuller and sleepier and sleepier and was wondering whether I couldn't just slip off, through the pantry. Nigel wouldn't notice, and neither would General Llewellyn. But just before the meringues and strawberries, we were given champagne. Peter stood up and knocked a glass with a knife to get people to stop talking. Then he announced my mother's engagement to Bruce Oldfield.

"Until that moment I had never head of Bruce Oldfield. When she married you, I had some sort of warning as you'd kept coming down to Runga all the time. But this time I had no warning whatever.

"From where I was sitting, I couldn't actually see my mother. She was hidden by General Llewellyn. We all stood up for the toast and then by peering I could see her, but I still didn't know which one Bruce Oldfield was. He might have been any of a number of people — for instance, a smallish man, rather solemn, with a mustache, who was standing next to Daphne for the toast; or a particularly thin man, a little like Nigel, whom I've already described, only older, of course. And there was a third man, too, who was bald, and he was standing opposite my mother, and looking at her across the table as if he knew her well and might have something special going with her. In fact, my mother was surrounded by men and any one of them might have been Bruce Oldfield. But eventually, when Peter had finished saying how long he and Daphne had known my mother, how she was their oldest friend and how happy they were for her, etc., everyone sat down again, except for a man with bushy eyebrows. I thought he must be on his way to the lavatory, but in a peculiar twangy voice he started to thank Peter and Daphne; and I realized, of course, he was it! He said this was a surprise to him and to my mother, too; that they had thought of themselves as *un*married people. They met for the first time in October and after that things had gone very fast. He told a rather involved joke about the telephone operator at Baluga, who kept cutting them off or joining in their conversations whenever he felt like it. These interruptions had very nearly killed the romance. While he was speaking, I couldn't see my mother's face because he was standing in the way. He offered a toast to her, and another to Peter and Daphne, and then we all sat down and finished our strawberries.

"At the end of dinner, when people had started back into the drawing room and Nigel was playing the piano again, my mother came over to me. Her face looked rather hot, and she came between the tables very fast, and I thought, She's going to explain now. But all she said was, 'Bruce wants to open the dancing with you!' He was just behind her and she took his hand and one of mine and joined us together. Clamped us together, rather, so I didn't have any say in the matter. We sped twice round the floor alone, while the others all grinned and stared at us. I looked at his chest and tried to follow what he was doing without tripping over the hem of my dress. Peter came onto the floor with Mum and lots of others came, too, so we were quickly hidden in the crowd, thank goodness. Bruce Oldfield said, 'You follow easily.' (He was trying to be nice, I know.) Then he said, 'Your mother makes me very happy. I've never met anyone quite like her,' and he gripped me tighter and did an unexpected twirl, which I weathered, though only just. 'I do feel honored,' he said, 'that she chose me.' And then he became quite gay. He'd been nervous up till then, almost as nervous as I. He told me he had a daughter back in Sydney. He's Australian, you see, which explains why he talks the way he does. He left because he was restless. (He must have been divorced, though he didn't mention a wife.) He simply set off round the world to have a look at things and came here quite by chance. He was on a boat from Bombay to Durban, and it stopped at Mombasa. He came ashore, he said, to see the elephants — he'd always wanted to see them in the wild, the ones in India were so dull and tame — and to look up an old friend he'd met in the war, and then he'd take the next boat on to South Africa. That was two years ago, and now he owns two butcheries and several shops, a garage, and a quarry. And he's going to marry my mother on Easter Saturday, which is her fortieth birthday, as it happens. After that, no more hotels. We're to live in his house here in Katari. It's got a swimming pool, he said (to tempt me!). He put it in himself. Before there'd just been a fish pond, only most of the fish had died because the old owners never had the water changed.

"Just then Nigel stopped playing and we were left standing in the middle of the drawing room floor. I saw Mummy advancing upon us, and I said to Mr. Oldfield, 'So glad to have met you. I expect we'll meet again soon. It's ten to twelve and I really must go to bed,' and I escaped before my mother quite reached us. I couldn't face her just then.

"I haven't digested any of this. I'm writing it down because I want you to know right away. It's ten in the morning and I haven't seen a soul yet except Jemima, who brought my breakfast. Perhaps when I go downstairs I'll find I dreamed the whole thing."

Marietta signed her letter and reread it quickly, then folded it and slipped it into the envelope she had laid ready on the tray beside her. She threw back the bedspread and was lowering her feet to the floor when the door opened and her mother walked in.

"Happy Christmas, Etta! Are you off somewhere?"

"I'm going for a walk with Peter. Last night we agreed to, at ten."

"There was no sign of him just now when I looked into the hall. He's not going anywhere yet." Virginia sat down on the bed. She patted the counterpane beside her. "Don't run away."

Reluctantly Marietta sat on the bed, but against the headboard, facing her mother, not beside her. They were going to have a brilliant dry-season day, with the rains not too long gone and the grass still green and growing. Marietta looked away through the window beyond the forest to the hills. In her mind's eye she spread her arms and flew off between the curtains that moved gently in the morning breeze, over the forest to the highest of the seven hills. From there she knew (because Peter had taken her up there once, long ago, when she was little) one could see all the wonders of the world. But between her and the gold and azure of the December sky her mother sat.

"Were you astonished?"

"Yes, as a matter of fact."

"And I suppose" — Virginia nodded at the letter on the tray — "you've been telling Neville all about it. Your great friend." Marietta said nothing. "He's so attentive. I remember how attentive he used to be." Virginia frowned quickly. "He was much too much for me."

"Why didn't you tell me before about this?" Marietta's voice was icy. "When I came back from school and said I wanted to go see Violet, and you said no, I must come down here with you, you'd already decided, hadn't you, and Daphne had planned her party and invited the guests. We had ten days at Baluga and you never said a word. Don't say you were too busy! This is just your way! You're always so full of secrets! I've a right to know a little in advance about changes in my life. If I hadn't found that newspaper account in the servants' quarters at Baluga, I'd probably still be waiting to hear that you were divorcing Neville. My mother works in most mysterious ways!" Marietta slipped from her pillow to the floor. "Excuse me, but I want to get dressed!"

Virginia said sadly, "I'm never quite sure I'll do something until I've done it." Marietta stopped in the middle of the room, a fistful of clothes clutched to her stomach. Her mother, seeing that she had her audience, said, "I make up my mind first round, as the Africans would say, and then wait to see what happens."

"Well, it's happened, hasn't it? You've announced your engagement. It wouldn't do for you to change your mind at this late stage. The way you did about Neville," Marietta added harshly.

"Oh, Etta, I couldn't bear that life! I felt ridiculous up there on that mountain, where everything hummed along the way it had before I got there, and for a time, at least, after I left. I can't tell you how awful it was being attended to, waited on, waited for. I have to work. Bruce understands that. He adores work, too, the kind which is never quite done." She grinned suddenly. "And you should see him! He dashes round Nairobi in an orange van. Daphne says she admires his energy, but Peter's horrified. 'Why d'you want to marry a shopkeeper?' he asked me. 'Because I love him, that's why,' I told him. But Peter kept on about shopkeepers being petty, narrowminded people. Poor Peter; sweet as he is, he's also a terrible snob. Well," she finished, searching her daughter's face, "you haven't told me what you think about Bruce."

Why should she care what I think? Marietta thought. What difference does it make? She's always done what she wants.

"Last night you seemed to be getting on so well . . ." Virginia's voice trailed into silence.

"Did we?"

"I saw you laughing at things he said. And you never laugh just to be polite. You're not that type at all."

"He talked about a tea planter he met on the boat from Bombay. His wig fell off into the curry at Sunday lunch."

Virginia looked at her hands.

All of a sudden Marietta let her clothes drop to the floor. Across the carpet she came to sit beside her mother on the bed. "Give me a chance, Mum." She covered her mother's clenched hands with her own. "It's just that I'm used to the *idea* of Neville, even though he's been gone for years. I hope you'll be ever so much happier this time. Not fenced in."

146

PART III

1964

10

London

More wine, Marietta?"

"No, thanks, I've had enough." Marietta covered her glass with her hand.

Lady Bilton put the stopper back in the decanter. "I must say, you're remarkably abstemious! I remember that at your age I was allowed exactly half a glass at dinner, though for my brother, Harry, two years younger, there was no such rule. I complained vociferously, but to no avail. 'Girls and boys are different,' my father said — different hearts, different livers. 'Can you prove it?' I said. And he couldn't, but still he wouldn't budge. So I swore that when my turn came I wouldn't discriminate between sons and daughters. I only had a son, of course, but now that a granddaughter of sorts has come my way, I intend to aid and abet her as much as I possibly can. Curtis!" she called over the back of her Hepplewhite chair.

Curtis wiped her hands on her apron as she came into the dining room. Her graying hair was pinned into a stout, untidy bun. She'd stretched her dark blue cardigan down in front by warming her hands in the pockets in the wintertime. Her heavy stockings wrinkled at the ankle and her shoes were loose. She always bought them a size too large because of her bunions, which pained her in wet weather, and August had been unusually wet. Nevertheless, she moved with purpose. "Why not use the bell, it's here," she said.

"Where? I can't see it."

Curtis sighed heavily. "Behind your water glass, just where it always is."

"I could've sworn . . . Oh well, do clear away. We're ready for our cheese. And bring the coffee. We all want an early night. We're getting up at four, remember."

"Is that a thing to forget?" Curtis said. "His bed's turned down. He'll want to sleep, after being in that airplane. Last time he said he didn't sleep a wink all the way from Montreal. Quite worn out, he was." She swept up Lady Bilton's plate and bore down on Marietta.

"The veal was delicious," Marietta said, "but I wasn't very hungry. I didn't do it justice, I'm afraid."

"It's excitement that's driven your appetite away. Not surprising, really." Curtis stood, a plate in either hand, beside Marietta's chair. "When was it you two saw each other last?"

"Four years ago last February."

"That's ever such a while then, isn't it. Did you say the Stilton or the Camembert, my lady?"

"Either. Both. Neither. Oh, Curtis, I believe I'm losing my appetite, too. Bring the coffee quickly." Lady Bilton fingered her pearls, four strands closed with an emerald-and-diamond clasp, which she wore turned to the front of her dress. Her eyes were emerald, too; her expression intent. White hair, cut *en brosse;* she didn't have time to take trouble. "I do wish Neville could have been here when you came on Tuesday, Marietta, but he had that meeting in Vancouver. Still, tomorrow's only Saturday. You've got a day or two before your term begins. Neville adores London. He'll rush you off your feet. I hope you're ready! You remember how he rushes?"

"I'm not sure what I remember," Marietta said. "It's been such a long time since I was at Itep. I've had hundreds of letters, but I think that sometimes he makes things up." She smiled. "Once he wrote me about a trip he was taking to Tahiti. He described in great detail all the people he met. A sailor with a hook instead of a hand, a Russian woman who'd had six husbands, and a planter with forty-two children by seven Tahitian wives, all living happily together. He described the view from the planter's front porch. The mountains and the sea, the surf breaking on the reef, the fishermen. And then a scarlet bird with black-tipped wings perched on the railing, ten feet away from where he sat. It winked at him and hopped nearer, winked again, and was just about to hop onto the table he was writing at when one of the seven wives appeared with a butterfly net and scooped it up. She gave it to him, roasted, for

150

his dinner. A year or two later, when I reread those letters, I noticed the Canadian stamps. I wrote and asked him, '*Did* you go to Tahiti or not?' and he wrote back, 'Does it matter?' And I don't suppose it did."

Lady Bilton chuckled. "He used to write exotic tales from school as well. His letters came out from England by sea mail, through Suez to Mombasa and up from the Coast on the train. Weeks and weeks letters took in those days. We'd open them and find that Neville had had polio and couldn't move his legs. Oh, the *panic*, until we thought to ask ourselves, Well, why didn't the school telegraph? And then we'd realize he'd made the whole thing up. He really was so naughty! However, he's accurate about timetables. When he writes that he's coming at five forty-five, he means it. Curtis!"

Curtis appeared with the coffee. "Didn't I show you the bell?"

"It's nine o'clock. So Sir Neville must have left Vancouver by now. Could you ring the airport, please, and see if the plane's on schedule? The number's on the pad next to my bed. Of course, I shan't sleep," she added to Marietta. "I'll imagine the plane coming over the prairies, down the St. Lawrence and out over the ocean. By the time it reaches Ireland I'll be dozing off at last, but then we'll have to be up and on our way."

Marietta didn't expect to sleep, either. She hadn't really slept since leaving Africa. She'd come on an adventure, but the adventure hadn't started yet. She was ready for it, though, and at five forty-five it would begin.

In the guest room she undressed, discarding each garment one by one across the blue-and-cream-striped bedspread. The curtains, made of the same material, were faded and their linings hung down below their hems. The Persian carpet had a rip in it near the door, and on either side of the dressing table stood piles of books, the overflow from Lady Bilton's study. Curtis, an inventive cook, didn't care for housekeeping, and Lady Bilton had far more interesting things to worry about. To Marietta, newly arrived in London, the crack in the water glass, the slightly crooked pictures, even the dust balls under the bureau, seemed charming. She put on her dressing gown and watched herself in the mirror as she brushed her hair. She and Bruce and Virginia had been at the Coast in August and her hair was bright from the sun and the sea. This September afternoon, walking with Curtis through Knightsbridge to get the veal for dinner, she'd carefully watched the English girls on the pavement. They were taut, aloof; they had an aura. At home, Rosemary Fullerton had tried for that aura but hadn't achieved it. It must take energy, Marietta thought, to feel so very much better than other people.

Of course, Virginia had warned her about the English, the real English. "Not colonials, like us," Virginia had said, pruning shears in hand in the middle of Bruce's roses at Katari. "They'll make you feel as if nothing you know or do is of any possible consequence. You'll want to jump up and down and shout, 'Look at me! *Listen!*' But if you're an outsider, they'll never pay attention. Not until you convert and see things the same way they do. Aunt Sophia's not like that, though. There's blood in *her* veins, not pond water. I hope you'll see a lot of her in England, Etta. She's not grand. The fact is, she's the only one of my relations who's given me more than the time of day."

"We aren't colonials anymore, really, now that we've got a president," Marietta said. "We're Europeans who happen to be living in Africa. Maybe I'll dislike England just as much as you do. I might bolt the moment my course is finished, or I might stay. I have to have a chance to draw my own conclusions, Mum!"

"You're getting your chance, for heaven's sake. Next Tuesday!"

"Won't you wish me luck?"

"Of course I wish you luck! I hope you turn into the best bloody painter that the Slade has ever seen! I hope you don't give a damn if people patronize you and talk about Mau Mau and King Solomon's Mines. And if eventually you want to stay, by then I hope I'll be used to the idea. Don't you realize, Etta," Virginia exclaimed, "it's not only that I object to the damp and the frozen people. If you were going to Mandalay, I'd feel just the same. You're going away, and you may never come back except for summers, if we can afford your fare. Then you'll be off again, and this" — she waved at the forest and the hills — "will be something you think of less and less. Instead, you'll put the colors in your paintings." Snipping off six dead roses and stuffing them into the gunny sack she carried with her, she added briskly, "There's another thing, apart from your going and probably never coming back. And that's Neville. Don't let him gobble you up!"

"He's not a shark, you know."

But Virginia went on, hurriedly, "If Neville'd had his way this

152

would've happened long ago. When you were twelve, ten even, he wanted to send you to school in England, but I always dug in my toes. And after he left Kenya, every year, in February, a letter would arrive: 'Will you let her come to Canada this summer? She'll be in the safest possible hands!' And I'd write back, 'Not this year. Wait till she's older.' Wait, wait, wait. But now you're eighteen, and you're dying to go." Virginia smiled wryly. "He'll do everything for you. He'll make himself absolutely indispensable. Before you know it, your life won't be your own. But then, *you* won't mind his lavishing attention. You'll thrive on it, not practically die the way I did." She went on quickly, "Don't get me wrong, I'm perfectly aware how difficult it would have been to educate you on my own. I'm grateful that Neville's been so generous, but I have to say I've always envied him a little. Somehow, you and he have more in common than you and I." She pushed her shears into her back pocket. Laughing suddenly, she added, "The thing is, you're both too brainy for me, a simple type from Rumuruti. I've got to go to town now. Want to come too? Is there some last-minute errand you should do?"

In her room in Cardigan Square Marietta got into bed. Virginia had never trusted Neville, not even on the day she married him. But what would she, Marietta, have done without him? She'd had two lives, really. One with Virginia and one with him. She'd never been to Jasper, Alberta, but if she went she'd be able to find her way to Neville's with her eyes shut. From the station you go past the post office and the bank, then to the right and up two miles through the forest, and left at the Norwegian church. By then the road's getting worse, especially in the spring before they've filled the potholes left by the frost. But soon the trees thin out and you come into a clearing. And there's the house built high, to get the view. So you go up the steps and in without knocking, and there he is, at his desk, writing his book about bird migrations. He laughs. You've come at last! After so many prevarications your mother let you come! Now tell me about the journey, Marietta. Who sat next to you on the train? I bet you got him to tell you his whole life story. Now tell it to *me!*

And he'd listen. Not like Virginia. As for Bruce, he didn't listen, either. He was busy making money. Just for the hell of it, to prove that he could do it — not to save or to spend or, like so many people he and Virginia knew, to send to Switzerland in preparation for the day when the whites would be ejected from Africa. In Australia he'd made and lost two fortunes and had been on his way to a third when he'd up and left after being cleaned out by Marilyn, his wife. Marilyn had hit the bottle so he'd been glad to let her take what she could get. He'd been glad to up and leave his daughter, too. Trixie liked surfing and not much else. Let Marilyn support Trixie's avocation; she had the means. He no longer did, though with time he intended to replace what he'd given up. This was a real challenge, he said — to start just when most other people were throwing in the towel. Getting rich in Nairobi would *really* amount to something. He was still a long way from getting rich, but he worked ceaselessly, and one of these days Peter Dawson might find himself laughing out of the other side of his face.

Bruce was boiled beef and mashed potatoes. Apple tart and custard. He didn't have flights of fancy. He was what he was, and it was obvious to everyone, even to Marietta, who had at first been reluctant to admit it, that her mother was extremely happy. The abrupt, sad silences that used to come between busyness and gaiety had completely vanished. She'd paid her debts, done her time, expiated her sins, whatever her sins had been. She'd finished with the bush, broken generators, the itinerant life. When people asked, she told them she intended to stay put, right where she was in the villa on Olduvai Road, with Bruce. "Third time lucky," she'd say, and Marietta had to concede that this seemed to be true.

The clock in the hall struck midnight. Where was Neville's plane now? Over Newfoundland, or past it. Over the Atlantic in the dead of night and humming toward the dawn. Marietta thought, Will he think I'm plain, or at least not to his taste? I write good letters, so he says. But letters are easy. I'm not shy on paper. I can cross things out and start again. But what if I *say* idiotic things? There's no taking them back. Or what if, once we see each other, there isn't anything to say? A car was driving through the square; it stopped and a door slammed. "Good night! And thanks!" a young woman called out. High heels tapped on the pavement and a key rattled. The car slid on.

For going to the airport, Lady Bilton had hired a limousine. A shiny Austin Princess, and a driver trying not to yawn. In the lamplight he blinked and rubbed his eyes. Having scarcely slept, Mari-

154

etta might have been yawning, too, but you don't yawn when your heart's in your throat and your stomach's surging. Lady Bilton got into the car first, Marietta next. Curtis was last, after making sure that the whiskey was out in the drawing room. "He likes it, first thing," she said, settling herself next to the driver.

Marietta shivered as they pulled away from the house. "We'll have to get you a proper coat on Monday," said Lady Bilton, who was wearing an aged fur. "That little jacket won't do you for autumn. And it *is* autumn already, though where the summer went, I'm sure I don't know."

"Forgot to come this year," Curtis said. "If I were you, Miss Marietta, I'd have stayed in the sunshine."

"Sunshine can get very tiresome," Lady Bilton remarked. "When we came home I was thankful to be out of it. George couldn't understand why. He loved it. He loved everything in Kenya. Leaving was dreadfully hard for him. If he hadn't needed that operation, he'd have stayed there till he dropped. But for all the years I lived there, I never felt quite settled. It seemed so artificial, somehow."

In her youth she'd fought for women's rights, after Oxford, where she'd viva'd for a first in Greats. But then she'd fallen in love with Sir George, of all unlikely people. "Give me one winter," he'd said, "to show you Africa" (a passion of his). "You'll be back at your work by the spring. I believe in your work, Alice. I truly do." So off they'd gone on a hunting honeymoon, and coming back from the Sudan in March 1913 they'd passed Mount Elgon, and George had said, "This must be the most beautiful place on earth! Any chance you could be happy living here?" For love, and thinking it wouldn't last, that passion of his, she'd taken a chance. Then Neville had arrived, and a few weeks after him had come the war, and good years and bad years, and then a second war; but still George's passion hadn't flaked one jot. "One got tired," Lady Bilton said dryly, "of telling oneself how challenging the outer edges were, when what one truly cared about was happening at the center."

Curtis had brought a thermos of coffee and some bread and butter wrapped in cellophane. At the Chiswick Flyover, she offered her provisions.

"No appetite yet," Lady Bilton said.

"Neither have I," Marietta added.

"We'll certainly be punctual," Curtis said. "I hope he is, too. Once there was a fog and the airplane went on up to Glasgow. Do you remember? He came down on the train and we met him at Euston in the evening. No fog this time, though," she added, peering up past the blaze of the streetlights into the still, dense darkness.

"I hate this getting up at four," Lady Bilton said suddenly. "It used to be boats that one met, and boat trains, at a sensible hour. Airplanes aren't sensible. They come when it suits *them*, not when it suits one. I hate this coming and going. Mostly it's going, of course. Perhaps," she said, brightening, "perhaps now you're here, Marietta, he'll think of staying. An old mother isn't enough to keep him in England. But you might be enough. That's what I'm hoping for."

"Yes," said Curtis. "He's traipsed about too much." Though she'd given him her frank opinion numerous times, Neville hadn't changed his ways. This Curtis held against him, because she was deeply attached to his mother. "I am," she'd said to Marietta in the kitchen, over tea. "She's been ever so good to me, and I've been ever so good to her, neither of us having that many people of our own. We enjoy ourselves, her ladyship and I, her with her causes, me with looking after her. Always meetings and do's and ten for luncheon. Believe me, Miss Marietta, she keeps us both on our toes!"

In the car Curtis said, "It would be nice if he settled. Had his own place. In Africa he used to be a farmer, didn't he? Well, why couldn't he be a farmer here, too? I don't fancy those Canadian winters myself. Milder in England, whatever else you might say about it."

"Farming?" Lady Bilton frowned. "He's done that once and I doubt he'd do it again. Neville doesn't do the same thing twice, you see. His enthusiasms wax and wane, and once they've waned, that's that. Stepfathering is what he's in the throes of now. He seems more set on that than he's been on anything in a very long while."

But what if he's disappointed in me? Marietta thought. What if, in the flesh, I'm disappointed in him? In her jacket pockets, the palms of her hands were damp.

The car slid into the underpass, a tube of blinding concrete. Taxis scurried past them. The plane's arrived already, Marietta thought. We're late, despite our getting up so early. But they weren't. Her watch said only half past five. Fifteen minutes to go yet.

Lady Bilton said, "We can go up to watch the plane come in. Then we'll have to wait for the customs, but one can have a little breakfast while one's waiting. I never feel hungry till I know he's on the ground."

In the terminal they pushed through a crowd of Jamaicans. The men wore light suits with broad lapels and pointed shoes, the women summery dresses, despite the autumn chill. They laughed and pushed and called to one another. Seeing the women and children, the men and the young girls, come to meet a plane from Kingston, Marietta thought, I know these people, they're familiar! Then she looked away. No, they don't move or talk or laugh like Africans, regardless of the color of their skin. They could as well be Japanese. She followed Curtis and Lady Bilton to the escalator.

They came to great windows overlooking the runways. The sky was pale now. Curtis said, "No doubt from where he is he can see the sun already. *We'll* have to wait to see it, though."

"They say his plane's on time?" said Lady Bilton, frowning at the flight board.

"A minute or two early."

"And it's mostly blue? So many to choose from! One can never be sure one's looking at the right one. Is that it?" Lady Bilton pointed at a plane taxiing at a distance to their left.

"No, that one's taking off, you see," Curtis said.

An Air France plane touched down, sped along the runway, slowed, and turned towards the terminal. "Red and green. That's not ours, either." A second plane plunged out of the sky. "There it is! That's it! Blue and silver underneath."

Marietta gripped the handrail. He'd promised they'd see each other again. He'd promised adventures. But she hadn't quite believed him. She wouldn't count her chickens. What if . . . But how foolish of her not to have believed him! His promises *did* come true, given enough time.

She watched as the blue and silver plane swept down the runway past suburban villas in the dawn. She waited for it to slow and turn towards the terminal, as the other planes had done. But halfway along the runway it careened to the left. Flames shot up above its tail as the plane pitched onto the dark grass. The scattering spectators gasped in disbelief. There was a second of silence, followed by a shriek of sirens through the thick plate glass.

That's not his, Marietta said to herself. It's only five forty-two. His hasn't come yet. As fire engines leapt onto the concrete and

157

raced toward the burning plane, she thought, Don't let them block the runway! Then he'll have to land in Glasglow and spend hours and hours coming down to London on the train. I've waited four years to see him; that's enough. I won't wait any longer.

"Curtis," said Lady Bilton quietly. "That *was* his, wasn't it?"

Curtis had her arm round the old shoulders. "Come, let's go downstairs. We'll find a place to sit. We'll have some coffee first, and then we'll have a chance to see what's what."

"Marietta!" Lady Bilton looked back. "Please come. You must have some coffee too. We brought three cups. We did, didn't we?" she said to Curtis. But Marietta remained where she was. To her touch the handrail was definitely hard. It anchored her above the ambulances racing past under a sky suddenly made pink by the sun, clambering up in time to illuminate disaster. A voice was saying something over the loudspeaker, a man's voice, harsh and cold, but Marietta didn't hear him. She couldn't listen; the conflagration on the runway demanded all her strength and her attention.

Lady Bilton slipped away from Curtis and came to Marietta. "No, no," she said. "It's horrible!" Her voice shook, though scarcely. "My dear, do come." She disengaged Marietta's hands from the steel rail — first one, then the other — and took her away through the crush of people flocking from ticket counters and refreshment bars to view and remember the spectacle so that they could tell their grandchildren about it. Like the war, really, it was. Like they'd gone and dropped a bomb and set the whole place on fire.

"Neville wasn't on that plane," Marietta said loudly, as she rode down the escalator to the main floor, emptied abruptly of travelers and tourists, porters and clerks, and littered with abandoned luggage. A Jamaican child howled in the middle of a great expanse of dark blue carpeting. His mother had run off upstairs to see the spectacle, and he'd been left behind. With eyes clenched shut and mouth wide open, his tears ran down his plump black cheeks onto a palm-tree-patterned shirt. He wouldn't survive to be reclaimed; he'd die of fright first, Marietta thought. She asked, "Are we going back to London now?"

"We're going to wait a little while," Lady Bilton said, "for any news of Neville."

Curtis led them to three upholstered chairs arranged round a plastic table. A cigar, still smoking, was lying in a heavy china ashtray. It isn't six o'clock yet, Marietta thought; it's much too early for cigars. The day hasn't started yet. Nothing's happened yet. We haven't even had breakfast! We shan't, till Neville's on the ground.

"This should do us fine. Miss Marietta, do you like milk as well as sugar?" Curtis said, taking the thermos out of her oilcloth bag. "And there's the bread and butter, too."

As they sipped their cups of coffee, the mother of the little boy dashed back to retrieve him. His eyes opened, his mouth shut, his tears were stanched on his cheeks. His howls dwindled to hiccups in an instant. She grabbed him, set him on her hip, and was off again, this time to the observation deck for the best view.

"Weren't those fire engines lovely!" Marietta's voice was taut and high. "So long and shiny and loud and efficient! The ones we have at home are dreadfully shabby and they always arrive too late to be useful anyway. But these London fire engines are really worth seeing." Carefully she put her cup down on the plastic table. "Thanks for the coffee. It warmed me nicely. Now I'm going back upstairs. I find fires thrilling. Always have. From what I saw of this one, it's going to be sensational! I wouldn't want to miss it." Her voice cracked. "It'll be like watching a small-scale end of the world."

Curtis said gently, "You stay here and rest with us, Miss Marietta. There's no sense in chasing after excitements. They only tire a person out, and we'll all be needing our strength later. Now sit down, please."

Lady Bilton sat in the dining room in her funeral clothes, a black wool suit and a crêpe de chine blouse and a black cloche hat, which she'd had new years ago for Sir George's funeral. Sir George died in January and one had needed a hat that hugged against the bitter wind cutting through the cemetery. But one never expected to wear that hat on a lovely autumn day at the funeral of one's son, who'd died, aged fifty, in an airplane disaster, leaving one childless at seventy-six. Cremation private, the notice she'd put in the *Times* said. Memorial service Tuesday, September 23, 2:00 P.M., St. Luke's, Chester Place; contributions to the Cancer Society. Neville's admirers would have their day, but the cremation should be for just the three of them — the only three, she thought, in whom Neville still provoked passion. On the table were four cakes, uncut.

159

Curtis had insisted, "You'll be ever so hungry afterwards, so I'm ordering in from Harrods. Grieving always takes it out of you."

"Such a terrible, terrible waste, having a son and not knowing him," Lady Bilton said. "Surely I knew him to begin with, didn't I? But we haven't even lived on the same continent for over forty years. He was wonderfully adept at avoiding me."

Neville had been eight and a week, she told Marietta, sitting opposite, when she'd left him at his private school in Surrey. "Then I drove back to London in a hired car. The boat for Mombasa sailed the following afternoon and I was on it.

"I'd given him fifty envelopes addressed to me. They'd last a year, I thought; after that he would have learned to write well enough to address his envelopes himself. But the notes he sent in those I'd left him didn't tell me anything, except about the food and football and a master called Chip. And the weather, which he seemed to fancy, funnily enough — most people don't, after all. My sister-in-law, Janet, was living in London then. She took him for the holidays, and went to see him in term time as well. She was devoted. I couldn't fault her on that. She sent me careful descriptions, careful reports, about teeth and height and appetite. 'Neville's never any trouble,' she assured me. 'Always happy in a world of his own.'" Lady Bilton sighed. "So her letters didn't tell me any more than Neville's did.

"After three years my husband found the time to get away from his beloved Kenya and we came to England. The boy we found waiting for us was very polite. No, that's not quite right. He wasn't waiting for *us*. He was a great deal more interested in butterflies than he was in us, but since we were taking him to the country for the summer and in the country there'd be butterflies, he was prepared to speak when spoken to by two grownups who were little more to him than strangers. We took a house in Suffolk, and there he gradually became less polite and somewhat more interested in his parents, but suddenly it was September and time to leave him for another three years. Then his letters changed. No more football. The master Chip had departed. Fewer complaints about the food. No comments on the weather. Instead, he was writing stories, tall tales, fantasies, call them what you will. And after a time or two of being taken in, I realized he was vanishing.

"I thought, How can I stop this, how can I bring him back? But there wasn't any way I could. It was far too late. In 1922 I had sent

160

him off forever." She shook her head. "Of course, we all did it. We thought we were doing well by our children. It wouldn't do to keep them out in Africa, with us. They needed England more than they needed parents. We knew which was more important, and when they were eight or nine, ten at the latest, we shipped them off to avoid the hazards of being colonials. When school was finished, there was Cambridge and London, which was, after all, the center of the universe. I'd made certain Neville understood that, and very soon there was the war. It was only after his father got cancer and he and I came home in haste and never went back that Neville found the time to live in Africa," she concluded sadly. "So you see, I haven't really known my son for more than forty years. *You* knew him much better than I did, I'm afraid."

In the square below, children were calling to one another in unexpected sunshine. That afternoon when the three of them were on their way to the crematorium in a stifling car, Curtis had remarked, "So summer came this year after all. With London looking its best, more's the pity that we're doing this. Death is for cold and sleet, not for precious summer." The dining room windows were open and voices floated in on the warm air. Children knew nothing about death, or about the chasms between past and future.

After a moment Marietta said, "Neville was . . . well, he liked quests."

"That sounds familiar," said Lady Bilton dryly. "And your mother? I imagine she didn't. Unfortunately I haven't got a very clear picture of her at all. She came and went so fast. She's beautiful, I'm told. Her mother was. I remember Sylvia Parkson quite distinctly. She was frail. Like some fleeting woodland flower that wouldn't last till morning. I take it, though, your mother wasn't frail. Isn't."

"No," Marietta agreed, "And she doesn't take the long view. 'What's the point,' she'd say. 'You'd only scare yourself to death, worrying about things that might never happen. Better to take each day at a time.' She's not one for great wide vistas, like Neville."

Lady Bilton nodded. "I believe Neville was the most romantic person I've ever known."

"Well, he told me he had to have very particular conditions. If he didn't, he got terribly restless. In every other way they were completely different, but in this one respect he and my mother

161

were alike. This restlessness, she had it too, and he wanted to warn me that I might have it as well. It generally comes out later, he said, after you've tried living the expected way and found that that doesn't work."

"And did he tell you what produces this mysterious condition?"

"Being brought up by servants."

"Weren't we all? Who wasn't, in those days!"

"He meant African servants," Marietta said. "They're the ones who washed us, nursed us, slept with us. They're the ones we loved. But as we get older we're required to behave as if none of that happened, or even if it did, it wasn't important. That leads to confusion. We aren't what we appear to be. Everything's out of whack, so Neville said. We aren't really white, after all."

"So that's how he excused himself?" Lady Bilton sighed. "What a thing to tell a child!"

"He wanted me to know before he went away, this theory of his."

"Which one wasn't obliged to accept, I hope!"

"He didn't mean any harm," Marietta said. After a moment she asked, "Didn't he say anything about it to you?"

Lady Bilton looked down at her hands, knotted and veined, on either side of her plate. She shook her head. "Dear me, no! After he went to private school in 1922 he told me nothing of importance."

Lady Bilton had an appointment with Carfax, the solicitor. Neville's will was going to be read. "Curtis and I should be back by one," she said. Once they'd driven off in the taxi, Marietta thought, Well, no point in saving up London, not anymore. She put her street map in her pocket, left a note on the table in the hall under the clock, and went out.

First she'd go to Foyle's, where all those books had come from, hundreds of them, wrapped in corrugated paper and then packed into boxes. They were ranged now on shelves in her room in Bruce's house on Olduvai Road. The last packet had arrived in July and she'd read the books at the Coast, all twelve of them, at night while her mother and Bruce went dancing. That's what they like, those married people, Marietta said to herself as she crossed the park, over bright green grass, past beds of yellow chrysanthemums. That's their idea of having a good time. Ever since she and Virginia had moved down to Katari to live with Bruce and his swimming pool and his roses, she'd been the odd one out. No matter, she'd thought, because soon I'm going out into the world. Well, she was in it now, wasn't she? At the center, in fact. Hadn't people always said that Hyde Park Corner was the actual center of the world? She saw pigeons and two old women sitting with their backs to one another, staring off into the trees. Didn't Kenyatta harangue his first crowds here? He was young then, with black hair, a black beard. He wouldn't have looked like a lion, or yet like a god; he was only a man in those days. But on this Wednesday morning that looked like rain, there weren't any speechmakers.

Marietta dashed across the street to Marble Arch. In the encyclopedia photograph at home it had looked much higher. But that picture had been taken at a clever angle to impress colonials. She walked slowly round the arch while the traffic roared. Perhaps she'd be marooned here forever, at the center of the world; but then the lights turned red and she escaped. The pavement in Oxford Street was dense with people. They swept you along, like the tide. No point in resisting, so she let herself go too.

Over her shoulder Neville said, You should always watch crowds. Looking into the faces you can learn so much about a culture, about its strengths and its weaknesses, the eyes tell you, and the way the mouths are set. The English, for instance, are always worrying about how small the cake is, and whether they're going to get a piece of it; that is their main preoccupation. They don't look up. They look down, ten feet in front. Never more, sometimes less, they're all the same, rich or poor, but the rich are the worst. They are so afraid!

Marietta replied, Your mother's not, except of you, whom she doesn't understand. Since you were eight she's found you inexplicable.

Since I was eight I've found her awesome, Neville said. Her standards are inexorable, as daunting for men as for little boys. May you measure up better than I!

Marietta turned into the entrance of a department store and stepped up against the display window, out of the way of women shoppers with their paper bags and strollers. She rested her forehead against the cold glass. You can't have conversations with someone once he's dead. Why not? Who's to stop you? Who's to care one way or the other? In the bright entrance she wept.

A few feet away a short man was selling brooches made of pheasant feathers. He had them laid out on a velvet-covered board balanced on top of an orange crate. "Just the ticket for your mum, or your auntie," he called to the women with their strollers. He saw Marietta through the display case and came over. "You shouldn't do that," he said gently, hands on hips. "Whyever should a girl like you be so upset? It doesn't do to cry out here." He wore a small felt hat on the back of his head and a jacket a size or two too big for him. "Did you have a row with your boyfriend, then?" He grinned and silver teeth gleamed. "You shouldn't bother about it," he said. "On again, off again. He'll love you tomorrow, you'll see. A pretty girl like you, how could he leave you?"

"But he did."

"That's what *you* think," the man said. "But he'll be on that telephone. Jabber, jabber. Can I come round? Wipe your eyes. Got your hankie?" Marietta blew her nose. "Better now?"

She nodded. "I'm sorry."

"You wasn't no bother to me, miss. I never care to see a broken heart. Come to do some shoppin'? Well, you get on with it, then." He walked with Marietta out to the pavement.

"I'm going to Foyle's, as a matter of fact."

"You're almost there, then, aren't you?"

But Marietta didn't go to Foyle's. No more books. Not today. Not for a long time. She walked through streets with familiar names, past buildings whose photographs she'd seen. This is the city people talk about after one home leave, all through the years until the next one. This is London, heart of Empire, so many monuments pushed up against each other.

At the Embankment she leaned against the balustrade and looked across the gray river. On the far side there were buses and barges and people, a little out of focus. Behind her she heard men's voices. They came nearer. Two Africans stopped just beside her. One was saying, "My mother is asking for money again. I have none but she does not hear me, or if she hears me, she refuses to accept. She believes that because I'm in the White Man's Country I can manufacture money. These old mothers are very bitter." He spoke in Ruba.

The other man said, "With me it is my brother. He wants to come to London. Do I have scholarships in my pocket? I have nothing, but he does not read the words I write."

They were slim young men. One had a gap between his two front teeth. Like Justin, Marietta thought, sneaking a glance sideways.

Maybe they know him, and her heart leapt to her throat.

"Where do you come from?" she said in Ruba. "From Galana?"

They looked at her in disbelief. "My friend's home is at Galana," Marietta added, searching their faces, "and on occasion I have visited her there. I know it very well. Is it your home also?"

The one with the gap between his teeth frowned. "How is it that you know our language?" he asked suspiciously, in English.

"I learned it as a child. From my friend, from her father. I came just last week from Africa. I am a stranger here, as you are. I have never been in London in my life before."

"Is that so?" the second man said. He wasn't so thin as his companion, and his trousers were tighter. Perhaps he didn't know what to do about his brother, but with women he was used to success. "I know this place very well. I have been here for three years." He crossed behind Marietta and propped himself against the balustrade on her other side. "London is a very interesting city. You must let me show it to you. Should we not go now, before the rain comes? I think it will rain, don't you?" He laughed. "It is not as it is at home, where people so often wait vainly for rain."

"Where exactly is your home?" Marietta said. "Is it on the island or the mainland?"

But he didn't want to talk about home. "If you come with me, I will cook for you," he said, staring at her breasts. "I will make *ugali*, we will have a very interesting time." He squared his shoulders. "My name is Ephraim. How fortunate it is that we should meet today! You will not find a better guide than I. May I know your name?"

Marietta looked away across the river. Once when she'd been waiting in a Nyanza market in the sunlight, outside a bar, she'd heard some boys joking about her buttocks. Too small, they said, like guinea fowl eggs, though her legs are strong. Her breasts are small, too, one said. But nice, another said. Let me play with them! They hadn't known she understood. Blushing furiously, she'd stalked off between the fish women and basket sellers. Perhaps those boys were these young men, come to London where a million girls with buttocks waited, a million nameless girls without past connections.

"I'm going back now," she said loudly.

"May I not escort you? Where is it that you wish to go? I will take you there."

"No," she said, meeting his bold black eyes. "I do not want to be escorted. I'll find my own way. I have a map." And she walked off.

But the two young men came after her. The one with the gap between his teeth said, "We are going this way also." Marietta walked faster, away from the river. At the corner the Africans caught up with her. "So you are lost! You must allow us to escort you. Then you will have no need of this," the one called Ephraim said, tugging at her map. She could smell the perspiration in his clothes. He put an arm around her waist. "Are we not friends?" he said.

But Marietta pulled away, and without waiting for the lights to change she ran across the street. She saw a taxi coming towards her and flagged it down. As she clambered in she burst into tears. I shan't talk to strange Africans again. I won't be so silly. She wiped her eyes. Her feet hurt. How stupid to walk across London in high-heeled shoes! She'd soak her feet in salt water and then she'd go to bed. When would she ever sleep again?

She had come on an adventure, but she hadn't expected to have it alone. "Can I stay? Am I up to it?" she said aloud.

They turned into Sloane Street. They were stopping at the lights. The taxi driver pulled back the partition. "What was that, miss?"

"That's the house," Marietta said, slipping on her shoes. "The third door on the right. Number six."

When she heard Marietta's key in the front door, Lady Bilton came out into the hall. "Where in the world have you been? Were you lost?"

"I should hâve telephoned. I'm sorry."

"You must've walked all over London! It's after three o'clock, but we kept some lunch for you. It's in the hot plate. Help yourself. Curtis is taking a nap."

"I'm not hungry. And anyway, it'll soon be time for tea. I'll wait."

"In that case, come into the drawing room. There's something you should know." Lady Bilton went to her desk and took out a heavy cream envelope. "Sit down, won't you," she said. "It's about Neville's will."

Marietta sat on the sofa with the blue chintz cover, Lady Bilton in the dark green velvet chair. "As you know, this morning I went to the solicitor. Now this may come as a surprise, but apart from Cousin Ivor in Saskatchewan, you are the major beneficiary."

"But I don't *want* Neville's money!" Marietta exclaimed. "Why should I have it? What about you? You should have it, not me. You're his mother. I'm only, well, a friend."

"But he didn't leave you money, Marietta. He explains why not in this." She waved the envelope. "You must read it."

"Won't you tell me?"

"All right, I shall, but you should read it for yourself later on. Neville believed that money isn't good for a young person. It wasn't for him, so he says here. He felt he wasted his talents, such as he had, through never needing out of financial necessity to commit himself to any particular thing. He wants to avoid that happening to you. So he's left you a block in the city of Westminster."

"A block! Of what?" Marietta looked dazed.

"Buildings of various sorts, shops, houses. Part of a hospital. But they're all let on leases which don't run out till 1996. How old will you be in 1996?"

"Fifty."

"He must have decided that by fifty you'll have had time enough to develop your talents and being rich won't interfere."

"I'll be rich?"

"Oh, yes, extremely, but till 1996 you'll have to live by your wits." Lady Bilton smiled. "That's not quite true. Neville did provide for your education. Money may be taken from the trust for 'reasonable educational expenses'! Going to an ashram in India wouldn't be considered reasonable, nor learning to be a parachutist — oh, there are numerous things which in my opinion aren't a necessary part of one's education, and my opinion does count since I'm one of your trustees. The other two are Carfax, the solicitor, and William Buchanan, from the bank."

"A block in the city of Westminster is utterly absurd," Marietta said, and began to cry.

Lady Bilton came and sat on the sofa beside her and patted her knee. "Having money is a privilege," she said, "but it carries obligations. You'll have to live more thoughtfully than other people do. And please don't worry about me, Marietta. My husband provided for me very well, and what's left when I die will be for Curtis and for cancer research. Neville never had children of his own, and he did so want them! But we don't always get what we want, Marietta, so we have to look about and see what else might come our way. He counted himself lucky to have got you, so to speak. You gave him much happiness. You should know that. Of course, he never expected to die. He thought you'd be a middle-aged woman by the time that happened, and then you wouldn't need trustees telling you what to do or not to do, and you certainly wouldn't have to deal with me because I'd be rotted away in my grave by then. There's a little jewelry, too, and that you may have now if you choose. But that's all. He left everything else to his second cousin. Ivor gets the title, too, of course, though I don't suppose he'll use it, being Canadian. Titles aren't very sensible nowadays. They get in the way. So I'm glad Neville couldn't leave you his. You might have found it a nuisance."

Marietta shook her head in wonder. "Millions of people do the pools each week. They fill them in and send them off and say to themselves and aloud as well, When I win, I'll buy a Rolls and move to Nice and never lift a finger again. Then, if it happens just as they hoped, they can believe it. They've filled out the form, no one else did it for them — they've brought about this miracle by themselves. But if it's never crossed your mind that you could be, it's ridiculous to find one day that you're rich, through absolutely no effort of your own."

"My dear, that hasn't happened yet, and won't for many years. In the meantime, you'll have to deal with a triumvirate whenever you want to spend more than a hundred pounds at once. You may get round Carfax and Buchanan, but I'm very strict." Lady Bilton chuckled. "George and I were very strict with Neville. That's how he happened to stay rich. He could have frittered his money away, together with his talents, but he'd learned good habits from us." She took Marietta's hand. "I'm glad you're the one to inherit. I've only known you for a week, Marietta, so I don't know you very well as yet, but I hope I'll get an opportunity to know you better. It's been a pleasure having you here and I very much hope you'll stay."

11

Folly Court

Marietta got out of the train at Swindon and looked about for her aunt. Sophia Twyford had sounded forceful on the telephone. "Of course you're coming! I've had you on my calendar since May. I won't let you back out!"

"I don't think I should leave Lady Bilton." It hadn't been a week yet.

"She might be longing to be left, haven't you thought of that? Besides, I've already sent a cable to your mother, telling her you're coming down to Folly Court. You deserve some distractions after what you've just been through. The train gets in at three forty-two. I'll be there. You're fair, I understand, like Virginia."

But Aunt Sophia hadn't said what *she* looked like. As the train rattled over the Downs, Marietta thought about the bride come out to spend the winter in East Africa with a husband called Jock and traveling cases full of shell-stitched underclothes — a fascinating creature, according to Virginia. However, the voice on the telephone had gone with a strong chin and florid cheeks. Port, at sporting events, would've done the damage, and the wind gusting across the Downs, as it was this afternoon. I'll have a hat with a feather in the band, Sophia might have said; or, You'll know me by my mackintosh to my ankles, which aren't slim anymore as they used to be; or, I'll hang a sign on a string round my neck. But she'd said nothing of the kind, leaving Marietta to scout her out.

She gave up her ticket at the barrier and went out into the station yard, where she immediately spotted a woman in urgent altercation with a policeman. It appeared that the woman had parked in a spot in which no parking was ever allowed.

"But I always stop here!" the woman insisted. "The policeman they used to have on duty here *believed* in making exceptions." Unmoved, his successor laboriously wrote out a ticket, signed the form, and dated it. "Here you are, Mrs. Twyford," he said as he gave her the original and tucked the carbon under his pad.

Mrs. Twyford was about to protest again when she saw Marietta with her suitcases at the curb. "What a bloody nuisance," she exclaimed, waving the ticket. "This, I mean, not you. I assume you're who I think you are. I told him" — she nodded at the policeman, who had resumed his usual position next to the newsstand — "you shouldn't make someone coming from Africa drag their bags across the station yard. But he didn't listen. I shan't pay the fine, mind you. They'll have to lock me up first," she added, thrusting the ticket into her handbag. "I'm so glad to meet you, Marietta. What a terrible time you've had! You look exactly like your mother, by the way. Come on, let's go before that creature strikes again."

Aunt Sophia did indeed have florid cheeks and a strong chin, but she was also very handsome, with firm shoulders and direct blue eyes. She wore a tweed suit, an amethyst cashmere sweater, and a regimental brooch on her left lapel. Her hair was covered with a head scarf across which foxhounds raced.

"Jock is sorry he couldn't come to meet you too, but he'll be in for tea. I hope you brought an evening dress. There's a do tomorrow night. The Red Cross ball. It's in the Assembly Rooms at Bath. Ever been there? No, of course not. Idiotic of me! Then you've got a treat in store. Even in the dark it's a rather lovely town. I'm on the ball committee and had to organize a party for it anyway. Your being here makes it so much more worthwhile. It'll give you a bit of fun, I hope. You should know, Marietta, how terribly sad for you we both are. I take it you ride," she finished abruptly.

"After a fashion," Marietta said.

"There's hunting in the morning. We meet at six, at this time of year. Cub hunting, you know. It isn't the season proper, yet."

"I didn't bring any riding clothes."

"Never mind, we'll find something to fit you. Pity to miss a peaceful jog round some pretty country."

Even though Sophia had been to Harley Street and Switzerland for consultations, treatments, and surgical adjustments, and once,

170

in secret, on a pilgrimage to Lourdes, she and Jock had had no children. Otherwise the marriage was a great success. Jock had Twyford's Ales & Stout, a brewery company, inherited, and Sophia had the Avon Hounds, of which she was joint master. The other master was a not very forceful man called Pinky Eglington. The Hounds devolved upon him from his grandfather, who'd started it in 1883, but Pinky didn't have quite the same sense of himself that Old Washy Eglington had had. When Pinky shouted "Hold!" people didn't hear, or pretended they hadn't, and they galloped on over winter wheat or bang through the middle of cabbage fields or over fences that shouldn't be jumped, fomenting bitterness among the farmers. So Pinky had been extraordinarily lucky, everyone said, to rope in Sophia, for Sophia had a remarkable voice. When she shouted, one couldn't pretend one hadn't heard, and she came with ample assets as well. For this, Pinky, whose trusts were dwindling, was particularly thankful. As a mother Sophia would have erred on the heavy side. Fortunate, perhaps, that she had never become one.

Soon they were out of the town and driving west. The clouds had cleared and the sun had spread across the hills. "Wiltshire looks like the country round Eldonia," Marietta exclaimed. "My mother's always said it did."

"How *is* your mother, by the way?"

"She's just started a shop. Interior decorating."

"Things *have* changed, haven't they! In my day there were Indian carpenters who could make a table for you with four equal legs if you were lucky, and tailors to run up your curtains, and that was it. No interior decorating. Now and then I run into people who've come back for good. Too frightened of the Africans to hang on any longer, but I take it that none of that bothers Virginia. She's all set to stay?"

"She says that if you believed half of what you read about Kenya, you'd think we'd all been murdered in our beds already, when in fact, so far, life isn't that much less predictable than it was before. No, Mum's not leaving. She's staying till she drops."

"And that husband of hers, Oldfield. He'll go along with her? They were with us for a weekend the summer before last. The weather was foul and Oldfield loathed being shut up in the house. Kept tapping the barometer. Obviously England didn't suit him. One assumes Kenya is more to his taste."

"It is. He came quite recently, in fifty-eight or -nine. He doesn't have the standard Settler views, if you know what I mean. He doesn't seem to bother about what color a person is, so long as he does the job he's been told to do. Bruce says he's made one move and he doesn't intend to make another if he can possibly avoid it. He and Mum are playing it by ear."

"Virginia's still living in the present, then. Never was a great one for worrying about the future. What about yours, Marietta? What's to be your future?" Better than her mother's past, I hope, Sophia thought. Uncanny how much they look alike, though this one seems a bit more on her mettle. Perhaps she already knows what's what, better than her mother did at least, at that age. "I understand you've come to study painting," Sophia added. "You'll go on with that, as planned?"

"I may go back to Nairobi and start the Slade next year. After what's happened."

On the telephone, Virginia had begged Marietta to come home. She'd heard about the crash on the BBC news on Saturday evening, and had read in the Sunday *Standard* about Neville's death. "They had a photo of him, the same one they printed after the divorce. And you were there and saw it all! Oh, Etta, your course can wait. One year won't make that much difference. You'll be better off at home. It doesn't do at such a time to be with strangers."

"Lady Bilton isn't a stranger," Marietta had shouted through the static.

"It's like falling into a hole. I fell into a hole, too, once, before you were born, and stayed there much too long." But the operator interrupted. Virginia had booked only six minutes and the time was up.

"Is that your idea, going back?" Sophia asked Marietta now.

"No." Marietta shook her head. "It's Mum's. I'd rather stay."

"What's stopping you?"

"Supposing I wasn't up to it, that's what Mum has in mind."

"Neville Bilton must have meant a great deal to you." Sophia had read the obituary with great interest, for although a trip home had been planned, Virginia and husband number two hadn't stayed together long enough to make it. The next time she'd come to England, Virginia had come alone and she hadn't had many words to spare on the topic of Neville Bilton. A Renaissance man, the *Telegraph* had called him — soldier, scholar, naturalist. (The *Times* was a shade less adulatory.) Sophia couldn't imagine Virginia lasting with anyone like that. But of course, she hadn't lasted.

Sophia came to a halt at a crossroads and looked to right and left. Her eyes met Marietta's. "Neville wouldn't think much of my going home," Marietta said. "He'd be outraged, in fact."

"Then don't go. Stay."

Folly Court was a seventeenth-century house set in celebrated gardens. But although the three gardeners had given an average of twenty-two years of dedicated service each, the Twyfords had had endless problems with their indoor staff, a succession of foreign couples who, apart from not speaking English, had odd notions of what constituted proper food. But since English servants were virtually impossible to find or keep, the Twyfords did their best to grin and bear it. Currently they were breaking in a Spanish couple, Rosa and Miguel. At dinner on Marietta's first night, Rosa produced gazpacho, paella, and flan. "We've had this menu three times in a week," Jock told Marietta, and as Miguel served the flan, Jock added with a sigh, "It seems that these days leg of lamb and bread-and-butter pudding are impossible to come by."

After dinner Sophia said to her husband, "Where are those photographs? Marietta would be so amused."

Jock brought out a blue leather album, tooled in gold leaf. He sat down next to Marietta. "I should say that when your mother saw them, she wasn't terribly amused. One doesn't necessarily relish looking at the past. But of course, you weren't in it." Jock had a round, red face. Apart from a narrow fringe above his collar, he was entirely bald. The backs of his hands, however, were astonishingly hairy. He was always chewing on a pipe, which he rarely bothered to light, but now he laid it carefully down in a Dresden ashtray and opened the album.

"Rumuruti, 1938" was written in white ink at the top of the first page. Underneath was a photograph of a low adobe house with brick pillars along its veranda. Between two of the pillars stood a bony man with a mustache, a young woman in a soft hat and jodhpurs, an older woman in a blouse and skirt, and a girl with bright hair. "Your grandfather, your great-aunt, your grandmother, and your mother, obviously," Jock said. He turned the page to a close-up of the man with the mustache, frowning into the sunlight. "Harold always looked fierce."

"He didn't just *look* fierce, either!" Sophia exclaimed. Her eyebrows shot up. They were almost hidden in her hair. "Grudges were your grandfather's meat and drink! He was perpetually at war, his own small vindictive war with every rock which stood in his way, every wretched Indian trader, branch bank manager, neighbor. Getting his own back was all he ever thought about. One wondered why he ever married. The last thing you'd think a man like him would need was a wife. He'd have done so much better with an African woman now and then, one who came in when he felt like seeing her and stayed out in her hut when he didn't, which would've been most of the time. He didn't deserve an audience for his rages. When I saw the rotten state of things in 1938 I begged my sister to come home with Jock and me. 'There's room at Folly Court and we'd love to have you,' I told her. 'Virginia's seventeen. She shouldn't stay a moment longer on this godforsaken plain; nor should you. You've forgotten how normal people live, people who aren't taken up with conquering nature and rubbing salt in their own wounds.' But Sylvia wouldn't do it. She'd been terrorized by Harold for so long, she wouldn't have known herself away from him. Jock, how about some port?" Sophia added. "I need mellowing. Thinking about Harold always gets me in a rotten mood."

"My mother doesn't talk about the past," Marietta said. "She prefers living in the present. You said so yourself."

Jock fetched the port and Sophia, fortified, went on. "Harold really had a screw loose, though that was nothing new, mind you. Africa hadn't done it to him. He'd had one all along. I remember the morning of the wedding. I was about eight. I was an afterthought, you see, Marietta, years younger than my sisters. That morning I found my mother crying in her room. Not doing the flowers or bullying the maids, but sitting with her head in her hands and her tears splashing onto the bureau. 'Because Sylvia's marrying Harold,' she said. 'Don't you like him?' I said. 'He's very good at polo, better even than Papa.' He had a handicap of six, by the way, Marietta. 'I know,' my poor weeping mother said, 'and he'll ride your sister into the ground, exactly the same way he does his polo ponies. Harold doesn't know when to stop.' And as you know, they *did* die in that extraordinary way."

"But I didn't know," Marietta said. "I thought they died of pneumonia."

"Now I've done it, haven't I!" Sophia sighed. "Put my foot in my bloody mouth. It's because you look so much like Virginia, like she

174

did, I mean, in 1938. I've been talking just as if I knew you, which I don't."

"You might as well tell her," Jock grunted. He pulled on the lobe of his right ear. "It was more than twenty years ago, for heaven's sake!"

"All right," Sophia said. "I might as well. I suppose you know the Rumuruti road, Marietta, from Thomson's Falls down the escarpment?"

Marietta shook her head. "I've never been to Rumuruti. When I asked to go, Mum always said, 'Why would you want to see that place? It's very boring.'"

"She says that? Poor thing! Your grandfather knew that road like the back of his hand; he'd driven it hundreds of times, in every kind of weather. But this time he drove bang off the edge and they fell two hundred feet down a precipice into a river. A couple of Samburu found them, but by then they'd both been dead for hours. Your mother was away in Abyssinia in the war, and I, of course, was here. We were notified, though not for several weeks, that they were dead, and that was all we knew until the war was over and your mother went back to Kenya. Then she had to go to Rumuruti to deal with the farm, which was being managed by someone the bank had put there. Davis, Davidson, I've forgotten his name. While she was up that way she found a note in their safe-deposit box in Thomson's Falls. It was written by Harold and dated August 3, 1942, which was the day of their death. I never saw it myself so I don't know what it said, exactly, but it was something about the government being against him, and his seeing to it that 'they' didn't get him. In the end, he really did go batty. Did himself in and my poor sister, too. And the sad thing about it is that if he'd hung on a bit longer he'd have got quite rich, like all the other farmers did who'd struggled through the thirties, dirt poor, and had their luck change in the war. As it was, this man, the one the bank had found to manage the farm, turned out to be a drunk and he let the place go pretty much to ruin. When it was auctioned off in 1945, your mother just about broke even, after she'd paid all the mortgages off. Hardly surprising she's never taken you back," Sophia added. "She can't have fond memories."

This time last week, Marietta thought as she pulled on Sophia's old breeches and pushed into her boots, Neville was alive, and then, surely, there'd been no weight in her chest, no pain behind her eyes. But seven days later she didn't seem to be breathing very well or seeing quite straight, and she couldn't manage to think about the future for more than a few moments at a time. She tied her tie, swung Sophia's jacket off its hanger, and went out onto the landing.

"You'll have coffee, won't you, and some toast?" Sophia called from halfway down the stairs. "We'll have a proper breakfast afterwards."

Marietta was given a mare of uncertain age. "She's perfectly placid unless she sees a bull, and that's not likely," Jock said. They left the stable yard and went out between the stone mushrooms that lined the drive. The air was very cold and their breath showed white. Marietta's watch said five forty-two. The dawn's rising, she thought, and the birds are beginning to sing. How can the world be peaceful again so soon?

Thirty horsemen and a handful of followers on foot waited at a crossroads. The hunt servants stood to one side in faded coats and the hounds darted about, in and out of the hedgerows. "They're young, most of them, new entries," Sophia explained. "They've got a great deal to learn. Everything entices them. Rabbits; moles; sandwiches, of course." She introduced Marietta to Pinky Eglington. His eyebrows were carrot-colored. His hair, though, was hidden by his bowler hat.

"How's the fox hunting in Kenya these days? Don't imagine the blackies are too keen," he added gruffly.

Blackies? "No, this isn't their kind of hunting at all."

"I was out there once," Pinky said. "Had some wonderful days in Limuru. Even though we only had a drag line, we had a lot of fun. What a life one could live there in those days! I was tempted to stay, and might have, too, if it hadn't been for these hounds here. Things wouldn't be the same there now. They aren't here, either. One can't stop things from changing, can one?" he said sadly.

He raised one orange eyebrow at Sophia, who cried, "Time, gentlemen, please!" The huntsman called to his hounds and moved off down the road towards a spruce plantation. "You stick with Jock," Sophia said to Marietta; "I have to go to work," and she surged ahead, knee to knee with Pinky Eglington.

As the hounds dashed in among the firs, Jock led Marietta away down the side of the plantation. "This is a very big place," he said,

176

"and there aren't too many out this morning, so we've got to spread about. You stay here under this tree and if anything comes in your direction, whack your saddle like this." He demonstrated. "That's to keep the young hounds in as well as the fox cubs. Got to keep their heads down. Mustn't let them get into the open field. I'm going on," he added, and cantered away.

For an hour Marietta was quite alone. She heard a hunting horn occasionally, but far away, on the other side of the plantation. She was hungry and her feet were starting to feel like ice. It won't hurt to trot about a bit, she thought, digging her heels into Sophia's mare, and if a cub or a hound escapes, that's just too bad.

Round the curve of the plantation, a young man sat on his horse, shoulders hunched. He frowned deeply at the grass. Marietta rode up to him. "What happens now?" she said. "Have they gone off without us?"

The man looked up. "Wouldn't that be nice! Then we could go home and have a decent breakfast." He had violet eyes and a beautiful mouth. But the mouth was down at the corners. "This definitely isn't my idea of fun," he said crossly. But then the young man smiled. "Am I being sacrilegious?"

"Why sacrilegious?" she said.

"Well," he said, smiling, "there are many in these parts who believe that sitting in a field on an icy autumn morning is the acutest form of pleasure known to man."

"But I'm not from these parts."

"I didn't think you could be. You're too pretty."

"It sounds like you don't fancy Wiltshire much," Marietta observed, studying his face.

"I'm in two minds about Wiltshire, actually." He laughed. "It tends to swallow one up."

"I wouldn't have guessed that. It looks perfectly harmless to me. No avalanches, no canyons, no rivers in flood. Nothing monumental. So far I like it. It's nice to find a bit of peace."

"But how far is so far?"

Marietta glanced at her watch. "Sixteen hours."

"See what you think after sixteen years!" he laughed. "That's how long I've been putting in appearances. I've come, head down, scowling, dragging my feet, but regularly just the same."

"Where have you been coming from?"

"Kenya, as a matter of fact," he said.

"I'm from Kenya, too, as a matter of fact."

"I thought it was you!" he exclaimed. "Better wait and see, though, and let her reveal herself. I'm Jonathan Sudbury. Do you remember, I was all het up and you calmed me down, one Christmas in the Red Lion in Eldonia."

Marietta said, "My mother calmed you down. I didn't."

"Was she there as well?"

"Oh yes." In a see-through blouse, without a brassiere, Marietta thought. One last revelation before she settled down with Bruce. Nowadays she was totally opaque in Airtex and Shetland wool.

Jonathan Sudbury shrugged. "I don't remember your mother. Only you. You're Marietta, Neville Bilton's stepdaughter. There's a kind of marigold called Marietta. It's red with yellow in the center. We grow them in tubs on the terrace back home. They're resistant to high winds and virtually all insects. When the rains fail, they thrive. They're the gardener's true friend. By the way," he added soberly, "the day I left Nairobi the newspapers were full of the air crash. There was a lot about Neville, too. What a dreadful thing to happen to a very nice man! He came to our place once, when I was young, and gave me a marvelous book about pyramids. I read it so often that it fell apart."

"It was years and years since I'd seen him," Marietta said flatly, looking away, "and technically I wasn't his stepdaughter, either." The hawthorn berries were scarlet in the hedgerow. Thrushes pecked at them in the early sunlight and darted off over the blackberry bushes. At this moment a week ago she'd been with Lady Bilten and Curtis in a hospital in Slough, the hospital nearest to the airport. With fifty or so other white-faced people they'd stood about in corridors, waiting to hear the worst about relatives and friends. And sure enough, the worst had happened to Neville. The doctors hadn't been able to save him; he'd died on the operating table. Their friendship, which had begun in Africa, had lasted the rest of his life, but *she* had a lifetime left over. She wasn't about to reminisce about Neville with this stranger.

"How d'you happen to be here now, behind this wood?" she said. "It's a long way from Eldonia!"

Jonathan Sudbury smiled. "I hoped to clear my head after a heavy evening with my uncle James. I've been spending some difficult days with him at Tresham. That's his place. It's the other side of this plantation. Don't tell me you haven't heard of Tresham! A truly remarkable example of early Tudor domestic architecture, surrounded by many acres of garden, all open to public view on Tuesdays and Thursdays, two to six, half a crown a head, four bob with tea. My aunt Elizabeth guarantees you'll get your money's worth. Her cakes are always made with butter, never marge. And what are you doing here, Marietta?"

"I'm staying with my aunt and uncle, too. Jock and Sophia Twyford. You may know them."

Jonathan nodded.

"Jock left me under a tree an hour ago," Marietta said. "I was looking for him. I hoped he'd have something to eat or drink."

"In that case, you must share my Cadbury's Fruit and Nut. I haven't any brandy, sorry." Jonathan broke his chocolate bar in two. "How long have you been in England?" he said, handing her half.

"Ten days."

"And how long do you intend to stay?"

"Perhaps forever."

"D'you like it here so much?"

"I may, though I've hardly seen anything yet."

"You didn't go to school here?"

"Heavens, no! I'm a bush girl. This is my first time. When I was a kid my mother came occasionally, but I stayed at home with the servants."

"Did you mind being left?"

"Of course not! For three months I'd do exactly as I pleased. But later I began wanting to see what all the talk was about. So here I am, at last, with an open mind. I haven't had years and years in English schools to put me off. You *are* put off, I take it."

"Put off? I've never taken it seriously!" Jonathan exclaimed. "I'm used to drought and locusts, to the topsoil being washed away and silting up the lakes and rivers, to the desecration of the earth. All this" — he waved his whip at the spruces, the high, wet autumn grass, the thrushes pecking — "it's trivial. I couldn't live in England! Unfortunately," he continued, shaking his head, "my uncle James has two delightful daughters, both married and both reproducing copiously. But they have seven girls between them. No sons. So Tresham will be left to me, whether I like it or not. And what in the world will I do with it? Divide it in half and give it to Polly and Patricia? They have a perfect right to it, in my opinion. But not in James's, and James believes that dead Sudburys would

179

clamber out of tombs and come after me — and him — with un-
sheathed swords if I walked away from my sacrosanct responsibilities!" He smiled apologetically. "I didn't intend to go into my dilemma at eight o'clock in the morning, but I was up till two
discussing it. Actually, we weren't having a discussion; that's too
elaborate a concept. I stated my position and Uncle James ignored
it. He lived in Kenya, too, when he was a young man, and came
back when Great-uncle William died. He always knew he'd come
into Tresham. So Kenya was just for fun. He can't imagine why,
given the choice, I would choose it over England. He's only interested in the preservation of the past, not in making something new.
I was sitting here reviewing what he'd said, what I'd said, line by
line, the futility of it, when you came along."

"Is that why you're here now," Marietta said, "to make your
point to your uncle?"

"Making one's point is a very long, drawn-out procedure. I make
stabs at it every year or so. One day he'll see the light. He'll have
to, as I shan't. I just stopped in to make my annual stab on my way
to Los Angeles, via New York, Chicago, St. Louis, Houston, and
Fort Worth. On Monday evening I'm due to dine with a posse of
multimillionaires in a duplex overlooking Central Park. I'm hoping to persuade them that until they've come to East Africa and
spent a hefty chunk of their millions hunting elephant with me,
they haven't really lived. Every so often," he said, smiling in self-
deprecation, "I exhibit myself in this rather ghastly way. The first
trip was so excruciating that I thought I might be better off after
all as a broiler prince at Tresham — Uncle James being the Broiler
King, you understand. He raises those chickens that turn on spits
in restaurant windows in Leicester Square. He's written a book
called *Chickens by the Million* and a companion volume, *Broiling*.
A guinea for the set and they're selling well. I don't suppose you've
seen them, have you? Anyway, after my first American safari I
thought, Which is really worse, chickens or being Exhibit A? And
at the time being Exhibit A seemed quite a lot worse. The clients
all wanted Hemingway or Stewart Granger, even at breakfast. But
by the second trip I was getting into the act, and now I'm off on
my third. If one insists on living in Kenya after the winds of change
have blasted through and turned everything upside down, one's
forced to go to certain lengths to finance one's bloody-
mindedness."

"I know quite a number of people," Marietta said dryly, "who wouldn't dream of leaving Kenya, but they lack your sense of the dramatic. They just carry on."

"Well, you're certainly frank, aren't you!" Jonathan chuckled. "I admit I can get pretty pompous about my dilemma. You see, I'm always composing speeches in my head, and then if I find a willing ear I can't resist the temptation to try one out."

For a moment they sat in silence. The sun was growing warmer on their backs. "By the way," Jonathan said, "what have you come to England for? Not just to meet the Twyfords, I don't suppose."

"I came to be a painter."

"You've made your mind up?"

"Yes."

"Not a shadow of a doubt? No Uncle James telling you you're mad?"

Marietta shook her head.

"No one to disappoint or let down? Then you're lucky. Don't let anyone distract you from doing what you want to do."

"I don't intend to," Marietta said.

"And where do you expect to do your painting?"

"At the Slade. I start on Wednesday."

"Wednesday," he said. "On Wednesday I'm flying to Chicago. I like Chicago. St. Louis I like less. That's next." He added, "What I meant was, where will you go once you have become a painter?"

"How can I say?"

"What about home? Will you go back there?"

"Where *is* home?" Marietta said. "I've never really had one. My mother liked to keep moving."

Jonathan looked at his watch. "I bet they've forgotten all about us. I could show you some English countryside, if you'd like. See that gate? If we go through it and over a couple of fields, we'll get to Tresham Park, my would-be home. There's an avenue of beeches, two miles long. We could gallop down it."

But round the corner of the plantation streamed the hounds, with Pinky Eglington and Aunt Sophia bringing up the rear. "Cut off," Jonathan remarked. "Damn!"

"Poor Marietta. What a deadly time you've had," Sophia cried. "Hardly a trace of a fox here. Are you frozen? Where's my husband? We're going on to Dixley now. Let's hope for better luck there."

"Dixley?" Jonathan said in disgust. "That's a lunatic asylum.

One stands about the shrubbery while the hounds chase after the patients. No foxes there, either, I bet you. I'm going back for breakfast."

"Good luck in America," Marietta said. "I hope you're a great success."

Marietta pulled on her coat and gathered up some books and a folder. She'd overslept. She'd have to take the tube this morning. She preferred the bus, sitting on top and seeing everything.

The telephone rang; Curtis answered in the pantry. "For you, Miss Marietta," she called.

"Damn," she muttered. "Now I *shall* be late." She took the receiver. "Hello."

"Can I see you tonight? I came back as soon as I could."

"Back from where?"

"Los Angeles. I was in that field in Wiltshire. Surely you haven't forgotten!"

"Jonathan! How were the multimillionaires?"

"Which? I've met so many in the last four weeks!"

"In the duplex overlooking the Park."

"One was tempted, one was convinced, a third wanted tigers, and there are no tigers in Africa, as you know, but he didn't, evidently. Can I see you tonight?"

"How did you find me?"

"I telephoned Sophia Twyford. She gave me your number. She approves of me. She doesn't care for chickens any more than I do. She's allergic to feathers. Are you busy this evening or not?"

"I'm not busy."

"Can I come at seven? I'll give you a delicious dinner and tell you my adventures."

That evening, when Marietta came into the drawing room, Lady Bilton was reading an Oxfam report. She was a trustee and she had a meeting the next day at ten. She glanced at Marietta over the top of her glasses. "How nice you look! I hope that young man appreciates you. Come from America this morning, you say? And what was he doing there?"

"Being Exhibit A. That's what he calls it. He's a white hunter. He goes to America to persuade rich people to go on safari with him."

"I wonder what Edmund Sudbury makes of all that."

"You knew his father?"

Lady Bilton put down the report. "Of course! It's a very small

182

country, don't forget. Philip Sudbury was there at the beginning. He bought a place called Olgolulu and had two sons. Edmund, the younger son, was the one who came into Olgolulu. He was so thin, practically translucent; one could just about see through him! But nevertheless he built a most substantial house. To last a thousand years, so he assured George and me when it was finished and we were bidden there to see it. He showed us everything, even the septic tank! He was *thrilled* with his creation. But in his own quiet way, mind you. He's a man of few words. James was the other Sudbury son. A very different type. Flaming red hair, in his youth, at least. Gregarious, a bit bumptious. Noisy, in fact. He left in 1939 and never went back. James played poker and a lot of polo, but Edmund didn't play either. He only cared about his farm."

The doorbell rang. "Now I shall see for myself, shan't I," Lady Bilton said.

They walked to a restaurant in Lower Sloane Street. "High-class Italian," Jonathan said. "You won't care for the Tivoli on Government Road after this, should you ever go back there, of course. No spaghetti Bolognese here." A grapevine was growing on a trellis above the heads of the diners and a fountain splashed in the center of the floor.

The proprietor greeted Jonathan effusively. "How are your lions, Mr. Sudbury? And your rhinoceroses? You and Victoria are well? It's too many months since we've seen you both." Then he saw that Marietta wasn't Victoria and spread his hands apologetically.

"You're known here," Marietta remarked when they were seated, facing one another at a table by the wall.

"I wouldn't take you to a place I couldn't count on, would I? I don't want to worry about food. I've got more important things to think about."

"Chickens? Millionaires?"

"No, *you*. I thought about you constantly. In airplanes and trains, in penthouses in Chicago, beside swimming pools in Texas. In the Sierras, at the Pacific. I thought, I missed her in Africa. I'm too late. She's gone for good. Then yesterday in the airport in Los Angeles I realized it didn't have to be that way. Changing my ticket was easy. I was routed through Rome, but I came to London instead. I'll go to Nairobi tomorrow evening. We've got a night and a day."

"I've got classes tomorrow."

"You'll skip them. You'll say you've got the flu."

"What makes you so sure I want to spend tomorrow with you?"

"Under the circumstances you might."

"What are the circumstances?"

"I think I'm going to fall in love with you." Beneath the vine in the patchy light he flushed. "Given the chance," he added. "Are you pleased?" He looked at Marietta steadily. He's charming, she thought, and he's not telling the truth.

"Do you often say that?"

"Only once before."

"To Victoria?"

Jonathan nodded.

"And what happened?"

He shrugged. "There was a certain amount of flying about. Then things came to an end. Now I'm saying it to you." He wasn't smiling. His mouth was set. He was telling the truth after all.

Marietta looked from the violet eyes to the hands, tanned against the tablecloth. What have I done? she thought, aghast. What does he imagine I am? All I want now is to try to become a painter. Can't he see that? But obviously he couldn't. She leaned across and touched his fingertips.

"Are you glad?" he said.

"It's very soon to tell." She added lightly, insisting on manageable proportions, "I'm slow. I have to consider things. I've never been in love, you see. Not even once." She smiled. "I've still got everything ahead of me."

Jonathan frowned. "I charged at you, didn't I? Like a bloody buffalo. Well, at least," he said, smiling now, "you know where I stand and I've got twenty-four hours to make my case. Tomorrow I'll take you to Richmond. They have fallow deer there, to remind one ever so faintly of home. And enormous oaks."

"I have life drawing at nine. I'd go *even* if I had flu," Marietta said. "You could pick me up at twelve, though."

"You're quite set in your ways, aren't you? I never guessed it that afternoon in the Red Lion. What an enchanting creature, I thought. How straightforward! When she's grown up I'll seek her out and naturally she'll be enchanted by me, too. That's the beauty of daydreams. One always gets what one wants."

"The fact is," Marietta said, "you never thought of me again until a month ago. But that's okay, because if you'd come looking for me

184

in Katari, you'd probably have regretted it. I didn't go to cocktail parties if I could possibly avoid them. I was very bad at tennis, the club bored me, and I didn't really approve of big-game hunting."

"It's a way to earn a living," Jonathan said.

"So," Marietta finished, "you'd have found me really rather tiresome."

"Then it was lucky that I waited, wasn't it!" Jonathan grinned. "Here in London I don't find you tiresome at all."

At breakfast Lady Bilton said, "Your young man looks like his mother. Eleanor had remarkable eyes. Came from Perthshire, I believe. What does he have to say for himself?"

"A lot. I'm going to spend the afternoon with him. He's leaving at half past ten tonight. He'll drop me off on his way to the airport, so don't expect me for dinner."

"He's another one for rushing about, is he?" said Curtis, slapping down the toast rack. "It's a wonder how their heads stay on their shoulders." That's right, Marietta thought, even if he's in love with me today, he'll forget me by tomorrow, so I don't have to worry, do I.

Jonathan, suntanned, wearing a beautifully cut tweed jacket made for Tresham visits to his uncle James and the odd rainy-season Sunday lunch at Olgolulu, jumped out of a taxi in front of the Slade at noon. Students poured past him into the street. The boys were mostly bearded, pale-faced, and untidy; the girls, tidier but equally pale, wore sludge and plum and grimy gray, colors that the youth of Britain had made their own suddenly that autumn. Searching student faces, Jonathan made his way up the steps and just inside the foyer found Marietta, dressed like her classmates in shades of gray and grape.

"Well, you certainly fit right in!" he said, smiling. "I'm so delighted to find you! When I didn't see you outside I was afraid you'd wheedled an extra hour out of your model and forgotten about me, desolate on the pavement with the sandwiches."

"The model didn't show up, so we used a skeleton instead. It droops down from a thing like a coat hanger. It's rather sad, but endearing in its way." Marietta added, taking Jonathan's hand, "Still, I've had enough of it. Where do we go now?"

They took the train to Richmond, where the leaves were turning. The park was deserted except for pale deer browsing in the sun.

"It's so green and quiet and empty here," Jonathan said. "I didn't find it until my last spring in England, and by that time, after thirteen years of exile, I was about to go home. You should know about it, though, so that if you ever have a longing for green spaces, you'll know where to find one."

"Why do you hate England so much?"

"I don't hate England. It's just that I hate being away from home. Now it's not that bad because I decide when to leave and how long to stay away, but as a kid I didn't have any say. I had to stay where I was put." They were walking over the grass towards a bench. "We could sit here," Jonathan said, "and eat our lunch. You must need reviving after a morning with a skeleton." He took two rolls out of a paper bag, two apples, and a large packet of potato crisps.

The worst time of all, he said, was the beginning of the Emergency. He'd been twelve when suddenly one October morning the newspapers in his private school in England were full of the word Mau Mau. He struggled through the *Times* reports. He didn't understand everything he read, but enough to grasp that this insurgency, rebellion, or whatever people chose to call what was happening in Kenya was viewed as a collision between civilization and barbarism, reason and chaos, light and dark. Soon Edmund and Eleanor Sudbury wrote that for safety's sake he couldn't come home for the summer holidays, as he had in other years. "I pleaded, I wept desperately across my letters home, so that the ink ran and the words were barely decipherable. But my pain, though obvious, didn't move my parents. They'd made up their minds. 'People are dying,' my father wrote. 'People are dead. People you know. It could be your mother and me next. If you came home, it could be you. Those we trusted all our lives, we trust no longer. We can't expose you to that.' Georgie Wickenden from Nyanga wasn't coming home either. He was going to stay in Sussex with his aunt. 'You two must get in touch,' my mother wrote. I didn't. Georgie couldn't have helped. Perhaps he thought the same about me. He never got in touch either.

"In July, instead of going to Africa, I went down to Tresham to stay with Uncle James. Polly and Patricia were already married, and Aunt Elizabeth was laid up with a bad back. I spent the summer in the chicken houses with James. He was just beginning. He'd been to America and got the idea and was starting up. He lived in terror of poultry disease. He hadn't thought of writing books. He

186

didn't know the answers yet himself. I'd look beyond the yard to James's beechwoods as I changed the deep litter and shoveled in the feed; I'd pretend those woods were the forests stretching up the escarpment above our farm at home. I thought, If I pretend hard enough, I'll be transported. I still believed in magic. I had to, or I wouldn't have survived. I've never been more wretched in my life than I was then."

But the following summer Kenya was declared safe enough again. For almost two years he'd been waking in the night in panic, certain he'd been banished from Olgolulu, certain that he was doomed to wander forever over the face of the earth. And so, on the long flight home, he was too excited, too unbelieving of his redemption, to sleep at all. "I remember peering through the plane window as it taxied into Eastleigh, and seeing British soldiers, Saint Georges sent out to slay the dragons of barbarism. And behind them were the parents, my own included, waiting to marvel at height and new teeth and down on cheeks that they remembered as the cheeks of children.

"My mother kissed me. Then she wanted to stare. She didn't, though. She could never be as pushy as that! So she glanced at me furtively, when she thought I wouldn't notice. My father shook my hand. 'What about lunch?' he said, not quite looking at me, either. 'Shall we give the Norfolk a try?'

"I'd forgotten how shy he was; I had a terrible feeling that I didn't know him anymore. I'd got used to Uncle James. James is big and broad and ruddy, and Dad slight and light, like his own wheat. His hair's been white since he was thirty. His eyes are a washed-out blue; you might think the wind and sun had bleached his eyes as well as his hair. That day in my honor he put on his linen jacket, normally reserved for agricultural shows. I hadn't expected such a flaxen figure; I barely recognized him. I thought, I've got to get to Olgolulu as soon as I possibly can, that's what I've missed, that's all I've come back for; and I said, 'Let's skip the Norfolk. Let's go straight on home.'"

"The fighting's far away now," Edmund had told him. "Up in the forest. Down here the war's as good as over." And yet, as they drove through the cloudy July afternoon, they passed stockaded villages, each protected by a watchtower. The government had forced these people, who, since the beginning of their world, had lived each lineage unto itself, to abandon their homesteads and withdraw behind barbed wire; for a few hours each day they were permitted to go out under guard to cultivate their fields. Jonathan glimpsed women weeding the young maize while at the edge of the fields, along the trash lines, soldiers stood watching them with automatic rifles. He wondered, What kind of peace is this?

At Nyanga they stopped to have the tires checked. Outside the hotel next to the petrol station European farmers and their wives greeted one another and talked on the front steps. They all carried guns. As they chatted, they explored pistol handles with intense fingers as if they were not used yet to being legally and lethally armed. Seeing his son stare, Edmund Sudbury laughed. "Here's mine," he said, and he pulled a revolver from under the driver's seat. "And your mother's got one. Pretty handy with it, too. I tell you, it's like the Wild West!"

The last twenty miles beyond Eldonia were unpaved. Rutted and hazardous at the best of times, the road was washed out in several places following a rainstorm. They got stuck twice. At least the war hadn't changed the roads.

Eventually, as the sun was setting, they reached Olgolulu. So often Jonathan had dreamed that it had been desecrated, the house left roofless and empty, the fields returned to bush. But instead the fields seemed wider, the house more imposing than ever. And Eleanor had extended her garden. Despite the Emergency she'd continued to receive seeds and cuttings from the Kentish nursery-man with whom she'd dealt for decades. In the dusk she pointed out the terraces she'd built. "I only put cuttings in last October. One still needs of a lot of imagination to picture what I have in mind. But by this time next year I won't have to apologize. I always wanted to make a fuchsia garden," she added happily, "but I never found the time before."

"Yes," Edmund Sudbury agreed. "After an initial scuffle, we've been wonderfully quiet here. It's odd to think that in those mountains" — he nodded towards the Aberdares, darkly rising on the far side of the Rift — "a war's being fought and won. Thirty miles away as the crow flies. Seems more like a thousand!"

And Jonathan, looking at the scarlet and purple blossoms, mere tokens of what, a year hence, his mother expected to see, almost wept with embarrassment as he remembered his lonely panic far away in England. If there'd been any confrontation between civilization and barbarism, it certainly hadn't happened at Olgolulu.

"After that," he said quietly to Marietta, "I swore I'd never be kept away from Olgolulu for so long again. Whatever happened there, I had to see it with my own two eyes. And for all the years since then, all the way through Harrow, all the way through Oxford, I insisted on going home in December as well as July; regardless of politics or the price of wheat, I bullied my way to a ticket twice a year." He smiled. "Once I even managed three trips home. I was up in Scotland, staying with my mother's cousins for the Easter holidays, and I made a killing at the Sterling races. I took that money and hopped on a bus to Edinburgh; then I took a night train south to London and bought an airplane ticket to Nairobi. From there I hitchhiked home with an Asian trader, and when Dad came in from the farm in the evening I was in the library, with his whiskey and soda all poured out and waiting for him! He practically had a heart attack!" Jonathan stood up and stretched, smiling into the soft English afternoon. "It's my land now," he said. "Since I was twenty-one. Dad still takes care of the farm while I take care of the cash flow. And with fair weather and a bit of luck, I'll be back there for lunch tomorrow."

"Your land, your land!" Marietta exclaimed. "Well, we never had any land. My mother didn't have a fuchsia garden. No one sent her seeds from Kent. She wouldn't have had anywhere to plant them. We were always picking up and going on to somewhere else. We lived from hand to mouth."

"But you were rich!"

"We most certainly were not. I wore second-hand dresses. Maybe they were fourth-hand by the time they got to me! We bought them for a shilling in the market, off a heap. They'd come by the hundredweight, squashed down, in cardboard boxes from Europe and America. Dresses people had thrown out, given to charity. Lady Bilton does a lot of work for Oxfam. Sometimes I smile to think that I might have worn some of those clothes she collected for the destitute. I never went to school until three years ago, and when I did, it was only because an old friend paid. Oh, yes, life's been one long adventure, seeing what might turn up next. Very ritzy, very lavish!"

Jonathan said gently, "But I wasn't talking about money, Marietta. Money has nothing whatever to do with it! You lived a real life. That's all I meant by being rich."

"I don't know what you're talking about," Marietta sighed, "and neither do you."

189

12

London

Marietta's hair darkened over a winter in which the sun scarcely showed its face. But she scarcely missed the sun. She had so many new sources of light. Propelled by all she devoured with her eyes, by the excitement of her classmates and the laconic comments of her teachers, she'd begun to cultivate refinements of awareness and perception she hadn't had the faintest notion of before. Technical accomplishment, however, was much harder to come by. Forget what you thought you knew, they told her, and start again.

She was sorting though the multiple layers of London. There was a lifetime's worth of seeing and doing here, and if necessary she'd take a lifetime. She didn't talk about Africa unless someone asked, and few did. She didn't often think to bring up her origins, which grew dimmer week by week. Perhaps she'd invent new ones, a credible English family, a credible English childhood.

Like Francis had. She met him at an opening. He was a portrait painter, lanky, bearded, twenty-five. He'd never had to fight the Philistines; he'd grown up in Chelsea near the river with a painter mother, a composer father, and four brothers and sisters who were equally divided between music and art. When Marietta went there for supper she soaked up all she could of what Francis took absolutely for granted. Ferocious argument, perpetual creativity. Children grew up and got quieter eventually, Francis said, and then they moved out, but not too far away. If they went abroad, they came back before too long. He'd been abroad himself, to Florence, where he'd been deeply influenced by Anigoni. Back in London, he surrounded his subjects with flowers and woodland creatures. These extravagances were popular and he had plenty of commissions. Marietta was impressed by Francis, by his origins, his knowledge, his technical accomplishment. Not his taste, though; she didn't care for Anigoni. Bridget Riley was her idol. Riley was declarative. She made important statements. Marietta intended to paint in the Riley mode, though the statement she had in mind to make still needed clarification. Meanwhile, she argued with Francis about form and purpose. "I'm a romantic," he told her. "Romanticism is a perfectly legitimate approach. You are a Burne-Jones bathing girl with your heavy hair, your languor. I can see you by the river, trailing fingers in the water, dreaming." Marietta thought, Who's this girl he sees? She wouldn't have described herself as languorous any more than rich.

Francis lived in South Kensington in a cluttered studio with a skylight and a bank of windows, a hotplate, a bit of a room off to one side in which he slept, and no central heating. In winter it was very cold. Marietta crouched next to the Primus stove while Francis painted. His powers of concentration were extraordinary. She was awed by his determination. He painted in his shirt-sleeves, regardless of the season, claiming not to notice temperature. He noticed color and shadow, French jazz, and certain kinds of food. His mouth was rather soft except when he was painting; then it straightened out into a steely line. Curtis liked him. "He's in no hurry, is he?" she said, and when he came to supper she cooked veal scaloppine. He'd had a passion for it, since Florence.

He wanted to sleep with Marietta, of course, but she let him think that off in those empty spaces beyond Europe in which he had no interest, she'd suffered a broken heart. Her heart would mend, he said. He wasn't so romantic as to believe that love or loss of it inflicted permanent damage. "I'll bide my time," he promised. Meanwhile, he seemed content to draw her. He always had her looking faintly medieval. For Francis, delay served to intensify romance.

But the ends he'd given her time to tie up stayed loose. The terrible longing she suffered from, was that a broken heart? She only knew her world had suddenly been blighted and she had no real trust that it would ever come to life again, except in her dreams. Several nights a week she dreamed the same dream about Neville.

She climbed the steps of his house in Jasper, Alberta, and there he was, delighted to see her. Tell me who you've met in London. Nobody, Neville, I was waiting for you. I know that, but I couldn't get away. And I couldn't wait any longer, so I came to find you. In the moment of touching him, she always woke up to the truth that he was dead. Though she dreaded the almost nightly sorrow of her dream, she cherished the precious fleeting certainty that Neville was alive and loving her.

Francis intended to go back to Italy as soon as he'd saved enough money. He thought he would be off in June and he wanted Marietta to go with him. They'd live in Fiesole, he'd get his old place back. Marietta liked the idea of Fiesole. She longed to see the terra cottas and the pinks, the laurel greens of Tuscany, and render them.

She received many letters from the Africa that she was methodically putting behind her. Virginia's letters were each a single page long, typewritten with a ribbon on the verge of exhaustion. Sometimes in midsentence she switched to red, which came out a little clearer. Mostly she wrote about business. Old whites continued to leave. New whites, who might order furniture and carpets, weren't coming very fast yet. Bruce, though, was convinced they'd soon be coming faster to this new Kenya that the worst of the bigots had left. Bruce read the World Bank reports. He had wind of investment schemes; meanwhile, he was buying property. Stone houses in Katari and Westlands and up in Tigoni, too. People were almost giving them away. Some came with tennis courts and thirty or forty acres. And they were all bought in Virginia's name, since she was a Kenyan citizen and Bruce was not. So here she was, a property owner, if only on paper. A far cry from Runga, and that rest house with the green iron roof!

"I thought you'd be interested in the enclosed," Virginia wrote in November. "This was in the *Nation* yesterday." And there was a picture of Mattias Ongaki, government chief of Keriki, North Nyanza, indicted, the article said, on ten counts of embezzlement, fraud, and intimidation. "Of course," Virginia wrote, "they'd been gunning for him. He didn't go down well in the new Republic, devoted servant of the Queen that he'd been, and of her father and of his father before him. I used to enjoy chatting with him at Speech Days at the Mountain School, getting all the Baluga gossip after we moved away. I wonder, have you heard at all from Catherine?

I hope she doesn't get caught in the crossfire. It wouldn't be fair if the father's sins devolved upon the daughter."

But Marietta wasn't someone Catherine bothered keeping up with. Painting, Catherine had declared, was irrelevant to an under-developed country in which hundreds of thousands of children suffered from protein deficiencies and parasites. They needed milk, green vegetables, beans. They needed piped water and medical care. Their mothers needed birth control and protection of their property rights.

"You're bright, you're energetic," she'd told Marietta. "A pity to waste yourself on trivialities."

Marietta had pointed out that she knew nothing about beans or how to grow them. Blood and pus made her nauseated. An effective feminist needed a louder voice than hers. "In your utopia, Catherine, won't it be possible for people to do what they have some talent for?"

But Marietta's point always seemed to fall on deaf ears. She'd departed from the Mountain School for her inconsequential life, leaving Catherine to prepare for the university entrance examination. Catherine hadn't considered for an instant staying in Africa. Nor would the British red bricks on which her classmates set their sights do, either. Nor would Cambridge. Oxford, she'd decided from reading biographies, nurtured the greatest statesmen, so Oxford was where she meant to go.

A week before Christmas during breakfast, after she'd finished her porridge and before she'd started on her toast, Lady Bilton crackled the *Times*. "One of your friends, Marietta!" And there in the list of scholarships awarded by Lady Bilton's Oxford college was C. Mattias, Mountain School for Girls, Kenya, in politics, philosophy, and economics.

"I knew her," Marietta agreed, "though she didn't go in for friends, being better than the rest of us. By the way, she's black."

This Lady Bilton found very satisfying. "For years," she told Marietta, "the odd maharajah's daughter was about as dark as they went. This, for them, is quite a radical departure." Perhaps she'd think about an increase in her annual contribution to the college endowment fund.

So Catherine had got what she wanted, despite the chief's disgrace. Well, Marietta thought, I won't be chasing down to Oxford after her.

In March Virginia wrote, "Terrible thing, would you believe it, Daphne's off and gone. After so many false alarms, it seems this time she's actually done it! He's Cuban, her young man, an emigré. She found him in a butcher's shop in Barcelona. He was buying pigs' trotters. She wasn't buying anything, just admiring the hams on her way to the cathedral. He's not a Spanish Cuban, either. Not pitch black, but by no stretch of the imagination is he white. She made a point of that in the letter she wrote me from a motel in South Miami. Perhaps, secretly, she's always been tempted. They say that in the Cape, which is where she's from, there must've been a great deal of surrendering to temptation in the past, since almost no one's a pure white. But if in fact she's just reverting to type, at least she's had the good taste not to do it here. Still, Peter's utterly distraught. He's been on a binge for a fortnight now. He's always been so fond of you, Etta; maybe *you* can cheer him up. I don't seem to be able to. The moment your term's over, do please come home! I'm sending your ticket at the beginning of next month. I have to say, I could do with some cheering up myself."

Justin's letters, written in Ruba and Swahili, were full of complaints. "The house is empty. The memsahb is never here. Always in her shop, like a *muhindi*, an Indian. It's wonderful to see her standing with the customers, measuring. She could be making trousers for them, not covers for their chairs. This Katari is a hard place. Maize is so dear. I am not happy living among Kikuyu. They are like weasels. You cannot trust them. So many whom you knew have left. Bwana Lewis down the ridge has gone to the White Man's Country, and his cook, Alexi, my kinsman, has returned to Galana. As for the Memsahb Daphne, she should have been a big lady by now, watching her sons become men. But as a barren woman, she had no one to stay for, so she's eloped. The Bwana Peter has no interest in another woman, only in *changaa*. I have gone there with your mother twice to encourage him, but he was not willing to open the door. I tell you, Mari, Katari is not a good place these days. I will stay to greet you when you come, but in September when you go away again I too shall go from here. I'll follow Alexi to Galana. For a long time you'd spoken of leaving, and yet I did not believe that you would really go. Sometimes I still do not believe it! I pass through the house looking for you. When you both were young I used to think, Violet must leave me; one day she will go off to her husband, there is no other way. Her

I must lose. But Mari I will have with me always. When she marries I will go with her, and her children I will care for as I have cared for her. But I understand now that you have a different idea, Mari. My intention of leaving, however, your mother does not yet know. Let it be our secret, yours and mine. Now I am ready to go home."

Marietta thought, Then who will there be left? Virginia done over, new, like the Uhuru postage stamp? Bruce, flying between the gateposts at Olduvai Road in his orange delivery van?

Violet's letters were written in Ruba and English. She'd weaned her second child, Rebecca, and her third was on the way. "At the time of Rebecca's birth you were in your boarding school, but this one will come in your holidays, so there's nothing to keep you away. These days the road along the lake is beautiful. The Ministry received a grader from the Israelites, a huge thing that groaned and roared, and when they saw it the children ran screaming to the bush. The fare from Homa Bay is four shillings. Don't forget, and refuse them if they ask for more. My boy Sampson has become so big since you were last here in July and when he sees your photograph he always asks, 'When is Mari coming, she is very bad, has she forgotten me?' Rebecca does not know you yet, though it is time she did. My mother, Boremo, and Lucia, my mother-in-law, both greet you, as do all the women in my husband's house. They are afraid the city has spoiled you, that you've forgotten our language and our ways. When you come here, Mari, they'll check you very carefully. I know you'll show them you remember everything!"

Then there were Jonathan's letters, written in black ink on crisp white paper in camp at the Tana River, in the Selous, in a clearing in the Mau forest, and mailed days later, whenever he happened to pass a post office. He wrote about his clients as he greeted them, lived with them in very close proximity, and, ultimately, bade them good-bye. He had a steady flow, month after month, with only a day or two between one client and the next. His American trip had paid off; he was fully booked until the end of the following year. Now it was merely a matter of enduring the consequences. At Christmas he took out a Hollywood film producer with five children from several previous marriages. "It's his latest wife, a model, without the faintest interest in children, who fancies herself the hunter. He just fusses about with cameras and film. The oldest boy wanted to spend Christmas at Sun Valley, the middle two, both girls, in Hawaii, and the youngest, twins, about ten, wanted a month at Disneyland. None of them wanted to come on safari. And they never let me forget it! On jaunts such as these I have to remind myself several times an hour: It's they who are paying your taxes, boy, and who are buying your fertilizer and your cattle feed for Olgolulu. If it weren't for them, you'd be in a nasty little bungalow out near Embakasi Airport. Even so, I came within a whisker of gunning down the lot of them."

But after that low point things had started picking up. The Sandersons had arrived from Lake Forest, Illinois. "Bunty was first in Tanganyika in her teens and apart from the war has been coming over every year for thirty years. Roger's her third husband. Before Bunty married him the summer before last, two weeks on a grouse moor near Inverness was as far as Roger dared go. But Bunty's done a major overhaul, and now he's even crazier about hunting than she is. This time he's staying on a fortnight after she goes home." Four hours after Roger's departure, the Viscount Hillingham arrived. "His mother comes from Oklahoma oil, on the strength of which she acquired a fairly seedy English earl and settled down to produce Patrick. I knew him at school, though not well, as he was five years older. Despite the prospect of great wealth, he didn't throw his weight about or try to sodomize one, either, and now that those prospects have become reality, he's still amazingly reasonable to live with. If the bath water's cold or the soufflé collapses or there isn't any petrol in Juba and one has to hang about for days for the tankers to come up from Nairobi, he doesn't seem to mind. And if he fires and misses, he just reloads. No face-saving maneuvers required, a mark of character which among oil heirs I've known appears to be quite rare."

Coming back from the Sudan with Hillingham, Jonathan had passed Mount Elgon. "For your sake, Marietta, I went up and had a good look round Itep. I'd never been there before, only heard about it and Neville's fanciful extravagances. Heart-wrenching to see it only now, after the Huns and Visigoths are in possession. It's a cooperative; I imagine you knew that. The tower's being used as a granary and the garden's completely gone. Pigs rooting under the poinsettias, calves tethered all over what used to be the lawn, and the ground floor of the castle itself given over to poultry. One sees cocks perching on the newel posts at the bottom of the stairs and hens laying eggs on the library shelves. And the stink is indescribable! The manager and his entire extended family live upstairs, regardless, and blacken the walls with the smoke of their cooking fires. It made me sick to see that extraordinary place so violated."

Jonathan wrote rarely from Olgolulu, for which he worked so hard. Once, when Edmund was down with bronchitis, he'd gone to a landowners' meeting in Eldonia. "The old-timers in tweeds and heavy knitted ties, holding battered hats from Locke on their knees, were heavily outnumbered by the new contingent, Kenyatta's boys, in natty pinstriped suits. Crying 'Uhuru!' they grab whatever they can lay their hands on. And they're giving up on wheat, because it's too much trouble; they're changing over to maize and destroying the topsoil at a phenomenal rate. Well, let them exhaust their land if they want! But we'll go on as before, conserving, enriching, taking great care."

"That Jonathan certainly took a shine to you," Curtis said, laying out the morning's post on the front hall table. "D'you give as good as you get?"

No, she did not. His need to have her be with him and see everything he saw seized her with dread. He wanted to get as good as he gave. In another correspondence, she'd given as good as she'd got, letter for letter, but she didn't have it in her to do that again. She began by writing two letters to his three. Later, one to three.

In early spring he wrote from Olgolulu, "The rains have started. The fields are the palest possible green. The dust's down, the view's as clear as can be. And I'm counting the days till you come back from dreary London so I can bring you up here and you can see all this for yourself."

But in June she'd be with Francis in a sunny room in Fiesole, and if things turned out well, she'd think up some excuse to stay all summer, not to go home to Africa at all.

One day in April when daffodils were bobbing in the park and babies born in the depths of winter were being pushed in their prams in the first warm sun, Marietta telephoned Francis from the Slade. "I can't draw another line. It's because of the spring. It's insidious. Do let's go to Richmond and watch the leaves unfurl! Can you be persuaded?" Francis said a forehead wasn't coming right, and why not go to Richmond? They'd come back and hear some music later on. "Meet me at home at two," Marietta said. "I'll leave my stuff there, then we'll go."

As she got off the bus and hurried through the square, she

thought of Jonathan. "If you ever want green spaces," he'd said. But the fact was, she hadn't until now. She'd been content in concrete and brick boxes, leafless city streets. She ran up the steps of number six and let herself in.

Beyond the hall in the drawing room she saw Francis, hands in his pockets. Head cocked a little to side, he was listening intently to a young black woman who sat very erect in Lady Bilton's dark green velvet chair. She wore an elaborate dress, red taffeta with silver threaded through it, a blouse with puffy sleeves, a long wrapper. She talked quickly and with much gesticulation, but from where she stood Marietta couldn't see her face, only the back of her turban and gold earrings swinging in rhythm with her speech. Neither she nor Francis had heard Marietta come in.

Curtis popped out of the pantry with doughy hands. She'd dispensed with her cardigan and the sleeves of her dress were rolled up above the elbows. She was making scones for tea. "You've got a visitor," she whispered. "She's been here since eleven-thirty. I told her, 'Miss Marietta's at her class. Her ladyship's out as well.' But she wouldn't go away. She wouldn't have lunch, either, she told me, with a look on her face as if she expected my chop'd poison her. I was ever so thankful when Mr. Francis came! I didn't fancy being alone with her all afternoon. Catherine, she said her name was. She was in that boarding school over in Africa."

"Oh, good Lord." Marietta dropped her belongings on the hall carpet. She's come a bit early, hasn't she? she said to herself. I thought Oxford didn't start until October.

"We'd no idea you were back!" Francis exclaimed as she walked into the drawing room. "We were so busy chatting."

Catherine stood up, hands outstretched. "Are you surprised to see me, Marietta, so far from home?" Her face beneath the turban shone. "I'm so very glad to find you!"

Marietta gazed at the red and silver, the kohl-rimmed eyes — like a Somali, she thought. Less than a year ago she was wearing knee socks and blue gingham. Her legs were too long, her arms too skinny. She had no breasts to speak of. But now she curves and her skin is gleaming.

"I wouldn't have known you," Marietta said in wonder, "you're all got up." But it wasn't her costume or her new figure or even seeing her here in Cardigan Square instead of there at the Mountain in the room they'd once shared. The fact was, Catherine actually did look glad! I'm relevant after all, is that it? Marietta wanted to ask. "You should have let me know you were coming," she said quickly. "Then I'd have been here to greet you. I'm sorry, I've kept you waiting a very long time."

"I wrote to you at your college. Didn't you receive my letter?"

"No."

"I thought that must have been the case, since surely you'd have answered, we're such old friends, Marietta! This morning I telephoned there and was told you were living at this address. Immediately I came on the Underground to find you, and all the time, I was thinking, How surprised Marietta will be! But I didn't pay close enough attention and all of a sudden I realized I was going in the wrong direction. Luckily the man sitting next to me noticed how confused I was. He wore a bowler hat and carried an umbrella, long and thin and black, rolled very tightly, the sort I've read about so often. But although he looked stern, in fact he was very kind to me. He took me off that train and through long tunnels until we came to another platform, where he waited with me till the right train came. So soon I reached your house, only to hear your servant say that you were out and wouldn't be returning until evening. I told her, 'Never mind, I'll stay here anyway, I don't want to go off and get lost a second time.' That didn't make her happy at all! She began to dust this room, although there was no dust. Oh, she was so busy making this clean room cleaner!"

"Curtis tends to hover," Marietta said. "It's just her way."

"It seemed that she was frightened I'd steal one of your ashtrays if she didn't keep a very close watch on me. But before too long Francis arrived and she was willing at last to leave me in his care and go back to the kitchen. Fortunately" — Catherine smiled — "Francis is not nearly so suspicious. He's a bohemian, so he tells me. Until today I'd thought bohemians were those dirty people who sing songs and beg for coins outside the New Stanley Hotel in Nairobi. But this one's not a parasite! He's an intelligent person. In your absence, Marietta, I've had a very interesting time."

"Even though I haven't sung a single song so far," Francis said, grinning. "Incidentally, Catherine's won a competition. Which is why she's here."

"Another prize!" Marietta exclaimed. "But I haven't even had a chance to congratulate you on your Oxford scholarship! I saw your name in the *Times* months ago and I meant to write," she lied, "but

I didn't know exactly where you'd be. What have you won this time?"

In the MacMillan Library in Nairobi, just before Christmas, Catherine had read that the *Daily Mail* was running an essay competition for Sixth Formers. They'd wanted four thousand words on Britain's prospects in the postcolonial period, so she'd entered and won. Two weeks in London and three hundred pounds. The judges hadn't expected the winner to be an African, she said. "They were rather surprised."

"I can imagine," Marietta murmured. "Incidentally, what are Britain's prospects — indifferent or disastrous?"

"That depends on whether she revitalizes her economy, and the present socialist government seems incompetent to do that. I brought a copy of my essay for you. Here it is." She bent to pick up a folder from the floor beside her chair. "I hope you like it," she added eagerly.

"Thanks. I expect to learn a lot. Right now, though, I've got to get something to eat. Are either of you hungry?"

"Nothing for me. I had a late breakfast," Francis said.

"Your servant brought me tea and biscuits. That was enough."

"But Curtis isn't *my* servant," Marietta said distinctly.

In the kitchen Curtis asked, "Is she a princess? Seems like she must be, from the way she carries on."

"No, not a princess; she has aspirations, though." Marietta took a plate of bread and cheese back to the drawing room and positioned herself on the sofa, opposite Catherine. With his eyes shut, she thought, even Pinky Eglington might be persuaded that she was white. She speaks just like Rosemary Fullerton. Same accent, only her diction's clearer. Is this what integration was intended to produce? A truly exotic English girl? I wonder, has Mrs. Tyson seen the result of all her efforts? Is she still teaching the parable of the talents in the Keriki Hills?

"How are things at home?" Marietta said, since home was easiest to start with.

Catherine shook her head. "Not so good," she said. The husband of her sister Elizabeth was an incorrigible drunkard, the only son of a mother who'd spoiled him from the moment he first drew breath. "First they tried to make me marry him, but I refused. I was interested in my studies, not in getting married, so then he asked for Elizabeth instead. I warned her not to accept, but she

200

didn't listen. He had a motorcycle and she imagined if she married him she'd ride about on it all day." Catherine snorted. "The girls he met in bars rode on that motorcycle, but my sister? Not even once!" On New Year's Day he'd fractured Elizabeth's skull in a drunken rage, and although now, four months later, she was recovering at last, surely he'd beat her again, and perhaps next time she wouldn't recover. This Elizabeth knew, but she wouldn't think of divorce. How could she? The cattle had been paid.

Marietta asked after Benjamin, who hadn't lasted long as a waiter and had failed disastrously as assistant cook. He'd left the Wayfarer under a cloud to become a conductor on a bus that ran between Narok and Eldonia. But he hadn't been happy collecting bus fares. He had ambition. He wanted to become a driver, with or without a license. One day he'd stolen the key to the ignition and started up the engine, and before he'd gone twenty feet he ran into another bus. For that he was imprisoned for a year. "They should have kept him there," Catherine said in disgust. "He's a child still and always will be!"

"That's what I liked about him," Marietta said mildly. "He was always so cheerful. He never got low like the rest of us."

They talked about this one and that one at Keriki. They talked about the Mountain School, too, and various Old Girls who were living in England now, some of them in London. "You'll let them know you're here, I'm sure," Marietta said.

But Catherine said she didn't mean to. She'd never found them interesting. She had a cousin, too, at Loughborough Technical College, in training as an engineer. But she didn't think he was worth a visit, either. "He used to thrash me when we herded sheep together." She grimaced. "He was a coward, actually. Should I visit a coward?" Miss Jellicoe, though, was living near Cambridge, and her, Catherine hoped to see. She'd been told that trains went frequently to Cambridge. She said nothing at all, however, about her father and his fall from grace. In Africa, Marietta reminded herself, you give people a chance to speak; if they choose not to, you let them be.

Francis, perched on one arm of the sofa, had been watching Catherine closely. Now he remarked, "One really ought to paint her there, just as she is. The red and silver and dark green, they're so compelling. The light's right and the lilies in that vase behind are perfect."

"All one needs are a few small woodland creatures, right?" Marietta said irritably. "But she has better things to do with her two weeks than sit for you, Francis." Then, feeling ashamed of herself, she added, "By the way, that dress really suits you, Catherine. You remind me of a model in *Drum* magazine."

"A Nigerian lady in Nairobi lent me three of her dresses." Catherine smiled. "They're rather postcolonial, don't you think?"

She'd arrived at London airport at six o'clock that morning and was staying in a hotel in Bedford Square with the three runners-up, a girl from Huddersfield and two boys, one from Manchester and one from Leeds. Under the direction of a Mr. Richard Craddock, an assistant editor of the *Daily Mail*, they were to acquire a first-hand knowledge of major British institutions. Today Mr. Craddock had arranged a bus tour of the city, but Catherine had excused herself. The real agenda would begin the following day. The owner of the *Daily Mail* himself had invited them to lunch at the House of Lords; afterwards they'd stay for the debate on old-age pensions. But Catherine wasn't interested in pensions. She intended to gain admission to the Commons debate on development aid to former British territories. "I expect you've been following the newspaper reports, Marietta. If I'm able to get tickets for tomorrow evening, will you go with me?"

"It's not really my kind of thing," Marietta said doubtfully. "You used to complain that I was politically illiterate. I haven't changed."

"I'm not only interested in politics, Marietta!" Out of her handbag Catherine brought several sheets of paper. "You see," she said eagerly, "I've listed everything I want to see under three separate headings: politics, history, literature. Though most of my afternoons are filled by Mr. Craddock, I have four free evenings and several mornings as well. We won't waste a minute, Marietta. We'll run about all over London! We'll see everything, you and I!"

Marietta put her plate down on the coffee table and brushed the crumbs off her skirt. "I'm afraid I'm rather busy right now. In fact, I've got half a dozen projects due. What about your runners-up? Couldn't you all go sightseeing together?"

Catherine shook her head emphatically. "They're provincials."

Marietta laughed. "Well, I'm from Songo, Tanganyika Territory. You couldn't be more provincial than that!"

"But Marietta, surely you remember the books of J. B. Priestley? Those northern industrial cities are exhausted. They make cripples of their inhabitants! This morning I spent an hour with my fellow prize winners, and I can assure you they have no imagination. As soon as I could, I excused myself and came here to you."

"I bet you terrified them." Marietta grinned. "I bet they've never met anyone like you in their lives! Anyway," she added, "you don't have to pack everything into these two weeks. You'll be back in October."

"No," Catherine said quietly, "I shan't be back in October."

"Aren't you going to Oxford?"

"I turned that scholarship down. I cannot leave my father, Marietta."

Marietta said she'd read about the charges. She'd been sorry to learn about the case against the chief, "but it's a tempest in a teapot. A publicity stunt. He'll get off, of course."

"No, he won't get off!" Catherine exclaimed. She sat forward in her chair. "You must know, Marietta, that this government has no interest in establishing the facts of the case, only in distinguishing themselves from those who preceded them. They intend to vilify him, and with him the past. Many people advise him: 'Go to Uganda, go to Tanzania. You are an old man, Mattias. Live out your life in peace.'" She shook her head. "With Uhuru my father may have grown more skeptical, but he is as courageous as ever he was. He'll never run away! Next month they will try him, they will convict him of crimes he did not commit, and he will fight, he will appeal, but in the end they will imprison him. But once his sentence is completed, he'll go home. He'll die where he was born, and he'll be buried where his ancestors were buried, not in some distant place among strangers! Those big new men, who grow daily richer at the expense of the common people, they'll learn that to destroy the spirit of Mattias Ongaki is impossible.

"As soon as the charges came against my father," she went on, "I knew that even if I won that scholarship I could not accept it. Nevertheless I thought, Let me sit for the examination anyway. Let me see what I can do. I did so not for my own sake but for my father's." She looked up at Francis. "You see, he was very much opposed to my going to school at all. Marietta may remember that," she said, smiling quickly. "My father's a man who's very set in his own ways. Each year it was a very fierce struggle persuading him to allow me to continue going to school. But finally he told me, 'Learn whatever you wish to learn, since that is your heart's desire. If you must, go and live among white people. You have my blessing!' So winning that scholarship was the most fitting way I knew to thank him for his generosity."

"But living among white people hasn't been easy," Marietta said. "I saw, I heard. Anyone less determined than you were would have given up. After all that, you can't turn round and go home!"

"I shan't go home. I shall go to Uganda, to Makerere College. From Kampala I'll be able to travel back to Kenya frequently, whereas perhaps from Britain I couldn't afford to go at all." She added, slipping into Keriki, "If for three years he never once saw me, then certainly my father would despair."

"But he's got more than a hundred children besides you. Let *them* visit him!"

"My father doesn't listen to his other children, Marietta. I'm the only one he trusts, the only one to keep him in good spirits. Besides, if I came here to study, I'd be worrying about him all the time, I wouldn't do well." She smiled gently. "When I was very young I watched him leave our place in a new uniform, with all his medals on his chest. People told me he was going to do homage to the Queen. 'Who is that?' I said. 'Why must he do homage? Is he not the King?' 'No,' they said, 'he is a great man, he is the chief, but he is not the King.' They showed me a picture of a young white woman. 'She lives beyond an ocean that you've never seen, in a city bigger than Kisumu. Bigger even than Nairobi, which you've never seen either. That city,' they told me, 'is at the center of the world. That is where your father's going.' Ever since then," she finished, "I've been waiting to come to London, and as you see, at last I am here! So let this be my consolation prize. In future there may be other opportunities, but for now I must take care of things at home."

If you have to give up the thing you'd set your heart on, Marietta wondered, does that make you more or less like other people?

"I'm sorry," Catherine said as she turned to Francis. "We were talking about matters that are at a very great distance from here, so we forgot, we began to speak my language. At school, too, we used to forget, just like this, and sometimes people were very annoyed with us. I suppose they suspected we were plotting against them!" She smiled. "But they were never indignant when two girls from Sweden spoke their native tongue together. It was strange, I used to think, that although we were living in Africa, African speech was so troubling to them."

"Your faces changed," Francis said softly. "You both looked different. What can it be like, I wonder, to belong to two such different worlds?"

But Catherine glanced at the clock on the mantelpiece. "See how late it is!" she said quickly. "We mustn't waste the whole afternoon. What was that place you spoke of, Francis? Oh yes, 'The Lass of Richmond Hill'! I'm only familiar with an English place if a poet or a novelist has mentioned it or if" — she laughed — "a Plantagenet monarch fought his rebellious barons there."

"Yes, Richmond," Francis agreed. "If you're not too tired would you like to come along? We'd love to have you. Or will your Mr. Craddock be frantic wondering what's become of you?"

"Thank you, I'd like to come. I'm not at all tired. Why should I be? I've been sitting ever since I left Nairobi at ten o'clock last night. May I use your telephone, Marietta? I'll leave a message for Mr. Craddock at the hotel."

"Richmond has green spaces and fallow deer," Marietta said dryly. "It might remind you of home. If we're really going, we'd better be off." She stood up. "There's a telephone in the study, second door to your right." Why did she have to single me out, she said to herself as Catherine went off, when there are half a dozen other girls in London whom she knows as well as she knows me? Well, whatever the reason, she's here now, and I'm going to have to put up with her.

At seven-thirty the following evening Catherine telephoned. "How are you?"

"Exhausted," Marietta replied. After Richmond and supper in a pub on Richmond Green they'd been at a jazz club in Leicester Square till three. "How was the House of Lords? You must be exhausted as well."

But Catherine wasn't. She'd got two tickets for the development debate.

"I suppose you asked Lord Rothermere?"

"Yes. He was very obliging. He sent his secretary right away to get these tickets for me. You will come with me, won't you, Marietta?"

"Sorry, I can't. I've got too much work to do."

But Catherine was saying, "I shall be outside the House of Commons in exactly one hour's time," and she hung up.

What was she to do, let Catherine wait until eventually the penny dropped that she wasn't coming? But she'd never been to the House of Commons, which, after eight months in London, was probably a mistake, so she changed her jeans for a more suitable skirt and took a bus to Westminster. And there was Catherine, a column of azure eyelet cotton, on the pavement. Heads turned in the Strangers' Gallery as she walked in. I bet they think she's a princess, too, Marietta thought.

Lord Rothermere's secretary had got them front-row seats. Catherine settled herself behind the balustrade and was immediately enthralled, but after fifteen minutes Marietta's mind was wandering. She began to draw a large member of Her Majesty's Opposition, a back-bencher with a mottled purple face. When she'd finished with him, she drew the lady on his right in a twin set and pearls, and so on down the row, while Catherine followed every word and every sally. She leaned far forward, her face still. Occasionally she nodded vigorously.

"We've got to go," Marietta whispered at ten twenty-three. "Won't she worry about you, that girl from Huddersfield whose room you're sharing?"

But Catherine only frowned and listened more intently. At midnight when the gallery was almost empty, Marietta attempted to leave once more. "We have to wait till Heath has finished," Catherine whispered back. Heath was extremely long-winded. Eventually they left, at half past one.

When Marietta complained about Catherine at breakfast, Lady Bilton observed, "In my day one didn't find girls like that in Kenya. I wish I had. Life would have been so much more exciting! I hope I have a chance to meet your Catherine."

"In my day one didn't find girls like her, either. She's unique. At least, I hope she is."

"I gather you're not fond of her."

"She knows what she's after and how to get there. She doesn't need me to hold her hand."

"She must appreciate your company."

"She does not! She believes that art is irrelevant, and since she's read every book about London that's in the MacMillan Library, I can't tell her anything she doesn't know already."

"She can still appreciate your company. I know I'd hate to have to share a room with a strange girl from Huddersfield, especially if I were black. Naturally I'd seek out someone with whom I had a little more in common. She's clearly very attached to you."

"That's a myth," Marietta retorted. "Catherine and I have never had anything in common, apart from the accident of having lived in the same African reserve."

The weather had broken; the streets were cold and wet. Catherine was spending the day at the Old Bailey and in the evening she and her companions were to air their views on Britain's future on television. Marietta, working in her room, forgot to watch. Curtis saw the first ten minutes, then switched off. "Your friend was doing all the talking," she told Marietta when she brought her a cup of cocoa before going to bed. "The other three were shriveling in their seats. She was a bit too quick for Mr. Dimbleby as well."

Catherine telephoned during breakfast. "We're off to the Bank of England," she said, "and before I left I wanted to speak to you about tonight."

"What about it?"

"I got tickets for the debate again. You'll come, won't you?"

"I'll read about it in the paper, thanks. Can't you ask one of your companions from the provinces?"

"They're going to see a play by Agatha Christie. They have different interests. Marietta, don't disappoint me, please!"

The last thing Marietta wanted was to spend another evening in the House of Commons. But perhaps Catherine really *was* fond of her, as Lady Bilton had said; only she, Marietta, was too mean-spirited to acknowledge this fact. "Oh, all right," she said peevishly. "One more session, then that's it. We also have different interests, you and I. You've pointed that out in the past."

But Lady Bilton was tapping Marietta's shoulder. "Wait a second," Marietta said to Catherine, then covered the mouthpiece.

"Ask her to dinner."

"We don't have to have her."

"It isn't a question of having to. Ask her for seven o'clock."

When Marietta came back from the Slade at half past five, Lady Bilton and Catherine, in yellow and green, were at the window in the drawing room. They were deep in conversation and didn't look around.

"She's here again, and her ladyship's taken a shine," Curtis said crossly in the hall. "They've been nattering ever since four."

"She wasn't invited till seven."

"I know, but she telephoned and asked to come early."

"She's very striking, isn't she, a remarkable presence in one so young," Lady Bilton said while Catherine was off in the downstairs lavatory.

"It's those dresses she's wearing nowadays," Marietta replied. "She never did before." And before, Marietta added silently, Catherine wasn't much for smiling and paying attention to other people, either, but now she's all flashes and gleams, and everyone's enchanted. Except Curtis and me. Well, Catherine treats Curtis like a servant, and why should Curtis care for that? But *me* she treats as if I were her closest friend — God knows why, when I've never even liked her! The fact is, I'm jealous. Not of her prizes, of being such a success. No. Of her and her father. I always have been, I suppose, from almost the first day I met her. They always seemed so delighted, so shamelessly pleased with one another. I'd hoped for something like that to happen between me and Neville. But it never did, quite.

"It's sad about that Oxford business," Lady Bilton went on. "I gather she's absolutely made up her mind and told them no. She's certainly one for looking on the bright side, though. She tells me it's very important to get to know one's contemporaries, and they'll be her classmates in Uganda. If she came and studied over here, on the other hand, she'd miss making essential contacts for the future. And she'll have a fascinating one, no doubt about it! I'm so glad you brought her to the house, Marietta."

Next thing we know, she'll be moving in here with us, Marietta thought in disgust. Aloud she said, "I didn't bring her here. She came on the Underground of her own accord."

Marietta didn't manage to drag Catherine out of the Strangers' Gallery until two o'clock in the morning. As they waited for taxis, Catherine said, "You're coming with me tomorrow, aren't you, Marietta?"

"I certainly am not."

"But I have to be at the Stock Exchange at one, so before that I thought we'd have time to go to the Docks and then to Inns of Court. They look quite close on the Underground map. I hope one day to be called to the Bar at Lincoln's Inn," she added, by way of explanation.

"There's something you've got to understand," Marietta said grimly. "I happen to have a project due in seven hours' time. Because I've been out almost every night this week with you, I've barely begun it. I'm going home now as fast as I possibly can. I'll drink two cups of coffee and stay up the rest of the night. Then I'll take the tube to class where I'll get hell for doing a rotten job. I'm not going to the Docks with you or to Lincoln's Inn either."

"Well, perhaps we could start out later and go somewhere closer by. We could go to the British Museum. I want to see the Benin bronzes, too. Let's leave the slums for another day."

"After I've been beaten to a pulp by my art history instructor, I'll doze my way through anatomy from half past ten till twelve, and then I'm going home to bed. I'm not going anywhere else with you, Catherine. Don't you understand," Marietta added in exasperation, "my own life didn't come to a halt when you arrived in London without warning!" and she jumped into the first taxi that drove up.

But as she was hurriedly buttering a slice of toast at twenty past eight, the telephone rang. "For you," Curtis said from the dining room doorway, "it's her royal highness."

"I forgot to ask you about Saturday," Catherine said. "I'm going to Cambridge to see Miss Jellicoe. Have you been down there, Marietta?"

"No, and I can't go with you, either," Marietta replied, "because I'm going to spend the weekend with my aunt." After a moment's thought she added more kindly, "But Francis's brother Billy is at Cambridge, and he spent three months in Dahomey, studying the music. It was a great experience, so he told me. He's hoping to travel again in Africa after he gets his degree. I bet he'll jump at the chance to show you round. But if I were you, I wouldn't take him with me when I went to see Miss Jellicoe. Billy tends to be argumentative. You'd like that, but Miss Jellicoe mightn't. I'll ask Francis to arrange everything."

"I'm sorry you can't come, Marietta."

"Really, you'll be much better off with Billy than with me. I've never set foot in Cambridge in my life. Do give my regards to Miss Jellicoe. Tell her one of these days I'll be down to visit her too."

That would get rid of Catherine for a couple of days. Perhaps after a weekend in the country and some sleep, Marietta thought, she'd start to feel more charitable.

*

A hundred miles away in Wiltshire Marietta found the spring in full throttle. The Avon Hunt had finished its season and Sophia had turned her horses out to grass. In ten days' time she and Jock would be off on a cruise round the Peloponnese before a summer of competitive gardening. Only Elizabeth Sudbury's garden at Tresham rivaled Sophia's. Every Tuesday and Thursday from Whitsuntide to the third week of September, the public oohed and ahed its way down the paths of Folly Court and Tresham. Since they were only four miles apart, one could manage both with ease in a single afternoon. In spring they were marvelous, but June, of course, would see the gardens at their peak.

On Sunday evening after three days of hyacinths and primroses, sheets of bluebells in the wild garden, and the earliest flaming ragged petaled tulips on the sheltered terrace, which faced south, Marietta took the train to Paddington and then the Underground to South Kensington. The time had changed and the evening was suddenly longer. The air was warm and lilac was coming out in the squares. Tomorrow she'd broach the subject of Italy to her trustees. She wouldn't say she planned to live in sin with Francis. Lady Bilton would guess, but she didn't have to be told straight out. Carfax, the solicitor, and Buchanan, at the bank in St. James's Street, didn't have to be told either. Still, with them, stern, dry men in dark gray suits with dandruff on their collars, one would choose one's words carefully. Why not spend the whole summer in Florence and go to Nairobi at Christmas instead, she thought as she turned Francis's corner. Up in his studio, now that the leaves were out, you'd think you were deep in a forest, not in London at all. The stairs were steep and she climbed them slowly. Her suitcase was heavy. She stopped at the second landing for breath, then more slowly went on up to the top. When she knocked at Francis's door, no one came, which meant either that he'd gone to his parents in Chelsea for supper or else that he was inside, concentrating furiously. At such times he didn't hear a knock the first time or even the third. If one kept on, though, he'd hear and come eventually.

She heard him crossing the room. Then the door opened and there he was, in his dressing gown. "You!" he exclaimed. "I thought you'd be at your aunt's till Monday."

"I came back," she said, and she kissed him. "The weather was marvelous in Wiltshire. I can't wait to go to Florence! On the way here, I was thinking about what to say to the trustees. I'm not used

to having to justify myself to strangers. I suppose I'd better learn."
She frowned. "Are you ill?"

"No, I'm not ill," Francis said. "I've been working. I never bothered to get dressed."

"Why don't you, and then we'll go out and have some supper. By the way," she added, as an afterthought, "have you any idea what happened to Catherine?"

"I set things up for her with Billy, that's all I know," Francis said.

"I felt pretty guilty about pushing her off on your brother. Really, I should have taken her with me to the country. Sophia wouldn't have minded. On Saturday night she'd have popped Catherine into an evening dress and carried her off to the Point-to-Point Ball, where she'd have been the object of enormous curiosity. But that wouldn't have fazed her in the least. She'd have danced with all the old reactionaries and chatted up the dowagers and charmed the lot of them. But the fact was, I couldn't face her for the whole weekend."

"She didn't want to go to Wiltshire anyway," Francis pointed out. "She wanted to go to Cambridge."

"I'd better ring her where she's staying and find out how that went."

But the hotel receptionist told Marietta that Catherine was out. She hadn't seen her all day. If she had, she'd have remembered, certainly. Marietta left a message that she'd ring later, and hung up. "I bet you she never came back from Cambridge," Marietta said, grinning. "I bet she's holed up with Billy in his rooms, teaching him a thing or two he didn't learn in Dahomey. When she wasn't in a boarding school for young white ladies, she was out scouring the brothels of western Kenya for women for her father. She said she always enjoyed their company. They probably gave her lots of tips."

As she talked, Marietta walked slowly through the room, glancing at canvases at various stages of completion. Francis's current oeuvre was of a handsome middle-aged woman, the Lady Mayoress of Portsmouth. A bear rooted in the bottom right-hand corner. "You'll be finished with this soon, won't you?" she said. "They'll be thrilled with it in Portsmouth. And then who's next? The merchant banker, or the property developer's children? Do hurry up and change, Francis, I'm starving. Oh, look!" she exclaimed "you did some sketches of Catherine!" There she was, in charcoal, her head and shoulders, hair tightly plaited. "When did you do these, the day after Richmond?"

Francis nodded. "While she was fresh in my mind."

"Clever how you got her hair just right! Really, it's a pity you can't paint her in that green chair. Lady Bilton would have been perfectly delighted. She's very keen on Catherine. Practically everyone is, of course, apart from me and Curtis. Curtis refers to her as her royal highness." She put down the sketch. "Poor Billy, I wonder how he is. Shouldn't we telephone him and find out? Catherine's a bit of a truck. I hope she didn't squash him flat," she said over her shoulder to Francis.

Behind her the bedroom door creaked open. Francis is going off to get dressed at last, she thought. But he wasn't. He was three feet from Marietta, hands in his dressing gown pockets, his face expressionless.

Marietta swung round. She saw a sleepy Catherine in the doorway, azure eyelet cotton hitched up under her armpits.

"Good God!" Marietta gasped. "What's she doing here? But it's obvious what she's doing here," she added bitterly, "isn't it?"

Francis said slowly, "Billy was off playing his cello. He couldn't be reached. Miss Jellicoe was ill. Catherine didn't go to Cambridge after all."

"And you took care of her instead." Marietta sat abruptly. "Is this the bohemian detour in her political itinerary?" She looked up. Catherine watched her in silence, eyes wide.

"Why should you care?" Francis said grimly. "It's art that excites you, not the artist. I thought, Is that your permanent condition, keeping yourself to yourself? Or mightn't you warm up in time? I came to the conclusion that the generosity one glimpses every now and then is an illusion. You're as icy in April, Marietta, as you were in November when we met."

Marietta jumped up. She grabbed for her suitcase and dashed to the door.

"Wait!" Catherine was running through the room. She dodged round easels, tripped over boxes, sent jars of paint and turpentine splattering across the floor. She stumbled over a stool and her wrapper came loose, but with quick fingers she fastened it again. "Wait for me!" she pleaded in Keriki to Marietta, who was struggling with the double lock. "What happened here is of no consequence. This man is of no consequence, either. He was eager, that

212

was all. It was not important. Our friendship, yours and mine, is important. Only that!" She took Marietta by the shoulders and tried to turn her round. "Look at me," she demanded. "Please don't run away!"

But Marietta pushed her off, wrenched the door open, and was through it in an instant. She scrambled down the stairs, four flights, suitcase banging against the spindles of the banisters. At last she was outside in the dusk. On the far side of the road the gate into the garden in the square was ajar. She crossed and went in. I keep myself to myself, she whispered, because I haven't stopped loving a man I don't even remember clearly anymore. A stone bench loomed whitish in the half-light. She sat down on it and wept.

Lady Bilton was going to spend a long weekend with her widowed sister-in-law. Janet lived in Cornwall, near St. Ives. She raised springer spaniels. Marietta was invited too, but she excused herself. "Curtis is going to Eastbourne," Lady Bilton said. "It's her annual treat. She's sat on the sea front in the same spot, in the very same deck chair, I dare say, for the last seventeen years. She wouldn't miss it even if it snowed. You'll be all alone here."

"I'll be perfectly fine. No excuses not to get my work finished."

"You won't stay all cooped up, will you? You'll see Francis?"

"No, I'm not seeing Francis anymore."

Lady Bilton frowned. "You had a falling-out?"

"We'd never really been in."

"I must say, he always struck me as being a bit vague," Lady Bilton said, "and I would have found that irritating over time. "Well," she added, "I hope you're not very upset."

"Not over Francis, no."

Early on Thursday morning Lady Bilton and Curtis set off in separate taxis, Lady Bilton to Paddington, Curtis to Waterloo. Marietta shut the front door and went to the kitchen for another cup of coffee. She was icy, Francis had said, though later he'd wanted to take that back. He'd telephoned and she'd been out. He'd telephoned again, and she hadn't returned the call. Then he'd come to find her at the Slade. It was just that he'd had Catherine on his hands, he said, and she'd been more than willing. It was her way of thanking him for showing her about. He'd taken her to Kenwood that Saturday afternoon, and to a concert, and then to bed.

But sleeping with Catherine didn't make any difference to his feeling about *her*. He'd been cruel, that Sunday night. It'd just come out, but she'd got him into a corner, hadn't she? Of course they'd go to Italy as planned. He even said he loved her.

"No," Marietta had replied grimly, in the corridor between life drawing and anatomy. "You don't love me and I don't love you. We took a long look at each other and things didn't work out. I'm not going to Italy this summer, and if I ever go, it won't be with you!"

More than willing, Catherine had been, had she? And who was Francis to stand up to her? Except if he was painting, he gladly fell in with the wishes of others. Marietta missed seeing his family in their big house in Chelsea where the chance to create was considered a necessity, a basic human need, but she didn't miss Francis. So far as she was concerned, he'd been spoiled — *oserererie*, Ruba people said, all used up. All used up by Catherine.

Catherine had telephoned, too. Marietta had taken the call in the study, shutting the door firmly behind her.

"I want to see you, Marietta, before I leave again for Africa."

"What's the point of our seeing one another? There's no point."

"I don't want to leave, and you still angry with me," Catherine had pleaded in Keriki. "Friends should not part this way."

"We've never been friends," Marietta had replied coldly in English. "We've tolerated one another. Now we shan't have to anymore. You've provided an excellent excuse to stop."

"It's you I care for, Marietta. Francis doesn't matter." Catherine's voice rose as Marietta put the receiver down.

Catherine was right: Francis didn't matter. Because Marietta hadn't had eyes to see or ears to hear, except from a great distance, she'd never given him a chance to matter. She kept herself to herself. Was that her permanent condition?

Marietta washed her cup and saucer and put them in the rack. Across the hall she heard someone at the front door, though no one rang. An envelope came through the letter box. A telegram. From Janet, probably. Or Janet's daily maid. She's had a heart attack. Oh Lord, Lady Bilton's almost at the station; how could one intercept her now? But the telegram was for Marietta. "Safari delayed," it read. "Coming to see you. Arriving Thursday, six P.M. Jonathan."

13

Galana

Marietta and Justin were waiting on the dock to cross to Galana Island. They'd arrived by bus from Nairobi at three in the afternoon to find the ferry boat marooned on the opposite shore. The ferry was hauled by winch and cable over the narrow channel, and in the mornings, with the wind blowing gently out of the west, crossings were easy. But at two (the eighth hour of the day, as the Africans counted), the wind abruptly changed direction and grew much stronger. Then the water surged and raced through the channel; the cables strained and threatened to snap. Until the wind died down again in the early evening, the men whose job it was to turn the winch slept under the big acacia tree, in front of the Galana bar.

Justin leaned against a pushcart loaded with cooking pots and Marietta sat on a box at his feet. Each had a bottle of Fanta, which Justin had bought in the market a little way back from the shore. Justin's was empty already, but Marietta had drunk very little of hers. "You take it," she said, "the sweetness makes me sick," and she gave her Fanta to Justin, who gulped it down at once.

"That road is wicked to the stomach," he said, "but with Violet you'll soon recover. You'll rest and she'll cook lake fish for you."

"I'm the one who'll do the cooking, Justin. She's about to have a baby. She won't wait on me!"

Virginia had objected to this expedition. "You've just come home and already you're dashing off to the end of the earth to deliver a baby! How d'you know Violet's calculated right? She's probably

215

not due for weeks, so you'll stew out there, gossiping and scratching for fleas. Is that what you came home for?" Maybe it is, Marietta said to herself. Certainly it wasn't to listen to the same old complaints about import restrictions and the lack of spare parts and thieving servants and blight on the roses, constants of Settler life ever since she could remember. And with Daphne gone, there wasn't even anyone to laugh with. Katari was a very gloomy place. "And anyway, what do *you* know about delivering babies?" Virginia said. "Violet's had two already without you. She'll have ten more, no doubt, before she's finished. With the Africans they just pop out. Heavens, I've known plenty who've had them all by themselves. They bite the cord and tie the child on the back and go on with their digging. There was a woman on the farm at Rumuruti. She must've had five on her own!"

"Violet doesn't need me to deliver her baby," Marietta said. "She's got sisters-in-law, four in fact, for that. She wants to see me and I want to see her, that's all."

To keep the peace, Bruce offered the Toyota, but Marietta said no thanks. She didn't want the responsibility. She wouldn't take a taxi, either. "Those drivers are all maniacs. I don't fancy getting killed. We'll go slowly on the bus, Justin and I."

"So he's going with you!" Virginia exclaimed. "All arranged without so much as a by-your-leave! It's extraordinary, Marietta, how you take things for granted! How d'you know I don't need him in the shop?"

"He dislikes shops. I doubt his frowns encourage people to part with their shillings, so a couple of weeks without him couldn't do your business any harm."

"What's the matter with you? You're so down on everything! You're just about as antisocial as your uncle Peter! And here I'd been, expecting you to cheer him up. What a hope!"

"Peter's got a perfect right to be miserable for the rest of his life if he wants," Marietta retorted. "In his shoes, I'd be too. Playing backgammon with one's goddaughter is no cure for a broken heart!"

From the Kisumu bus depot Marietta saw the Baluga road threading up the escarpment. After Virginia left and married Bruce, Ian and Nancy MacDonald had carried on for Hamilton and Muir. But soon they'd tired of the Wayfarer, just as they'd soon tired of tea, and they'd set off for New Zealand to raise beef. An

Asian had been hired next, but when the toilet seats got broken, they stayed that way. Mr. Nag didn't have what it took. With so many European farmers gone, there was less and less call for up-country hotels anyway. The tourists wanted the Coast and the game parks. So Hamilton and Muir had cut their losses and sold out to Chief Mattias, who'd been waiting a decade to get his hands on those eleven acres of rich alluvial soil. He'd moved three wives into the hotel and planted coffee.

They must have cut down the dogwoods where we used to play at weddings, Marietta thought. But she wouldn't go back there, ever. She couldn't bear to see it as it would be now, coffee bushes in regular, weeded rows.

"Although you don't seem interested in anything in Kenya any-more," Virginia had said, "I saved this clipping for you. They got the old boy, just as I thought they would." Although it could not be proved conclusively either that he'd smuggled maize into Uganda in 1960 or that he'd tampered with ballots in the local elections of 1961, Mattias Ongaki was convicted on the twenty-eighth of May, 1965, of eight of the ten charges brought against him by the government. He would appeal, but his chances for reversal were said to be slim. There was a newspaper picture, too, of the chief outside the court in Kisumu, and behind his left shoulder was Catherine's round-eyed, anxious, cherishing face.

Justin said sharply, "What are you dreaming about? The bus leaves now," and he picked up her duffel bag stuffed with towels for the baby and shirts and dresses for Sampson and Rebecca. Marietta, stiff after the night and dizzy, too, climbed into the bus behind him. Eight hours later they reached the Galana ferry and found it beached on the opposite shore.

When the birds were wheeling before the sunset, the wind died and enough men awakened to work the winch and bring the ferry to the mainland. The crowd of people who'd been waiting lifted their bundles and boxes to their heads and went aboard.

On the far side Justin spotted one of Violet's brothers-in-law, who'd come to do business with a trader by the dock. Justin put Marietta in his charge. "Greet my daughter, Mari," Justin said, and set off alone to his own homestead. Only when her baby had been safely born could he visit his eldest daughter. He'd have to sacrifice a chicken if he came sooner.

217

Violet lived on the other side of the island, facing the open lake. The narrow path twisted between yellow-flowering hedgerows. Round every bend Marietta was greeted by children who shrieked and ran to join her as she passed. Soon there were thirty children thronging down the path behind her. "The wife of Daniel is very huge," the bravest of them told her. "You've come in time." He raced ahead to tell Violet of Marietta's arrival.

In a gap in the euphorbia hedge Violet stood shading her eyes. She held Rebecca on her hip and Sampson danced in front of her. She wore a flowered blouse and a length of cloth wrapped round her waist and up over her belly. Her bare head was shaved. When Sampson saw Marietta coming down the rise, he scampered away from his mother and ran to greet her.

"What a big boy you've become," Marietta cried, as she took his arms and swung him from the ground. "So heavy now that I can scarcely lift you!" She put the boy down again and they came hand in hand to Violet. Rebecca burst into tears and hid her face against her mother's breast.

"She's not a wild beast," Violet laughed. "She's my sister! So you came," she added in wonder. Her eyes were wide and her face was densely black. "Mari, my dear friend, you came home. I was afraid you'd gone forever!"

I know where I am now, Marietta thought. "How have I managed without you?" she said softly. She put her arm round Violet, bringing the shaved head to rest against her own. "So your little fellow waited for me. Tell him he may come out to greet me now!"

Violet's husband, Daniel, was working at the Coast. He had come for two weeks' leave in October, Violet said, white teeth flashing. She herself had no wish to live among Arabs, so Daniel had left her here at home. It was better by the lake with her husband's family, who now came flocking across the compound to greet Marietta.

"You've changed," said Violet's mother-in-law. "Did they do something to your skin in Europe? Did they bleach you? And you're so thin! Did they starve you there? Don't they treat strangers well in Europe, even though they're rich? Is it true that they marry only with grade cattle, never with zebu, as we do here?"

Marietta shook her head. "No, not with grade cattle either."

"Goats, then? Like Kikuyu? Ruba people don't accept goats."

"In Europe people marry freely, as they wish. They marry for love. Only love is important there. A man pays nothing for a wife."

The old lady snorted. "You know better than to give yourself like that. You'd never bear a man's children, cook his food, dig his garden, for nothing!" Indignantly she turned away and Marietta heard her shouting orders in the dusk. "Three chickens we shall kill and eat. Where are onions, tomatoes? What of flour? Clementina, bring me firewood!"

Violet led Marietta to her own hut. "You shall sleep here with me. Or these days," she teased, "must you have sheets and a mattress five inches thick?" She pulled out two chairs and they both sat down. Sampson had run off with his grandmother. Rebecca was asleep on her mother's back. Violet untied the cloth that held her and lifted the child round onto her lap. "So tell me, now that those chatterers have left us, what did you become in Europe?"

"Do you have to get your answer so soon, while my brain's still rattling from the journey? What did I become in Europe!" Marietta smiled. "Next to you, I feel like a small girl still."

Violet was stroking her daughter's head, then her neck, her shoulders. "The mother of Bilton was kind?" she asked softly.

"Yes, she was very kind. She asked me to stay with her in her house, but I'd never lived with anyone so old before. I thought, I'll have to be very careful and polite. I'd rather live in the hostel with girls of my own age. But she insisted I remain. I'm glad I did. She doesn't chatter the way most old people do. She talks very little unless she has something of importance to say."

"Yes," Violet said, "that other kind I know. Always you must nod your head, or else they scream, 'Are you deaf? Why aren't you showing me respect?'"

"Although she has lost the people she cared for most, she isn't bitter. She says, 'What's done is done. Now let us see what else will come. Perhaps the future will suit us as well or even better than the past.' When I'm old," Marietta added, "I hope I'm like her."

"And your teachers, were they kind also?"

"Not at all! They said, 'Whatever you learned before you came to us is useless. In three years, in five, in ten, perhaps, you'll know something!' It is hard to hear every day how ignorant you are. All of us felt worthless, but soon we became accustomed to their harshness and we began to learn. In ten years' time, you'll have five children, or six or even seven, while I, with luck, may have finished a little work of which I may be proud."

"I have your stories in my box, still, those you sent me when first I came here to my husband. And the pictures also. Such care you took with them! Now you no longer send them, Mari."

"I don't write them anymore. I scribbled those in the afternoons to make up for losing you. Didn't you notice" — Marietta smiled — "that they were all about you?"

"That girl you wrote of was Luo, Mari," Violet said sharply, "and I am Ruba. Ruba people don't marry Luos or eat with them either, if they can avoid doing so. That girl of yours was not at all like me!"

"I had to alter things a little. I was writing only stories, not the truth." Marietta laughed. "In the morning we'll get down your box and read some of them again. You'll see, that girl, Rose Achola as I called her, was really you!"

They were silent for a little while, then Violet said, "Did you find new friends in London?"

"None to replace you."

"I was thinking of young men."

"Some whom I like. None whom I love."

"That's good," Violet said. "I would not care to have you marry there."

"Why should I marry?"

"To get children, of course."

Marietta laughed. "You'll have enough for both of us!"

At cockcrow Violet got up from her bed and came into the kitchen, where Marietta lay on a mat by the fire. As Violet knelt to blow on the coals, Marietta stirred and opened her eyes.

"I should be doing that," she said sleepily. "I didn't come here for you to wait on me." She threw off her blanket and knelt beside Violet. "Oh, no," she groaned, and crept back to her sleeping mat. "Why should I get sick now?"

"So these days you've got a European's stomach," Violet teased. "Our food's no longer good for you."

By the time the sun rose, Marietta was feeling better. As they sat cradling cups of tea on their knees, Violet remarked, "This child will be born tomorrow, the twentieth of July. I'm not one of those old women who measure according to the moon. I follow that calendar hanging on my wall." The pains had started in the night, she said. "But the child is lazy. He comes like a snail."

"What will you do today?"

220

"What I did yesterday, and the day before. Is today the Sabbath, Mari? Rest if you like, but I have work to do."

After they'd swept out the hut they went to the garden to pick beans. Then they took the children and went to the lake to wash clothes. They knelt at the water's edge while the children played behind them on the beach. Pounding and scrubbing, Violet sang Swahili love songs she'd heard on the radio, and occasionally, when a pain came, she gasped, but she didn't stop scrubbing. They finished the clothes and waded into the water to wash themselves. Violet lathered her arms and neck and plunged down to rinse herself. As she rose again, water sluicing off her shoulders and her belly, Sampson said gravely, "Mamma, you are a hippo."

"Only for a few more hours!" Violet laughed.

They brought the wet clothes home and laid them out on the grass to dry. Later, when they'd slept a little under the shade tree, they went visiting. Women said to Violet that surely she would nurse the child soon, but Violet shook her head. "I have a long way yet to go," she said. "At the end of next month I will nurse my child."

"And there you are in labor!" Marietta exclaimed, once they were back in Violet's hut. "What a liar you are!"

"They know that," Violet said. "They're not blind. But should I count my chickens? If I told them, 'Yes, tomorrow you will see this child,' they'd say that I was crazy."

"You told *me* the truth."

"Are you Ruba?"

Marietta smiled wistfully. "I used to hope I'd be when I grew up."

Next morning Marietta vomited onto her mat. Afterwards, as she lay back, her hair clinging in tendrils round her face, Violet stood over her, hands on hips, and observed, "It's not a European's stomach that you have, but a European's child. Who is the father of this child?" she demanded. "One whom you liked but did not love?" Marietta didn't answer. "Should I believe this came like thistle seed upon the wind? Even Sampson knows better!" Violet pulled out a stool and sat down. She took Marietta's hand and held it against her cheek. "So this is what became of you in Europe! I thought it must be so when I first saw you on the path. As you were coming, I saw your breasts. They are no longer as they used to be, a girl's."

Marietta said grimly, "If my period is late, that's because of traveling, of leaving Europe and coming home. If my breasts are sore, that's because of the fever I had in Nairobi. If I vomit, that's because of the journey. That bus could make anyone vomit, even old men. I've never wanted to have children!" she burst out, and wrenched her hand away from Violet. She sat up. A chill breeze came off the lake and under the plank door. She shivered. Violet reached for the blanket and draped it over her shoulders. "Hold it close," she murmured. "You aren't well."

By the gray coals of last night's fire, Marietta rocked back and forth. "How can you be kind," she whispered, "to someone who hates her own child?"

"But this one is only just beginning. You have many months in which to know him. When he's born, you'll love him. How could it be otherwise?"

Marietta continued rocking. "I'll hide from him; he'll look at me, at my hands, my hair, my face. He'll look into my eyes and see I've run away!"

"I don't understand you," Violet said. She knelt and blew on the coals, and added kindling, twig by twig, until the fire was up. She poured water from a tall earthenware pot by the door into her kettle and put it on the fire for their morning tea. Then she sat down.

"My grandmother Bosibori knows about these things," she said quietly. "If that's what you want, she will help you. She'll give you medicine that will hurt you. I've seen how it hurts! A girl came once when I was there at home. She was with child by her cousin, but Ruba people do not permit marriage between cousins. Her child would have been an outcast, unclean, defiled. She had to rid herself of it even if she died in doing so. Although she knew it was a sin to do so, my grandmother helped that girl because it would have been an even greater sin to allow such a child to be born. At first the girl was very ill, but later she recovered and went to her home and married in time, but I heard she never could have children. Is that what you want also?"

The kettle boiled and Violet made the tea. In Marietta's cup she put four spoonfuls of sugar. "Drink this," she said. "Let it bring you to your senses!"

At noon Violet sent Marietta to fetch her mother-in-law, Lucia. The old lady had been drinking beer for several hours while she shelled beans in her front yard. When Marietta told her the news she cleared her throat loudly and spat in the dust. "Wait, you will escort me."

222

She was slow, the old woman. She poured her beans into a basket, which she put away into the rafters. Then she searched for a bandanna to cover her gray hair. One that she pulled out from her box was rejected, then another. She was showing Marietta how much her son Daniel esteemed her, since all these head cloths were his gifts. The third she took out, smoothed against her hip, folded, and tied about her head. Then she went looking for her chickens.

"Should the rats take them?" she asked rhetorically. "This child may idle in the mother's womb. Should my chickens, then, be left to the rats?" She took a stick to beat the grass. "*Ero, ero, ero.*" Marietta joined her and two, three, five lean chickens pelted out of the grass. The old woman waved her arms, corralling them into her hut.

She saw fit, now, to come. She swooped ahead of Marietta, clapping her hands, flapping her elbows, dancing across the compound, her headtie knocked crooked so that the knot hung down over one eye. "The seed became a plant," she cried, "the plant bore fruit, the fruit is ready to be plucked." Her daughters-in-law on the beach and in their gardens heard her trilling and left their work to come with her to Violet's hut.

Violet had set water to heat on the fire and taken off her clothes. She was walking up and down, wrapped in a blanket, while her children sat wide-eyed against the wall. "Go with Mari," Violet said. "She will take you to your baba's house and draw pictures for you. By suppertime you'll have a little stranger to play with. But he is shy; he will not dare to come if you two stay and watch for him. Mari will bring you back to greet him soon."

Violet gave birth to a daughter an hour before sunset. Lucia, who had been sending off for condensed-milk cans of beer at intervals throughout the afternoon, sang a praise song in the living room, while in the kitchen her two eldest daughters-in-law held Violet's arms and the two younger ones her legs. Clementina, who had married the Christmas before Violet, received the baby as she slithered out onto the earthen floor. She slapped the child, who opened her mouth and screamed.

"More hands to help you," Lucia cried as she came dancing in. "More cattle for your sons to marry with!"

Violet lay back on a pile of blankets while her sisters-in-law washed her daughter and cleaned up the afterbirth. But in a few moments she sat up and took her baby in her arms. To Clementina she said, "Fetch my children, will you? And my friend."

223

Later, after the women had gone back to their own huts, Marietta said to Violet, "All day I've been thinking about what you said to me this morning. I shan't go to Bosibori."

"Ah, you have come to your senses."

"My child isn't tainted like the one you spoke about. He'll be born, he'll be loved, he'll grow up. He'll have sons of his own."

"So you will marry his father."

"No, not that. Europeans marry for love, Violet, and I *am* European, not Ruba," she said sadly, "as once I thought I was. And I don't love his father. In fact, I scarcely know him."

"Did I know Daniel when I married him? Did that prevent my loving him later?"

"It's not the same," Marietta said miserably. "I will go back to Europe and my child will be born there and I shall give him to a married woman, one who cannot bear children of her own. In Europe, Violet, girls do make arrangements of that sort. It's quite common. Bilton's mother will help me. Oh yes, no doubt she will think very harshly of me, but she will help me all the same. It's for the best. I couldn't manage on my own." She stopped. Of course her mother had managed. Presented with the choice, husband or child, Virginia had chosen her child, and managed. But she hadn't been alone, not really. She'd always had Justin from that day to this. But in London she, Marietta, would have no one, and she hadn't the courage for that.

Violet lay by the hearth with her baby asleep on her breast. Her eyes glinted in the firelight. "Is this the Mari I have loved, as my sister, as my own life? No, this must be some other creature" — her voice rose — "one who gabbles nonsense! Your father charged Justin with your care, Mari. Justin could have refused that responsibility. Any year he could have come back to Galana and forgotten you, but he did not. He has loved you as his own child, Mari, that is true, but before loving you he already had a purpose. And that was to honor your father, until such time as you could honor him yourself by bearing children in his memory so that he might not vanish entirely from this earth! Did Justin ever think that when you became a woman you would turn from us, from what we have taught and you have learned, and hurry off to please yourself?" She went on harshly, "If you carry a child in your womb, a treasure moving, growing, if you bear this pain, the tearing, all I have borne today, and after that you give him to another woman so that you

224

may continue playing with your paints and pencils as a little girl might play, then you are like one who burns her own house and lets her harvest spoil. You are unnatural, you're mad!"

On the long journey back from Galana, Marietta and Justin sat side by side virtually in silence. Next to the window Justin dozed and woke and stared at the head of the man in the seat in front and out at the plains and forests and mountains they passed through, but he scarcely looked at Marietta. When the bus stopped he bought her mineral water. "Here," he told her, "since Fanta upsets your stomach." He who'd watched her a whole childhood and later seen her body change when she came to adolescence, of course he noticed that her breasts were larger, her stomach not quite so flat as when she went away to London. He knew perfectly well she was going to have a baby, but respect and shame would prevent him from ever mentioning it. As for Marietta, she longed to take his hand and say, Don't pass judgment on me, Justin, not yet! But looking at the stern, sad profile, she felt her own shame, her own dread of being disrespectful.

And so they rode in silence to Nairobi, where they took another bus out to the Katari crossroads. From there they walked down the ridge to Bruce's house, and all the way Marietta was telling herself, like an incantation, It's up to me to make the decision, it isn't up to them! It isn't Justin or Violet's business, it's mine!

A Land-Rover stood on the gravel. "Your mother is still in her shop and the bwana is gone," Justin said. "Who is this stranger and what does he want? Karanja should have told him to come back another day."

Barking furiously, Bruce's Rhodesian ridgeback leapt out from the boys' quarters, over the lawn, past roses in full bloom. He dashed up to Marietta. "It's only us, Jacko," she said. "We're not thieves." Round the corner of the house Karanja hurried in his white uniform.

"Welcome," he cried. "How was your safari? Do they have rain in Rubaland? There's none here. The wells are almost dry. There's someone here to see you, Mari," he added. "I told him you were in Nyanza, but he wouldn't go away."

Marietta went through the garden to the veranda, out of the sun. Clematis was growing furiously up the pillars — white and purple and a pink one, too. Virginia had had the cutting from Daphne just before she'd taken off. Marietta stopped on the threshold to adjust her eyes to the shadow. I'm not ready, she thought, but there's no more time. It's run out.

"So you came back after all!" Jonathan's face shone in the dim afternoon room. He looks like a knight in a picture book, trusting in his quest, Marietta thought. "I drove in last night from Isiolo. Four weeks I've been up there, counting the days, and when finally I'm finished and everyone's dropped off and accounted for, I come out here and your houseboy says you're gone to Galana to deliver a baby. Can that be true?"

"More or less."

"So I thought, having waited so long and come so far, I'm not budging until I've talked to your mother. Are you glad to see me?"

"Of course."

"I'm never sure with you. Maybe," he added lightly, "I'm doomed to unrequited love."

"I *am* glad to see you," Marietta cried. She lifted his hand and kissed the palm. "I've been in a muddle, that's all."

"I haven't done anything straight myself, these last few days," Jonathan said with a grin.

"Did Karanja give you a drink?"

"I don't want a drink. That's not what I came for. I just want you."

"I've got to talk to you, Jonathan."

"What are you doing now?"

"Not here. Somewhere else. My mother and Bruce will be home in an hour."

"We'll go to the hills, then, and never come back!"

As they drove towards the hills, they passed women with hoes on their heads coming from the fields, young men with cattle, children coming from the power mill, all hurrying home for the evening meal. They don't have to make choices, Marietta thought. They're links in a chain, and the obligation to continue it is never questioned.

Soon the farms stopped and they came to open country. In front ranged the seven hills, guarding the Highlands against the barbarians of the Rift. It had rained recently and the track was slippery. The vehicle slid back, steadied, and climbed on. Below them the country fell away green, less green, and then brown, to the shining

226

surface of Lake Magadi. They reached the top, and Jonathan turned off the engine. "People have been murdered up here, you know. We won't stay after sunset. I'd rather live for love than die for it." He slipped his arm behind Marietta's shoulders.

"I've got something to tell you, Jonathan," she said.

'You've joined the Flying Doctors. You've fallen in love with another man."

"I'm pregnant," she said.

"How clever of us!" He laughed and kissed her. "We're going to have a son to inherit Olgolulu."

"You're crazy, Jonathan!"

"Crazy? Why? Olgolulu's a magnificent place. I'm taking you there tomorrow, then you'll see it for yourself."

"But this child's never going to see Olgolulu. I'm going back to England. I'll have it there and then I'll get it adopted."

"Christ, what a monster you are!"

"Monster?"

"Yes, *monster!* I happen to love you. Baby or not, I want to marry you."

Marietta shook her head. "I'll be nineteen the day after tomorrow. Can you remember being nineteen? Could you have married anyone then?"

"If I'd known you then, I might have."

"You didn't want to go out and see the world?"

"Not bloody likely! I'd been out in it for too long already. I couldn't wait to get home!"

Marietta's shoulders drooped. "I couldn't be anyone's mother. Don't you see?"

"I don't, as a matter of fact. But I do see that you don't love me, and therefore, obviously, you don't want my child. Well," he said evenly, "I do. If you're looking for someone to adopt him, how about me?"

Marietta covered her face with her hands. "Violet said I was unnatural. You call me a monster."

"Violet?"

"My friend at Galana."

"I have an ally, then!"

"Oh, yes. And you'll have many more, I expect. I'm the one who won't have allies."

"You don't seem to need any," Jonathan said bitterly. "Of course,

I can't claim you misled me. Last September in Wiltshire at eight in the morning you said you meant to be a painter. I'm not deaf. I heard you perfectly. Mind all made up. Eyes on the future, not on the past. That you'd swept under the rug. 'Africa? Where's that?' But this girl is for me, I told myself, whatever she says, and I came chasing back six thousand miles. And what did I hear that time? 'Life drawing's more exciting than you are, Mr. Sudbury. Pity you came so far out of your way!' But I'm like a ferret, Marietta. Once I take hold, I won't let go. So back I came and it looked like I was getting somewhere: you consented to sleep with me. Proposed it, no less, and seemed to savor the experience. In fact, you volunteered just before you ran off to anatomy that you'd been happier those past few days than you ever remembered. You held my face between your hands and said it. You're no liar, Marietta. You don't fabricate or flatter. Truth's your specialty. I saw that at the beginning. No, I'm the one at fault, not you. I'm not a strictly literal type, you see. A straw in the wind I tend to turn into a tree. 'I've been happier with you than I've ever been before' was merely a statement of fact. It wasn't a promise. It didn't lay claims on the future. Only I'd fallen so goddamned in love with you, I thought it did! But you were just getting into your stride. You'd chalked up one good experience, expecting many more. You'll have a fast, happy life, Marietta, skating along on the surface, never going deep." Jonathan turned on the engine. "There's no point sitting here, is there? Let's go right down to Nairobi and call on Dr. Rajwani. She's a nice Indian lady who takes care of young women in your situation, young women who don't want to mess up their well-planned lives. If it's too late to catch her at her surgery, we'll find her at home. She lives along Highland Road. There's a big sign out in front of her house. You can't miss it."

"*Am* I monstrous?" Marietta stared miserably at her hands. "I need time to think."

"If that's all you need," Jonathan said as he turned off the engine again, "I'll give you plenty."

PART IV

1966

14

Lake Forest

Jonathan had warned Marietta, "Bunty Sanderson comes on strong, but after the initial rush she'll back off and give you air. She was my first client and mercifully a very indulgent one; in spite of my running out of petrol seventy-five miles from the nearest pump, she came back the next year and the next, and she's sent a good many of her friends my way as well. I think you'll like her. I do."

At Gate Twenty an athletic-looking woman in linen slacks waited at the front of the crowd to meet the New York plane. "Welcome to Chicago, both of you!" she cried. "Marietta, it's great to see you in the flesh at last! I was perfectly disgusted that I had to miss that last safari, and Roger's going on when he got back about Botticelli and madonnas only had me feeling worse. There I was in my hospital bed, having had my insides out, and all he talked about was you! By the way, he's been held up. Some meeting's going on too long. He's so disappointed not to be here. Don't you hate airports? Let's get out of here!"

Bunty came from Texas. She'd started young on quail and black-tailed deer, and shot a cougar in the High Sierras before she turned fifteen. This feat was noted in the *Southwestern Hunters' Yearbook* for 1934. Amazing, people said, the way Roger's come along since marrying her. Stodgy Rog, they used to call him, but no more. Last January, while Bunty had her uterus removed in St. Luke's Presbyterian, Roger had gone out to Kenya on his own.

At the curb a chauffeur waited. Marietta was first into the Cad-

231

illac, then Bunty. Jonathan got in last. "Hot, isn't it?" Bunty said. "That's Chicago for you in October, worse than Houston, even. We'll have the air conditioning on. Now tell me," she said, settling herself, "about your little boy. Charles Neville. Why not Jonathan junior?"

"My father's name was Charles," Marietta said.

"And who was Neville?"

"My stepfather. Not my mother's present husband. That's Bruce. Neville was the one before. He was killed in a plane crash the year before last."

The Cadillac edged through the rush-hour traffic. On either side and in front were huge trailer trucks. It was dark in the car. Like being caught in a ravine, with no hope of getting out. The pain in her chest and behind her eyes had dulled to an ache during the last two years. The grief that she had no words to describe or account for was apparently a permanent condition, except in fleeting instants in the dream. She never talked to Jonathan about Neville. She wouldn't have known how to begin, nor, worse, having started, how to stop.

The truck in front moved into another lane and suddenly there was light again. "I weaned Charlie a week ago today," she said suddenly.

"You nursed him? Well," Bunty said, amused, "I guess that's the way to go in Africa! I had all my five on bottles, thanks. I was far too vain to give them me." She glanced sideways. "Though you seem in pretty decent shape, I have to say. Of course, after five, things might be different."

"Any European who has five kids in Africa these days would have to be insane! Who knows what's going to happen to any of us." Marietta sat a little forward on the deep, soft seat and gazed at the autumn yards along the highway.

"Coming as visitors," Bunty said quickly, "being taken care of so well, we tend not to think about the future. Of course, it's quite different for you, being natives."

"But that's exactly what we aren't! We only like to think we are."

"Marietta and I disagree about this," Jonathan said. "It's almost our oldest argument."

In the last heat of the year the elms along the Sandersons' driveway shone. Asters and chrysanthemums filled the beds on either side of the front door.

232

"It's like Olgolulu," Jonathan exclaimed. "The same gray stone, the rather solemn look."

"Solemn!" Bunty laughed. "You should've seen it when I first came up. This place was like a tomb! No flowers. Just evergreens and ivy. A regular meatpacker's mausoleum. You're in the south wing, overlooking the lake. Lake Michigan isn't quite the Indian Ocean. No reef, not much of a beach, but it's the best we can do."

"Have a drink, won't you?" she said once they were inside. "While Ruby unpacks your things."

"I'll have Scotch, if I may," Jonathan said, but Marietta wanted a nap before the party.

Upstairs in the south wing, she removed her new shoes and lay down. In New York, Jonathan had urged, "Go on, buy yourself some clothes."

"But we've only got two days here and I want to look at paintings, not fritter my time away in shops."

"Don't girls have trousseaux anymore?"

"I'm not a girl. I'm a mother. Too late for trousseaux."

"Well, Charles would appreciate a pretty mother."

"Charlie takes me any way I come."

"Actually, I prefer you without any clothes at all. But if you're smashing in Chicago and St. Louis, your admirers will admire you even more. Secretly, mightn't that please you?"

So she'd spent her second precious morning going back and forth across Fifth Avenue. Invariably assistants said, "I love your accent. Where are you from?" And when she told them, they exclaimed, "Isn't it scary living with those Africans? You've had a lot of trouble over there." In the end she got wise and said she came from London. "I've a niece in London," the sleek assistant said. "You should know Marsham Road in Golders Green," but Marietta didn't. Filling three shopping bags by one o'clock she'd made off to the galleries on Fifty-seventh Street. Jonathan was lunching with a client in the Harvard Club. At five they were both due above the Park for cocktails. That left Marietta four hours for the galleries and a race through the Museum of Modern Art.

In Lake Forest while Marietta rested the maid hung up dresses and put underclothes away. Her hair was pinned in smooth, oiled sausages round her head. In the dusk she looked down. "Should I run a bath, ma'am?"

"No, thanks."

The woman left.

Marietta thought, At Olgolulu it's three in the morning, and Jerusha's taken Charlie into bed with her. Charlie, Charlie — her breasts still filled at daybreak and at dusk, although in North America dusk came shortly after breakfast, daybreak during dinner. But not for much longer, according to the book Virginia had brought her the month before she'd given birth. "You might find it helpful," she'd said. "I know I would have, if only Daphne'd thought to bring it. It's a miracle you survived, given all I didn't know about infants."

A week after weaning, so this book said, her breasts would dry up, and that would be that. She hadn't wanted to leave her red-haired son, the spitting image, her mother-in-law assured her, of James Sudbury, Broiler King. Apart from the eyes, which had immediately darkened to violet. "Well," Virginia had exclaimed, "where were you when this child was conceived? Not a trace of his mother anywhere!"

"But he may yet develop my character," Marietta had replied. "We'll have to wait and see."

And waiting and seeing was what she'd have been delighted to do indefinitely, if Jonathan hadn't insisted on her coming with him to America for a fortnight. "Charlie's had you long enough. It's my turn now," he'd said. And then he'd added, smiling, "I came first, don't forget. It's because of me you got him."

So Charlie and his ayah and Justin had moved out of the cottage at the bottom of the farm road and into the big house at the top and into the charge of Eleanor Sudbury, who believed in babies sleeping on their own, in separate rooms, down corridors. She'd had a Scottish nanny for Jonathan, passed on from the Ashfords up at Thomson's Falls. Jonathan hadn't been slept with ever, or even very near. But to Jerusha, setting Charlie off by himself behind bars was abject cruelty. She'd do things her way, with one ear cocked, so that if she heard Eleanor's slippers on the stone floors, quick as a whip she'd have Charlie back in his own bed, squalling. "He peed," she'd say, shrugging, back turned on Eleanor, "and so he cries."

Charlie. He'd inextricably compounded the original dilemma: to stay or to leave and start again, under a pale sky, suitable for white people. You don't want this child, this man, this continent, a voice

234

in her head had urged in August just a year ago. You're monstrous, then. Unnatural, mad, another voice had answered. Both voices at her ceaselessly, awake and in her dreams.

The day after her return from Galana she'd gone, as bidden, up to Olgolulu, built to last a thousand years. It crouched above a lake rimmed with the pinks of water birds, a huge sentry guarding the Rift. Jonathan explained to Marietta that Tresham, where his father had grown up, had narrow, niggardly windows designed for defense against the crossbows of the Wars of the Roses. Edmund, wanting something just as massive in Africa, but lighter, had chosen an Elizabethan house, with wide banks of windows facing the sunrise. "He's not by nature what you'd call poetic, my father," Jonathan said, "but about those windows, when I was a kid and he'd just built them, he waxed positively lyrical!" The house was skirted by Eleanor's garden, which after the long rains stretched orange and scarlet, purple and pink to the east and south, and beyond them were farm buildings and two long rows of tin-roofed stone cottages for the laborers. Edmund Sudbury, sun-bleached, light like wheat, the skin of his face and his forearms broken by ten thousand tiny lines from forty years of equatorial elements, walked Marietta up the hillside at a great rate. At the forest's edge he gave a history of his struggles against blight and pestilence, then marched her down again into the library, crammed with scientific journals, shelf on shelf. Shyly, just before lunch, he showed her reprints of his own articles. After lunch Eleanor took her round the garden, shrub by shrub, and pointed out the six roses that she'd bred herself.

"They talked your ear off, didn't they?" Jonathan said afterwards. "If you'd been out from England, they'd hardly have had a word to say."

"They're awesome," Marietta exclaimed. "So are you. You're all so utterly determined!"

"Yes, thank God!" In the barns, with a ragged line of laborers' children straggling out behind him, Jonathan knelt, hand on heart. "I offer you the risk of turbulence, an uncertain livelihood, humor, and much cherishing."

"You're so extravagant!" she cried, and took him by the shoulders, raising him from the straw so that the children giggled, crowded in behind them, big babies clasped on little hips. He made so many promises that he'd keep, given the chance; she

235

ought to be falling in love with him, but she didn't believe she could ever fall in love with anyone.

"Extravagant, awesome. Such epithets!" But Jonathan didn't seem in the least bit hurt. To him, he told her, she made the difference between dark and light. She was skeptical. Could she be so important? Had she ever mattered that much to anyone before? Violet would say, Not to the living, but most certainly to the dead, for we are even more beholden to the dead than to the living, Mari.

All through the month of August, whenever she was with her mother, at dinner, in the garden, on drives into town, Marietta was always on the verge of asking, Were you beholden? Is that why you chose to have me, because assuaging the despair of your husband had to come second to providing your parents with the hope of a future? But she never did ask; she dreaded her mother's mockery, her denial of any such bush notions, though the truth might be that she believed them utterly and had lived her life according to them.

On the last day of the month, as Jonathan and Marietta were bumping down the Fort Hare road after they'd been up to Meru to see a man who had some tents to sell, Marietta said softly, "You win," at which Jonathan swerved and came to a halt under a thorn tree, and Kamau and the cook and three trackers spilled out of the back of the lorry.

"No petrol?" Kamau peered in at Jonathan. "There's a jerry can behind."

"Scram," Jonathan exploded in Kikuyu, "hop back up!" In English, laughing, he said, "Why am I so honored?"

"You're so charming. Could I possibly resist you?" she said, laughing back.

"Epithets again." His shoulders drooped.

"Jonathan, dearest Jonathan, you make things all right."

"For who?"

"For me."

"Should I take it that your plans have changed?"

"I shan't be on that plane next Saturday. I'm staying. Yes, my plans have changed. I'll marry you. That is, if you still want me to."

Kamau was at the window again. "No water, is it? Shall I open up the front to look?"

"Plenty of water. Plenty of petrol. Always poking in your nose, Kamau. For Christ's sake, hop back up and stay there this time!"

They drove on down to Katari to tell Virginia, back from her shop after a good day. Bruce's prediction had been correct. Kenya was safe, Kenya was a friend of the West, and Kenya was ripe for development. A new breed of whites was trickling in; soon there'd be a flood, all needing sofas and carpets and curtains and chairs for their patios.

"Oh, Lord, I'd better have a gin and tonic," Virginia exclaimed. "Hadn't you as well?" Jonathan and Marietta shook their heads. Drink in hand, Virginia turned to face Marietta. "You were going to be the greatest female painter of the century. You had your mind made up."

"I'm going to have a baby instead," said Marietta distinctly, three steps in front of Jonathan. "And Jonathan's responsible."

Virginia sat too quickly, spilling her gin. "Well, I never did! But how could he be," she added, frowning, "living on a different continent?"

"I was over at Whitsun," Jonathan said. "Yes, I'm responsible, I'm delighted to say. I'll take good care of your daughter."

"I thought you'd gone for good, Etta," Virginia said, "apart from duty visits to your poor old mum. Now you're back, all three of you." She laughed suddenly. "I must say, I'm delighted, too!"

Jonathan had to go into town. When he'd driven off, Virginia asked, "Are you in love with him?"

"He loves me."

"That I can see! But that's not what I asked." Virginia shook her head sadly. "You're taking a big risk, Etta. You don't have to go through with this. It's not too late to change your mind."

"You're a fine one to talk!" Marietta flared. "When were you ever sure beforehand about marriages? You weren't even sure about Bruce!"

"He's so young," Virginia persisted.

"What about *me*?"

"You, young? Not like he is, no. You never have been." Then, after a moment, "He so wants to take care of you, just like Neville did."

Was that it? A year before, she'd set out to see the world and render it. Now she was giving it up. For the sake of the child, for the sake of the dead. But mightn't it be for her own sake, too, because at bottom she hadn't been up to having an adventure on her own? She thought this as she wrote the necessary letters to Lady

Bilton, Aunt Sophia, the Slade. Lady Bilton cabled, "Amazed, good luck, I'll miss you, letter following, all love." A statement arrived from the Slade: Marietta Hamilton owed fifty-three pounds ten. "Students who withdraw after the first of August are subject to . . . Immediate remittance would be appreciated." Aunt Sophia sent three shell-stitched silk nightdresses, airmail.

After breakfast on the morning of the wedding, when Bruce was in his study on the telephone and Virginia in the kitchen finding fault with Karanja's cold fish soup, Marietta took a bottle of vodka from the drawing room and went upstairs. She shut her bedroom door and filled the tooth mug from the sink with vodka. She drank, shivered, drank some more, and carried the rest to the dressing table. There Justin found her when he brought in her bouquet of gardenias. He picked up the mug and sniffed it.

"*Changaa,*" he said, grimacing. "Why?"

"Leave me alone."

Justin took the mug to the sink and poured the vodka out.

"Where's the bottle?"

Marietta didn't reply. He spotted it, though, behind the curtain on the windowsill.

"I shall return this to its place," he said softly. Then, with one gnarled hand on her shoulder, he told her, "Mari, you're going to a good man."

Marietta looked up at him, at the deep furrows in his forehead and the slightly bloodshot eyes. "Yes," she cried, "he's a good man, and his parents are good, and you and Violet, my mother, Bruce. And all you good people want the best for me. What's best, Justin? *You* think you know, but I know I don't."

"Change your clothes now, it's time." Justin turned away. At the door he stopped again. "When she went to her husband, did Violet's fears last long?"

So Marietta put on the cream silk dress made in haste and drove with Bruce and Virginia under scudding midday clouds to Katari Parish Church. Peter Dawson waited to give her away. "I'd rather have Peter do it," she'd told her mother. "Bruce is so new by comparison. Do you think he'll mind?" Why should he, though? she'd thought. I've given myself away already, haven't I? It's because of that that I'm here.

At the church door Peter whispered, "Daphne's sick of America. She's coming home," and he sped off up the aisle with Marietta on his arm. He whipped her past Edmund and Eleanor Sudbury in the front pew, reassured of their son's good sense by his choice, in the wake of Victoria, of a Kenya girl, and on up the chancel steps to Jonathan. At lunch on the veranda at Olduvai Road, Peter's speech started out about Jonathan and Marietta, but soon it turned to himself and Daphne, and what she'd looked like on *their* wedding day, "a hundred years ago, before this young lady had even been thought of!"

Afterwards Jonathan and Marietta would have three days in a borrowed house at Tigoni; then Tiny Templeton was coming in from Dallas for his third time out with Jonathan. "What are you waiting for?" Jonathan called from the front door to Marietta on the evening lawn at Tigoni.

She pointed south and then north. "The light is right. You can see both of them, Mount Kenya and Kilimanjaro."

"That's auspicious, surely," he said, laughing, as he came down again to take her hand. "Let's go in now." In the house he said, "I'm so happy. You've made me so happy!"

"I'm so terrified!" She searched his face. "Jonathan, tell me, what have we done?"

"Whatever it is, it doesn't terrify me at all!" Then he swung her up and carried her off to a great big bed. In the firelight he smiled joyfully.

It's as if long ago he made a fortune, Marietta thought. He hoarded it, he never used a penny of it, and now he's free to spend it lavishly in the promised land. He knew the secret of how to get in. But I don't know the secret. I'll never know it.

His head between her breasts, he said, "The flame tree didn't flower in vain. Though I'd almost given up hope, the rains came after all, the earth turned green, and I found you on it. Bright and light as you are, you're real. You're not going to vanish."

She went with Jonathan and Tiny Templeton into Tanzania and was gone three weeks. When Tiny left an English couple came, and she went out with them as well. After that safari, Eleanor Sudbury said, "That's enough. You'd be mad to go again. You could come to dreadful harm out there in the bush."

"I'll risk it," Marietta told her. "Once the baby's born Jonathan's life won't change, he'll still go off for weeks on end, but *my* life will be completely different. I'll be staying here most of the time, so now I want to be with Jonathan as much as I possibly can," she finished doggedly, hands clasped across her stomach.

Eleanor, touched by her daughter-in-law's devotion, conceded,

239

"Well, so long as Justin's with you." For Justin hadn't retired to Galana after all. "I shall go with you to your husband's home. I always promised so," he'd said. But once there he hadn't taken easily to the Olgolulu servants. He was happy to be off with Marietta, jolting through January wastelands, against the better judgment of Dr. Bryce and her mother-in-law. Even her mother objected. Within reason, Virginia believed in people having their own way, but it wasn't reasonable in one's eighth month to go with Roger Sanderson into the Sudan. "She's tough, she's a Kenya girl. Let her go," Jonathan had said, and so she'd gone.

But it was terror rather than devotion that kept this young wife with her new husband, terror of the child inching its way closer to life. The child would be a daughter — this Marietta never doubted. Fair, blue-eyed. A replica of Virginia and herself, insisting on the same distances. Night after night in their tent she'd whisper, "I'll be frozen. I shan't be able to touch her!" And Jonathan would hold her in his arms and tell her, "You're going to be fine and so is he." She didn't believe him, not one word, but she stayed with him anyway — she couldn't have contained her dread alone.

In March, a week after returning from safari in the Northwest Frontier District, she'd had Charles without any problem in the Eldonia hospital, and she, who thought she could never fall in love, had fallen in love with his pink face, his pink fists, the rash over the bridge of his nose. As he gazed at his infant son and heir, Jonathan crowed with delight, "How clever we are, and you especially!" He laughed. "You with your fear of motherhood! The moment I set eyes on you I knew you'd make a marvelous mother."

"Liar! You knew nothing of the sort," Marietta said, but she laughed too.

"I was so afraid," she wrote to Violet a few hours after the delivery, "but you were right, there wasn't any need to be. I'm calling him Charles Neville, in the Ruba way, after those who are dead."

Virginia had her reservations. "Neville, maybe, but does it have to be Charles? If you insist on an ancestor, why not Philip? Philip Sudbury was worth memorializing."

Marietta stuck to her guns. She'd chosen those two names with awe, pity, sorrow, love, and hope that, being so honored, the dead might rest in peace and allow her also to live peacefully. But this she didn't explain to her mother. Instead she told Virginia, "Philip Sudbury has seven great-grandchildren already. Charles Hamilton

240

and Neville Bilton have no descendants whatsoever, except my son."

The Sudburys, thrilled with a male heir, were agreeable to whatever names his mother fancied. Jonathan said, "You can call him Maximillian if you want."

"Or even Basil," Edmund added, laughing.

Justin, who'd spent the night of her labor next to Jonathan on a bench in the Eldonia hospital, head down, elbows on his knees, cracking his knuckles hour after hour, came the following day to visit her. He stood by the bed, speechless with delight, patting her hand. He smiled so widely that his mouth almost cut his face in two. He'd done what he'd promised her father he'd do, he'd fulfilled his obligation. When Dr. Bryce let Marietta leave the hospital she asked Justin to hold the baby. "The road's so dreadful. So many potholes. He'll be more comfortable and safer with you."

And that's where Charlie was, with Justin, an ocean and two continents away, while she, Marietta, was trying to nap before the Sandersons' buffet supper for ninety of their closest friends. A great deal of money was made in Chicago and a great deal was spent on French impressionists and yachts and villas in Mexico; why not on African safaris, too? After cocktails and a buffet supper, there'd be dancing in the library. "Too late in the year to dance outside. The dew's so heavy in October. It gets you in the joints," Bunty said.

In the south wing, overlooking the lake, glinting orange and black under an early moon, Jonathan stood in front of the looking glass. "The public wants an English lord. In dark green velvet I give them a reasonable facsimile, don't you think?"

"I once saw Lord Delamere at the races. Apart from him, I don't know any lords," Marietta replied. Her dress was white chiffon. "You're young," the assistant had urged in Saks. "You can handle it. You've got to be young to wear white in the fall."

"You're well-cast, too," Jonathan said. "I'd take you for a lady any day."

"You despise them so!"

"Who?"

"The Sandersons. Those people in New York."

"No, not them, but I do despise *myself* in certain situations."

Downstairs Marietta said she didn't want a drink quite yet. Jonathan asked for Scotch again. Bunty slipped her arm through his. "I'm a sucker for dancing, will you dance with me, Jonathan, when the moment comes?" Bunty wore flowing pajamas and pearls practically the size of plovers' eggs; Roger, black tie and flowered slippers. A little color at his feet, Bunty had decided. Roger didn't care for petit point. There'd been nothing the matter with his old patent shoes, and these things pinched his toes. But the thought of January in Zaire, going after bongo, soothed him.

"What a sight you are," he said gallantly to Marietta. "Who do I prefer, the madonna or the fairy princess? Or can I have both?"

The Sandersons' friends began to arrive. The men stared at Marietta and moved on. The women tended to linger. They asked about primitive life in the wilds. "But it's not the wilds anymore," Marietta would reply. "And you'd hardly call Olgolulu primitive. There's a baronial hall, a library as big as this one." The piano was already being played; no dancing yet, though. "There's a piano at Olgolulu, too. It came to Eldonia on the train in 1925 and the rest of the way by bullock cart. They'd removed its legs in London and sent them in a separate crate. Which arrived years afterwards, so I'm told. The piano's horrible to play and worse to listen to. The tuner only comes up every second year."

"And what do you do?" they asked. "You surely have time on your hands with all those servants!"

"I used to paint. Now that my son's bigger, I'll be getting back to it. I'm thinking of doing a children's book."

"Were you trained?"

"I'd just begun and then I married."

"Dropped out?" A woman nodded disapprovingly. "My daughter wanted to, when she was twenty. I told her, 'That Mount Holyoke diploma's nothing to be sneezed at. What if you're widowed, divorced, abandoned? Your father won't support you your whole life!' So she stuck it out, graduated, and married a different boy. I never cared for the first one."

"Painting?" said another woman, in turquoise brocade. "You should be in politics! The Kenya experiment can't succeed if the whites withdraw from the political process. It's immoral," she went on grimly, "to retreat to the back and make money. You should actively build!"

"Tell me, how do *you* do it?" Marietta said evenly.

"What?"

242

"Build."

"Dorothy's secretary of the Illinois chapter of the ADA. She's frighteningly advanced!" someone said.

"By the way," Marietta said, looking her attacker in the eye, "have you spent much time in Africa?"

"Never been there, though I do intend to go. One's so busy. Hard to get away."

Bunty edged over. "Is Dorothy bullying you? You mustn't let her. She has exacting notions about how the world should be. I'm flattered you made time to come this evening, Dorothy, my dear. She usually spends Saturdays marching," Bunty explained to Marietta. "We went to school together. She campaigned for Jews in those days, as there still weren't any blacks. They came much later. To Smith, I mean."

"Where's the lavatory?" Marietta said.

"In the front hall. Two doors on the left. Shall I show you?"

"I can find my own way, thanks." Marietta turned to Dorothy. "I'm so glad to have had the chance to hear your views. I'm not always brave enough to be moral. How I wish I were!"

She went through the hall and the dining room, where caterers were setting out the supper. Wild boars stared ferociously, whole salmons, an enormous ham. A chef was sharpening his carving knife. She went through French doors onto a terrace, out of the light, down steps, and onto the grass. Instantly her shoes were soaked, but the air was warm. She held up her long skirts and walked away under the catalpas and the elms. At the edge of the lawn she found a bench, screened from the house by a huge tree. Below was a narrow strip of sand under the moon, and then the water stretching black and orange to a lighter sky. It's five o'clock at Olgolulu now, she thought. Not dawn quite, although the moon has set. You wouldn't see that other lake yet, despite the cocks crowing and the smell of wood smoke from early fires. At Olgolulu. Why not "at home"? Because it wasn't *her* home; she wasn't a Sudbury. She wondered, Will Charlie be like them, requiring a particular setting, a world built to his own specifications? Or will he be like me?

A man came over the grass. He passed twenty yards away from Marietta, and at the edge of the lawn he stopped, outlined against the glinting water. Then he turned back towards the house again and Marietta saw that he was black; at that same instant he saw her, too, her white dress spread across the bench under the great catalpa tree.

"Good evening," he said. "Am I disturbing you? I hadn't realized anyone was here."

"You're not disturbing me. I was looking at the moon over the water."

He came closer. "I live near this lake, but down where I am, I'd be murdered if I sat and looked at it." He wore horn-rimmed glasses and a lightweight suit. He wasn't American. Almost, but not quite.

"It's very dangerous there?"

"On the South Side of Chicago there are murderers everywhere! Didn't you know that?"

"I only arrived this afternoon. I know nothing about this city, apart, of course, from Al Capone."

He smiled. "The first time I came here I expected to find him waiting for me with a gun. When I didn't see him, I was just a little disappointed."

"Won't you sit down?"

"No, thanks," he said easily. "I've been sitting all day long in the laboratory. What special occasion is this? Look at you, in your beautiful dress! The friends I came with never told me they were coming to a ball!"

"Mrs. Sanderson has guests from abroad and this party's in their honor."

"Mrs. Sanderson? Oh, yes, when I arrived she took my hand and said, 'I've so many questions to ask you! But now I have to see about the food,' and off she ran." He laughed. "So I ran off, too. It's not every day I have the chance to walk on grass, under trees, in the dark in safety and alone."

"If that's what you want, there's plenty of room for us both. Look," she said, pointing along the edge of the lawn. "See that willow tree? If you stood under it, you wouldn't notice me. You could look at the lake in peace."

He turned towards the water. After a moment he said softly, "When I was a boy I lived near a lake. It was some miles off, but on bright nights you saw the moon, like this, reflected in it."

"I've lived on lakes, too," she said. "Where was yours?"

"In Africa."

"But you speak like an American!"

244

"That's because I've been here many years."

"Where did you come from originally?"

"From Kenya. I was born in the Great Rift Valley."

"Is that so!" She wanted to declare herself, to claim kinship with him, coming from the same distant corner of the earth. But of course he'd deny kinship. What was she to him? A woman, with breasts and buttocks, to be appraised on account of them, and a European Settler. Could a young man who remembered Settlers in the old Kenya, but had never seen them powerless in the new, look at her with anything other than contempt? And so, not wanting to create a gulf instantly between herself and him, she said, "Did you leave a large family at home?"

"All Africans have large families," he said, smiling. "And when I get back they'll all want help. School fees, a roof over their heads, three meals a day. No, not lunch, but breakfast and their dinner."

"Why go back, then? You may get eaten alive!"

"But I don't belong here," he said gravely. "I'll leave as soon as my research is finished. In June, if my parasites die as they're supposed to. If they live, then I've miscalculated, and I'll have to do the experiment again. But one day soon I'll finish, and then I'll go home."

"How many years is it since you left?"

"Eleven."

"A lot must have changed."

"I'm used to changes." After a moment he said, "When I was young, my parents moved very often. My father was a mechanic and he went from farm to farm. There was a certain place in the reserves which he called home, but we only went there once. I remember a dog with a narrow black face and an old woman without any teeth. But a dog and a toothless old woman don't amount to a home."

"We were like that, too, my mother and I," Marietta said eagerly. "We also went from place to place. We were endlessly packing and unpacking. We lived in hotels. My mother managed them, you see." She added, "Your parents will be so happy to have you back after all these years!"

"My parents are dead," he said harshly. "They died a long time ago. The only ones left are relatives I scarcely remember." For some minutes he was silent. Perhaps he's forgotten me, Marietta thought, but then he went on in a quite different tone, "My father could repair anything with parts that moved. Generators, tractors, lorries, grandfather clocks. 'He's a genius,' the Europeans used to say. 'And to think his grandparents still lived in trees!' Oh, yes, they admired him very much. They were always scheming to get him to come to work for them. They'd come looking for him in the fields and say, 'I'll give you ten shillings more a month. What do you think of twenty, and a house with an iron roof?' If I was there they'd reach deep into their pockets" — he demonstrated — "as if they had some treasure and bring out sweets for me. But one particular farm had a milking machine. It was famous. Everyone had heard about it, and that's where my father wanted to work. As he went by that farm on the bus he'd look up at the sheds and imagine that machine, taking it apart, putting it together again; and eventually he got his wish: the European who owned it offered him thirty shillings more each month and my school fees, so we moved again." He added, "If I've ever had a home at all, it was that place. It overlooked a lake, and beyond that were the mountains. It was a more beautiful lake than this one, flat like a plate to the sky."

Marietta wondered, Who would have had such a machine twenty years ago? The Wickendens at Nyanga? She opened her mouth to ask and shut it again. You know of them? he would have said, and turned cold at her deception.

"May I sit down now?"

She brought her skirt close, making room for him beside her, one arm draped along the back of the bench. "Go on with your story, will you please?"

He smiled. "I have so many. Which particular one do you want to hear?"

"Tell me about the farm that looked across the lake to the mountains."

"The farm or the farmer?" He chuckled. "Both were remarkable. Every day of my life I'd heard Europeans shouting, 'Hey, you, come here, go there, watch out!' But this European was different. Diseases interested him more than anything in life! Fungus, mold, insects of all sorts. His own true enemies, he called them. He was a fanatic! He was always reading and trying out ideas. 'I believe I've discovered the secret,' he'd say. 'We'll get those little buggers! We'll double our yield in two years' time, we'll triple it!' He had a son, about my age, whom he wanted to teach what he'd learned, but that boy's mind was on other things, and anyway, he was off at

246

school in England for most of the year. But I was always there, and for some reason, who knows why, it was insects that intrigued me, not those machines that my father loved so dearly. Little by little this European and I became friends, and little by little he taught me much of what he knew. Not everything, of course; I was only a kid, ten, twelve, fourteen at the most, but he had a gift, that man, for explaining difficult ideas. So many teachers, by mistake or perhaps intentionally, shame their students; they make them feel 'Ah, I know nothing,' as if that ignorance of theirs were a permanent and irremediable condition! But this man never shamed me. Instead, he transmitted to me, pure and undiluted, his own passion for discovery" — he smiled — "and so you see me now, an entomologist myself."

"Does he know that?"

"Oh, no. We haven't seen or heard of one another for fourteen years. Do you remember the Emergency in Kenya? That's something you're familiar with, perhaps."

"Of course. I'm English."

He tapped his ear. "I heard. I'm being very careful," he said, smiling.

"That isn't necessary."

"No," he nodded, "for you had nothing to do with it. You were a child then, as I was, too. But at that time, all Kikuyu people — and I and my parents are of that tribe — were ordered off the farms and sent back to the African reserves. After that I never saw my friend again. He may have gone away to England where he'd come from as a boy. Although it wasn't a place he was too fond of, he had relatives there." He sighed. "In fact, it's very difficult to imagine him anywhere but on that farm, so perhaps he's still there after all. But one thing I'm certain of," he said with a wry smile, "that son of his will have left. He was a real *mzungu*, that one! He could never be comfortable nowadays in Kenya. How he despised Africans! And yet, he spoke our language very fluently. When he swore he was really something to listen to! I listened, you see. I knew better than to answer him. Except once. I lost my temper, too; I swore back at him. For an instant he was shocked. He couldn't believe what he was hearing. But then he took out a hunting knife, a long one. Like this." He showed Marietta. "Perhaps not quite so big, but it seemed very huge to me, with only my hands to protect myself. He got me here" — he touched his right forearm.

"If my father hadn't heard me yelling and come straight and caught that boy, he'd have put an end to me! I still have the scar." He stretched, yawning a little. "Excuse me. I was up very early this morning. Anyway, all this happened long ago."

But Marietta persisted. "Why did he try to kill you?"

"Because he believed his father loved me more than he loved him."

Marietta thought, That's what Violet used to say: It's *you* Justin favors. He cares for you more than me! We fought so many times about it, until we got too old to fight and left it at that. More, less? He loved both of us enough, and that's what counted in the end.

Suddenly, without knowing quite why, she asked, "May I look at your scar?"

"In the dark like this? What would you see?"

"There's a moon."

"Well . . ." He glanced at her, amused. "If you wish." He slipped off his jacket, pushed up his sleeve. He drew one finger from inside his elbow down his forearm almost to his wrist. "He just missed the artery. I was very fortunate, they said." Then quickly he buttoned his sleeve again. "In those days I was very simple-minded. I thought, Since the father has become my friend, surely the son will, too, and I looked forward to July when I knew he would return. The first time I saw him I greeted him. 'Shall we go swimming?' I said. But he turned and went away. Later I went up to him again and this time he was proud and cold. 'Who are you to invite me to swim in my own river?' he replied. The only Africans he cared to be with were Dorobo people, who lived in the forests. They are outcasts. They have no language of their own. If once they did, they've lost it. They speak a dialect made up of the languages of all the thieves who, over hundreds of years, have fled from justice to the forest. They stay in one place for a little while, and on they go again. They are hunters, they rarely stop to cultivate. Anyway, these people were this boy's friends. Perhaps they accepted his arrogance in a way that the rest of us who lived with him could not. Of course, I haven't seen him for very many years, but I seriously doubt he's changed. A fellow like that would've gone away as soon as there was talk of independence. To South Africa, probably. They'd appreciate his sort down there."

He got up and walked out from under the tree. "By the way," he said, turning back to Marietta, "why are you sitting out here in that beautiful dress? You didn't tell me."

"You didn't ask."

"No," he said quietly. "All I've done is talk about myself. I'm a rude young African, as the British would say."

"I ran away from a self-important woman who was talking at me about politics. I know I should be going back."

"I'll come with you, then." As they started towards the house he remarked, "It'll be interesting to find out what happened to those people. And most particularly, what happened to their place. In those days only Europeans could have farms like that; but now our turn has come."

"Yes," said Marietta, "so I've heard." She looked up and saw her husband on the floodlit terrace. Bunty was beside him, peering into the dark.

"Marietta," she called. "Marietta!"

"God, Etta," Jonathan exclaimed, as Marietta emerged from the shadows. "Why didn't you tell someone you were going off? We were frantic!"

"We thought you'd gotten sick," said Bunty. "You disappeared so suddenly and couldn't be found."

"It was hot in the house. I didn't mean to worry you. I'm sorry."

"Well, the main thing is you're fine. And I see that you and Dr. Kagia have found each other! But of course you men haven't met yet, have you?" Bunty added hastily. "Jonathan, Dr. Michael Kagia. Dr. Kagia, our guest of honor, Jonathan Sudbury. Seeing you're both from Kenya, you should have plenty to talk about!"

Marietta looked sideways at Kagia. He was staring at Jonathan in his velvet suit. What on earth does Kagia make of him? she wondered. And what does he make of me?

"Kagia?" Jonathan frowned. "Where are you from?"

"Fort Hall."

"I see." But what did he see? His face was flushed. Though in Kenya he drank very little, to get through these trips he needed two drinks before lunch, three before dinner. "It's the part," he'd told Marietta. "Off my own turf I can't be what they want, stone cold sober."

"You'll have such a lot to talk about," Bunty said again, "but right now we should all go eat!"

In the dining room people were helping themselves and being

helped by white-coated waiters to shrimp quiche and caviar, cold roast beef and Virginia ham. They were drinking hard and laughing loudly and many were shouting in order to make themselves heard above their fellow guests. Jonathan and Marietta were surrounded as they came in from the garden. "We're so delighted to see you after all the stories we've been told . . . Such an enchanting couple . . . D'you think you'll have time for us in April?" In the crush Kagia was separated from the Sudburys. Or perhaps he separated himself.

When supper was over, Roger Sanderson started the dancing with Marietta. After four turns round the floor, a man in a silk tuxedo cut in. "I've been talking with your husband," he told Marietta. "I'm serious. I said, 'When's the soonest you can fit me in?' You'll be along as well, I hope. You're a very lovely young woman; you know that?" Fleetingly Marietta saw her mother in the Wayfarer on Saturday nights, being claimed by strangers. Had they pressed themselves against Virginia like this man was pressing himself against her? Over his shoulder she saw Kagia watching her. Help, she signaled with her eyes.

Kagia slipped through the other couples on the floor. "Excuse me," he said to Marietta's partner. "I wish to dance with Mrs. Sudbury."

"Hold on, we just this minute began."

"Even so."

Gratefully Marietta disengaged herself. "Thanks for coming to my rescue," she whispered, but Kagia didn't reply. He held her lightly as if he might change his mind; any moment he might let go again. "You're annoyed with me," she said. "Why? I suppose I know why," she added. "But out there, if I'd told you where I came from, you'd have shut up like a clam! So long as you refuse to look at me, I can't apologize. Besides," she added, "I dislike talking to the side of your head!"

"Okay." He turned to her at last. "What have you to say for yourself, Mrs. Sudbury?" He was only a little taller than she, and he was brown, not black. Over the years, in the long winters and the laboratories of North America, perhaps his skin had lightened.

"If we passed in the street in Nairobi, I'd wonder, How do you see things? But you probably wouldn't even notice me. To clever young men like you, people like me don't count. We're simply of no interest. Even though we might wait in the same queue in the

250

post office, or sit in next-door seats in the cinema, despite Uhuru, it's unlikely we'd ever know each other. So the only chance I get to satisfy my curiosity is in a foreign place like this one. In the garden just now, by keeping quiet about myself, I'd hoped to find out if there was anything else we had in common, you and I, apart from being guests at the same party."

"I'm sorry you thought that you'd annoyed me," Kagia said quietly. "Because that isn't so. And whatever you might think, I find some Settlers very interesting. I believe I told you that at considerable length."

He was a little aloof but not disapproving, she decided. He was merely taking his time. Then suddenly he held her tighter and spun her round twice and she grinned.

"Why are you smiling?"

"Because I do count, after all! And also, I'd been thinking about the last time I danced the quickstep with an African. At the school I went to back home, we had ballroom dancing classes every Friday night and my partner was always a Keriki girl. At that time, she was the only African in the school and she tried to be the best at everything, even ballroom dancing. She made me practice with her every morning early, before breakfast, one two, one two, round and round the music room, to a wind-up gramophone. Each record was only three minutes long; we'd just get going and the tune would end and she'd dash off to start it again. But at the end of the term, we won first prize, two tins of Johnson's Baby Powder."

"Unfortunately, I've never taken ballroom dancing lessons," Kagia said, smiling. "In the high school I went to, all we danced was rock and roll. So as you can tell, I'm not quite the expert your girlfriend was."

"Where was that high school?"

"In Toronto."

"Toronto! Why?"

"That's a very long story, Mrs. Sudbury."

"I wish you'd stop calling me that!"

"All right." Kagia nodded. "When I see you in the street in Nairobi, I'll call out 'Marietta!'"

"It's more likely that you'll walk straight by me! You don't know what it's like there, do you? There's a certain spurious chumminess, which is new, but underneath it's the same old story. Three camps. African, Asian, European. When you're a kid you can ignore

251

the fortifications, the moats and ditches. You can go where you want and be friends with anyone you choose, but then one morning you're likely to wake up to find you've been fenced in with your own kind."

"That happened to you?"

"Of course!" Marietta laughed. "The minute she discovered I had a crush on one of our houseboys, my mother whipped me off to boarding school!"

The music stopped. "Thank you. I enjoyed my first dance with a Settler lady." Kagia smiled. "But now I have to ask you a great many questions. This time it's my turn to keep quiet."

"Then will you explain why you went to high school in Toronto?"

"Perhaps."

But Bunty was making her way towards them round the dance floor. "There are so many people dying to meet Marietta," she cried. "I'm going to have to tear her away, I'm afraid."

"We could try to make a dash for it," Marietta whispered. She felt wonderfully at ease with this man, Kagia, as if she'd been traveling in a crowded train full of jostling strangers and all of a sudden she'd come upon someone very familiar, waiting in a carriage reserved just for him and her. But now someone was demanding entry. "Let's pretend we didn't hear!"

"I don't think so," Kagia said, amused. "Go with her now, but never mind, we'll see each other later."

So Marietta was led away to do her duty. She glimpsed Kagia from time to time, being talked at, listening politely. Dorothy, in the turquoise brocade, kept him longest. Undoubtedly she's much more pleased with him, Marietta thought, than she was with me. How distinguished he looked among these garrulous white people, most of whom by now had drunk too much. Later she scanned the crowd and didn't see him. She realized he'd left without speaking to her again and for an instant she felt hurt. Then Jonathan came up to her. "May I have the pleasure of dancing with my wife?"

At half past one the last guests went into the autumn night. Bunty sank onto a sofa. She took off her pearl-and-diamond earrings and lined them up on the coffee table. Then she shook off her shoes, put her feet up, and lay back, massaging her ear lobes. "Well," she said to Marietta, "you sure were the belle of this ball!"

"A nightcap, anyone?" Roger asked.

"By the way, Jonathan," Bunty said, "did you ever get to talk to Dr. Kagia?"

252

Jonathan shook his head. "I didn't, no."

"Neither did I," Bunty sighed. "That's the trouble with one's own party. One's always in such a rush!" She went on, "Brad and Betty Harley brought him. Brad's a trustee of the university. He spent a lot of time on the Copper Belt in his younger years, and he's always interested in the students who come over from Africa, but Michael's been unusually close to him and Betty. They're sorry he'll be leaving for home before too long. I gather both his parents died during the Mau Mau. The father was shot by mistake and the mother died in a prison camp. Or was it the other way round? You know how it is, if you hear these stories third-hand, you never get them straight. Anyway, he was more or less adopted by a Canadian couple, medical missionaries. He was simply their houseboy, to start with, but they were so impressed that when they left the country, rather than leaving him to an uncertain future they took him with them. To Uganda first, and from there back home. After he'd finished college up in Canada, he came down here to school. He's a biologist, and quite outstanding, so I've heard."

"He studies parasites," Marietta said.

"But of course! You had a long talk with him, didn't you? My friend Dorothy, whom you met, told me she was very taken with him, and Dorothy isn't taken easily with anyone. When she left she said, 'That young man's simply fascinating. We've got to keep an eye on him!' I told her that I meant to," Bunty said with a yawn, "but not tonight, alas. What did you make of him, Marietta? Will it be Kagia after Kenyatta?" She yawned again. "Oh, *dear*, I'm afraid I've had it." She picked up her shoes and her earrings. "No more talk. Sleep. This gracious hostess is throwing in the towel. You two must've had it as well. All this dancing on top of jet lag!"

Upstairs in the south wing, Jonathan said, "You found him pretty fascinating, too."

"Who?"

"Kagia."

Marietta said lightly, "He didn't talk about Mau Mau, if that's what you mean. Mostly he talked about a friend of his. A European farmer who taught him all about pests and fungus. I was dying to ask, was it Major Wickenden? Unfortunately, the man's son didn't care for him at all. In fact, he went for Kagia once with a hunting knife! He showed me the scar. It went from his wrist to the crook of his arm. It's a wonder he isn't dead, too, as well as his mother and father. I kept thinking, Georgie Wickenden's such an easygoing

253

fellow, I can't see Georgie doing that! But who knows, he might have a murderous side one's never seen." She added as she got into bed, "I swear Bunty made me dance with every single man at her party. I hope my feet recover before our next gala event. It's on Tuesday in St. Louis, didn't you say? This being on show really takes training, doesn't it? I remember when I met you and you were on your way to the States, how you complained, and I thought, What's he making all the fuss about? Well," she said, sighing, "I'm beginning to understand."

"I gave Kagia that!"

"You gave Kagia what?"

Jonathan said harshly, "I was the one with the hunting knife. I gave Kagia that scar at Olgolulu in September 1952."

"You!" Marietta sat up in bed. "It couldn't have been you!"

"I don't seem like the type to knife an African any more than Georgie Wickenden, do I?"

"Did he show any sign of knowing who you were?"

"Of course not! A sly little bastard like Michael Maruga would never let on!"

"Maruga?"

"That's what he called himself then. But in the fifties a Kikuyu boy whose father was in a concentration camp and whose mother had been shot as a collaborator hadn't a hope in hell of getting a passport if he used his father's name, so naturally he changed it!"

"Out there on the terrace did you recognize him?"

"He's fourteen years older and several inches taller; his voice has broken, he shaves, he wears shoes and a nice blue shirt with a button-down collar. He'd almost pass for an American, wouldn't he? Of course I didn't recognize him! But under that nice blue shirt, he's still got the scar, right down the inside of his forearm. He showed it off to you! Rolled up his sleeve and flashed it in your face!" Jonathan sat suddenly in the chair over which Marietta had laid her evening dress. He covered his head with his hands.

"I asked to see it," Marietta said quietly. "I don't even know why I asked."

"But I do," Jonathan's voice was cold with hatred. Of her, of himself. "You'd already guessed I was that European boy."

"It hadn't entered my head. That's not my idea of you at all," Marietta said wearily.

Jonathan sprang up and began to pace the room. "He was always there, Michael Maruga, the mechanic's son, hanging about, waiting his chance. He got my castoffs. He had narrower shoulders and shorter arms. Last thing, as Dad drove me away to catch the plane to school, I'd see him in my old pants, my sweater which covered his wrist bones but not mine anymore. And as soon as I'd gone he was king of the castle again!"

Jonathan stopped at the window. The curtains were drawn back, and beyond the lawn and the catalpa trees the lake glinted under a setting moon. He pressed his forehead against a pane. Watching his back and his narrow fingers splayed across the glass, Marietta was afraid. Afraid of his past, and of her future. "How did it happen?" she asked finally.

"Dad's passion is making things grow. Wheat, calves, vegetable marrows, anything, everything. I'm no farmer. I never was and never will be, and I can't remember a time when I wasn't already sure of that fact. I've always wanted what I can't quite see; in the forest, beyond the horizon. Of course, there's no law that sons must follow their fathers, but I never even tried to."

He stepped back from the window and resumed his pacing over the deep beige carpet, past Marietta in the satin quilted bed. There were yellow rosebuds in a vase on the mantelpiece. When eventually they opened, they'd be lavish, but that was days away; for now they were still shut tight.

He went on, "When I was young, Dorobo people lived above Olgolulu. Sometimes when they came down to herd cattle on the farm, I'd play about with their kids. One day, I was eight or nine, a couple of them took me back to their village in a forest clearing. The next afternoon I went again, and then again and so on, until I was spending almost every waking moment with them, and sometimes I slept there too. Towett and Taita were their names. Taita was my age, his brother some years older. Their father had herded for Dad on and off for years. My parents assumed I was okay with him, although the fact was, I rarely saw him. I slept in the boys' hut with his sons and at first light we'd be up and gone. Those boys taught me how to use a bow and arrow and a sling, how to live as they did in the forest. And the day before I left for school in England, they told me, 'You're one of us. Don't forget, you're Dorobo now! Outcasts, wild ones, the people in the valley call us, but as for ourselves, we know that we are free. We move as we wish, we have no masters.'

255

"One of them! Until then I'd always been the wrong color, or even if the right color, wrong nevertheless. Different from my parents, different from other kids, black or white; the extra piece of a jigsaw puzzle, fitting nowhere. Once I asked my mother, 'Did you adopt me?' and she laughed and said, 'Looking like me, the dead spit, how could you imagine that!' 'I didn't mean my eyes or nose or hair,' I said miserably. 'Such fanciful ideas you do have, Johnny!' 'Is it bad blood, then?' That infuriated her. 'I really don't know what you're after,' she said. But now, miraculously, bad blood or not, these people claimed me.

"Away at school I submitted to being organized and ordered about. I didn't care, because it was only a matter of waiting ten months, six, four, and I'd be with my friends again. And in July I was, and the next year as well, but when I came home the year after that, I found they'd gone, they'd fled before the loggers up the escarpment into the high forest, leaving no trace, no promise to return in a year, two years, ever. I was on my own again. It was then that it dawned on me what had happened. While I'd been preoccupied, my father and Maruga's boy had become inseparable. They fitted together. They mimicked one another's gestures. They even smiled the same way! It was as if they'd unearthed evidence disinheriting me, proving Michael the true heir. There wasn't a thing I could do about it! Or was there? Just as I was due to leave for school again, I decided to teach him a lesson. I put my knife on my belt, the same knife I'd hunted with the year before and the year before that. I didn't intend to use it, though. I just wanted to scare the daylights out of him. Then I hid behind some straw bales in the barn next to the milking shed. I knew he'd be passing through, sooner or later. And sure enough, he did. I jumped out and knocked him down and broke his glasses. Dad had taken him to have his eyes tested and bought him those glasses; it gave me enormous pleasure to see them shattered on the concrete floor. According to my plan, at this point he should have begged for mercy, but instead he pulled himself up and lunged at me and there we were, going for each other! It was then that I pulled my knife on him."

Back and forth Jonathan paced, from the window to the door, to the door, to the window. He never looked at his wife, wide-eyed with sadness for two boys, now two grown men. "My parents took him to the hospital, bleeding to death, as I supposed. They stayed overnight in Eldonia so as to be near him and I didn't see them again. Bill Bryant, our farm manager, drove me down to Nairobi the next day and I took the plane to England in complete disgrace. The following month the Emergency began, and for two years my parents wouldn't let me come home. For safety's sake, they told me; but that was a lie. Other parents let their kids come home, despite the war; mine didn't. They knew damn well I was frantic to see Olgolulu with my own two eyes, that second-hand reports couldn't do the trick; all the same, they didn't let me come home. They wanted to teach me a lesson I'd never forget, you see."

Can that be true? Marietta thought. Did that quiet man, that shy, careful woman, both so cautious and correct, really want to teach their son a lesson he'd never forget? She knew them at times to be distracted, unheeding, even obsessed with getting things done now, not later. But deliberately cruel? It was hard to imagine. She shook her head; how could she know what once went on?

At the window Jonathan was saying, "My only source of satisfaction during those years was knowing that Michael Maruga had been sent back to Central Province with all the other Kukes. At night in bed at school, I'd think, I'm in exile, but he's gone for good! If ever I get back there, even if it's all in ruins, I'll have Olgolulu to myself again! Meanwhile, Dad had to hire a Kipsigis mechanic who hardly knew pliers from a wrench, and when the combine broke down, it stayed that way for weeks on end, and half the wheat was spoiled.

"Eventually, when they thought they'd punished me enough, they let me come home. That first evening, Bill Bryant said, 'By the way, I just heard from that policeman pal of mine that Maruga's been picked up. My friend was in the agricultural service before the Emergency, and he remembered Maruga as a loyal, hardworking fellow. So when they brought him in, at first he thought there'd been some mistake. But no, they'd got the right man. Evidently Maruga'd had a clever little operation going. He'd have one lot attack sentry posts to clean out the guns and ammunition. They'd get the stuff up to him and his boys, and from there they'd take it to the guerrillas in the Aberdares!' In the future, Bryant said, he was going to try to be more patient with that Kip. When the pump broke down, it was a hell of a time mending it, but at least we were alive, which we might well not be if Maruga hadn't been handily removed by Her Majesty's Government. After a month or so, I got my courage up enough to say to Dad, 'I'd like to talk about what happened between Michael and me.' 'There's nothing further to talk about. You did what you did.' To this day I remember his voice, dry and cold like a desert in winter. And that was that, so far as he was concerned. He never mentioned Michael's name to me again.

"A long while later we heard Maruga had died in prison, and the mother was dead as well, but of Michael there was no trace. I remember Bryant saying he was ready to bet that Maruga's boy had joined General China in the forest; maybe he'd been killed too. Good riddance! Bryant hadn't cared for Michael, either. Perhaps," Jonathan said, smiling wryly, "he'd been a bit jealous, too."

He stopped, his back to the fireplace and the spiky roses. "So there you have my nasty little secret."

"Why didn't you tell me before? You could have!"

Far from her Jonathan said, "But you see, Dad's never really forgiven me. Why should he, after all."

"Because you were his son and only twelve years old!" Marietta ran to him. "Whatever Kagia was or is or will be, has nothing to do with it. Fathers *have* to forgive their sons!" She took his hands. "Things always seem so much more dreadful in the middle of the night, Johnny. Please come!" But Jonathan pulled away.

"The fight with Michael," he said bleakly, "the fact that I hadn't fought fair, that I'd used a knife and he'd been unarmed, was actually a red herring. What Dad has never forgiven me for is that he's stuck with me as a son, instead of Michael. Eventually, since the war had swallowed Michael up, he was forced to take another look at me and renegotiate. But I wasn't his first choice. I was just the runner-up." He shrugged off his jacket and threw it at the chair where Marietta's dress already lay. "So I have to prove myself worthy, don't I? If, for the sake of his beloved Olgolulu, I sell my soul nine months a year at home and another month in America, mightn't I convince him I deserve to be his son? I'm afraid I've roped you into a fairly desperate enterprise, Marietta. It's to alleviate bitter disappointments that we chatter half the night with strangers and I wear this ridiculous suit and your feet ache, my love."

15

Olgolulu

After Fort Worth, they went to Colorado, where the sun was brilliant. There was snow on the peaks but hardly a soul in the lodge. The ski season hadn't started yet. They walked through the woods bare of leaves and on up above the tree line.

One day as they walked Jonathan remarked, "One gets so tired of trying to recreate a past one was born much too late to have been part of. That's what the clients want, though — the Africa of Count Teleki gunning his way north from the Coast to Abyssinia before the turn of the century. Teeming herds plus the odd Samburu warrior. No poachers, no *shiftas* with automatic rifles mowing down elephant and rhino, no Kukes suddenly planting maize slap in the middle of a shooting block." He grimaced. "It's a strain, year in, year out, massaging other people's fantasies."

"You don't have to keep doing it. Any time you wanted, you could stop. You've got all sorts of connections; I bet you'd have all sorts of opportunities, too, as soon as people knew you were willing to consider something else. You could leave Kenya, go to Australia, come here or anywhere else you chose."

"No, I couldn't," he replied. "You know quite well why not. And besides, I *want* to stay. Kenya's where I belong, and fortunately, one gets a second wind. A third, a fourth. A twentieth, if necessary. One tires and one recovers."

On Monday he was going to San Francisco for two more weeks of the rich life. Marietta was going east again, and back to her son. When they made love Jonathan was especially tender.

"It's been wonderful having you back," he told her.

"Back? You're the one who's gone most of the time."

"Back from Charlie," he said. "Since the moment of his birth you've only had eyes for him, admit it!"

"You were the one who wanted him," Marietta teased. "I just fell in with your plans."

"I suppose that's true, but I had no idea you'd make such a thorough job of it." He smiled faintly. "Lately I'd been thinking, Maybe, so far as Etta's concerned, that's all I'm good for, siring sons for her to fall in love with."

"No," she laughed, "that's not all. Look how your public adores you!"

"But I'm talking about *you*, Etta."

"You've changed my life, you know that."

"Not necessarily for the better."

"*Yes*, Johnny, without a doubt for the better!" He'd made her many promises and all of them he'd kept.

"I'm never sure. That's why I had to ask. I never quite know what you're thinking."

On the last night they were together Marietta said, "I won't mention Kagia to your father."

"Whyever not?"

"Wouldn't you rather tell him yourself?"

"You're the one who talked to him, not I."

"Even so . . ."

"No," Jonathan said. "As far as I'm concerned, Michael Maruga's dead. This Kagia fellow's someone different."

"But this Kagia fellow's going home soon. You heard what Bunty said."

"Why should he bother us?"

From Denver, Marietta flew to Chicago to catch an evening flight to London. Over Nebraska she thought, Shall I tell Edmund I saw only one sort of American, the sort who's secure, predictable, complacent, and therefore foreign? The others I barely glimpsed as I was driven in and out of cities. In fact, the only person I met who seemed at all familiar wasn't American at all. You remember him? I heard that once you loved him more than your own son. Why did you love one and not the other, or the other less and not enough?

260

In Chicago she had fifty-five minutes between planes. She changed terminals, checked in her luggage, bought two magazines, and looked up KAGIA, MICHAEL in the telephone directory. She dialed the number. Eight times it rang, and just as she was about to hang up and so, through no effort of her own, be saved from committing treason, a man's voice answered. "Michael's not here. He'll be home from the lab at six-thirty. D'you want to call back?"

"Tell him . . ."

"What's that? The line's not good. Are you calling long distance?"

"From the airport, how far is that?"

"So you're passing through?"

"That's right."

"What's your name? What can I tell him?"

"Nothing, no message. They're calling my flight now. I've got to go." Not treason, then, just a very petty sin.

Had he been there, what would you have said? That would depend. Depend on what? On him. But this was your idea, not his, so what did you have in mind to say? That I'm so glad I met him, that I look forward to meeting him again!

In London she stayed one night in Cardigan Square with Lady Bilton, whom she hadn't seen since the summer before last, before she married. You mustn't come to meet me at that hour, she'd written. I'll take a taxi. At five minute to seven, Curtis was on the front steps fetching in the milk.

"May I kiss you?" Marietta said, but Curtis held back, squinting off into the square. "What's the matter? Am I on your blacklist now?"

"What've you got in this one?" Curtis said gruffly, hauling a suitcase to the door. "Iron bars?"

"Presents. One for you, one for her ladyship, and lots for my son."

"We liked his picture," Curtis conceded. "Ever so cheerful, he looked." Her ladyship was still in bed, nursing a cold. After her meeting last Friday she'd been caught in the rain and got her feet wet, and it'd gone to her chest immediately. "You go right on in, miss. Madam I should say now, shouldn't I? She's ready for you. She's been awake since five."

Lady Bilton sat back against pillows, in a shell pink bed jacket with lacy sleeves. "At last!" she cried. "What a pleasure it is to see you again! Curtis, you can bring my breakfast, now she's on the ground."

When she had her tray and was pouring out the coffee she said lightly, "Is it a success?"

"It?"

"Your marriage. I was surprised you married — stunned, in fact. It wasn't at all what I'd expected. Forgive me, won't you, for saying so."

"I was pregnant. I wrote and told you that."

"There were alternatives."

"I know, but by doing what I did, I pleased a good many people."

"Ah. Did you please yourself?"

"Charlie's the best mistake I ever made. He brought me to my senses. I don't know how you stood me," she added. "I was so utterly self-centered when I lived with you."

"But mustn't one expect that of the young? And it's all to the good, provided it doesn't last too long. In my opinion, you could have done with a little more of it!" The emerald eyes narrowed. "And your husband, are you pleased with him?"

"Jonathan takes good care of me."

"I think of you often," Lady Bilton said quickly, "and I think of myself, at Itep in 1914, with a baby and" — she smiled wryly — "a demented husband, whose passion for that particular spot on earth showed no signs whatever of abating. Had I known at the time that it wouldn't either, not for thirty-four years . . ." She shook her head. "But luckily I didn't! It's a great mistake to assume on the basis of a few superficial similarities that another person's experience bears any resemblance to one's own. All I really have to say, Marietta," she finished, "is that you've made me a great-grandmother of sorts, and that pleases me enormously."

Not wanting her first visit to Tresham to be without Jonathan, Marietta had written that she didn't have time to go down to Wiltshire on this trip, she had to get back to her infant son. So James Sudbury, Broiler King, was coming to dinner in Cardigan Square. Aunt Elizabeth wouldn't be joining them; her back had given out again and she was laid up at Tresham on the sofa in the little sitting room. But she'd sent a pair of hairbrushes backed with ivory and engraved with Charlie's initials and the Sudbury crest. "Two!" Marietta exclaimed, taking them out of tissue paper. "Will he ever have enough hair for two?"

262

James loomed by the fireplace in his country suit. *His* hair was mostly white, though there was red still at the edges, above his collar and over his ears. Eleanor Sudbury had insisted that Charlie was the spitting image of James. Did that mean Charlie would grow up to look like Henry the Eighth with small, shrewd eyes and a thunderous laugh that stopped short in the middle? Marietta thought, Uncle James is used to getting what he wants. For all his tweeds and bluff ruddy face, his congenial squire-ishness, he's a bit of a bully. She imagined him on long evenings at Tresham, refusing to listen to Jonathan. She sincerely hoped Charlie *wouldn't* take after him in looks or in anything else. Couldn't Charlie just be himself, starting out new!

At dinner, taking up one side of the table, James boomed, "I remember your grandfather. Enormously brave in his way, though one was bound to wonder to what end. Once he stuck his toes in, there wasn't any budging him. What they used to call a character, was Harold." He asked a great many questions about Olgolulu. Some Marietta could answer, but many she could not. Then he talked to her about Tresham. With purpose, she realized that. After dinner, in the drawing room, he stood with his back to the fire and showed his hand. "So which will Jonathan choose?"

"He's chosen. He's made up his mind. He's staying put," Marietta replied, looking straight into the small, shrewd eyes.

"And the younger generation?"

"When I left, Charlie was just beginning to crawl. You shouldn't count on him."

Turning away from her, James said, "Harold Parkson did everything arse backwards. I'd say you've got another like him on your hands."

"More coffee, James?" said Lady Bilton gently, from the sofa.

Edmund Sudbury was at Embakasi Airport before dawn. "Had a good trip?" he said, kissing the air next to Marietta's right ear, and then, not waiting to hear if she had or not, "Mind if we don't stop in and see your mother? I'm expecting the vet about ten. Got to get on." So they drove past the signposts to Katari. In the first light the bougainvillea along the highway was sumptuously in bloom. Through the city they went, and out again through coffee plantations where laborers were already threading through the trees, up to the pastures of Tigoni. And all the way beside her father-in-law, hands clasped in her lap, Marietta marveled at the tumult this familiar road aroused in her. Trumpets, kettledrums, bugles, horns; all together, a cacophony, a wild glee. She was almost home! Could that be? She'd never thought of Olgolulu as home before. Had something happened to her in America? Was she settling at last?

At sunrise they reached the edge of the escarpment and the great wide sweep of the Rift. In the gold of early morning one could forget the uncertain future. The beauty of the valley and the mountains demanded all one's attention. Before them Longonot rose imperiously from the Masai plains, bald shoulders rising to a yawning crater, while to the north Lake Naivasha gleamed.

"I'm always astonished," Edmund said softly, "though I've seen it ten thousand times before," and then, matter-of-factly, "By the way, Eleanor and I are thinking of going to stay with my brother at Christmas."

"When was the last time you were in an English winter, Edmund?"

"Nineteen twenty-three."

"Why not wait until the spring? Already it's cold there, the sky hangs low, it's dark by five."

"But December's a good time. By April we'll be ploughing. I'll be very busy here. Last week I wrote to James. Didn't he mention my letter? No, well, perhaps he hadn't got it yet."

"When he does, I'm sure he'll be delighted," Marietta said. "He asked so many questions about Olgolulu which I couldn't begin to answer. Now he can ask you."

"There was a time," Edmund said, smiling, "when James didn't have a sensible thought in his head, let alone questions or answers. If we met he'd say, 'Eddie, how's the battle against rinderpest?' Eddie! No one ever called me that except my nurse! 'And how's the polo handicap?' I'd say. But he came to his senses in the end. He practically reinvented the chicken! He's the real pro now!" He went on, "Tresham used to be arctic in the winter. Nothing new in the way of heat since the house was built in 1488. But James has done so extraordinarily well, he can afford the swishest sort of central heating now. You see, we aren't the least bit worried about being chilly."

They drove on in silence for a while, until Marietta said, "We met an old friend of yours in America. Michael Maruga. Do you remember him?" But Edmund's eyes were on the road ahead and he showed no sign of having heard. "His name is Michael Kagia now," Marietta persisted. "He came to a party someone gave for us in Chicago. These people hadn't known, of course, that he and Jonathan had any previous connection. He's a scientist. Because of you, mainly, he told me. You started him off."

Edmund slowed carefully, edged the Land-Rover onto the verge, and stopped. "What happened in Chicago?" he said. "Now tell me."

"How did Jonathan take it?" he asked, when she'd finished.

"He said that to him Michael Maruga was dead, that if in fact he was alive it didn't matter one way or the other."

Edmund stared up the narrow road, empty at this hour of the morning, although on the ridge buck grazed, tails flicking black and white in the early sunlight. He's not thinking about Jonathan, Marietta thought, he's remembering the boy he hasn't seen for fourteen years. He's remembering his face and his hands and the way he smiled and what it was like to be at ease with him the whole day long. He's wondering what it would be like to be with him now. Should I tell him, He's a little stern, perhaps, but gracious, and when he smiled my heart sang?

At last Edmund said, "If I wrote to him, what would I say? No, no, I'll wait. He'll be home next year. What's one more year when it's already been so many? If he answered, his letter wouldn't give me the whole picture. It wouldn't be like seeing him face to face. He'll come back home," Edmund added, as if he were talking to himself, "and I'll show him all the improvements." Suddenly he chuckled. "I bet he has a thing or two to teach *me* now!"

"Yes," Marietta said softly, "you'll show him everything, from the road up to the boundary fence, and he'll hardly believe what you've done!"

They drove on to Olgolulu, where Charles, in Jerusha's arms at the front door, screamed at the sight of his mother. For a week he continued to scream whenever she came near him. "You little tyrant," Marietta cried, in tears. "What have I done? Why do I deserve this?" But on the seventh day he sat in her lap to play with the crested hairbrushes. He squashed them together, dropped them, fretted till his mother picked them up, squashed them together, and dropped them again. This game he found quite thrilling. Now he could crawl at a great rate across the hardwood floors, over the lintel, out onto the lawn and away, red curls bobbing, if you didn't watch him every second. He was growing, if not quite up.

Marietta brought out paper and ink. She would start with the Ruba stories Boremo used to tell. She'd go to Galana in the New Year and get Boremo to tell them all again. She'd borrow a tape recorder from Bruce, who used them for dictating letters. Then she'd come back here and translate, and edit and illustrate. By the beginning of the rains she might have finished! But she wouldn't send it to one of those Nairobi presses that printed true confessions on spotty yellow paper. This book would be published properly in London. Perhaps one of her old teachers at the Slade could help. She'd use a pseudonym, of course: Marianna Hill. What aunt or granny, looking through W. H. Smith's for a suitable present — colorful, interesting, instructive but not too hard — would resist such a book? She wasn't Bridget Riley yet, but what was wrong with being the Beatrix Potter of the Rift for now? She smiled as she drew a crocodile in the mud of a river bank, one eye open, one eye shut.

Ten days after Marietta got back to Olgolulu Jonathan returned from California in good spirits. He'd had twice as many people after him as he'd have time for in the coming year. In December, when Edmund and Eleanor had gone eagerly to England, the Hollywood producer and his wife arrived; this time the offspring from the previous marriages had gone their different ways, and Jonathan told Marietta that he was bringing the two of them to Olgolulu for a weekend before he left with them for the bush. "Dad doesn't do very well with Americans. Mum doesn't either, but having charmed your way from New York to Texas, you're an old hand. It's always a lot easier having clients up here when my parents are away. They'd adore a taste of feudal life and after four times out with me these people certainly deserve one."

They were duly impressed by the gargoyles, lizards with tongues extended, carved by Italian prisoners of war brought down from Abyssinia expressly for this purpose, and by Eleanor's ancestors in the hall and the dining room. The ancestors had come, peeling, from Perthshire because Eleanor, having no brothers, had been left them and had the walls to hang them on. On the equator in the dry Rift air the peeling had accelerated rapidly. However, by candlelight one hardly noticed.

"Is this all necessary," Marietta said, "this lighting of candles?"

Jonathan laughed. "We're lucky we can still afford the candles,

Etta. Besides, it all looks lovely, you have to admit. Once in a while it's nice to put on a show."

The wife, Loretta, formerly a model, now a movie star, had set out from Live Oak, Alabama, a decade or so before to make it to the very brightest lights. The true facts of her origins had been obscured in the process and in place of the unpainted drygoods store of her childhood had arisen a pillared and porticoed moss-hung mansion, full of devoted family retainers. Olgolulu caught her fancy instantly. She exclaimed over each new sign of faded elegance and hugged Marietta at the slightest opportunity. But what sent her into paroxysms of delight was the glimpse she caught after breakfast of Justin carrying nine-month-old Charlie on his shoulders across the front lawn. In the South, she told Jonathan and Marietta, when she was just a little bitty girl, her daddy had been so busy running the plantation and her mother's health had been so poor that really she'd been closest to Priscilla, Mother's old mammy, and the steward, Saul. Of course she'd respected Mother and Daddy, but Saul and Priscilla were the ones who had time to play. These bittersweet memories brought tears to Loretta's eyes, and she had to have a vodka and tonic to settle her. Then she was up and looking for Charlie. She didn't want children and certainly not stepchildren, but Charlie and his circumstances seemed to have potential. There might be the seed of a movie in all this, with Sidney Poitier as Justin and herself as Marietta — never mind that Marietta was a blonde and she a brunette.

She found Charlie with Justin in the laundry room. Justin was ironing and Charlie was sitting on the floor in his red dungarees, gnawing his teething ring. It was Sunday, the ayah's day off. "*Jumbo*," Loretta said, and squatted beside Charlie, who howled, dropped his teething ring, and threw up his arms. Eyes shut, tears pelting down his fat cheeks, he waited for Justin to extract him from Loretta's overwhelming perfumed presence.

"I didn't mean to scare you, sweetheart," Loretta said. "It's only Auntie Lori come to say hello."

Justin, who was holding Charlie against his shoulder and patting his hiccupping back, said grimly in Swahili, "He doesn't like strangers."

"What was that?"

Justin repeated himself. He could have said it in English but he wanted to get rid of the woman, not engage her further. It wasn't

267

only Charlie who disliked strangers. If they had to come to Olgolulu, Justin thought, then they should be told to stay in the front
of the house. Bwana Edmund should have a sign painted, like the
ones in the Nairobi parks, telling people to keep off the grass.

"*No comprendo*," said Loretta. In reply Justin pointed one thick
black index finger first to her and then at the door, whereupon Loretta squared her shoulders, tossed her gleaming hair, and removed herself from the laundry room as gracefully as she could
manage.

When she left Olgolulu on Monday morning she gave Marietta a
gold bracelet to remember her by. It weighed eight ounces on the
kitchen scale.

"No, no," Marietta protested. "I really can't take it." But Loretta
insisted. Marietta asked Jonathan to slip it back into Loretta's luggage, but he told her, "I can't do that. Think of it as a very high-
class tip for performing a very high-class service that you didn't
especially enjoy. If you don't want to, you'll never have to wear it."
Marietta put the bracelet in the safe, and after Jonathan and Loretta and Loretta's husband, Bobby, had gone off to Tanzania, she
lay on her bed and laughed till she cried.

Jonathan would be spending Christmas in the Selous and Justin
was going to Galana, so Marietta took Charles and went down to
Katari to meet Trixie, Bruce's daughter, who had come from Sydney by way of Singapore. She hadn't seen her father for ten years.
"We need help," Virginia had pleaded on the telephone, "if you can
spare it. You'll see why."

Trixie's straw-colored hair was in pigtails and she wore jeans
with the legs cut off, very short, and no underpants. No bra, either,
under her thin white T-shirt that her dark nipples showed through.
She told Marietta that the old man had pushed off when she was
seventeen. What a break! They'd never got on. She was twenty-
seven now, and she drank beer on and off all day, from the bottle,
with her feet up on the arms of chairs, to Karanja's consternation.

"I wouldn't leave my kid with an African," she said, seeing Charlie on Jerusha's back. "Why can't you look after him yourself, fucking lazy all you people are. In Australia we do our own work,
thanks!"

"Bruce certainly works," Marietta said mildly. "You've scarcely
seen him because he works so hard."

"Him!" The corners of Trixie's mouth drew down with disdain.

268

"I like Bruce," Marietta said.

"You're welcome to him!"

"If you dislike him, why did you come to see him? He's rather out of your way."

Sprawling across the sofa Virginia had just recovered with pink and yellow birds on white, Trixie shrugged. "I wanted to see what he was up to." She giggled. "That Karanja in his fez at lunch! They wouldn't believe it back home. And your mother, like some blinking film star from the forties, the way she does her eyelids. All that blue! Never mind, on Boxing Day I'll be off to London. You been there, Marietta?"

"Oh, yes."

"Then why in the world did you come back to this dump? You must've been bats!"

Peter Dawson had them to dinner on Christmas Day. Early in December he'd gone to meet Daphne in Paris. "He went off so full of beans," Virginia told Marietta, "but of course she changed her mind again, and back he came, desperately sad." She shook her head. "Your godmother's a wicked woman, the way she's kept that poor man on a string! I hope that this time she's sent him home for good. If only she'd just make up her mind and stick to it, and give him a chance to get over her."

New trophies were up on all the walls. An elephant, two buffalo, a lion, half a dozen antelope. He's hanging them up for company, Marietta thought. How sad, how mad. Peter crossed the marble hall to greet them. "So good of you all to come to dine with an old recluse like me," he said, and he kissed Virginia's hand.

"What's this about being old, Peter? You haven't a gray hair on your head."

"I'm the old one," Bruce laughed. "I'll be sixty-two on Friday. You're a mere spring chicken, Peter, next to me."

"Age has little to do with it," Peter said.

Trixie whispered, "They give me the creeps, all those monsters hanging up, don't they you?" She had on a halter top and a sarong, bought, she told Marietta, on the half day her boat had put in at Penang. Her hair was done with combs and hibiscus blossom. "I used to sing with a rock-and-roll band," she explained, "and I did my hair this way then." At dinner she sat between Bruce and Peter. She was quiet during the smoked sailfish, more talkative with the soup. By the time the turkey came, she was in full swing. "Tell me about your war, Peter. Tell me all about your girls. At home they say the French were the best, and the English a pretty close second. That ladylike crap was only a front. Once you got in there, the English girls were just as hot as the French. And you could talk to them if you wanted, and get an answer back." She'd had four glasses of champagne. Peter had too.

"I wasn't in Europe much," he said. "I was in the Middle East."

"I saw some belly dancers in a club in Singapore. They were terrific," Trixie said. "All the men were peeing in their pants. They even turned me on."

"Egypt *was* fun," Virginia said.

"You were there as well?"

Virginia laughed. "Peter and I met in Cairo, as a matter of fact."

"What was she like then, Peter? How did she rate?"

"We were only friends," Virginia said quietly. "How did Mwangi marinate this turkey? It's delicious. Did he use papaya leaves?"

"She was extraordinary," said Peter. "They both were. The first time I saw them was in the Gezira Sporting Club at a table a little to one side. They wore exactly the same expression. As if" — he looked intently at Trixie, with the hibiscus nodding in her hair — "they were waiting for a curtain to swing open on their lives. Their faces were all lit up. But another chap beat me over there. He got the first one and left Daphne for me."

"I've heard she was quite a one, that Daphne," Trixie said.

"Gone now, as you see."

"You never know. She might be back."

"She won't," said Peter flatly, pouring more champagne for Trixie. The others shook their heads and he served himself. "The day she left she told me she'd never intended to stay in Africa. She'd been born here, she'd grown up here, and the war had given her the chance she'd been waiting for to escape the daily hypocrisies which, as a white on a black continent, she'd been obliged to live by. If she hadn't met me in Cairo, she'd have made her getaway the minute the war was over. But instead she married me, and hung around for twenty years, thinking of the life she might have led if she hadn't, out of pity, got involved with me."

"She didn't pity you, Peter," Virginia said, red in the face and very close to tears. "She loved you. She often said so, to me as well as to you. You made up the part about pity."

"She was *fond* of me, Virginia. But mostly she was sorry for me,

270

and for herself for botching her chances. One man was never enough for her. The moment I left, I wouldn't know who'd be in this house. I never knew who I'd find when I got home. At first she went for one's friends, so at least one had some sense of what the attraction might be; then it was people who worked in banks or flogged tractor parts, and after them she started on the young. One's friends' sons. There was one especially — Nigel. We met him in Hampshire. Do you know Hampshire, Trixie?"

"Never been to U.K."

"Marietta remembers Nigel. He played the piano." Peter turned to Marietta. "Nigel gave her a very good time, she always said. I found that hard to believe, though. Not one for bed, Nigel, I wouldn't have thought, would you, Etta?"

"Don't, Peter, don't talk about those times. They're done with," Marietta said.

"But those are the only times I've had," said Peter bitterly. "What else have I got to look back on? It's all very well for you, with your life ahead of you." He finished his fifth glass of champagne. "Who was that chap you danced with in the Gezira, Virginia?"

"Blowed if I could say."

"No, you wouldn't remember. How could you? You and she were the same," Peter said carefully, "like two peas in a pod. In Paris, Daphne had a Jamaican. Collar and tie and crocodile shoes. Got rid of the fellow from Cuba. Not black enough, I don't suppose. Are you on to fancy black men, too, Virginia? Is that why you sent Justin packing?"

"Watch it," Bruce said. "Watch what you're saying, Peter."

"She doesn't deny it, does she?" said Peter, pushing back from the table and elaborately crossing his legs. "You all come to them sooner or later. Used to be, you could control yourself longer so you took your time getting there. But times have changed. No need to hold back now, with blacks all over everywhere, running the show. How about you, Marietta? Are you onto them as well?"

White man, black man, brown man, yellow man; rich man, poor man, beggar man, thief. Her face burned.

"I'm going to warn that husband of yours, he'd better watch it," Peter taunted. "Poor chap, I suppose he thinks he's keeping you racially uncontaminated, up at Olgolulu, under the eye of your mother-in-law, but I'm going to tell him, he's got another think coming. Eleanor's not going to stop her, nobody can."

Flowers bouncing, eyes round, Trixie looked from Virginia to Peter and back. "Blimey," she said, grinning, "things can get personal at Christmas, can't they?"

"Trixie?" Peter smiled. "That's an intriguing name. Can I give you more champagne?"

"Who's Justin?" Trixie said. "Sounds like a real dog."

"Dog?" Peter nodded slowly. "That's it! I was trying so hard to remember! I had a spaniel called Trixie once. Wonderfully affectionate. Used to lick one's face when one was sad. Justin isn't a spaniel, no, not at all! He has a much better way of getting your stepmother's spirits up than poor Trixie ever did. He screwed Virginia to kingdom come for almost twenty years!"

On her feet, Virginia cried, "You're disgusting!" She leaned across the dismembered turkey. "I've done plenty of things I'm ashamed of in my time, Peter Dawson, but never that! How could you say it? How could you even think it?"

"I've every reason to do both, my dear. I've been watching you with interest since 1943." He leaned back in his chair, smiling gleefully, then suddenly he waved his napkin. "Get out. All of you. Don't let me catch you coming here again!"

In the car as they drove under dark trees banded with white paint, Trixie remarked, "Funny old geezer, all by himself in that great big ugly house. Not what you'd expect to find in Africa, really." And then, leaning along the back seat, she whispered to Marietta, "You mean, Bruce didn't know about that fellow Justin till tonight?"

Edmund and Eleanor came back from England with new Aquascutum raincoats. "So clever," Eleanor said, hanging hers up. "You just zip the lining in and out."

"Much too warm for East Africa," said Marietta.

Eleanor had new twin sets, too. One blue, one green. "One needed them," she said, placing them carefully with mothballs in a tin box. "Though I didn't find it as cold as I'd imagined. It's a question of attitude, really."

Jonathan and Marietta had dinner with Edmund and Eleanor on their first night home. "James and Elizabeth were both so terribly kind!" Edmund said. "Elizabeth, poor thing, can stand or lie but cannot sit, not since her spinal fusion." The daughters, Polly and Patricia, had come to Tresham and been frightfully kind as well. "All those girls they've got between them!" Eleanor ex-

272

claimed. "But still no sons. Everyone was so keen to hear about Charlie! You'll have to take him over for inspection very soon."

After chocolate mousse, Edmund made his announcement. "James is getting on," he said. "He can't manage Tresham on his own. He asked if we'd be interested in helping out. Eleanor would do the books. After all, she's done them here for thirty years. I'd manage the farm and he'd concentrate on the business side. We said we needed time to think. But after a week, we'd made up our minds. We'd hate it at the Coast in some villa at Malindi, rusting away in the salt air. We neither of us care for bridge or fishing. We've got some good years left and Tresham seems the place to spend them usefully."

"James has offered us a nice little house," Eleanor said eagerly, "with a garden. It's quite sheltered. I went over every foot of it. It'll be fun to see if fuchsias do well in Wiltshire, too."

"We asked James to give us a year," Edmund said. "We need a year to train Marietta."

"Me?" Marietta gasped.

"Jonathan's occupied elsewhere. He has to be. Farming's so problematic. One year up and then two down. You have to have another source of income, don't you? Besides" — Edmund fiddled with his fruit knife — "farming's never been Johnny's bent."

"I couldn't manage Olgolulu!" Marietta cried.

"Whyever not? Look at your mother. She's a superb manager. It's in your blood, I bet you."

"But I'm not my mother. I'm me, I'm a painter."

"I know. You can't make a living doing that, though. Not here, anyway," Edmund said reasonably.

"Dad's not leaving tomorrow," Jonathan said. "You can learn an amazing amount in a year."

Marietta turned to him. "So you knew all about this?"

"I can't say I thought they'd go to Tresham, no. But I knew they wouldn't stay on here forever, and then we'd have to pitch in."

"In theory," Edmund said, "you could hire a European manager. But I don't know where you'd find a competent one these days, and if you did, I don't see how you could afford him. Such people cost a fortune." He patted Marietta's hand. "I'm going to have to learn about chickens overnight, myself, and the old brain doesn't go as quickly as it once did. I remember perfectly," he said with a laugh, "everything I heard and saw before the Second War, but anything since then's quite murky. At your age, though, you get the hang of things so easily, and then you don't forget." He sat back. "We told James we'd be at Tresham by next Christmas. He's planning a big expansion after that. He'll need our help, you see."

"And you think we don't!"

Edmund stood up. "We ought to have left sooner. We were only waiting till Johnny settled down. Now he's got you, there's no reason for us to hang on, is there?"

As they were walking down the road to the cottage, Marietta exploded. "Of course, this is perfectly fine by you!"

"Dad's right. They probably ought to have left sooner. We've put off facing up to what would happen next."

"Let me tell you," Marietta shouted, "if I'd known I was going to be pushed into this, I'd never have married you, Charlie or no Charlie! I can't tell a Jersey from a Guernsey or wheat from barley. 'Farming's never been Johnny's bent,' your father says. Well, who says it's mine either?"

"You're amazing with the laborers," Jonathan said evenly. "They eat out of your hand. You've got the knack. Like Dad."

"You knew exactly what you needed, didn't you! A bush girl! Who else could stand this life? Who else would be dense enough! Marietta, simple creature, she'll put up with anything! That's what you thought!"

"We'll find a manager, then."

"And pay him with what?"

"You've got more money than I'll ever have."

"Money? I haven't a penny to my name!" Marietta stormed. "If you think for a second I could convince Carfax and Buchanan, let alone Lady Bilton, to whom life in Kenya was anathema, that hiring a manager to run your farm was a legitimate educational expense, think again! Your rich wife, Jonathan Sudbury, can't buy her way out of her own or other people's problems until 1996 and by that time she'll most probably have died of rinderpest!"

As the Land-Rover lurched over a pothole, Charlie shot from Justin's lap against the back of the front seat. "Bumped me," he wailed, rubbing his forehead; "hurts." Marietta sighed. She'd better get onto Esmail about a load of gravel right away. On Saturday, Jonathan was bringing up three plutocrats from Frankfurt. It wouldn't do to bump them, too. One night they'd spend at Olgolulu, between Isiolo and the Mara. One night with candles and the Sudbury plate and linen sheets with Eleanor's monogram embroidered in one corner. There were only eight such sheets left, and five pillowcases. These were kept on a special shelf, reserved for clients. The family, and guests who didn't pay, used rough cotton sheets and pillowcases bought on Biashara Street in Nairobi.

On the main road, about two hundred yards to the left of the gate, Marietta saw a battered cream Volkswagen pulled up on the verge. It was loaded to the roof inside and boxes were roped to the rack above. An African leaned against the hood. Arms folded, he was looking up at the great house on the ridge. As she changed gears and turned right towards Eldonia, Marietta remarked, "Wasn't that Joel? I wonder why he didn't come to greet us." Justin's nephew Joel was a Nestlé salesman; he stopped in frequently on his way to and from Nyanza in his company VW.

"That's not he," Justin replied. "Different license number. That one's a stranger. What can he be after, staring up the hill?" Although at first he'd complained vociferously, with time Justin had taken to farm life, and since the older Sudburys' departure he'd grown quite protective of Olgolulu, which he referred to nowadays as "our place." He didn't care for strangers snooping.

Round a bend they came suddenly upon a dense herd of Masai cattle, hundreds of them, blocking the road entirely. Marietta slowed to a halt and blew the horn. In response, half a dozen herdsmen in sweeping ocher togas shouted and waved their sticks and the cattle crowded more closely together than ever. In the back seat, Charles struggled. "Charlie chase those *gombes*, too!"

"Charlie's not big enough. He stays with Justin."

"Chase them too," Charles retorted, struggling harder.

In the mirror, Marietta saw the cream Volkswagen come bobbing into view. It slowed and stopped just behind them. The driver sprang out, slammed his door, and came up to see what could be done. He should know it's useless, Marietta thought. One rages and one waits. She snapped on the radio and fiddled with the knobs. She heard an advertisement for aspirin and snapped it off again.

"Mrs. Sudbury, do you remember me?"

"Michael Kagia. Oh, good God!" She gazed at him. "The parasites didn't die so you had to do the experiments all over again."

"You *do* remember!" He smiled, one arm along the edge of the window. He'd grown a mustache, which swept down below the corners of his mouth. Like a Tartar, Marietta thought — he's come out of the north, bent on conquest. For a warrior, though, he seemed extremely friendly. "When did you get back? What's it like to be home? What are you doing here, for heaven's sake, and at this hour?"

He laughed. "Can I answer so many questions all at once?" Then, eyes narrowing, he looked beyond Marietta into the back seat. His face stiffened. "Who is this boy?" he said.

"My son, Charlie."

"Ah." But a path was being cleared through the cattle at last.

"We'd better go on, or we'll miss our chance," Marietta said.

"Where are you going?"

"Barclay's Bank. It's payday. I'll be getting the wages."

"Then I'll meet you in town," he said, nodding, and ran back to his car.

"Who is that foreigner?" Justin asked immediately. "A black American?" He'd seen such people in Nairobi and he didn't approve. They talked loudly, they showed no respect.

Marietta said lightly, "He's an African, just like you."

"No, not like me," Justin said. He added, "Does the bwana know him also?"

"Since boyhood."

"Then that's another matter."

"Another matter from what?" Marietta asked. But Justin didn't elaborate.

In Eldonia he and Charles were dropped off in the Hindu playground in which there was a swing and a splintery seesaw and a sandpit not quite empty of sand, and a bench for Justin to sit on and read *Tafaya Leo*. Down the street several hundred people waited in front of the bank for the clock to strike nine and the doors to swing open.

"We'll have a battle today, Marietta," said Jim McKinley, a wizened Scot in shorts and kneesocks, with dirt under his broken fingernails. For thirty years he'd farmed up the ridge from Olgolulu. "This used to be Edmund's job, of course, scrumming for the cash. I tell you, I was so sorry to see him go! In these parts he's sorely missed. I hope that brother of his appreciates him."

"He does, don't worry." Marietta slipped past McKinley and on round the edges of the crowd. After a few moments she spotted Kagia, hurrying along the pavement.

"I was looking for a boy to watch my car," he explained. "I didn't want to leave it unattended and full of my belongings."

"Where are you going with them?"

"Kampala. I'm going to Makerere University."

"In that case, what were you doing at our place? It's twenty miles of unpaved road out of your way!"

"I was hoping to hear news of an old friend."

"Edmund Sudbury?"

Kagia nodded. "That's right."

"Well, he's gone. He left for England last December. His wife's gone, too. They went to help his brother with his chicken farm."

Kagia breathed out slowly, "This is a permanent arrangement?"

"They have no plans to come back here." Then, looking at him squarely she said, "That night in Chicago, why didn't you tell me who you were?"

"As I remember, I told you a lot about myself."

"But not that you knew my husband or my parents-in-law. Or that the farm you'd spoken of, overlooking a lake, was in fact our farm!"

He said quickly, "Should I have made an announcement to you right there in that crowded room? I disagree! I'd hoped to speak to you alone and then, as you may remember, I didn't get an opportunity."

The doors of the bank strained open as the clock began to strike nine. "I have to go now," Marietta said, turning away. She pushed forward with the rest of the crowd and jostled into line between a Sikh garage owner and a shopkeeper from Moro. He'll get into his car and drive off, she thought, and perhaps I don't care. She'd wanted him to tell her about the past, willingly, of his own accord: this is how things used to be and how they are now, this is the truth. She didn't want to dig for information and hazard guesses and be left wondering. So early in the day, and already she felt weary.

She was sixth in a queue at the mercy of a pale Asian clerk in a frayed white shirt who handed over the cash with enormous hesitancy, as if he were parceling out fractions of his own slight soul.

"I'm afraid that one will keep you waiting a very long time."

Marietta looked round. "I thought you'd driven off to Uganda and that was that!"

"You won't get rid of me so easily!" Kagia laughed. Ten feet away in the next queue, Jim McKinley was watching them with intense interest. Turning her back, Marietta said softly, "Can you meet me somewhere else? It would be better, don't you think?"

"Much better, I agree."

"There's a restaurant next to Bata Shoes on Entebbe Road. The Pavati, it's called. It has a blue sign above the door. I'll come there as quickly as I can."

"Okay." Kagia shook her hand. "Greet those at home for me," he said loudly for McKinley's sake, and made his way out of the bank.

"Haven't seen that one before, have I?" said McKinley, frowning. "Quite a chap."

"We met him in America," Marietta said casually. "He's just come home. He was born and grew up in this part of the Rift, though he's been studying abroad for many years."

"They're showing up in droves, aren't they, these bright young men. Been swotting up all over the place, Germany, France — I heard of one from Russia just the other day. Learned to be a midwife, would you believe it! What a waste of rubles! They've all been getting ready for their big chance. Well, now they've got it, haven't they? So let's see how quick they wreck this bloody country!"

At ten twenty-five, Marietta left the bank with a leather pouch full of notes and silver under one arm. Down the street she went past straggling oleander bushes, dusty in the heat of March, and into Entebbe Road. Kagia's car was parked in front of the shoe shop and as she came up he climbed out.

In the restaurant, chairs were still upside down on tables. Two old men were drinking tea in one corner near the door; otherwise, the place was deserted. The Indian proprietor hurried forward. "You are here so early, memsahb, and this time without your little boy. Is it that you have special business to attend to today?" he added, eyeing Kagia.

"That's right." Marietta accepted the chair he swung down for her. They ordered Coca-Colas and the man scampered off.

"In case you've forgotten," Marietta remarked, "there's no privacy in Africa. Nothing you do goes unobserved and everything's remembered by someone other than yourself. But at least it's practically empty here, and they have cold sodas." She leaned back in her chair. "Michael Maruga," she said, "the mechanic's son."

"How did you know that?" The collar of his shirt was open and his sleeves were rolled up above the elbow, showing the whole length of the scar on his right arm. "Well," he said with a shrug, "I suppose it wasn't difficult to put two and two together. Your husband hadn't forgotten me?"

"He remembered you at least as well as you remembered him!"

Kagia smiled faintly. "When we were boys he scarcely noticed my existence."

"Oh, he noticed you all right!"

Kagia nodded. "I suppose," he said, touching his scar, "this proves it, doesn't it?" After a moment he asked, "Where is he now? Why were you in the bank and not he?"

"He's on safari. He's a professional hunter."

"Yes, I'd heard. My friends in Chicago told me. So he's not at home too often, is that right?"

"Not too often," Marietta agreed. "He's very skilled and much sought after. Those Doroba people taught him well."

"And you, Mrs. Sudbury, how do you spend your time?"

She grinned. "Snipping dead heads off my mother-in-law's roses! No, in fact, I stand in queues. I get fences mended and potholes filled. I rush about like a headless chicken thinking disaster's struck, and then I find it hasn't, after all, but still might yet. In other words, when Edmund left he handed everything over to me."

"Not to your husband?"

"Farming doesn't suit Jonathan."

"Then he hasn't changed."

"In that respect he hasn't, no. It wasn't my cup of tea, either. To begin with, I wasn't interested in learning about fertilizer or yields or pest control. In fact, I was furious about having to and fought tooth and nail against it, but eventually, because I had no practical alternative, I swallowed my fury and started listening to what Edmund was telling me. He's a very fine teacher. I remember you saying so yourself. But just when I was really starting to enjoy myself, he left for Britain and I was on my own, sink or swim."

"Which is it?"

She smiled. "I'm swimming. Maybe I'm only doing the dog paddle, but I'm swimming nevertheless." She gathered her long fair hair, tangled from the ride into town with all the windows open, and twisted it into a knot at the back of her neck.

"Don't do that!"

"Don't do what?"

"It's much more beautiful loose."

She blushed and thanked him, but she didn't untie her hair. "It's hot this morning," she said quickly. "It's got to start raining soon! Don't you find it hot, coming suddenly like this, from the depths of winter?" He said nothing. He was watching her steadily, waiting for her to reveal herself. What does he expect, she wondered, what does he want to hear? She hurried on, "There are still a few people left at Olgolulu from your time. Do you remember Siele? He's our livestock foreman now. He's stiff and gray, but very wise."

"Missing two fingers of his left hand?"

"That's him," she nodded. "He lost them in a border dispute with the Masai before he came down from Kipsigis country. That's his story, anyway; perhaps the truth is he lost them in a bar."

"I heard the Masai story, too. He used to act out for us children exactly how it happened. Somehow," Kagia said, smiling, "the details were never quite the same twice."

"Well, he's still telling stories. Or myths, perhaps, about how things used to be. 'In the old days they did this and this, in Bwana Philip's time.' Mind you, Bwana Philip died in 1931. 'Then Bwana Edmund went to the White Man's Country and brought back three grade cows on the airplane!' In those days there weren't airplanes, and Edmund got his cattle from Nyanga; even so, Siele insists on his version. 'You weren't here. You came so recently. Can you know all that they knew?' 'Maybe I can't,' I tell him, 'but one thing's certain, they aren't here now and I am. Do as I say, Siele, not as you remember them doing all those years ago.'"

"And then what happens?"

"With a great deal of sighing and frowning and shaking of the head he gives in. But it's just as if there's a column of ghosts lined up behind him, and all of them frowning and sighing together. Who are you, they seem to be saying, you're still a stranger. You only came here yesterday!"

The proprietor pushed through a beaded curtain with their sodas on a tray. The smell of curry wafted after him. The beads clicked. "Not so cold," he said, placing two Cokes on the table. "This morning there was no electricity. No fan, no fridge. Not my fault, you see," he added, hitching himself up on the next table, between two upturned metal chairs. "From overseas are you," he said comfortably to Kagia, "and posted here in Eldonia? What office? Ministry of Fuel and Power? Always trouble we are having with the electricity! Perhaps you will improve it? Or are you working in the hospital? Mrs. Kakar, who runs the x-ray machine, is taking maternity leave. Are you the one to replace her?"

"Dr. Kagia has just come from the United States," Marietta said distinctly, "with news and messages from my husband's friends. He stopped in for a very short time to speak with me on his way to Kampala."

"That's right," Kagia said. "I've got an appointment early in the morning. In fact, as soon as I've finished this soda, I'll be leaving here, so now will you excuse us?"

The proprietor shrugged. "Doctor? They are short of a doctor, too. That Lebanese has gone back home. Did you hear?" As he turned to go, he added to Marietta, "Next time be sure to bring your son. Tell him Rama has something for him in the kitchen."

When he'd gone, Kagia said quietly, "I hadn't known before that you had children. In America you didn't speak of having any."

"I only have one, the little boy you saw on the road," Marietta replied. "Right now he's in the playground down the street getting sleepier by the minute. It's time I took him home to bed. You're coming back to Olgolulu with us, aren't you?"

"I haven't got time, I'm afraid."

"Of course you have!" Marietta exclaimed. "Didn't you tell me if ever you'd had a home it was there? I've been expecting you to turn up at Olgolulu for at least a year!"

"But I have an appointment to keep in Kampala. Nine o'clock sharp with Professor Tillman, who belongs to the old school."

"He shouts, you mean."

"Sometimes, certainly. But he happens to know more about waterborne diseases than anyone else in Africa. I met him when he came to the United States some time ago and we've corresponded ever since. You see, we have very similar interests, and I've been fortunate in getting a lectureship in his department, starting tomorrow."

"Then let's hurry! Olgolulu's twenty miles in the wrong direction, and as you probably noticed, the road's just as bad as ever it was. But if we leave now we'll be out there by twelve. It'll take me half an hour to do the wages. Then we'll have a bit of lunch and I'll give you the grand tour. You'll be on your way by four."

But Kagia was shaking his head. "Not today. I only came in order to get news of your father-in-law."

Marietta's face fell. And not to see me? But of course not! she thought. When your drama took place I was still down in Tanganyika in a rest house with a rusting iron roof. The patch of *shamba* behind it produced okra and the odd tomato. Everything else withered and died. No riches there! I didn't have a patrimony to win or lose. I wasn't even in the running. I have Olgolulu by default, because my husband, your old enemy, would rather die than be bound by the exacting and repetitious demands of the agricultural cycle.

"And from you," Kagia was saying, "I've learned that he's gone and won't be coming back. So now I must hurry to Kampala. I ought to have arrived there last September, but my research took longer to complete than I'd anticipated and my report took longer to write. Meanwhile, I've received four letters and six telegrams from Tillman, the last of which said, 'See me at nine on the first or contract canceled.' That's why I can't accept your invitation, Mrs. Sudbury."

She looked down. For months she'd imagined watching his face as he went with her round his old home, hers now, and considered the splendors of it. After a moment she said, as matter-of-factly as she could manage, "I told Edmund that I'd met you. He'd been hoping to see you before he left. In case you ever go to England, you should have his address." She wrote it on a page torn from her diary. "Here."

"Tresham," he read. "What is that?"

"I've never seen it myself, but I'm told it's very large and very cold; the Sudbury family has lived there since the Middle Ages. Jonathan will probably inherit it one day."

"And then he'll go to live there also?"

"Oh, no! He has no interest in it whatsoever. He says he was born here and he intends to die here, too. Perhaps my son will go there, though."

Kagia said slowly, "From what I knew of him, I thought your husband wouldn't care to live in Kenya nowadays."

"People sometimes turn out to be different from what we thought they were," Marietta said dryly. "I, too, am late. I'm sure the laborers are already lined up waiting for their wages." As she rose, she added, "By the way, I know a young woman at Makerere. Her name's Catherine Mattias. She's extremely intelligent. Most people think she's beautiful. She's also very fierce."

"In that case, shouldn't I stay away from her?" Kagia smiled.

"I imagine she's got a soft spot somewhere. It's only a matter of finding it. Believe me, she's most unusual. Unique, I'd say. But so are you. You might suit one another."

Outside on the pavement they shook hands. "Greet your husband. Ask Siele if he remembers me, and if he does, greet him as well," Kagia added, unlocking the door of his car.

"Wait!" Marietta cried. "Don't go yet."

He looked up. "What is it?"

"You haven't told me what you thought!"

"When? About what?"

"In Chicago, having realized who we were, Jonathan and I."

"I thought many different things. But can you expect me to describe them here?" He was silent for a moment. "I was glad and I was very sorry. But after some time" — he smiled faintly — "I began feeling glad again. Now I must be going, and so must you. Take good care of Olgolulu!"

He's going to his own kind, she thought. Was she glad or was she sorry? With the wages heavy on her hip, Marietta walked off. Behind her she heard the VW shake into life and move slowly, faster, away to the Uganda road. She found the Land-Rover and went to fetch her son.

16

Dobson's Gorge

Jonathan was going up to Dobson's Gorge to camp by a river over-hung by high red rocks. He'd be gone for the month of February. "This time, Etta, will you come? When we went to the gorge before Charlie was born, you loved that country. You haven't been there since."

At the library table, making lists, Marietta answered without looking up, "But Kabir's promised to start digging the new well on Monday. I can't leave until he's finished. We're making a big investment, Johnny. We simply can't afford to make a mess of things."

"When was the last time you came out with me? August? July? It was so long ago I can't remember."

"Can I be in two places at once?"

"Occasionally you could be in my place rather than yours."

"Is Olgolulu mine?"

"It seems so. You've taken it over."

"But that's just what you wanted!" Marietta exclaimed in exasperation. "You and Edmund. It was my part in the grand plan. Anything else I had in mind to do was by your lights trivial and unworthy. And I started from scratch, remember. I've made dozens of silly small mistakes and a handful of important big ones. Once every week or so, I still get into a cold sweat — oh, my God, what did I do, what *didn't* I do that I should have done?" She pushed back from the table. "First you wanted an heir for your Eden, and after that a caretaker. I've provided you with both, haven't I? What more do you want?"

At the window, high above the lake, flamingo-ringed on a dazzling morning, Jonathan said, "You've done marvelously. You do marvelously. I can't imagine anyone doing better. Only I scarcely even see you!" Hands in pockets, leaning up against the sill, he added quietly, "I imagine this arrangement suits you, though."

"Exactly what d'you mean by that?"

He shrugged. "Once it was Virginia, you, and Justin. Now it's you, Charlie, and Justin. In your scheme of things husbands and fathers just drop in and out. Yesterday when I got home I went and found Charlie. 'Let's check over the lorry,' I said. 'The engine's been knocking. Don't you want to help me find out what's the matter?' Small boys are mad about lorries, aren't they? All except my son! 'Can't come with you,' he said. 'Justin's waiting.' 'Let him wait,' I said. 'He's not your father. I am.' '*You're* Johnny,' he said. He was standing on the ground, heels dug in, head down. 'Well, how about coming with me anyway?' So he straggled after me and climbed up and looked in the engine, but in ten minutes, when I went into the workshop to fetch something, he was off. Later on I saw him with Justin. They had their heads together on the kitchen steps. They were looking at pictures in an old newspaper, chattering away in Ruba, and they weren't about to switch to include me."

Marietta folded a note to herself and put it in her shirt pocket. She stood up. "You're wrong," she said quietly.

"Wrong? How?"

"I mean about Charlie. He spends half the day pretending to be you. He talks about you constantly."

"He doesn't talk *to* me, though. He can hardly wait to get away."

"I was just like him," Marietta said slowly. "After Mum ran away from Neville Bilton I was always talking to him in my head and coaxing Violet into playing games of make-believe about him. I didn't know where he was or if I'd ever see him again." She looked down at the faded blues and oranges of the Persian carpet on the library floor. "And when I did see him again, I was tongue-tied. I couldn't fit the real man in. Actual conversations were so much more difficult than imaginary ones. Neville could never have guessed from my behavior face to face how much I idolized him. I was a good deal older than Charlie, of course, but probably he suffers from the same sort of thing."

"Charlie doesn't suffer!" Jonathan said bitterly. "I'm the one who's suffering."

"I'm sorry."

285

"Sorry! No, you're not! You dislike the life I lead. You can't stand most of the people I lead it with, and you have an ironclad excuse for staying as far away from it as you possibly can. You're *always* needed here, whatever the season. So if *I* need you occasionally, that's just too bad!"

There had been a time when she had taken Charlie and gone out in the bush with her husband every month or two and never thought twice about leaving Olgolulu. But after Edmund and Eleanor left, she'd moved out of the cottage, up the hill and into the big house, into her parents-in-law's room. After some months she'd stopped dreaming the old dream of searching for Neville and finding him alive and loving her; she'd stopped waking, grief-stricken, to the truth that he was dead and had been dead for years. In the great carved bed she slept a dreamless sleep and awakened refreshed in the morning. She rarely thought about that other world which with such pain and disbelief and turmoil she'd once watched vanish over the curve of the earth. She cared very little for what happened beyond her own horizon now. Olgolulu was what had her attention, and the unremarkable events occurring on the length and breadth of her land.

"I'm always afraid," she said ruefully, "that things will fall to pieces if I'm not here, but I hugely exaggerate my own importance. Siele can manage perfectly well without me for a week or so." She went up to Jonathan and kissed him quickly. "You can see I'm getting more like Edmund day by day. I'm obsessed, just like he used to be." She laughed. "Do you know, when I think about myself I see a house on a mountainside, surrounded by fields!"

"I don't. I see a beautiful girl who could never by any stretch of my imagination be transformed into a house. Look," he said softly, arms round her, stroking her hair, "you're stringently single-minded. That's the thing about you which got me in the first place. It's just that from time to time I find myself feeling a bit left out. I get jealous, and I whine. It's very unattractive, I agree."

Slipping away from him, Marietta went to look at the calendar that was tacked to a narrow strip of wall between tall banks of bookshelves, still stuffed, two years after his departure, with Edmund's journals. "Kabir will be here on the fourth and I should allow ten days for the well. Let's see, that'll take us to Thursday, the fourteenth." The calendar bore a colored photograph of President Kenyatta addressing the Kenya Union of Farmers. Marietta

286

had been proposed as secretary of the Eldonia branch by Jim McKinley. "We *wazungu* have to show form," he'd said, "and you're the only fresh face among us." She hadn't a hope in hell of winning, since there were exactly eleven white farmers left in this part of the valley. Eleven votes; ten, if Humphrey Smith was drunk on the day of the election. But McKinley insisted on her standing nevertheless. The vote was scheduled for the first week of March. She had to be back by then. "Who'll be out with you?"

A fellow called Noble, Jonathan told her, and assorted friends. Six of them; Noble would be the only gun.

"What in the world will they do with themselves for a month in the bush?"

"I imagine they have something in mind. It seems unlikely they'd spend a fortune just to hang around for Noble to come back at night. Maybe they play poker. Or chess. Maybe they take exquisite photographs."

"Noble hasn't been out before, has he?"

"Not with me, at any rate. He was sent my way by Clive Van Wyck, who's his brother-in-law. Clive's been after me for a long time about taking Noble on, so when the Sandersons canceled, I thought, Might as well give him first refusal. I wrote, and got no reply for ages, and then a couple of weeks ago a cable arrived from Calicut."

"Calicut? Where's that?"

"India. That's where Noble is, or was. He'll be at the Norfolk tonight, together with his crew. I'm picking them up at nine tomorrow morning."

"I remember Clive," Marietta said, grimacing. "He gleamed and glistened. He took extravagant care of himself."

"Rich people tend to, since their principal passion is usually themselves. That's true of the rest of us, too, I suppose; only they have greater scope than we do for indulging their passion."

"Must you be so cynical, Johnny," Marietta teased.

"I think I must," Jonathan said dryly. "In this business cynicism's the most essential item in one's kit."

Virginia was coming for the night. She'd be up for lunch, she'd said on the telephone. She was sorry to be missing Jonathan. "Hardly seen him in months. How much have you?"

At twelve o'clock Charles was hopping about outside the front door. When he spotted a cloud of dust down the farm road he dashed to the laundry room and pulled Justin away from his ironing. The two of them were on the steps as Virginia drove up in her sky blue Datsun truck with "Oldfield Interior Designs" stenciled on the door.

"What did you bring me! What did you bring!"

"You ought to cut his hair. The child will get cross-eyes," Virginia remarked, brushing red curls off Charlie's forehead.

"When I bring the scissors he screams. You'd think I was a murderer."

"Then get his mother to do it."

"He screams louder than ever with her. He knows what he does and does not want, this boy."

"You spoil him rotten, Justin, just as you spoiled my daughter. You always let her have her way. And now it's him. The only one you never spoiled," Virginia murmured, "was me. What've we got here?" she added, holding up a plastic bag of toys, and the three of them sat on the steps to see.

Marietta found them racing cars across the terrace. Mum never did that with me, she thought. She never had time to play, not even Snap. But I hardly ever have the time either, do I? Virginia had pronounced, "Until a certain stage, it's wise just to look and wait in hope," but once she had confidence that the danger of Charlie's depositing his lunch on her lap was past, she'd taken to being a grandmother in earnest. Everyone in the know in Nairobi wanted an Oldfield interior — the smart, bright fabrics, the plump cushions, the wall hangings — and Saturday was her busiest day, but she'd shut her shop this Saturday, disappointed dozens of people, and sped to see her grandson with a bag full of Japanese toys. Apart from Bruce, Charles was the only human being able to distract her from the task at hand for more than half an hour. "Charlie, Charlie, shine my shoes?" she'd sung a hundred times, rolling her eyes, pointing to her toes, and a hundred times Charlie had hiccupped with laughter. She let him ride horsey on her back, holding her hair as reins; she had rolling races with him down the sloping lawn on Olduvai Road, covering her Italian blouses and her smart flared linen skirts with grass clippings, laddering her nylons. She bashed out songs on the Olgolulu piano, which had languished, untuned, for half a dozen years. "I never heard you play when I was young. I didn't even know you could," Marietta told her.

288

"*Then* I couldn't. I'd forgotten. It's only now that I've remembered." And at bedtime she told amazing tales of derring-do in the old Northwest Frontier District.

By the library fire, when a thoroughly overexcited Charlie had fallen asleep at last, Virginia shivered. "What a barn this house is! I'm never so cold as I am here. No, that's not quite true. Itep was worse. Besides the cold there was the damp and that smell of incipient decay. I can't understand this compulsion for living in huge houses on windy mountainsides! And here you are, just the three of you, and mostly only two." She sipped her whiskey. "You don't see much of Jonathan." A statement and a question.

"We both have a lot to do."

"An odd life, though who am I to say?" A moment later she said, "I see you're about to have an election."

Marietta nodded. "It's a ritual, really. With yours truly as the sacrificial lamb."

"Good gracious! You're standing too?"

"It's Jim McKinley's idea."

"Then why aren't you listed in the paper?"

"Local union politics are hardly of national interest. The vote's on the first of March. There's a big Kikuyu from up Sabukia way who'll win hands down."

Virginia shook her head. "That's not what I was talking about. I meant the Parliamentary by-election. You know, to fill the seat of that Kimoja fellow who was killed in the car accident on New Year's Day. In this morning's paper there's a list of candidates."

"Really? I haven't seen today's paper." Marietta grinned. "No, I'm certainly not standing for Parliament. Jim McKinley may be slightly deranged, but he's not so out of it that he'd try to make an MP of me!"

"There's a Dr. Michael Kagia who sounds interesting."

Marietta held out her hands to the fire. "It *is* cold, isn't it?" she remarked, "and fires don't help. All the heat goes up the chimney. Sometimes I long for one of those gas fires they have in London, the shilling-in-the-meter kind you can roast your front by." Then in a carefully noncommittal voice she added, "Kagia? Funny, I met a Michael Kagia the time I went to America with Johnny."

"Could this be the one? The paper said his father died in the Vanga camp. The police tried forcing prisoners who'd taken the Mau Mau oath to go through a sort of expiation rite, but this man's father was one of the few who held out. Eventually the superintendent made them dig their own graves and had them lined up and shot. And buried right there, in the graves they'd dug themselves. There was a terrific *shauri* when it all came out. It had the whole Empire, or what was left of it, shaking in its shoes."

They'd been living at Baluga when the Vanga news leaked out. Marietta had still been doing the course from Pietermaritzburg and one early morning she'd run up to the market to buy exercise books for Dr. Vorster's compositions. The stall where you bought them sold newspapers and magazines as well, and she'd had to wait to buy what she needed while the proprietor unloaded a pickup truck just in from Kisumu. After a night of slow rain there'd been mist in the hollows and banana stands below the town, and Marietta had watched as the Africans coming up from the valley broke into the sunlight and laughed to see the bright blue day. At last when the bundles of newspapers were in place at the front of the stall and he'd sold a couple, the proprietor turned to Marietta. She wanted two hundred-page notebooks this time, she told him; the fifty-page size got finished in a flash. But behind her an orderly from the Baluga hospital was reading the newspaper headlines aloud and translating them from English into Keriki. People passing stopped and almost instantly a crowd gathered, pushing up to the man, demanding that he translate the columns underneath as well. Beside him, Marietta had listened to every terrible word. Which side was she on? Was she even free to choose? Surely these frightened, angry, staring people would make her go with her own kind. But they totally ignored her, and after a few moments of gesturing and fierce discussion the orderly folded up his paper and went off to his shift at the hospital. The crowd drifted away, Marietta's racing heart slowed, and she paid for her notebooks and left. She hadn't been forced to take sides, not then, not later. Even after all these years she still trod the same fine line.

"Being the son of a freedom fighter your friend will get plenty of mileage, I'd say," Virginia remarked.

"He's not my friend," Marietta said quickly.

"Well, anyway, it seems he's expected to win, in which case knowing him might come in handy. You can never tell when things'll get tough for you up here. So far you'll admit you've led something of a charmed life."

"Charmed!" Marietta exclaimed indignantly. "We produce more milk per head of cattle and higher yields of wheat per acre than

any other farm in Rift Valley Province, including Kitale and Eldoret! We're still here not because of charms or magic, but because
the government has to feed twelve million people and they can't
afford to let us go!"

"I didn't mean to cast aspersions. May I help myself?"

"Go ahead."

When she was settled again by the fire with a new drink, Virginia
said quietly, "Bruce hasn't been at all well, I'm afraid." Four
months ago he'd awakened in the night with a sharp pain in his
chest. It had gone away within an hour, and being Bruce he hadn't
done anything about it. He hadn't got time to go to doctors. On the
third of January he'd had the pain again, and Virginia had herself
driven him to Dr. Hewitt. After tests, Hewitt told them that Bruce
had had two heart attacks.

"Small ones," Virginia said, "but nevertheless, this puts a different light on things. Hewitt insists that Bruce cut down drastically,
but he couldn't bear to sell out and stay on watching other people
make money off the business he built up. Or even worse, watching
as it went to pot. He'd go barmy." Carefully she lit a cigarette. "So
to cut a long story short, we've decided to leave Kenya. As you
know, Bruce has always said that having come here rather late in
life, he wasn't willing to go anywhere else, except at gunpoint.
When everyone was doomsaying, still he wasn't put off. But he re-
alizes now that if he were to cut down and stay on afterwards, he'd
be absolutely wretched and in no time he'd be off and running and
back at his old pace again. In some new place, though, I might just
be able to keep him quiet." She smiled. "I'll cross my fingers,
anyway."

"You of all people, Mum!" Marietta stood in front of the mantelpiece with the Sudbury arms carved in the center. She added,
shaking her head, "I can't imagine you anywhere else."

"Neither could I, until a month ago."

"Where will you go? Rhodesia?"

"Oh, no! We shan't stay in Africa. We're thinking of Spain. Bruce
went there once and fancied it. The summer's hotter than hell, but
the winter's short. The living's cheap. We shan't be allowed to take
much money out. So we shan't be able to live as we do here, but
at least in Spain there are doctors of sorts and hospitals if need be
and enough British types for company. Even a few one knows from
here."

"It sounds grim," Marietta said.

"It wouldn't appeal to the young. But we aren't young." Virginia smiled. "To tell you the truth, I'm quite excited. I'm a bit tired of Oldfield Interiors. The first dozen cushioned benches were fun, but now everyone wants cushions on their benches. They won't consider anything else. In Spain, I shan't do hotels or shops or residential property or anything I've done before. Next time I'll start a travel agency." She grinned. "Oh, I know there are already hundreds on the Costa del Sol. Everyone's starting this and that, but I've come up the hard way. Spanish time couldn't be slower than Kenyan time or the Spanish more maddening than the Africans. I'm extremely hard to daunt." She sipped her drink. "So what do you think, Etta, of two middle-aged people, one with a dicky heart, going off into the world?"

"And without a backward glance, right?" For a few moments Marietta was silent. Then she said, dryly, "Well, with you I shan't make the mistake I made with Edmund and Eleanor. The first year after they left I'd write them long letters full of news about the neighbors. Then one day it dawned on me that they weren't interested in Mrs. Strang's corgi having puppies or whether the Butlers' cook turned out to be a thief, even though they'd eaten his Yorkshire pudding every other Sunday for twenty years! Don't worry, I shan't bore *you* with details from your old life."

"Look at me!"

"Wasn't I?"

"No, Etta. You were looking at my feet. We've had our ups and downs," Virginia said softly. "That's been more my fault than yours. When you were younger I was like a dog worrying a bone. I wouldn't let well alone."

"Let what well alone?"

"Those three deaths."

Marietta drew in her breath sharply. "Whatever do you mean?"

"It wasn't just your father's. There'd been my parents', too." Virginia closed her eyes. After a moment she went on, "I was off in Abyssinia when I got the letter from the bank in Thomson's Falls. I put it in my suitcase, changed into my newest dress, and went out and had a drink. And then I more or less forgot about it, about them. I didn't miss them. I hardly thought about them. I'd run away from them in 1939 as fast as my two legs could carry me, and three years later, when that letter came, I was still running. But grief sometimes plays odd tricks on you. It lurks about and dodges

292

in and out of dreams and for years you aren't aware it's waiting for you. It wasn't till the war was over and I came back south that it caught up with me. I hadn't intended to break my mother's heart, only to insist on a life of my own. I'd meant one day to tell her that, and to tell my father that I didn't hate him, I truly wished him peace. But I missed my chance to tell them anything, and there I was, adrift. Charlie wasn't enough of a mooring. Neither was Africa, despite the old familiar life and landscape.

"I was just about at my lowest when I found out I was going to have you. I hadn't meant to be pregnant — not then, anyway. I'd been taking precautions. But I knew immediately that I had to have my baby, there was never a doubt in my mind. I tried to explain to Charlie that it was the one hope I had of making peace. 'But you've only enough life for one, Virginia. Husband *or* child, not both. For you a child may mean a new beginning, but for me it's the end.' And he meant exactly what he said. I didn't believe him and I should have. Two months later he was dead."

"How could you have believed him? How could you have known?"

"Because he'd done the same thing before. Tried to, rather, only he'd bungled it, shot himself through the shoulder instead of the heart and put himself in hospitals of various sorts for the best part of a year. Oh, and I knew that! Daphne had told me up in Cairo and later he'd said so himself. But I thought, It won't happen this time. It can't. He's different. He's not that way anymore. He's ever so much stronger than he used to be. On the Italian front he'd won two Military Crosses for bravery!" She sighed deeply. "I didn't tell him to his face that I was leaving. I didn't dare. I left a letter and walked out, and within half an hour of reading that letter, he was dead. I might as well have pulled the trigger, mightn't I?"

Marietta said softly, "You really thought his dying was your fault."

"Then I did. Despite all the signs that he was heading for disaster, I turned my back. I left him for another man. Someone who'd protect me, so I hoped. But how could anyone do that? Your father was my responsibility; and after he was dead it was up to me to take the consequences. Up to you, too, of course, once you'd been born. We both had to do our time. Fifteen years, as it turned out." She paused. "D'you know who finally convinced me enough was enough? Geoffrey Lucas!"

Marietta frowned. "Why him?"

"I'd dragged you from one flyblown town to another, I'd scarcely let you out of my sight. I'd chosen you over Charlie, so my job was being a mother to my child. I'd made my bed, I'd better lie on it. But of course you weren't going to remain a child forever. It was only when Lucas appeared, though, that I realized that; before he came, I'd had plugs in my ears and blinkers on. But what happened between you and him made me see you were practically grown up! There wasn't any point going on with our hair-shirt existence, then, was there? You didn't need me anymore, or hardly. In fact, you couldn't wait to get away! But what in heaven's name would I do then? That's when the miracle occurred. In a downpour outside the city market I ran into Bruce. Literally. I skidded my old Land-Rover into his van. Bashed in the back." She smiled faintly. "Oh, there was a *shauri*, too! Anyway, that's the way we met, though how or why or what I did to deserve him, I don't know. I'd never had much luck with men before." She added gently, "Believe me, if it were up to me I wouldn't dream of leaving Kenya. It's only for his sake that I'm going, Etta, otherwise I'd stay."

Marietta knelt to put a new log on the fire. "I should be used to being left by now," she said gruffly. "On this road nowadays the Strangs and the McKinleys and the Sudburys are the only Europeans. I don't know how many farm sales I've been to in the last eighteen months, or how many lifetimes' worth of blankets and baling wire and crockery and circular saws and God knows what else I've seen sold off." She stood and poked the log with her foot and sparks flew. "No one in their right mind would stay."

"Why do you?"

"For Johnny, leaving's never been an option."

"But for you?"

"I hold the fort."

"While he's off making the money for you to hold it with."

"Correct."

"Why do you put up with it?"

Marietta opened her eyes to see her mother watching her expectantly and without malice. "For my own sake," she said. After a moment she went on, "Although I had no experience of belonging in any particular place, I had a yearning for exactly that. After Edmund and Eleanor announced that they were leaving, I started to spend almost all my time on the farm, and gradually I began to see that Edmund loved this place almost as if it were a human being. I would watch him and marvel, and envy his resolve, and his joy, day in and day out, even as he took his leave. One evening, very near the end, we were coming down the hill together. The clouds were low and you could see the light on over the front door. He was humming under his breath. When we came to the railing beyond the drive, he said, as he swung one leg over, 'I've been extraordinarily happy here, Marietta; it's my sense you will be, too.'"

She shrugged. "One reads in novels about women pining for their lovers. They're in a state of alert misery because they're forced to be alone. Well, I've never experienced that — except over Olgolulu. The truth is, I'm quite lost away from here! Those few weeks in England each July seem endless. I'm glad to see Neville's mother and Sophia, of course, and I'm glad the other grandparents have a chance to see Charlie growing up. But I'll be thankful when he's big enough to be put on a plane without me. Because the fact is, I feel dreary away from home. Off kilter." She smiled faintly. "Unplugged."

"Thank you," Virginia said.

"For what?"

"For having your say."

"I have a great deal of time to think and nobody much to talk to." After a moment's silence she said, "You are off to a new life in a new country." She hesitated and finally, in wonder, finished, "But you settled your account. Wherever you go, Mum, good luck!"

The well was finished on the fifteenth and Marietta set off to meet Jonathan at Dobson's Gorge. North of Kitale on the Kapenguria road a policeman waved her down. He wanted all her papers, even the log book. But why that, too? "Let me see it," he said officiously. As he scrutinized it page by page, he remarked, "You are going to Lokot?"

"To the gorge."

"That is close to Lokot," he said. "I will go with you. I have home leave. I haven't been at home since May." He climbed in beside her, removed his hat and with it his officiousness. He began telling her about his brother, who'd been wounded by Somali *shiftas* in a cattle raid. "Last year he was well. Now he cannot walk. And he has six children. Who will pay to educate them? I, of course, and I have seven of my own." A few miles further on he spotted a kinsman with a cardboard suitcase outside a crossroads bar. "Let him come also," he said. They went on three more hours to another cross-roads by a dried-up river bed, where the men got out. They'd walk the ten miles to Lokot.

Marietta reached camp after dark. Hearing the Land-Rover far down the gorge, Jonathan had come out to meet her.

"You missed the sunset. The blood red rocks. I'd almost given up on you. But you made it after all, thank God."

"How are you?"

"Hanging by my fingernails. Buxton Noble's a different type from his brother-in-law."

In a large screened tent six people sprawled, waiting for their supper. The sweet smell of marijuana hung in the air.

"Lovely to see you." A sun-scorched giant bore down on Marietta. His hair was tied back in a ponytail and he wore a pendent elephant god round his neck. "I'm Buxton. Great you could take the time away to see us," he said expansively, as if the tent were his and the gorge as well. Behind him sat Theo and Victor in kurtas, heavily beaded. They had fair, fragile faces and narrow wrists. "They look like twins," Buxton said, "but they aren't. They're together." Luna, curled on a cushion, was black. Later, uncurled, she turned out to be six feet two inches tall. "We used to be together," Buxton said. "Now Ogden takes her photograph." Ogden wore white jeans, a purple shirt, and two gold rings in the lobe of his right ear. "And Brooke's with me." Brooke had dark curly hair and a length of cloth wrapped under her arms, across her breasts, and behind her neck. "We're having a wonderful time," she said. "Jonathan's so super" — only she said "thuper."

For supper they had herb omelettes and bread and cheese. They were vegetarians, Brooke explained. Since Orissa. They'd been living in an ashram in Bubaneshwa, but abstinence hadn't suited Buxton and the sleeping mats were all too short. "It didn't suit me either, really," Brooke put in.

"They didn't like her sunbathing on the kitchen roof," Theo said.

"And after all his preaching purity the guru made a dead set at Luna."

"I thought *darshin* meant lookie no feelie," Luna said, "but that guy said it depended on one's karma. Nude." She grimaced. "He was a real runt, once you got those robes off him."

"So we quit and went to Goa and the beach. And came on here

296

from there. We like Africa," Brooke said. "In India there were far too many people. They'd be coming inside after you, and you'd be thinking, Well, surely when the house is all filled up, they'll stop. But they just kept on packing themselves in. Kind of dumb, don't you think?"

"And when this safari's over, where will you go then?"

"We might just stay," Brooke said. "Get our own place in Katari. We know some neat people there. But Ogden's going to the States. He's doing a book, you know, the Goddess Luna. It's got to be a smash, and maybe we'll go on back with him. It just depends on where we're at." Brooke jumped to her feet. "Right now I wanna dance."

"That's Brooke's thing, really," Buxton said. He took out a tape recorder and turned on the Rolling Stones.

Luna curled up on her cushion again, her head on Ogden's knee. Theo and Victor rolled joints and offered them around. "Kamba gold," Victor said, "the best in the hemisphere. I'd kill for it."

Brooke began to dance, dark hair sweeping through the lamplight. "She's a great girl," Buxton said, leaning back in his canvas chair, legs outstretched. He wore no shoes. "Once she was working in a topless bar on the Coast. Up in a cage, you know. Spectacular! Her old man heard though, and flew out. Hired some sort of Mafioso — you know, scowling, with a lump under his jacket where the revolver was. The two of them burst in and dragged Brookie out. Covered her up in a great big bath towel and carried her off. She fought like a tigress, but what could she do, really, against that hood? She's never danced professionally since then. A shame, I think. You can see how talented she is. She's had bad luck, I tell you. In Orissa they wouldn't let her play her tapes. That was a real drag. For us as well as her. We missed her show."

"Dance with me, Johnny," Brooke lisped, reaching out to him. "You're such a super dancer."

Later, sitting on the edge of her cot in Jonathan's tent, Marietta said, "Why did they come here?"

"They'd run out of other scenes, so they got into mine, as they'd say."

"And who or what is Noble?"

"He's rich, obviously. From pharmaceuticals. He dabbles in politics and Broadway shows. One he backed was a great sensation.

Feet, it was called. Luna was the star. Ogden did the sets. Buxton found Theo and Victor in India."

"And what about Brooke?"

"She ran away from prep school with her father's chauffeur. There was a huge to-do. It was all in *Newsweek* and the *Daily Mirror*. 'Heiress elopes with Yardman,' that sort of thing, and pictures of Brooke sitting on this fellow's lap in Puerto Vallarta."

"You saw them?"

"She's got a file with all the clippings. She'll show them to you if you're in the least bit interested. I wasn't actually, but she showed them to me anyway. She took up with Buxton after the annulment. But Buxton, by the way, is in love with Ogden."

"You've had an earful, haven't you?"

"Indeed I have," Jonathan said, yawning.

"Brooke seems about to switch to you."

Jonathan shrugged. "I'm just one of the facilities. Like a chair or a vehicle. Here to be used."

"Or like a yardman." Marietta began taking clothes out of her duffel bag.

"On the whole," Jonathan said mildly, "they don't take much advantage of the facilities. When we first came up here I took Buxton out twice. He's got a license for leopard and we'd seen some about, but he's not interested. 'Just because I've got a license doesn't mean I have to shoot the fucking thing,' he said. 'It's hot out there in the bush. I've been hot enough in India.'"

"So what do they do all day?"

"Ogden gets up at five-twenty to take his pictures before the sun's too high. That girl Luna poses in a gold bikini and sometimes stark naked. The Turkana herdsmen are mesmerized. I told Ogden, You can't do this, not in front of Africans. Why not? he said. They're naked themselves, so what's the difference? I said, There *is* a difference. That's not my problem, he said; tell them to fuck off. But this is their grazing land, I told him, and what you're doing is offensive. You're kidding, he said. Luna's a terrific shape.

"The others smoke dope and I'm out all day. Mostly I've been going after leopard. The difference is of course that when I've pursued him for the best part of a week and finally I'm up close, I take a good long look and walk away instead of killing him." Jonathan smiled. "Awful as they are, I can put up with a lot worse than No-

298

ble and his friends because a hundred yards away from camp I totally forget about them. I only have to contend with them at dinner."

Marietta told Jonathan about Bruce's heart and the plans for Spain.

"Should we envy them," she said, "a little?"

"I don't," he said.

"But they're free to go."

"I don't envy anyone," Jonathan replied, beginning to make love. "Why should I? I've got my girl."

"There's one more thing."

"Now?"

"Let it wait, then," she said, but she stiffened.

"Okay, what is it, then?" he said.

"Michael Kagia's standing for Kimoja's seat in Central Rift. He's been campaigning for a week already. His picture's in the paper every day."

Jonathan lay back. "What are we supposed to do? Hang out the flags to welcome the returning hero?"

On the way home the radiator sprang a leak and Marietta had to get her Land-Rover towed to a garage in Kitale.

"Today's Thursday," the mechanic said. "You'll have it on Monday at half past four. No cars to hire here, either; you'll have to take a taxi." But as she wouldn't risk her life in one of those, she took a bus going to Nairobi and every crossroads in between. She climbed in, edged all the way down, heaved her bag up on the seat beside her, and sat back. In the heat and clamor she hovered on the edge of sleep. But suddenly she jolted awake to see a huge old man in a felt hat and long black overcoat pushing his way through the bus.

"Watch out," the old man grumbled, prodding with elbows and staff. "Aye, move, let me pass!" He eased himself into the seat beside her, and with an enormous sigh rested his chin on the carved handle of his staff.

"Chief Mattias, *mboyore!*"

"What's this!" he exclaimed, surging to life again. "Miss Marietta! I heard that you'd married a rich European from Eldonia. Now have you run away from him?" Throwing his head back, he laughed, eyes shut in the old way.

"Not such a rich man," she said, smiling, "and now his vehicle's broken down. I've had to leave it in a garage here. He won't be happy when he has to pay for the repairs."

"Vehicles are far too costly," Mattias said emphatically.

"How are things at home?" Marietta asked.

"Not good at all." But that she'd known, of course. For eight counts of embezzlement and fraud he'd been sentenced to two years of hard labor, which, owing to his age, had been commuted to two years making doormats in the Kisumu prison. At the front the conductor shouted and clanged the door shut. But they remained in the lorry park nonetheless while the conductor made his way through the bus, taking the fares. "Eldonia," Mattias said, counting out the coins carefully.

"You also?" Marietta said. "What takes you there?"

"I hope to recover a debt," he replied, bringing his face so close to Marietta's that she smelled the sour breath. "Many people are in my debt from the old days. Now they are wealthy, and I, who helped them once, am as you see."

The bus started up at last and off they went, past the market and the bank, past the Kitale Club. In her mind's eye she saw Neville watching her across the table as she ate her filet of Thomson's gazelle. "I hope you'll fatten her up. The kid's too thin!" "I'm doing my best." Neville laughed, smoothing his hair, gray at the temples. How elegant he is, how distinguished he is, and he'll be mine forever, she'd told herself, despite already knowing with every bone in her body that in fact her time was running out, she should be getting ready for the end. But he'd never been hers, not even in the first place. He'd been Virginia's, and so had she; for all his promises, he hadn't moved a finger to stop Virginia from taking her away. And supposing her dream had come true, supposing she'd made her way to Jasper, Alberta, and through the town and through the forest and up to the wooden house he built with the view, she'd have found that while she loved him, he'd only loved the idea of her. She'd been a small girl once with whom it had pleased him to spin fantasies. But grown men aren't content to live with memories of a small girl, warmed every week or two by letters from one who's growing up. For her he'd been the only one; for him though, she'd been only one in a procession of enchantments.

But they were beyond the club now, bumping over the plain,

with Elgon crouching to the west, a mastodon of a mountain, black against the sky.

"You have sons?" Mattias said suddenly.

"One," she said. "He's almost four years old."

"Young still, and therefore kind," Mattias said. "When sons grow they cease to be so kind."

"Where is Benjamin?"

"Dead."

"I'm sorry. I did not know. I have had little news of Keriki since I went to my husband's home. How did the death occur?"

Mattias's eyes narrowed. "That property I bought from your mother in Baluga town, I planted with coffee and passion fruit and tea. But just as the tea was ready to be picked, I had to put a man in charge and go away." To prison, Marietta said to herself. "When I returned, I came to town to check, and I found Benjamin there. 'What do you want?' he asked me, roughly, as if to a stranger. 'To see my property,' I replied. 'Yours? But you are mistaken. The records show this place is mine.' So I knew that while I'd been away, through bribery he'd had the title changed. Then I cursed him, 'You are no longer my son! I never knew your mother or your sisters! It is as if you had never been born!'" Mattias's mouth moved vigorously. He's tasting his bile, Marietta thought. "I sent my sons to school. I gave them land and cattle to marry with. I behaved to them always as a Keriki father should, and yet all, each and every one of them, has turned against me!" He cleared his throat and spat on the floor of the bus. "Remember this, Miss Marietta, a son's betrayal is more bitter than anything in life!"

"But your daughters have remained your friends."

"What good are daughters?" Mattias growled. "They marry and they go! Afterwards they forget their father. They have sons of their own. It is they whom my daughters love. They don't remember me, except in times of hardship. When they come, craven, asking for maize, they never look me in the eye, they're too ashamed."

It was five years since that April night in London when Marietta had last seen Catherine, in azure eyelet cotton, sleepy from Francis's bed. For five years, such a very long time, she had never once sought news of Catherine, though it would have been simple enough to get it. Her die had been cast that night, so she'd come to believe. Betrayed, yes, and humiliated; she'd felt both. But far more painful was the sense that in some way she'd been punished for clinging to a grief which had kept her cold and to herself; and that grief for the loss of a man she'd really not known very well was out of proportion and therefore unjustified. All this she'd thought in May five years ago, but rather than struggle with her loneliness she'd looked for an escape, and she'd found a haven in Jonathan. She hadn't become a painter of declarative works; she hadn't had shows or won prizes or acclaim. Instead, she'd become a link in the chain. She'd acquired a past and the promise, through her son, of a future, which gave her the courage to ask the old giant sitting next to her, "How is Catherine? Surely she, of all your children, has not forgotten you!"

Mattias laughed mirthlessly. "Perhaps not, since twice a month I receive letters from her still. But who is left to read them to me? I do not even open them! They will stay in my box until she comes. And if I were to read those little words that run like chickens across the page, what would I learn? Nothing that could give me pleasure." He cleared his throat and spat again. "Would that she had been like you, Miss Marietta. Would that she had married a rich farmer in the Rift!"

"It's not quite what I had in mind to do," Marietta said softly, more to herself than to him.

He went on, "Last year she came to tell me that the time had come for her to go to the White Man's Country. Since she was a very small girl always she has been reading books. Here and there and in Uganda. Yes, she studied in Kampala as well, did you not know that? 'Isn't that enough?' I said. But no, she told me, 'I have stayed back these three years for your sake; now it is time to go to London. I must read more. I shall become an advocate.'" He paused; then, shaking his head, he added sorrowfully, "Surely she will marry there and have half-caste sons who cannot know Keriki? She will marry a *mzungu* and I shall never see her face again! I tell you, Miss Marietta, sons and daughters, all of them, they forget you in the end. You have one son, you say? Then one is enough!"

Violet, on her way to Mombasa to visit her husband, Daniel, had demanded why there was still no other. Her fourth child, a boy called Festus, she'd brought with her. He was ready to be weaned, just as soon as Daniel could provide him with a follower. "And where's *your* follower?" she'd asked Charlie.

"I don't like babies," he'd replied. "They're always wetting on

302

you and vomiting and making too much noise. So if my mother has one, Justin and I shall go down to Katari to my grandmother's house. My grandmother doesn't like babies either."

"It's time you had another, Mari, that boy's too proud," Violet had urged.

"He's not so proud," Marietta had said mildly. "He merely tells the truth. Babies are just as he says. Besides, the time is wrong."

"And when do you think it will be right?" Violet had retorted. "When will your husband come home? When will your responsibilities decrease? If you wait for that, Mari, you'll wait forever."

"But children bind you, Violet," she'd replied, "and I'm bound enough as it is."

"Perhaps you're right," she said softly now to Mattias. But he had fallen asleep. His head hung to one side; mouth open, he snored. His staff slipped to the floor. Marietta picked it up and wedged it between his knees, without waking him. So Catherine had got her second chance, after all. Five years later, she was precisely where she'd had it in mind to be! And as the afternoon sun beat through the window on her arms and neck, Marietta was soon asleep as well.

They reached Eldonia a long time after sunset. "Where are you going?" Marietta asked Mattias. Moro, he told her. "I have to telephone for someone to come in the other vehicle and fetch me. Moro's on my way. I'll give you a lift home." So they walked out of the lorry park and along Entebbe Road. They went into the Red Lion together, the European woman in her stained bush shirt, her fair hair in a knot at the back of her neck, and the old African, with his staff tap-tapping across the tiled floor.

The lobby was full of people. "Candidates," Mattias snorted. "Whose friends are they? What difference do elections make? Are we not always robbed, regardless!" Yes, Marietta thought, smiling to herself. And in the old days you took your share of the spoils. "Wait here," she said aloud, "I won't be long. Then we'll drink beer together."

She turned into the crowd. A broad back blocked her path and she stepped to one side and slipped by. In front of her a group of men sat, heads forward, elbows on knees, hands clasped, listening intently to their candidate, Dr. Michael Kagia.

Kagia glanced up and saw Marietta. He stopped in midsentence, his face suddenly still. Then he called out, "Mrs. Sudbury, now it's your turn to surprise me!" To his companions he said, "An old friend of mine has come, so let me greet her," and he hurried across the circle. His suit was crumpled and he needed to shave. His eyes were bloodshot from lack of sleep and dusty dry-season roads. "I haven't seen you for so long!" he exclaimed. "I've been in Uganda and only recently returned. How are you? Why are you here at night like this, so late?"

"My vehicle broke down up in Kitale. I came down on the bus from there and just got in. I'm about to ring Olgolulu for someone to fetch me home."

"Is your husband with you?"

She shook her head. "I'm on my way back from Turkana country. Johnny's still in camp up there. In fact, I'm traveling with an old friend, Chief Mattias Ongaki."

"Ongaki?" Kagia said sharply.

"Why, yes. He's waiting for me over there. See that old man in the hat in front of the reception desk? Do you know him, perhaps?"

"Not at all."

"No? I thought from your expression that you did. He's one of the old school. In North Nyanza when I was a child, he was rich and powerful; his enormous American car with tail fins went six miles to the gallon. But after Uhuru he fell from grace and now he takes the bus like everyone else. That's the political life for you," she said, shrugging. "It has its ups and downs. And you're on your way up, I understand. The papers say Dr. Kagia is one of the new school. He takes nothing for granted. He runs a provocative and brisk campaign."

"Will you wish me luck in the election?"

"D'you need it? You're expected to win hands down. Yes" — she smiled — "I wish you luck."

"You're still up at Olgolulu?"

"Of course. And we expect to stay. It suits us. Both of us, regardless."

"Of what?"

"Of the changes that one sees."

"You're looking very well, at any rate," Kagia said.

She laughed and said, "After eight hours on the bus, can that be true?"

"And that small son of yours, is he well, too?"

"He's no longer so small and he's much more talkative. He has very strong opinions about almost everything."

"Once this election's over I'll come to visit you. Then we'll see how well I stand up to your boy! Now I must go back to my companions." He smiled. "I've discovered that if you don't plan each day carefully, a provocative and brisk campaign loses momentum very fast."

17

Olgolulu

"Charlie," Marietta sighed, "please play with your train outside. I've got to finish my sums and I can't think straight with you roaring and crashing round my feet."

"Ever since breakfast you've been doing sums," Charles said, on hands and knees on the office floor. "And I don't see why, on Sunday."

"Because tomorrow's the last day of the month and everything had better add up right by then."

"But I've got no one to play with."

"There's Siele's Jennifer. Go and find her."

"I hate girls!" Charles sprang to his feet. "What I want," he insisted, "is for Johnny to come home! He's been away so long he doesn't even know we won! When he does come," Charles added, "I shall put the cup right next to his plate at supper. I want him to see it first thing of all."

A week ago Olgolulu Shining Star, by Naivasha Robin Hood out of Olgolulu Stella, had been judged by a panel of three, including Brigadier Deering from Gloucestershire, to be the number one Guernsey heifer at the Eldonia Agricultural Show.

"Deeply impressive," Deering had told Marietta. "One rarely sees such quality anywhere, even in the U.K. However do you do it," he'd added, in a lower tone, "in this day and age?"

"We take great care," Marietta had replied. "Ever since Bwana Edmund brought out our first three head on the back of a silver bird, before the war of the second King George, only the greatest care has been taken."

"What's that? I didn't quite catch," he said, and Marietta, light-headed from standing so many hours in the equatorial sun, had laughed.

"I was telling you the mythic origins of the Olgolulu herd."

"It's the real ones I'd prefer to know," Deering had replied, as he'd tied a red rosette with "First" in gold across its center to Shining Star's halter. Later, when the Kikuyu ladies had done their dancing and the Air Force band had played the national anthem all through twice, the prize winners had filed up, one by one, to the podium to receive their silver cups. Although it had been announced that the president himself would give them out, he'd been ill the night before, so the new Member for Central Rift had had to take his place.

"You! Why you?" Kagia exclaimed as Marietta presented herself in Siele's oversized dairyman's coat, trailing around her ankles, sleeves rolled up.

"Like our president, Siele's sick," she said, grinning. "I'm a mere substitute. Congratulations," she added, "you won, too."

Kagia nodded. "We ran a good campaign. I enjoyed it, and I'm very glad indeed it's over."

"So you're reaping the rewards! Prize giving, fund raising, hearing constituents' complaints."

"That's right."

"This constituent has a complaint," she said boldly. "You never came."

"I shall," he said, smiling. "Now I shall." She turned away. "Wait, don't go," he called. "Take this. We forgot it." He handed her a tarnished trophy, eighteen inches high. Afterwards, reading the list of names engraved on it had been like reading a chronicle of Settler times.

In the Sunday morning stillness they heard a car on the farm road. "Johnny's back!" Charles cried. "I knew he'd come!" He grabbed the cup from the table by the window and dashed to the door.

"It can't be him yet, love," Marietta called. "It's only Mrs. Strang bringing strawberries for lunch. Tell her I'll be over in a minute."

She went down her column of figures again. Twenty-seven thousand five hundred and sixty-three shillings and twenty-two cents. Last time it had come to sixteen hundred shillings more.

"Am I disturbing you?" Kagia stood in the doorway. He was wearing a dark blue suit and a red-and-blue-striped tie — the

307

clothes of a big man who meets with bigger men yet, even on a Sunday.

"It wasn't Mrs. Strang," Charles said breathlessly, slipping past. "Has she forgotten?"

"I'm sure she'll bring the strawberries later on." Marietta stood up. "So at last you're finding time for us," she said to Kagia. "You've already met Charlie."

"Not officially." Kagia smiled and offered his hand.

"You're the man who gave Mummy our cup," Charles said. "I saw you. Did you see me? I was up on Justin's shoulders, as near as we could get."

"I'm afraid I didn't see you. I was far too busy worrying about who should get which cup!"

"Charlie, Dr. Kagia lived here when he was little."

Charles said, not yet letting go of Kagia's hand, "My mother wants me to play with Jennifer, but Jennifer makes me be her husband and I hate that! Or else I have to be her little boy and I hate that, too. What did you and Johnny play when you were little boys?"

"War," Kagia said.

"That's what I'd like," Charles said eagerly. "Did they let you play in here?"

"Never. If I came in here I had to sit over there" — Kagia pointed to the table by the window, piled high with papers and periodicals — "and be quiet. I'll show you something I did do, though." With Charles two steps behind him he went to the table. He picked up one pile of papers and then another. "Do you know your ABC?"

"I'm not a baby," Charles said scornfully.

"Then which letters are these?"

Charles studied the initials carved in the table top. "MM. What's that?"

"Michael Maruga. That used to be my name. I carved these letters once when I was sent to sit and be quiet."

"Who sent you?"

"Your grandfather."

"Did you get a spanking when he saw?"

Kagia smiled. "I don't believe he ever noticed."

Charles leaned back against the table, arms folded. "Why did you go away?"

"My father and mother were leaving and I had to go with them."

"Were you sad?"

"I was very sad."

"Well, you came back in the end. You'll be all right now."

"Do you think so?" Kagia said.

Marietta came from behind the desk. "You'll stay for lunch, of course."

"I should be getting on to Nairobi. I have an appointment there."

"Not that again! Charlie, run and tell Justin we'll have lunch early. Would twelve be soon enough?"

Kagia raised his hands in resignation. "If you insist."

"This time I do."

After Charles had gone, tracing MM with one finger, Kagia said, "He has his father's eyes exactly, doesn't he? It's strange to find those eyes watching me again. But in character he resembles you."

"I hope you're paying me a compliment."

"Why, yes!" he replied, and glancing up, she saw that the expression on his face was very serious.

She said quickly, "I can't imagine I deserve it!" What could he know about her character? But skeptical as she was, all the same for an instant he made her heart leap. Then the facts reasserted themselves. "You should have telephoned ahead so we could have arranged for you to come when my husband was here, too. He'll be back on Tuesday."

"He's just as busy as before?"

"Oh, yes! And soon he may be famous, too. An American called Dalton is writing a book about him: white hunter, Old Harrovian, Oxford graduate, bearer of an ancient name. That sort of thing. There was quite a fuss here over Christmas. Photographs and interviews and tape recordings. Dalton had everybody very het up. We're not used to dealing with writers at Olgolulu! Siele had the time of his life, naturally. He got his chance to tell how things used to be, with simultaneous translation by me. Some of the tales he told were outrageous, but I was absolutely faithful to the task. I decided it wasn't my job to tone down the lions and the Masai. After Dalton went off with Johnny to Uganda, it took us several weeks to settle back into the old routine." She smiled. "Johnny's used to having people hang on to his every word, but the rest of us aren't."

"So this book will be about you as well?"

"Oh, not really! Just a paragraph or two, and the odd picture.

I'm not as glamorous as my husband is. My past's quite shabby!"
She laughed. "It's full of people and events it wouldn't do to read
about. No, my role in all of this consisted mostly of combing the
dukas in Eldonia for olives for Dalton's martinis and watching like
a hawk to make sure the cook didn't put milk in anything. Dalton's
allergic to it, you see. Maybe he'll put a sentence in the foreword,
thanking me."

Kagia walked slowly round the room. He stopped now and then
to examine the titles in the bookshelves. "It's strange without him."

"Without Johnny?"

"I was thinking of his father, in fact."

"Have you been to England?"

"Several times, to scientific conferences. I was last there in
November."

"But you didn't go to see Edmund, did you?"

"No, I never did." Kagia turned towards her. "I knew him not as
an old man but in his prime. I prefer to remember him that way."
He tapped his forehead. "That is the man whom I have with me
here."

"But he's not old at all! He's never looked better. He works fourteen hours a day and thrives." Then, after a moment, she added,
"Or is it that he's become an ancestor?"

Kagia nodded. "That's right. One reveres, but does not meet with
them."

"And the property of the ancestors," Marietta said lightly, "do
you want to see what the descendants have done with it?"

"By all means."

So out they went, through the yard, past the barns and the workshop to a line of stone cottages. "That one at the end was ours,"
Kagia said, pointing. "It seemed very beautiful after the huts we'd
lived in before." They passed women gossiping together, calling to
children who darted up and down the hillocks, in and out between
the washing laid to dry on the grass in the sun.

On doorsteps men sat with eyelids lowered, cradling beer in tin
mugs. One said, "See, it is Kagia! Why does he come here?"

"Now that he's a big man, like other big men, he, too, must have
land."

"And Mari, will he take her as well?" They laughed as they rose
to their feet to shake the hand of the new Member for Central Rift.
A man came running out to Marietta. His daughter, who would

have died, he insisted, if the memsahb hadn't taken her and the mother to hospital, had recovered and was ready to come home. A relative had arrived last night from town with the news. Would the memsahb go to fetch her today — this afternoon, in fact? On Wednesday, Marietta said. Not sooner? The other children needed their mother. Three weeks they'd been without her. They were suffering. They had nobody to wash their clothes, or cook.

"I go to town on Wednesdays," Marietta repeated. "Except for emergencies. Is this an emergency? No! You have received good news, not bad. If you want your wife at home any sooner, then go to meet her on the bus yourself!"

"I shall wait," the man said sheepishly, stepping back.

"You know my language better than I do myself," Kagia remarked admiringly. "In North America I almost forgot it. I'm told that now I speak it like a stranger or a very young boy."

"While you were out in the world, I was here at home. Why should I forget?" Side by side they went up the long slope towards the forest. Kagia took his jacket off and swung it over his shoulder. Marietta saw smooth muscle under his shirt. Like a thief, surreptitiously, she looked away again.

"This used to be wheat," Kagia said. "Three hundred acres from the lawn to the boundary fence."

"We plant potatoes now. We finished harvesting in the middle of last month and soon we'll plough and plant again. We get two crops a year. Jim McKinley, three farms up the ridge, did very well with potatoes, so I thought I'd try them, too. There's a big market for them in Nairobi now, and we send them over to Kampala and down to Zambia, too."

"You decide such things? How to use three hundred acres?"

Marietta smiled. "Isn't that the African way? The man goes out and finds work and the woman takes care of things at home."

They were at the edge of the forest now. "Could we rest here?" Kagia said. They sat in the shade against the boundary fence, carefully apart. Far below them, Marietta saw Charlie, a tiny figure crossing the yard. When he was gone there were only crickets in the grass, pale yellow cows with great brown eyes grazing round the new well, a buzzard two hundred feet up against the blue. The world's empty, Marietta thought, ready for a new creation.

Kagia said lightly, "I've imagined this ten thousand times, the house, the lake, the mountains rising to the sky, just as it appears

311

today, with a few small white clouds. But it's only lately that I've put you in this landscape, too." They were silent.

"Why didn't you come before?" Marietta said at last.

"I wasn't prepared before."

"Prepared for what?"

"To disturb Johnny." After a long moment he asked, watching her steadily, "Are you happy?"

"What business is that of yours!"

"It *is* my business. I consider it so."

"You don't know me, Michael."

"No? But I believe I do," he said gently. "Not only that, but I love you, which is very serious, isn't it?" He smiled. "So now we must decide what we should do."

At noon on the equator she was shivering. "Like a Tartar," she said, "come out of the north, bent on conquest."

"Who's that?"

"You," and she sighed immensely. "Down there on the road the year before last I thought of you that way. But you vanished. You got in your car and drove off. At first I was angry, but not for very long. Soon I was thankful." She turned to him. "I didn't want to be disturbed."

"We must decide what we should do," he repeated patiently.

"Have you no family?" she said, as if she were drowning and given over already to despair.

"My parents are dead. I think you know that."

"No, no, not them. I know about them. Everyone does! During the campaign, it was all in the papers, day after day. Where is your wife? Where are your children? A man like you, brilliant and effective, why should you want me?"

"I'm not married," he said simply. "In town I live in a rented bungalow beyond the station, on Dedan Road, number fourteen. I have a houseboy and an *askari* who sleeps from midnight until dawn. In Nairobi I rent another bungalow. My father's widowed sister takes care of things. And you, of course, are here, where a hundred pairs of eyes watch you all the time. Even now, on this hillside, those eyes are searching for us. Here in the shade, we're hidden from them, but we shan't be for long. As you once told me, nothing in Africa goes unobserved. So what are we to do, Marietta?"

Watching the empty stretch of gravel far below, Marietta prayed,

Charlie, won't you run out again; for my sake, for your mother, who imperils you! "Nothing," she said. "I shan't do anything. I daren't risk losing what I have."

"And what is that?"

"Some sort of peace, with my child in this place."

"You love me?" he said quietly.

"Can I afford to, given who you are, you of all men, Michael!"

He got to his feet and brushed the dry-season grass from his clothes. "I'm used to waiting," he said, "though perhaps your cook is not. Shouldn't we go down now?" He slipped on his jacket. But Marietta still sat at his feet, hands clasped round her knees. He leaned down and touched her hair, then her cheek, softly. "Come along," he said, "you haven't shown me the garden yet. Those fuchsias you spoke of, and those roses."

PART V

1972

18

Olgolulu

In the first faint light of morning, as the mountains peaked black against the eastern sky, Marietta unlocked the office door. She knew exactly where the letters were. She ran to the table by the window and seized the pile of papers covering them. But they were further to the left. Yes, there they were! MM. No, *not* MM. The second M had been carefully erased and in its place she saw the letter K, pale, splintery to the touch, freshly carved. Since yesterday. He'd come in the darkness to change the old times for the new. And he was here still, she was certain, hidden nearby, waiting for her in the dairy or the tractor shed. And the laborers had gone, all of them, and the doors of their cottages swung slowly in the wind. Taking Charles by the hand, Justin had gone too, down the farm road and away into the world.

There was nobody left to help her now.

She could hide in the forest. There she'd be safe. No, slowly she shook her head. She couldn't live, scarcely seeing the sky. Better to stay here. Better to face him. So she sat at the desk and on a new page she wrote, "The stars are dead, the moon has set. No sun has risen yet to take its place."

But the office door flew open and Charles raced in. "I shouted from across the pool but you were fast asleep!"

"Was I?" On a lounge chair under a flame tree, Marietta opened her eyes. "I'm glad you woke me, Charlie. I was having a bad dream."

"Can Anthony come to our house to play?" Charles said urgently, water trickling from his hair.

"Anthony who?"

"I don't know his other name."

Marietta swung her feet to the ground. "Where is he, your friend Anthony?"

"Over there." Charles was pointing to a small brown boy in turquoise bathing trunks whose hair stood up round his head like a halo.

"We'll have to ask his mother, Charlie." Marietta glanced round the Katari Club swimming pool. On this September afternoon there were a dozen children, a few women, and one lone man who sat reading with his back to the sun. Apart from Anthony and two waiters with their trays in front of the pool house bar, everyone was white. Up at Olgolulu, apart from Charlie and me and sometimes Jonathan, everyone used to be black, Marietta thought.

Charles skipped off and came back shortly with the small brown boy. "He sits next to me at school," he explained. "We swap lunches."

"I don't like Marmite," Anthony said, "and he does."

"He gives me his potato crisps," Charles said, adding, "he lives in the house with the turrets."

Marietta's eyes widened. "In Mr. Dawson's house?"

"No," Anthony replied sturdily. "We live in our own house."

Katari had once been a stronghold for the colonial gentry, but with Uhuru the names at the ends of the driveways had begun to change. Soon they were almost as likely to be Japanese or Pakistani as British, for Kenya's reputation for stability in contrast with the turbulence of the rest of Africa was attracting a new type of *mzungu* who wasn't necessarily white. And these international birds of passage tended to live in Katari with its mansions and gardens and views of green hills, for although they'd come to foster the new Kenya, in the meantime, living in the illusion of the old was highly desirable. If not quite so firmly as before, nevertheless the stronghold had held after a fashion, until one day the house Peter Dawson had built for the bride he'd brought home from the war went up for sale. After Daphne left him, Peter had lived alone there for a few more years, and then one Easter Sunday he'd fallen down dead on the terrace just before lunch. To settle the estate, his lawyer sold the house to Dr. Nelson Otieno, surgeon, Minister for Wildlife and Tourism. After the first panic passed, the neighbors told Marietta, down from Olgolulu for news to transmit to Spain,

318

that on Christmas morning Dr. Otieno had read the second lesson awfully well. "His father's an Anglican archdeacon, by the way," one of the neighbors said — that helped explain the aura he generated among the congregation in St. Elizabeth's. The congregation seemed to be warming also to his British wife, and to their coffee-colored sons who'd been observed in the *dukas* at the Katari crossroads. "They weren't snitching chocolate bars, at least," old Lady Forrester remarked, adding generously, "and she has astonishing red hair! She's Welsh, you know, though she might strike one more as Irish. With an artistic bent, it seems. She's opened a picture gallery behind the Standard Bank." Soon the Otienos were followed to Katari by a Kikuyu businessman with two Kikuyu wives ("Perhaps there are others on the farm he's got at Kinangop. Bought Tony Bellows's place, you know. Poor Tony went to Perth") and Lady Forrester and her friends resigned themselves to peaceful coexistence. "After all," they said to one another and to Marietta, over tea, "it *is* their country now and one doesn't have to dine with them just because one lives next door."

Marietta realized that Anthony was one of those coffee-colored children whose capacity to withstand the temptation of Mars bars had been noted with relief by Lady Forrester. "Charlie says you've got a lorry and I'd like to play in it," said Anthony, sounding Welsh.

"The trouble is," Marietta replied, "my husband's taken it out and he won't be back till a week from Saturday."

"I don't have any school on Saturday. I can come then, too," Anthony said. "Today I shall play with your dog instead. I like dogs very much but my father doesn't. We've only got a cat. Cats run up trees and won't come down." He added, wrinkling his nose, "They aren't half so much fun as dogs."

Marietta smiled. "Who did you come here with, Anthony?"

"My mother, of course."

"And where is she? I can't take you to my house without asking her if it's okay."

"She's playing tennis. I'll get her if you like."

"No, don't do that! We'll wait till she finishes her game. You two can go back in the water for the moment."

Marietta lay down again and closed her eyes. So Charlie's made a friend, she said to herself. He's set. For him, Olgolulu's just the place where we used to live and now we don't anymore. He's ready to begin a different life. You're that way when you're six. Not when

319

you're twenty-six, though. At my age you might never stop missing the certainty of Olgolulu, of knowing what's to be done, when and how and why.

"Am I disturbing you?" A small woman in a tennis dress stood over Marietta. Her red hair was tied back. She had sea green eyes and a thickly freckled face. She carried a racquet and a bottle of Coke with a straw sticking out of it. "Our sons have been making arrangements, I hear," she said. "By the way, I'm Flora Otieno." She added, pulling up a chair, "Last week Anthony told me, 'There's a boy in my class with hair like yours, Mum.' 'Well,' I said, 'I hope you don't tease him like they teased *me* at school.'" She laughed, and her gold hoop earrings swung. "Carrots, they called me. Rottie, when they wanted to be kind." She sat back. "Is this your boy's first term at Saint Paul's?" Marietta nodded. "Just out from U.K. then."

"Oh, no! I was born out here, in fact. We moved down from up-country three weeks ago. We're living on Olduvai Road."

"Is that so! Where exactly?"

"Did you know my stepfather, Bruce Oldfield? It's his house. He and my mother went to Spain."

Mrs. Otieno nodded. "I remember the Oldfields well. I even bought a sofa from your mother once; it's stood up wonderfully to three small boys, I have to say! How are they liking it in Spain?"

"Bruce grows roses and my mother runs a travel agency. They both speak Spanish very fast and with an appalling accent, but people understand. They seem to like it very much there."

"They don't miss this place?"

Marietta shrugged. "If so, they don't let on. Most of their British friends complain about the Spanish winters. The rain, the damp, and so on, but not Bruce or my mother! When I went over there last year I told them, 'If you left Madrid in the morning and changed planes in Rome you'd be in Nairobi for dinner. You ought to think about coming for Christmas.' 'Can't spare the time,' they said. The truth is, though, they haven't got the interest. You'd hardly know they'd ever lived in Africa at all. One day they picked themselves up and took off from here and that was that." She went on quickly, "You bought Peter Dawson's place, didn't you? My mother and Daphne Dawson used to be best friends. I spent my childhood in and out of that house, but after Daphne left him Peter had it in for my mother, rather, and in recent years we never saw

320

him at all. I really missed going there. Peter built a house for me in a jacaranda tree behind the kitchen. That was 'Africa' and the gazebo on the lawn was 'Europe.' I used to play going abroad and coming home again for weeks on end!"

"The treehouse is gone," Mrs. Otieno said, "but the gazebo's still there. I'd like to pull it down, but we kept on Mr. Dawson's *shamba* boy and he's an old mule when it comes to change. If you want to put zinnias where nasturtiums used to be, he throws a fit. So after a few collisions," Mrs. Otieno continued, waving her Coke, "I gave up. Indoors I get my own way, but the garden's Gregory's. He claims he planted each and every shrub himself." She laughed. "They're like his arms and legs; he can't part with a single one of them."

Peter would have called her "a little person," Marietta thought. She could just see him, looking askance. But Daphne would be glad to know that this lively woman was living in her house. Daphne was in New York now, orchestrating charity events. She was tired of white men, tired of black men. She had a charming homosexual friend, an up-and-coming Costa Rican dress designer, whose lover was out of town a lot. It's tremendous to be living by my wits at last, she'd written to her goddaughter, not just according to my hormones!

"Gregory and I used to race snails in an enclosure near the compost heap. Late June was the high season, towards the end of the long rains. We betted like fiends, too."

"You'll be glad to know he's still at it. He makes extraordinary clucking noises to encourage his snail to go faster. He sounds just like a chicken about to lay three eggs at once."

"Yes, I remember those noises." Marietta smiled. "I'm not sure how effective they were though, since my snail won at least as often as his did and I never made any noises at all."

Looking firmly at Marietta, Mrs. Otieno asked, "So where were you upcountry?"

"Near Moro."

"Farming?"

"Yes."

"And you sold out."

"We were forced out," Marietta replied carefully.

"How?"

"It's a long story."

321

"It always is. What happened?"

Marietta reached for her bag. "Do you smoke? No?" She lit a cigarette. "Our place was six miles the Nairobi side of Moro. I shouldn't say our place. It was my husband's. He'd inherited it from his father, who'd inherited it from *his* father. When I got there seven years ago there were still a couple of dozen European farmers left along the valley. From year to year we never knew if our permits or our licenses or our insurance policies were going to be renewed. We were always awaiting the pleasure of the powers that be. Will they, won't they, will they, won't they? The government's only consistent objective, so it seemed, was to keep us dancing like cats on a hot tin roof. One by one our neighbors got tired of trying to make a go of it against such odds. They didn't wait for the end. They gave up and gave in ahead of time. It took more than exhaustion, though, to get rid of us. Since living anywhere else had no appeal at all, perhaps we could put up with more than other people." In a low voice she went on, "So long as the battle was mostly one of nerves and irritations, we managed, but eventually someone came along whose purpose was to get rid of us specifically. Another farm up or down the ridge wasn't what he was after. Of all people, it was only us whom he wanted to uproot.

"In the end," she continued, smiling wryly, "that was rather simple. Although in most dry seasons our own well provided an adequate water supply for our dairy herd, in exceptional years we had to use the bore hole dug by the government a hundred yards outside our property. And that required a permit. Last year *was* an exceptional year. In March, just as our own well was running dry, we were refused access to the bore hole. We appealed, and our appeal was rejected. That same day we received an offer, and unless we chose to shoot our livestock, we had no alternative but to accept it. The day our well ran dry, we *did* accept; that evening our stock went to the bore hole and we had five months to pack up."

"Who bought you out?"

"The Moro Farmers' Cooperative."

"Isn't Michael Kagia chairman?"

"I believe he is."

Mrs. Otieno said lightly, "We've known him forever, practically. We met him in the States when he and Nelson were in training over there. I've always liked him very much."

Is that all? Marietta thought in wonder. You don't hate hate him, you don't love him? He's just a friend to spend a few hours with every month or so, if and when you both can find the time! Such a benign response she found impossible to imagine.

"But then," Mrs. Otieno said, touching her hand, "he wasn't after *my* farm, was he?"

Last March, the day after they'd made the decision to sell out, Marietta had found Jonathan in the library with a half-empty bottle of Courvoisier at three in the afternoon. He rarely touched brandy, even after dinner. "I'm celebrating," he told her. "Imagine! No more whoring to the rich! We've been slaves to this place, Etta. Now we're free! We can go anywhere on earth we want. What do you think of Oregon? Last year they were after me about running that safari park, remember? I believe I'll take them up on it."

"What about James?" Marietta stopped, confused. "This is exactly what he's been praying for all along. How can you *not* go to Tresham now?"

"Bloody-minded I may be," Jonathan laughed, "but not utterly insane! I've spent every minute since I was twelve years old obsessing about one piece of Sudbury property, and I'm not about to repeat that folly. I've written to James already. I told him that although my circumstances have changed, my original decision hasn't. I don't intend to join him now, nor at any other time." He sipped his brandy. "I've always found England too manicured and precious. Too endlessly worked over. While we're about it, Etta, why not go to the New World?"

Oregon? Where was that? It didn't matter. Marietta had only wanted an assurance that after August they'd be off. The only thing she knew she couldn't face was staying on. Whichever world they went to, she'd manage when the time came. People did. Virginia, Edmund, so many others. They landed on their feet somehow.

But then in June, back from his penultimate safari, three weeks in Tanzania with two Bolivians, Jonathan was drinking brandy at eleven in the morning. "What are you celebrating now?" Marietta asked in alarm.

"I've ironed out my itinerary. My dates suit everybody fine."

"Your dates? I don't understand."

"I'm leaving for America on July the twenty-first."

"How can you!" she gasped. "The closing isn't till the tenth of August."

"I'll sign all the papers and leave them with the lawyer." He

323

went on, "Apart from the delightful occasion of our meeting in Chicago, I haven't laid eyes on Maruga's boy since the afternoon I almost killed him twenty years ago. A record of a sort, wouldn't you say? And one I intend to keep. If there's any hobnobbing to be done, Marietta, would you mind doing it for both of us? I'm not quite up to shaking hands and going out for a drink afterwards. I'd prefer to leave ahead of time, if that's okay with you."

"Go, then!" she shouted furiously. "You should have gone long ago, before Jim McKinley, before the Strangs! You should have gone before your father! You might have had a real life, then, not this make-believe you've been living all these years!" Seeing the dreadful bleakness in his face, she stopped. "I'm sorry!" She took his cold hand and rubbed it, hoping to put warmth into him and into herself in place of the disbelief that had frozen her in March, and froze her still, with the closing only weeks away. "Yes, we'll do it your way. You go first. Then I'll pack up and join you in Oregon later. Your contract with the park said you'd be starting on the first of September. Now they're wanting you earlier, is that it?" She shook her head. "If only you'd told me that, Johnny! Sometimes you're terribly obtuse!"

Jonathan withdrew his hand abruptly. "I'll be going to California first," he said, staring past her, "and working my way east. Colorado, Chicago. The Maryland shore. I've never been there before. It should be interesting. I'll give Texas a miss this time," he finished, "but I shan't be going to Oregon. I have no intention of running a safari park there or anywhere else."

"What d'you mean?" Her heart was in her mouth. "What's this you're telling me?"

"I'm not leaving Kenya. Those Oregon people had been after me for a long while, and in March in the heat of the moment I thought, Okay, I'll do it. I wrote off and they wrote back right away and sent that contract I showed you. But I never signed it." He smiled to himself. "Where were you that morning? In Eldonia, I suppose. It was exceptionally still. No wind. I burned the contract on the terrace. It was fun, watching the paper flame and curl into a small, neat pile of ash."

Hands pressed to her forehead, Marietta moaned. "When exactly did you do this?"

"Before I went out with the Bolivians. Beginning of May, I believe." He held his brandy to the light. "So you see, I'll be home by the end of the third week in August. Olduvai Road will make an excellent base. Quite a stroke of luck, your parents letting us have it, though at the time I thought, Oh, no, another white elephant! It's very convenient to the airport, and since Bruce built that shed at the back, I won't even have to add on. There's plenty of room for the truck and all the gear. I've got three Italians due the first week of September. The Dobson's Gorge hunting block's booked for the sixth. I'll take the other road up. Lucky it's paved now. I shan't need to come past here again."

"Why didn't you tell me this before?" Marietta said in a strangled voice.

"You wouldn't like it in Oregon, anyway. Rains most of the time."

"You're an ostrich!" Marietta exploded. "Your head's stuck fast in the sand."

"Not an ostrich," Jonathan said lightly, "a Neanderthal. I require particular conditions that aren't to be replicated elsewhere. Kenya's my corner of the world, my ecological niche, if you will. I'll go on doing what I'm suited to do until" — he shrugged — "until one day I drop in my tracks. You see, it doesn't really bother me that what I do for a living's a joke. You can take out a license for lion or rhino and reserve a vast area in which to pursue your prey. You've got your piece of paper all signed and sealed and paid for and you put it in your pocket and out you go into the bush. But the chances of finding a single lion or rhino are slim and getting slimmer every day. The Somalis are poaching from the north, the Masai from the south, and what they miss goes to our president's lady wife and her relatives and friends, including, so one's heard, the Honorable Minister for Wildlife himself. But I can stand being the butt of the joke. If all things were equal, there are a few luxuries I'd like to hold on to. The farm I was born on being one. But if I lose those, I'll manage with whatever's left. A fresh start doesn't appeal to me, though I grant you I've had plenty of time to consider one. How long is it since Maruga's boy resurfaced in his button-down collar and tie? Five years? Six?

"Oh, yes, I've had plenty of warning. I've known all along that sooner or later he'd get his own back. But he's a complicated fellow and vengeance and idealism aren't easy to combine. They make for crablike movements. It would have been far simpler if he'd only been out for himself. Then, no doubt, he'd have got us thrown out of here a good deal quicker. But he's a cut above your usual politician. He doesn't use his status for private gain at the expense of the common man. Not on your life! Maruga's boy's the high-minded exception who proves all the rules." Jonathan smiled bitterly. "The only honest man in the whole gang of cutthroats who run this godforsaken country! So at last, after years of machinations, Olgolulu is being taken from the white exploiter and given to the people. Soon the cattle will start dying — from neglect and ignorance, this time, not thirst — and they won't be replaced. A few seasons more, and they'll give up wheat as well. They'll divide the place up into five-acre plots and they'll plant maize up the hillside. In ten years' time the soil will have washed away in the rain and blown away in the wind and all Dad's efforts and yours, too, to conserve it will have come to nothing. Only rock will belong to the people then. And where will I be in ten years' time? Somewhere about. Maruga's boy can drive me off my land, but not out of my country. That degree of satisfaction, at least, I can deny him! Besides, life's long. Who's to say I won't get even with him one day? At any rate, it's an idea to play about with. And now" — he stood up — "I'd better be off. I promised Charlie I'd help him with that fort he's building out behind the fish pond."

For twenty-three thousand pounds sterling, a sum considered adequate by the government evaluators who oversaw the sale of European-owned agricultural land to Africans, the Moro Farmers' Cooperative would acquire Olgolulu, lock, stock, and barrel, including the ancestors on the walls and the Chippendale chairs and Hepplewhite tables, all made, oversize, to elaborate Edmund Sudbury's dream. They wouldn't have fitted into the villa on Olduvai Road. That was already filled with floor samples from Oldfield Interiors.

Jonathan, leaving for America, promised to bring his son a half-size surfboard from Santa Barbara. One of these days they'd get a chance to try it at Malindi. To Marietta he said, "My itinerary's on the big desk in the office. You'll know where to reach me if need be." He thrust his briefcase along the front seat and slid in behind the wheel. "Thank you for doing this, Marietta," he added quietly, looking up at her. "You can't know how grateful I am!" Then he put the car into gear and drove off slowly over the patchy gravel, which wouldn't be replaced this year as it had been in all other years after the long rains. Once through the gate he picked up

326

speed and bounced away down the hill, over the potholes. He flew out onto the main road, swerved, skidded, missed by a hair's breadth a lorry lumbering up from Nairobi, and disappeared. Marietta, shielding her eyes from the morning's glare and hiding her tears from her son, thought with certainty like lead, For all his obstinacy, his bravado, he's lost hope. So long as there was Olgolulu to work for, he still had a chance to set things right with Edmund. Selling his soul ten months a year would all be worth it if, in the end, being who he was turned out to be good enough. But this *is* the end, his time's run out. He's given up hope of ever being the only one. For so many years, that's what I mostly thought about. I never got what I wanted either, and for a long long time I felt like I was lost in some wilderness, with no chance of finding my way out. But I *did* get out eventually. I suppose I can manage anywhere, if I have to, but can Johnny?

A week later Charles and Justin left Olgolulu for Galana. Charlie would come to Katari later, after his mother had pasted over the break with the past as well as she knew how and had ranged his toys along the shelves of his new room on Olduvai Road. Marietta saw them onto the bus at Eldonia and waited through the excitements of departure. She waved as the bus pulled off, round the beds of canna lilies, westward. In her mind's eye she went with them up the escarpment, over the mountains, down at evening to the lake shore. But I'm not ready to go yet, she said to herself as she left the lorry park and went to find her Land-Rover.

These days members of the Moro Farmers' Cooperative were coming steadily to Olgolulu. They'd get out of vans and pickup trucks in their best clothes, to stand in awe of their purchase. In the house they craned their necks to see the gargoyles and to watch Marietta on her knees in the pantry wrapping candlesticks and christening cups in newspaper.

"Welcome," she would say, getting quickly to her feet. "My husband is away from home. Let me greet you in his stead." Then she would shake them by the hand, ask their names and where they came from. They huddled together, not caring for this ritual, but she insisted on it. Into your hands, she said to herself, I commend the spirit of this place. And to do that I must touch you. Then she'd kneel down again and they'd watch her a little longer before straggling off through the corridors to gaze at the great beds and the

327

huge baths, like sheep dips. Soon families of ten and twelve would be living in each of these rooms and Eleanor's peeling ancestors would look down on goats and children scampering through the hall. But not quite yet. A few days before the closing the pickup trucks stopped coming, and after a day and a half without visitors, Marietta realized with relief and gratitude that they were leaving her in peace. Though they craved the land, they honored sorrow nevertheless.

Early on the last morning she oversaw the loading of the two moving vans that would take what was salvageable from sixty years down to Katari. There wasn't a great deal: Edmund's books and papers, bound eventually for the MacMillan Library in Nairobi, Jonathan's guns, a few worn Persian carpets, pots and pans and photograph albums, and an outsize globe on a mahogany stand, which might come in handy when Charlie started asking about a wider world. All other trappings of grandeur were being left for the new owners to do with as they saw fit. After the vans had lumbered away she'd still have time to walk up to the forest and back and through the fuchsia garden and round to the Land-Rover parked outside the office in the yard.

Siele, who'd started long ago as under-dairyman and progressed to dairyman and ultimately to foreman, came up to Marietta. "I am going now, Mari. My brother's come to take me home," he said — home to the six Jersey cows he'd bought with his Olgolulu wages. He'd be a wealthy man at last, respected for that and for all he'd learned about cattle from Europeans on the Rift. The brother waited impatiently in his battered Morris. Drumming his fingers on the steering wheel, he watched the leavetaking in his rear-view mirror.

"I give you my thanks, Siele, and the thanks of Johnny and Bwana Edmund, too. Go well. Live well," Marietta said.

"Soon you'll come to greet me."

"I'll come one day, Siele."

Then he, too, was gone, and she was alone with her dog, Gelda, loping up the hillside ahead of her. At the top, Gelda slipped through the boundary fence to the fascinations of the forest, while Marietta looked for the last time over the blues and pinks on the bottom of the valley to the mountains beyond. Clouds were coming up. By early afternoon it would be raining over those mountains, but she wouldn't stay to see the rain.

328

Far below a small car was jolting up the farm road. It's not theirs yet, she thought. Not until this afternoon at four. Calling her dog from the thickets, she ran in rage down the hill. She slipped, fell, got to her feet, ran on. The car reached the house and an African emerged.

"Get out," Marietta shouted, "it's not your time yet!" But she was still a long way off. Her voice cracked in anger and the wind snatched it away. The intruder tried the front door and went inside.

She scrambled over the fence between the fields and the garden and ran across the lawn and the gravel, past the small car, its fenders thick with red dust. In the entrance she paused an instant to bind her rage before she walked in. But the terrace door stood open. The intruder had escaped the scrutiny of the ancestors who lined the walls and gone outside again. He'd be standing there now, among the fuchsias, looking at the lake and the rim of water birds and the heavy gray thunderclouds coming over the mountains. She set off to confront him, reciting under her breath as she crossed the hall, "You had no business coming here today. Soon you'll have all the time in the world to celebrate your victory. But I had only an hour for making peace with what I've lost, for pulling off the last small hands. Even that you couldn't spare me!"

At the far door she saw there was no one on the terrace. He'd vanished into the garden that Eleanor had planted in the midst of a guerrilla war. The garden was high and lavish now, and somewhere in it he was already thinking of how best to root out the bushes and clear the space for pigs and chickens. With Gelda at her heels, Marietta ran across the terrace into a winding avenue between mounds of pink and purple, but no one sat on the stone bench. At the end she rounded a great promontory of scarlet and came upon him. Gelda dashed up to him, barking furiously, but he spoke to her and immediately the barking stopped.

"She knows a friend when she sees one, your dog," Kagia said, fondling her ears.

"Friend!" Marietta threw back her head. "Good God! You were so eager, you couldn't even wait until I'd left!"

"I didn't know you were still here. I saw Siele in town and he told me that you'd gone. And when I drove up just now, I saw no other car. Don't quarrel with me, Marietta," he pleaded.

"One careful step after another," she mocked. "All the way up to your prize! But you won't get my congratulations." And in the bright sun before the rain she wept.

"Don't quarrel with me, Marietta," he said again, shaking his head through the blur of her tears.

"What will become of us, now that you've destroyed our peace? Do you wonder? Do you care?"

"I love you," Kagia said softly. "I told you so two years ago, and that's not changed."

The clouds had been small and white that morning. They'd danced over the mountains. Incredulous as she'd been, she'd believed him all the same, and dreaded the consequences. But today, in a different age that he himself had brought about, how could she believe him?

"You don't love me! Only *want*. The same way you wanted the house and the farm, the cattle, the combine harvester! But I don't come with the property, Michael! I'm not part of your deal!" She stretched out her hands to draw him to her or to send him away, she didn't know, and then she whirled about and ran off. Across the terrace she went, past the empty house, and a voice in her head repeated, "Your time's run out, your time's run out," and just before her heart broke she reached the Land-Rover, packed to the roof with odds and ends of a life she'd fallen into by chance, not by design, and which, nevertheless, she'd made her own. She wrenched open the door and jumped in. She turned on the ignition, and while the engine warmed, dug in her pockets for her handkerchief, but she must have lost it running through the fields. So she pulled out a rag from under the seat and blew her nose on that. Then she let off the brake and drove out of the yard, over the patchy gravel, past the great stone house. Kagia stood by the front door under the Sudbury coat of arms, VIRTUTE, a unicorn rampant, three scimitars, lichen-covered. She thought, He'll try to stop me, he'll try to speak to me, and I'll drive on. But he stayed where he was, by the open door. As she leveled with him, he raised one hand in farewell.

By the Katari swimming pool on a September Sunday afternoon, Marietta said to Flora Otieno, "We were set to go to America. We were going to make a fresh start. My husband had a job lined up there, but he changed his mind." She tapped cigarette ash into the palm of her hand and blew it away. "He's a hunter. He was never

330

much at Olgolulu, anyway. He decided to go on as before. Hunting is what suits him. As for myself, I haven't decided what to do. I expect it'll take a while to get over leaving the farm. In fact, sometimes," she added quickly to this sympathetic woman whom she scarcely knew, "I wonder if I ever shall."

"It's amazing what you do get over," Flora Otieno said. "That sounds heartless, doesn't it? But really, I believe it's true."

19

Katari

Jonathan stood by the boundary fence as the hills disappeared into the night. The scent of the long white trumpet flowers on the bush behind him was heavy and sweet. His head ached. He stared into the forest on the far side of the wire. It used to be full of game, but there was little there now. At dusk or in the early morning one had seen buck, even giraffe occasionally. Sights one used to take for granted were very rare these days.

Marietta came over the lawn in the starlight. They were due at eight o'clock at the house of their neighbor, Dr. Nelson Otieno, and already it was seven twenty-five. If Marietta had sent Justin to remind Jonathan that they were going out to dinner, he'd have answered, to appease, "Tell her I'm coming," and then not come. He wanted to stay at home and drink his own brandy.

In the bush he still managed a semblance of his former self, the man of the myth and of the book with the glossy cover which was selling briskly in England and America, but at home, now that Olduvai Road was home, Jonathan made no pretense: he drank steadily. But he didn't slur his words or stumble about. To Marietta he was courteous, and increasingly remote. He came to bed very late and sometimes not at all, or he'd sleep the two hours before dawn on the study sofa.

"Please talk to me," she'd begged him, coming into the study without knocking as the sun rose. "It seems like the end of the world, but it isn't, Johnny!"

Red-eyed, unshaven, he'd challenged, "And how are you going to prove it?"

332

He wouldn't talk to her, he wouldn't touch her. He was engaged in a struggle, and whatever the stakes, win or lose, it was only *his* struggle, he'd let her have no part of it. He wanted to be left alone, but when for one reason or another she wouldn't let him have his way and got him to come out with her, she was taking a risk, for he drank steadily away from home as well. He'd be mild and amusing to begin with but he was only biding his time. As other people started to relax he'd go on the alert for the hasty global statement, the innocent unsubstantiated claim; when one came, he'd turn on the offensive. A month ago he'd gone for Julian Forrester at a cocktail party following the Ngong Races. The son of a long-dead Uganda High Court judge, Julian was a congenial fellow who raised lilies that he air-freighted twice a week to Covent Garden Market. After a couple of whiskey and sodas he'd happened to remark that his cook's eldest boy had been accepted at the university, and smiling broadly he'd added that the *watu*, the common people, seemed to be on the up and up. "My God, that boy never wore shoes till he was twelve, and that first pair I bought him!"

"What in the hell do you know about the common people?" demanded Jonathan, two quick, quiet drinks ahead. "One kid in a hundred thousand gets a halfway decent education and the rest are just as ignorant and exploited as they were before. Only now it's their own kind screwing them, not us. Don't tell me you believe that crap about progress and justice you read in the newspapers, Forrester? Or is it that to keep on getting your export license, you've agreed publicly to kiss old Kenyatta's arse?"

There'd been two dinner party incidents as well. Each time Marietta, knowing what was brewing, had tried and failed to cut him off before the damage was done. Later, with jars of homemade plum jam in hand, she'd visited old family friends to apologize for Jonathan's behavior.

But then again, sometimes Jonathan would be just as mild and amusing at the end of an evening as he'd been at the beginning. As she passed the haycocks that the laborers had made that morning, Marietta wondered about the odds of this being such a lucky evening. Not good, but one never knew ahead of time.

"Johnny," she called as she came to the tennis court. In the dense darkness near the boundary fence she saw the glow of a cigarette. Jonathan's shirt emerged, pale against the forest. His back to her, he stood with his arms folded across his chest. "Johnny, remember we're going out."

"Christ!" He stubbed his cigarette against a post. The sparks sank into the grass. "I'd done my best to forget. When are we due?" He felt his chin. "I should shave, shouldn't I?"

At four minutes to eight, with a cut still bleeding under his chin, Jonathan joined Marietta in the car. She was smoking a cigarette.

"How extravagant you look! New dress, is it?"

"Yes, new," she said. "New for our new old life. You can't wear Wellingtons and jeans to a dinner party in Katari."

"Despite the wars you've been through lately, you're still astonishingly lovely, Etta. I trust you won't be seated next to the minister though. I'd rather he didn't paw your knee."

Marietta threw her cigarette out of the car window. "I'm curious to see how the Otienos live in that house," she said evenly. "I hope they got rid of the elephants. Peter had three heads up in the dining room."

"Seems right for the Minister of Wildlife, though I have to say, he looks like an advertisement for aftershave lotion. One couldn't imagine him near an elephant unless it were stuffed. Remind me why we're honored with his company?"

They'd been through this before when the invitation arrived. Jonathan had said then, "Since when did we dine with Africans?"

"We've been doing it all our lives," Marietta had answered.

"Since when did we eat *with* Africans, rather than in front of them?"

"We've never been invited before, but now that we are, we should accept. For one thing, Dr. Otieno's Ministry gives out all your permits."

"And I should keep in with the authorities, right? Only this authority's a self-congratulating fool. I know. I spent an hour in a tent with him last year at the Nairobi show. I earn my living with people of his ilk. White, maybe, but generally as trite. I'd rather spend my evenings off alone." And he'd pushed the card into a drawer.

Eventually, receiving no reply, Flora Otieno had telephoned. "I thought the post office had failed again," she'd said cheerfully, "so I had to check." Marietta apologized — Johnny had been out on safari, he'd only just got back (he'd been back twelve days, in fact). She was so glad Mrs. Otieno hadn't given up on them. If it wasn't too late, they'd be delighted to accept.

"One of Otieno's sons is in Charlie's class at school," Marietta told Jonathan in the car. "He comes over to play quite often, but so far you've always been out. He's Charlie's great new friend."

"What's the mother like?"

"She's got bright red hair. You couldn't miss her. She happens also to be very nice."

"Tea and sympathy on the veranda, is that it?"

"No, she's not that type. Anthony gets dropped off by a driver. His mother's far to busy to fetch and carry him herself. She owns the Casuarina Gallery. If there is such a thing here as a center for the arts, that's it. But this evening has nothing to do with art. We're invited because the Otienos are entertaining the warden of an American national park, and a big-game hunter is just the sort of person the warden of a national park would want to meet in Africa. I accepted because it seemed the sensible thing to do."

"Without you to make up for my deficiencies in tact," Jonathan said dryly, "whatever would become of us?"

At the door they were received by the minister and his wife, who greeted Marietta warmly, taking both her hands in a quite un-British way.

"I'm so pleased you both could come! I was afraid your husband might have vanished into the bush again!"

Dr. Otieno, six feet tall and inky black, bowed over Jonathan's hand. "We met, I believe, in February a year ago." It seemed he knew exactly how long Jonathan had been in the safari business, that his preference was for forest hunting, that in '67 he'd been up on Lake Albert, culling crocodiles. Probably how much he earns as well, Marietta said to herself. He must have underlings whose job it is to unearth obscure facts. These Otieno would have written on an index card and memorized while he changed his clothes. Obviously he did his homework thoroughly.

In the country at large, despite his cosmopolitan glamour and his conspicuous wealth — acquired, it was widely rumored, from the smuggling of ivory to Hong Kong and Macao — Otieno was regarded as a mediator, a steadying influence after the inflammatory leadership that in past years had drawn all manner of punishments upon his tribe. During those hard times he had discreetly pursued his education in Britain and America. On his return, although there had certainly been a place for him in academic medicine, the benighted Luo had made stronger claims on his talents, and so he had abandoned the university for politics. These days his life was devoted to power: to its uses in Nairobi and its wellsprings in his Nyanza constituency. Only when politics allowed or dictated did he spend an evening in Katari. But tonight's party was to repay a debt of hospitality he'd incurred when he'd been the guest of Big John Bridges, who last June had struggled for a week to interest him in the habits of the American bison.

Otieno led Jonathan away to the living room, but Marietta hung back. At the bottom of the staircase she told Flora Otieno, "I used to slide down these banisters. You started slowly, came with a terrific whoosh round the curve, and then flew far out onto the marble floor. Don't your children love it?"

"Of course! Nelson forbids them to do it, but he's away so much they do it anyway."

The lion skins had vanished from the floors, the antelope and elephant heads from the walls. Instead, Flora Otieno displayed paintings and silkscreen prints from her gallery. "It's lovely," Marietta told her. "This house was almost uninhabitable before."

"It *was* a bit like a zoo, wasn't it?"

Half a dozen people, including the guest of honor, in string tie and cowboy boots, were already in the vaulted living room.

Dr. Otieno came up to Marietta. "Let me make you a drink." He watched her boldly. He expected admiration. His gray suit fitted him perfectly. He'd had it made in London. Indian tailors in Nairobi couldn't have done him justice. Marietta looked down, an act of self-protection that was also an admission of his splendor.

"I'd like Lillet if you have it." As a good guest, Marietta had no business asking for something she guessed her African host wouldn't have. They drank Lillet in New York these days, Jonathan had told her. Not in Nairobi yet. She should have asked for gin, but Otieno's obvious pleasure in himself made her defiant.

For a moment she saw him puzzled, then annoyed. "Of course," he said. "But I don't see it here. I won't be a moment." He vanished through a door.

Jonathan caught Marietta's eye and smiled. He seemed at ease. From time to time he surfaced unexpectedly from the morass which these days claimed him. Marietta smiled back.

Dr. Otieno reemerged with an open bottle of Chablis. He poured some into a glass and handed it to Marietta. "I'm sorry I kept you waiting. I could not find exactly what you requested. This is acceptable instead, I hope." You're a foolish woman, his look told her.

"I like your house," Marietta said, to mollify him. "I like the changes you've made."

336

"I also like it," he said steadily, forcing Marietta to hold his gaze. "I was the first African to buy property in Katari. I understand that certain people objected when they heard I'd showed an interest in this place. I'm told they tried to prevent the sale. But they were altogether out of date. The time was over for such games. Although there are a number of us here now, I was the first. It suits me." He smiled coldly, dismissing her, and turned away to another guest.

Flora introduced Marietta to a Nigerian in flowing robes. Mr. Ibrahim Olipo was delighted with Nairobi. How happy he'd been to leave Lagos! "That city is a place for beasts, not men. And the heat! You would not believe how hot it is! But this is paradise! The air is cool, the people are polite. When you use the telephone, you do so successfully."

"If you're prepared to wait," Marietta added, but Mr. Olipo chose to ignore her.

"And you, madam, are on a visit, or your husband is in business here?"

"This is my home."

Mr. Olipo looked closely at Marietta. "Clearly you agree, then, that this is a paradise. Many Europeans left when this country got its freedom from the British, but you have remained. You stayed to enjoy the benefits of good government. Do you know that in Nigeria we have anarchy! But here, life is so peaceful. In the post office, people stand in lines!"

No one but the most naive, the almost blind, Marietta thought, would consider this paradise. But I suppose that if you live carefully, unlike us, you may preserve the illusion that you can hope to thrive here. She looked across the room at Jonathan. He appeared from thirty feet to be at his rare best. No doubt Mr. Olipo would latch on to him in due course and find in him what he needed to reinforce his preconceptions about Kenya as a multiracial temperate society.

Jonathan was talking to a black woman. Around her head were twisted colored ropes of cloth, Lawrence of Arabia, Paris style. She wore a wonderful embroidered robe. Her fingernails were long, and the color of cranberry juice. Marietta looked about for a possible husband. A short Kikuyu stood near the fireplace with a woman, obviously his wife, right next to him. There were two archeologists with beards and scorched faces, an Arab diplomat, a gray-haired African with a paunch. No one worthy of such glamour.

337

Mr. Olipo spoke urgently about an experience he'd had in Geneva. He asked, "What would you have done in my place?"

Marietta, hoping for clues, received none, and replied lamely, "I imagine I'd have to have done the same thing."

Mr. Olipo appeared discouraged, but Dr. Otieno came over to refill his guest's glass and quickly involved him in a discussion about oil.

Released, Marietta went up to Jonathan. "You must meet Miss Ongaki," he said. "My wife, Marietta, Miss Catherine Ongaki."

Marietta marveled at the curve of the cheek, the proud tilt of the chin, the wide all-seeing eyes, and felt just as scrutinized and just as woefully deficient as she ever had. "In those days you were Catherine," she said, "but not Ongaki. You've taken your father's name."

Miss Ongaki smiled, showing very white teeth. "And you, Marietta, have acquired a new name, too. You married here in Kenya? I'm surprised. I thought you'd gone for good."

"So you're the Catherine I used to hear about!" Jonathan exclaimed.

"What have you heard about me?" Miss Ongaki said archly, and then, "I've been away so long, in Uganda, Britain, the United States. I only returned at the beginning of the month. Tell me, Marietta, when did you marry this charming man?"

"My son is six."

"Your son! I, too, have a son. Mattias is his name."

"He was born while you were overseas?"

"Of course! His favorite foods are fish and chips and hot dogs." Miss Ongaki laughed. "He has to learn to take *ugali* now."

"And your husband, where is he from?"

"I have never married, Marietta."

Jonathan said quickly, "Miss Ongaki was just telling me that she read for the Bar in Lincoln's Inn."

Marietta nodded. "You always knew what you wanted, didn't you? You're Kenya's first woman barrister and one of these days you'll be her first woman judge, just as you used to say."

"I did? Well," said Miss Ongaki, smiling, "at that age, one had very splendid ideas!"

"Your father must be delighted to have you home."

"My father died last August," Miss Ongaki said softly. "The tenth, it was."

That was our day, too, Marietta thought. The day of our capitulation. Did many people's lives change forever on the tenth of August, not just ours? "I'm so very sorry," she said. "I hadn't heard."

"I was still in London then. I'd so much hoped to see him again. Most especially, I'd wanted him to know my son. Since the day that boy was born, I'd imagined bringing him home, and seeing my father's expression and hearing him say, 'Aye, have you come to greet me? I've been so lonely for your company! What's kept you away?'" After a moment she went on, "When I got home, I took my son straight to Keriki. There I found my father's house, empty, and Ongeso dead. There aren't many left of those whom I knew best. The school where you and I both studied has been taken over by the government. It's no longer neat and tidy as it used to be. It's very strange to be away so long and then to return." In a low voice she added, "Perhaps it would be wiser to hear of the changes and not to see them. But what about you, Marietta? Did you paint those bold pictures that were stacked up in your head, so impatient to jump out and onto the canvas?"

"No," said Jonathan distinctly. "She married me instead, a decision she's coming to regret. I'll let her tell you *that* story herself."

But suddenly, mercifully, Flora Otieno appeared beside them. "Won't you come into the dining room? Of course Mrs. Sudbury knows the way. I'm sorry to interrupt. It looked like you were having a grand old time, but we'd better go in while the soup's still hot. There's nothing nastier than tepid crayfish bisque."

"How clever you were to arrange this meeting between old friends," Jonathan remarked. "I suppose you knew that Miss Ongaki and my wife grew up together."

"I had absolutely no idea!"

"Oh, yes! They were the leading lights of North Nyanza. Unfortunately, only one of them's fulfilled her promise. When I met her, Marietta had great ambitions, but for my sake, alas, she gave them up."

Mrs. Otieno looked from Jonathan to Marietta and back again. "Well," she said gaily, "some of us are late developers. I know I was. It's a question of the time being right. Go on in, won't you. You'll see the place cards."

There were four courses served by houseboys in white gloves. Jonathan sat at one end of the long table on Flora's left; Marietta was between the Arab and a permanent secretary. Miss Ongaki sat between the minister and the guest of honor. She's too much for

339

the warden, Marietta thought. He'll have indigestion. Flora should have asked that pretty, pale young English girl instead, the one who bottle-feeds the lion cubs at the animal orphanage. Bridges would have coped much better with her. Otieno's more in Catherine's league, though. They flash and gleam together. They make quite a pair! And Catherine's living the life she intended. She never wanted to marry. How could I? she used to say, when I have so much else to do in life! But she has her own son even so. The princess got her little prince.

At five past eleven, Miss Ongaki got up from the table. She had to be at work early. She was in the attorney general's office. Chief assistant, appellate division. "I should be on my way as well," Bridges said. He was off to Lake Turkana in the morning. Otieno's driver was called to run them back to town.

On her way out, Miss Ongaki stopped at Marietta's chair. "Let us see one another again. I was very amazed to see you here, Marietta. I thought you'd gone long ago and forgotten this place altogether. But it was I who went and you who stayed! There must be so much you could tell me about our country. You know where our office is? But do telephone to let me know when I should expect you. I wouldn't want you to come and not find me there," and with Otieno at her side she swept away.

She's the star, Marietta thought. So it always was. Nothing I have to say would interest her.

Justin came out to call Marietta to the telephone. "It's the mother of Anthony. But should I take a message?" he asked, seeing Marietta's muddy hands and feet. She was transplanting Swiss chard seedlings. When the Oldfields left for Spain, the garden had quickly gone to ruin. Now Marietta had set about reviving it. Once Neville had told her, If ever they destroy the world you know, go on and imagine another they can't touch. You have the knack, he'd said. But the truth was, she didn't. And so, somehow, she'd have to come to terms with the world as it was. In the face of a cataclysm all *she* knew was how to plant a garden.

"No, I'll speak to her myself," she replied, plunging her hands in a bucket of water. In the study a few moments later she said into the telephone, "I had a very interesting time the other night."

"But I never got a chance to talk to you! Will you have lunch with me in town one day this week?"

"When they met on Thursday in the Casuarina Gallery, Marietta said, "It's so glamorous in here. Just like Bond Street. The leather and steel, the lighting. I've passed often but never dared to set foot inside."

"Glamour's meant to attract people, not drive them away," Flora Otieno said, laughing.

"I wanted to be a painter once myself," Marietta said. "But I married and had Charlie. He needn't have stopped me, really, but when he was a baby I took over the farm. Even that needn't have stopped me. There were times when I wasn't that busy, but somehow I'd lost my nerve, or whatever it takes to deal with the blank of an empty canvas. So whenever I passed your gallery, I'd think of what I hadn't done. Coming in to look at what other people had succeeded in doing . . ." She smiled. "But now that I've taken the plunge and got through your door, I want to see everything."

"Certainly you shall. We've got plenty of time since we have to wait for Rose. She's my assistant. She's all I've got at present. I used to have a Swedish fellow, too, but his visa expired in September. He'd already had one extension and couldn't get another. He'll be back, I hope, but meanwhile Rose and I can't both be out to lunch at the same time."

Part of the gallery was taken up with paintings and wall hangings. "By my regulars," Flora said. "They show with me all the time." In the front section there was a sculpture exhibit, massive birds in pinkish stone. "You may know Kiro's work already. There's that wonderful piece of his in the lobby of the National Theater. I came across him a few years ago at Makerere. Before Amin, of course, when the fine arts department was still intact. From there he went to Rome and when he returned I asked him to do the show you see here." She handed Marietta a glass of Dubonnet. "I hope this will tide you over." Then, abruptly, she said, "Tell me, how do you know Catherine?"

Marietta smiled. "I tell you, it was quite a surprise, seeing her again — shock might be a better word. How do I know her? When we were eleven, we sat at next-door desks at a Quaker mission school. To be exact, we sat at the same desk, Catherine and I and her sisters. Later on we were in the same class again at the Mountain School for Girls. Everyone called her H.R.H., Her Royal Highness, in those days. The last time I saw her was in London. Seven or eight years ago. She'd won some competition, first prize, two weeks in the U.K. She arrived without warning and turned my life completely upside down. To be precise, she seduced my boyfriend. Since that great event, I haven't been in touch with her at all. The fact is, she mostly despised me, or disapproved of me, at any rate, for not being dedicated to the people's welfare. And I mostly envied her. It seemed she always got what she wanted. She reminded me rather of a caterpillar tractor. Implacable. Now I've gone and done it, haven't I! You're about to tell me she's your dearest friend!"

"Not mine. Nelson's."

Marietta stared. "D'you mean it?"

"I certainly do!"

"What an affliction!"

"Oh, I don't know. Things could have been so much worse," Flora said matter-of-factly. "They met at a conference in London a few years ago, and since I was there as well I had a ringside view. From the start it wasn't a secret. Of course, after that, Nelson took every chance to travel abroad so he could see her, but at least she wasn't *here*. And she wasn't in any great hurry to come home, either. After she passed the Bar she went to Harvard on a fellowship and it looked like she might stay there. While she was making up her mind, Nelson was very difficult to live with. But she decided to come home after all, and here she is! However, despite the little boy, she isn't interested in getting married. And even if she were, Nelson wouldn't marry her. There are only two people on this earth he's afraid of: the President and his father. The President's over eighty and in poorish health, but Nelson's father's only sixty-four and as strong as an ox. He's an archdeacon, you know; he may be made a bishop yet and he'd take a panga to Nelson if he left me."

"*You* could leave *him*."

"But that would mean leaving the children. These Kenyan men, they never let go of their sons, and the divorce laws are entirely in their favor. Tribal custom, you know. When was the last time a mother got custody of her children? I'll tell you, if it's ever happened, it was before my time! But supposing I left anyway, on my own, where would I go? U.K.? I'd be a foreigner there."

She'd married Nelson right after leaving the university. As soon as he finished at St. Thomas's they left for the States. In those days Nelson had just wanted to get on with becoming a doctor. *She* was the radical, not he. She'd grown up listening to her father's diatribes against colonialism. "He was a sociologist, a Marxist, naturally, but he never *did* anything, except lecture at his students. *And* at me. In my not very humble opinion, he was a dreadful hypocrite. I couldn't wait to do battle myself, and show him up! But that was a thousand years, well, fifteen, anyway, before Women's Liberation. So," she said, shrugging, "I married Nelson. Eventually *he'd* do the fighting. Meanwhile, he needed to be taken care of. He was rather shy and grateful, with enormous bony hands and feet, immensely tall, pitifully thin. Your princess wouldn't have looked at him twice! The Nelson you see now is a later edition who evolved" — she gestured graphically — "after he became a politician." She sighed. "Of course, along with the power and influence came all kinds of women, though none of them lasted. Until Catherine. When I saw that this time he was really hooked my hair started falling out, I lost a stone, I was a wreck. But after a bit I calmed down enough to take a longer look, and I saw that Catherine's an exceedingly ambitious young woman. Nelson's what she wants for the moment while she's getting started, but once she's set, she'll be up and on her way.

"The fact is," she went on quietly, "Nelson still has those great big hands and feet and he's still grateful to me sometimes. I sort of brought him up, you see. It'd be foolish to go stumping off now he's amounting to something. Besides, polygamy's the African way, or so everyone insists, apart from my father-in-law. One had just better get used to it, right?"

She poured herself some more Dubonnet. Marietta shook her head. "No, thanks, not for me." Her head was spinning. Faced with Catherine as one's husband's lover, how could any woman be cheerful, energetic, practical, or kind? And yet Flora managed all that, and probably much more. As Flora screwed the top back onto the Dubonnet bottle Marietta watched her in awe. "Go on," she said.

"With my soap opera?" Flora grinned. "I imagine that's what it must sound like to you. Well, okay. Nelson spends Monday and Tuesday nights in town with Catherine, Wednesday and Thursday in Katari with me. The rest of the time he's out in Nyanza. He's devoted to his constituents. I bet you he'd give up both of us sooner than neglect them." She stopped. "Do you have any idea how horrified you look! But really, Marietta, one knows much more awful situations. Elizabeth Kibaki's, for example. There she is, with three sons, just like me, living in the same bungalow with her sixteen-year-old illiterate co-wife. They go off to the *shamba* every morning, *jembes* at the ready. I've seen them, digging together! And Elizabeth got her Ph.D. in medieval German literature at Stanford! I went to her graduation. Thank heaven Nelson isn't one for farming. He lets me do whatever I like. Even if life in a country free of the colonial yoke isn't as inspiring as my father had me believe, I like it. And in my way," she added, waving at the stone birds, "I believe I'm making a contribution."

The Bihar restaurant on River Road served only vegetarian curries. "All you can eat for six bob," Flora said. "It's not at all bad, either." She'd developed a taste for curry when she'd been a student at the London School of Economics, but in Palo Alto, California, where Nelson had taken his surgical training, there'd been no Indian restaurants. "It was wonderful to get back here. Incidentally," she remarked once they'd ordered, "if you've got time on your hands, how about filling in for Lars?"

"Lars?"

"My Swede. He should be back in May. If he isn't, then I'll have to find someone permanent, but in the meantime, would you like to help? The tourist season's just beginning, and I don't quite know how Rose and I can struggle through it on our own."

"But I don't know anything about buying and selling art!"

"You don't have to buy. I do that. As for selling, all you'd do is chat people up a bit, and look attractive, which you certainly are. Then I have a party every couple of months or so. The next one's just after the New Year. Nelson rarely comes. My parties aren't political enough for him. Lars was pretty good at parties. How good are you?"

Marietta grimaced. "I've been living in the bush."

"Well, that bit's not important. Mostly you'd be having your patience tested by women who want something just exactly right for their living room in Shaker Heights, Ohio. After running a farm, helping in a gallery will seem like very small potatoes. But it'll be a different slice of life from what you're used to. And, as you saw just now, not everyone's painting lions and naked tribesmen or views of Kilimanjaro. There are some exciting things being done out here these days. You'll be paid, of course. Salary plus commission."

344

"No one's ever offered to pay me before." Marietta smiled. "Can I begin next Monday?"

"Settling in, are you?" Jonathan said, when Marietta told him in the study on Olduvai Road. His brandy bottle was three-quarters empty. "I thought you'd be off soon."

"Off? Where to?"

He shrugged. "Do I know what goes on in your head? You've never been one for revelations."

"I'm not going anywhere."

"Whatever can be keeping you?" he mocked. "Not fear of the unknown. Or is it feeling for your husband, this poor sot?"

She said quietly, "Has something happened I don't know about?"

"You mean you don't care for my belligerence? But you see me as I have become, Marietta! I'm not the charming chap I once was. Why hang around? Why waste any more time on me? I'm not your type. Of course you never claimed I was, did you? Even at the beginning. You weren't quite up to turning me down, though. I don't deny that you've appreciated me — that'd be the right word, I think — as you would some esoteric work of art, perhaps. If pressed, you'd offer a favorable critique. But always with the reservation: given the type of man I am." He added, "Not your type."

"I won't listen to you, Jonathan. You're drunk." She turned to go.

"Oh, no! You sit down. It's high time you listened to me." He leaned back in his chair, his head and shoulders sharply outlined against the bright afternoon beyond the window. "I put things off. I admit that. It was always such a source of anguish that you didn't love me, not as much as I loved you. Before you, I'd never treasured another human being. I'd been too busy worrying about myself, would I measure up? — knowing, ultimately, I couldn't. But I felt different with you. I'd worry about you, not just about me. Whatever I had would be that much better for being shared with you. I'd lavish love upon you. And I did, but the return I'd hoped for simply never came.

"It's been a strange humiliation, being jealous not of a man you were creeping off to behind my back — someone who screwed you and got life from you, not the arctic air I got — but of my own farm! Passion I don't doubt you've got, Marietta. I've seen it. Oh, yes! Sweeping over the land. *My* land, as it happened. But never passion for me! However" — he smiled grimly — "to my surprise

345

I've found of late that I'm not as sorry for myself as I used to be. If I haven't got precisely what I'd hoped for, I haven't lost out all together. I wanted an heir." He shrugged. "That's all over, isn't it. Nothing to inherit now. But I wanted a son much more and he, thank God, I've got. So there's no need to hang about here, Marietta, doing make-work when you could be out in the real world, as you'd call it. I'm an ostrich by nature, so you've said. With my head stuck fast in the sand. But *you're* not!"

"You're inviting me to leave you, is that it?" Marietta said, palms like ice.

"Not inviting. Telling. That's what you've been waiting for. A little push from me. I've seen you looking at me, Marietta. I've seen you thinking, What in the hell am I doing here with him? Got to stick it out, though. He won't survive alone. Well, maybe I shall. Maybe I shan't. It's up to me, not you." He poured himself more brandy. "Charlie stays with me, of course," he added carefully. "So sorry." He looked up. "I never offered you a drink. Want one? No? Well, fortunately I don't mind drinking alone." He sat back again, and looked at Marietta over the top of his glass. "Quiet, aren't you. Should I take it you accept my proposition? That surprises me. I'd imagined being in for a terrific *shauri*. But maybe I misjudged you. Maybe you see just as clearly as I do" — his voice rose — "that it's essential for me to have my son."

"We'll fight," Marietta said at last, "over how we've failed one another, but not over Charlie."

Jonathan jumped up. He came round the desk and jerked her to her feet. He shook her savagely, like a dog would shake a rat, and her long hair fell over her face. "Your righteousness appalls me! I've had all I can take of being judged by you. Get out!" He flung her towards the door. "Go to that common little friend of yours! I hope she meets your standards!"

"I'm not going anywhere, Jonathan." Marietta shielded herself with her arms. "I'm not leaving Charlie here with you. God knows what you'd do!"

"That's a chance you'll have to take!" He opened a desk drawer and out of it he took a small revolver. "You heard." He pulled Marietta to one side and wrenched the door wide. "Get out of here!"

A car was coming up the driveway. It stopped. They heard Charlie's voice saying, "See you in the morning!" He appeared in the doorway, a small figure in khaki shorts and shirt. Seeing his parents he cried, "I've got to take a shoebox to school tomorrow. Where d'you keep them?"

"Ask Justin," Marietta answered. She stood just in front of Jonathan with his gun cold in her back.

"But it's Justin's day off. Can't you help me look, Mum?"

"Of course, today's Thursday! I'd forgotten. Yes, I'll help you look. But just give me a hug first."

He dropped his satchel and came to Marietta, who put her arms tightly round him and buried her face in his curly hair. "It's wonderful to see you, Charlie."

"You saw me at breakfast, didn't you?" Charles retorted, wriggling. Then he stiffened. "Hey, Johnny, I never saw that before," he said as he slipped out of Marietta's arms.

"I got it because of the burglaries down the road last week," Jonathan said lightly. "I was just showing it to your mother."

"Is it loaded?"

"Good heavens, no! That'd be a stupid thing to do, to keep a loaded revolver in the house! You never know who'd find it. I was just about to put it in the drawer by my bed. If any thief gets past Gelda and the *askari* I'll get after him with this. *He* won't know it isn't loaded. Don't you go telling him, either!" Jonathan laughed, then turned and went up the stairs.

At supper he spoke very little. Afterwards he disappeared into the study, but when it was time to go up to bed he came into the drawing room. "As you know," he said to Marietta, "Sunday I'm off to Tanzania with the Hillinghams. I'll be gone till the beginning of January. While I'm away, you should think very carefully what you want to do. Staying here may prove to be more difficult than you imagine. I'm capable of living under extraordinarily adverse conditions. Without love, for instance, and with very little hope. But you, after all, are used to being loved by me. Shan't you miss that? I wonder." Then he went back into the study and closed the door.

20

Nairobi

M rs. Otieno's at the Coast," Marietta said. "She'll be back on Monday. Can I help you?"

"I wrote well ahead to say when I was coming," a stout British woman replied indignantly. Her bosom was swathed in shell pink linen and she carried a massive handbag made of zebra skin. "By the way, don't remember seeing you before."

"I'll get Rose. She's in the back."

"I've dealt so much with Mrs Otieno in the past. It's really very disappointing not to find her here."

Snow was falling in Europe and America. But in Nairobi bougainvillea tumbled over walls. The Casuarina Gallery was thronged with the first tourists of the Christmas season. Marietta slipped between sunburned Germans in identical blue shirts, identical blue jeans. In the storeroom she found Rose checking a shipment just in from Dahomey. "There's a woman insisting on Flora. Can you pacify her? It seems I can't." As she followed Rose back through the crowd she was intercepted by a man interested in a stone bird for his country house on the Baltic. But what arrangements could be made to get it there? "I'll have to look in the files. Could you wait just a minute?" At the desk the British woman looked happier already. She remembered Rose from the year before and Rose claimed to remember her as well. Marietta opened a file drawer labeled "Shipping."

"What are you doing here?" Michael Kagia smiled at her across the desk. "I saw you through the window and I came right in."

For an instant Marietta stared. "This is where I work," she said hurriedly. "What are *you* doing here?"

"In Parliament they're debating an increase in the postal rates. Yesterday it was the same, and probably tomorrow as well. So I thought I'd take a walk. I was looking at a piece of sculpture in the window and suddenly, behind it, there you were!"

She'd found the list of shipping regulations. "It shouldn't be too difficult," she told her customer. "By when would you want this piece?"

"June. I won't go up there before June. Who would? The weather's very unpredictable. One more day I shall think about it and then I shall inform you. It's the wings I like. But then again, perhaps not," he added, and went off to look at his bird again.

Kagia said, "Are you busy, Marietta?"

"Extremely. Can't you see that!"

"Then I'll have to wait until you're finished. I'd been hoping for a chance to talk to you, you see."

"But I don't want to talk to *you*. Not now. Not later. I want you to leave me alone. Go away, please." She went by him and on to the back of the gallery. Kagia watched her for a moment, then he took out a card and wrote on it.

"Will you give this to Mrs. Sudbury?" he asked Rose. "Greet Mrs. Otieno for me when she comes. Tell her this place looks very interesting. I had not realized that she kept such treasures in it."

"This is for you," Rose said when Marietta reappeared. "That man, Flora's friend, he did not wish to wait." But on the card he'd written: Botanical Gardens 6 o'clock. In the evening only vagrants and beggars went into the gardens, and European hippies coming north, going south, wanting somewhere to smoke their marijuana. I'm afraid of that place in the dusk, Marietta thought. I'm afraid of *him*. And I'm afraid of myself and the harm I might do to my husband and my son.

She helped Rose tidy up. She counted the cash, locked the safe, barred the windows, greeted the watchman. Rose's sister was waiting at the Thorn Tree. They were going to the pictures later on. "Since your husband's gone again, d'you want to come with us?"

Marietta thought, We've never had a beginning, he and I. Given who I am and who he is and *what he has already done*, there won't be a beginning, either. Not now, never. This I will tell him. Suddenly everything seemed so simple. "Not this time, Rose. There's something I must do tonight. Thanks anyway."

Rose glanced into her pocket mirror. Her hair was done in several dozen stiff braids. She tweaked a few, applied dark red lipstick, zipped up her shoulder purse, and left.

Marietta dialed the Katari number, and when Justin answered she said clearly, "I've just run into someone I haven't seen for a while and there are matters we need to discuss so I shan't be home for dinner. Could you read to Charlie, please?" Then she went out into the street. It was the gentle time, after the day, before the night, when birds wheeled above the city. She found her car behind the mosque and drove out onto the avenue. She turned not west into the setting sun, towards Katari, but east.

Some schoolboys straggled to the gate of the gardens. Their bags were heavy with facts to be memorized perfectly by morning, or else what would become of them? They argued and shrugged and straggled on again. No time for chasing down the avenues.

But Marietta went through the gate. He was waiting under a tree festooned with vines. "So after all you came," he said joyfully. "Welcome!"

She ignored his outstretched hand. "I decided it was time you know what you've accomplished."

"What is this, Marietta?" He shook his head. "Aren't we friends now?"

She said in fury, "How could Edmund have resisted you? You weren't in England. Shut up in a boarding school. You were right there, next to him. And *you* knew how to listen, how to answer. *You* knew how to please!"

"Did you come to talk about *that*?" Kagia looked at her incredulously. "I was a child then, Marietta. Can you be so harsh about a child? He had so much to teach and I had so much to learn. And it was all so long ago. What have he and I to do with you and me?"

"I'll tell you!" she cried. "He was always a shy man. Ill at ease with people, and especially children. He couldn't pay attention to more than one boy at a time. It was you or Jonathan, one or the other, and you saw to it that he chose you!" She breathed out deeply and went on, "When I see him he never asks after you. But I know he's waiting to hear. I've thought, All right, if he won't ask, then I shan't tell him. I'll punish him for what he did. I'll punish him for loving someone else's son more than his own. I'll punish

350

him for setting that terrible sadness on Jonathan! But I'm never quite able to be that cruel to someone who's always been so kind. To me, at least. So eventually when we're alone together, five thousand miles and twenty years from the scene of the original crime, I say to him, 'By the way, Michael's been made senior lecturer. He's written a book. I can't make head or tail of it myself. You'd understand it, though. Order it from Blackwell's, why don't you?' Or else I say, 'He stood for Parliament. And won, yes, by a landslide. He's a very popular member. People like him because he doesn't behave like a *mtu mkubwa*, a big man. They think he cares about them, and he probably does, too. It's not just show, to ensure his reelection.' Then Edmund's hand shakes a little as he lifts his cup and the tea may spill. And he says, quietly, 'He did turn out so well, didn't he.'"

They weren't alone in the avenue. Four young men in bell-bottoms and wide-buckle belts were watching. "Her husband was no good for her and so she wandered, but see, this black one cannot satisfy her either. She's telling him, 'You're useless, too.'" They rocked with laughter.

"I haven't seen Edmund since your latest triumph," Marietta said. "So I don't know what he thinks about that. But I do know that when he was young he had a vision of how Olgolulu could be and his life's work was to make that vision real. And then to pass it on to his son and his son's son. But you squelched that one! So what's left?" She said bitterly, "I'll tell you what's left for my husband. A bottle of brandy a day. Less in the bush when he's earning his living, but not that much less!"

"It is he who spoils himself," Kagia replied gravely. "It is his choice and his responsibility. Not mine, not Edmund's; not yours, either, though I'm sorry for the burden that it places on you."

"I don't believe you care!"

"If that's so, why did I ask you to come here?"

"Because you wanted to know how we've taken defeat. Well, you've got your answer, haven't you? Not well at all."

"I hadn't thought you hated me," he said sorrowfully. "I hadn't expected that."

"Did you expect me to *love* you?" she cried.

"I thought so."

She hung her head. "I don't hate you," she said wearily. "I never hated you. I'm jealous, that's all."

351

"Of me?" Kagia exclaimed. *"Terrible* things have happened to me, Marietta!"

"But you've survived them! Edmund was right to love you," she added. "You had what it takes."

"What's that?"

"Knowing your own worth, regardless. At Olgolulu things were simple. There I knew exactly how much I was worth. Now what's left?" She smiled bleakly. "Not much."

"I see things differently," Kagia said. "I see that you were bound and now you're free. We may want something, Marietta, because only that can soothe and heal us. For a time, being in a certain place, doing what we know, nothing else, nothing more. That's all that interests us. I, too, was like that once," he said softly. "In North America I thought, I shall stay here. I'll never go back where those things happened. I shall forget what I used to be. I felt as if I'd lost my life and had no option but to start a new one. But in fact I hadn't died, only suffered greatly, and after a long time I noticed I was getting better after all. One day I *was* better, and so I left and came back home. It's often disappointing here at home. But I prefer it, even so. Once you're healed you get impatient and that safe place no longer satisfies you."

Marietta said, "Did I need healing?"

"You told me that you needed peace, so I went away. But peace becomes tedious in the end. That place, Olgolulu, it was Edmund's vision, his dream. Not yours, Marietta, unless you are a peasant who craves the land, not to be healed but in order to live at all."

"What makes you think I'm healed now?"

"You came to meet me," he said in triumph. "This time you didn't turn away! How many years have I known you?" He took her hand.

"Let me be, Michael," she said, and she made as if to pull away.

"No, we shall count together. It was October, wasn't it? The moon was very orange and the lake was very black. And that's one, two, three, four, five, six years ago. I'm becoming gray here," he said as he touched his temples. "Is your hair as bright as it used to be? We'll be old people soon. I tell you, Marietta, I am tired of waiting. But see," he added softly, "we have our audience here. It is always so in Africa, as you said."

"Do those boys know you?"

"Oh, no. I'm not such a big man, Marietta. My picture isn't so often in the papers. How could they recognize me?"

352

"And I'm only a white woman. Which is a perfect disguise."

"All the same, I'd rather leave them." Smiling a little, he added, "Away from them, you may be kinder to me."

So they went down steps and round a fish pond clogged with lily pads and up to the top of the ridge as the shadows grew long.

"You stayed in Kenya after all," Kagia said.

"Were you worried that I wouldn't?"

"Worried enough to drive out to your house once."

"You did! When was that?"

He shrugged. "A few weeks ago. I meant only to ask your *shamba* boy, as if I were interested in buying the place, Are they leaving? When are they leaving? Your son was playing outside and with him was Flora Otieno's youngest child. Since he was a baby he has known me. He danced and jumped and shouted and that dog of yours came barking after me again. And then your servant came, the Ruba man."

"Justin."

"He wasn't happy to see me." Kagia smiled. "He told me, 'You've troubled them enough, let them live their lives in peace here.' So I drove away again, but I'd heard what I had hoped to hear, that you weren't leaving Kenya."

"Anyone in their right mind would have left," she said, and her head began to swim with the happiness that she'd feared and hidden from for such a long time.

"You're not in your right mind?"

She stopped as the path entered a thicket of bamboo that reached up fifty and sixty feet into heavy vines looping low from the branches of great mahogany trees. "I don't believe so," she said, laughing, and she took his face between her hands. He was just her height and wonderfully familiar. "I used to be afraid of you. I've forgotten why, but I was more afraid of myself than of you." Then she kissed him. She felt his warmth and his hardness and thought, I want this man for myself, for my very own.

"It isn't safe in this place after dark," he said softly. "Let us go from here." In the dusk she looked into his eyes and knew that his head, like hers, swam with a rough, wild joy that things were coming to pass, despite such odds.

They went back past waxy lilies, closed till morning, and up the long stone steps. Their audience was gone from the avenue.

He lived beyond the hospital in a house behind the mansion of a very rich Ismaili. "I'll lead the way in my car and you stay close

353

behind me," he said, and in the shadow of the wrought iron gate, a relic of the Empire, he kissed her quickly.

They drove through dimly lit streets lined with high walls that were topped by broken glass. Thieves were the obsession of this city in which the poor grew ever poorer, despite Uhuru. Kagia turned off at a heavy stone archway. They waited while dogs barked and a watchman struggled with the padlock. Slowly he opened the left side of the gate, then the right, and stood back to let them through. A hundred yards past a stucco house they came to a green bungalow set on short brick piles, surrounded by frangipani trees. A single light bulb shone on the veranda and under it an old woman sat on a straight-backed chair, reading the paper. She wore an orange nylon shirtwaist dress splattered with blue cabbage roses, and an old green cardigan, unraveling at the wrists. She folded her newspaper carefully and stood up. "Who's this you've brought to me?" she said in Kikuyu. She'd been scratching her scalp at the back and her head cloth had pitched down over her eyes. She looked suspiciously at Marietta, and spotting her wedding ring, added, "Why, Maruga, should you make trouble with some white man's wife?"

"It isn't only his trouble," Marietta said. "It's mine as well. But this is what we choose."

The woman stared. "You know our language! Are you then an African?"

"Will you tell me what I am?" said Marietta, close to tears. "Let us greet one another. Mari, they called me in my home."

"Mari? Mary. I, too, am Mary. It is good that we have the same name." She led Marietta across the veranda, through the battered screen door. The bungalow had two rooms. It had been built as the guest house of the mansion. The kitchen was separate, off in the back. In the living room, books were everywhere, jamming the shelves, in piles on tables, and on the floor as well. In front of the fireplace was a worn Turkish carpet, a lumpy blue sofa, and a huge armchair. On the walls were two Canadian Pacific Railway posters of the Rockies. "I shall bring Tusker," Mary said, and hurried out.

Kagia smiled. "Mary likes you."

"Is she particular about your woman friends?"

"I don't bring women here. I like to have a quiet place."

"So am I specially honored?"

354

"I hope you know you are."

Mary came back from the kitchen with two glasses and two bottles of beer. She made space for them on a table. "Shall I cook for your visitor, Maruga?"

"Not now. Next time she comes you will cook for her."

"In that case," Mary said, tying her head cloth tighter, "I shall go to visit my friend." She added, looking straight at Marietta, "Will you be happy together, you two? I hope so, yes!" She went out through the screen door and they heard her on the steps. She went softly away over the grass.

Kagia took Marietta's hand and bowed just a little. "Will you come now, Marietta? Does it suit you?"

"It suits me exactly. Better than anything ever before!" She went with him into the bedroom. It contained a large iron bed, a dresser, a chair, one small lamp, and many more piles of books.

"Not what you're used to," he said.

"I'm tired of that."

He undressed her carefully. He had difficulty with the buttons on her blouse.

"I'll help you," she said.

"No, no!"

When she was naked, he said, "Now your hair." She let him loosen it and it fell heavy and bright to her waist.

"It's my turn now."

All her life she'd seen black men washing in the river. With Violet she'd washed herself beside them, although she'd stopped once she felt shame. Later she'd said to herself, as she drove over bridges and along the river bank, They're beautiful, those flanks, those backs, the deep rift of the spine. Now that she had a black man for her own, she thought, I'm used to him, it was the other I was never used to; and she smiled.

"What is it?" Kagia said.

"I'm pleased, that's all. So pleased by you!"

It was time, then, to make love.

"Where shall we start?"

"At the very beginning, of course," she said, "and we'll go on for as long as it takes."

"This year, next year."

"Even forever."

"Then we shall begin again."

But at midnight she had to get up to go home. She sat on the edge of the bed, and stretched.

"Are you tired?" he said, propped on one elbow, watching her. "I've made you very tired, I think. How will you drive your car?"

"I'm not tired," she said. "I just woke up, don't you see?" She knelt over him, laughing. "I've been asleep all my life till now." His hand went over her stomach, over her hips, to her breasts. She held it over her heart. "D'you feel it, the way it laughs along? It used to stumble from one beat to the next."

"That's a story."

"But it's true. How is your heart, Michael?"

"Strong," he said. "Far stronger than it used to be. When are you coming back, Marietta?" He pulled her down beside him. "You must promise me a time, or I shan't let you go," he said, and he began making love to her again.

When she got back to Olduvai Road the *askari* was crouched on the porch with Gelda at his feet. He greeted Marietta sleepily. Inside the light was on on the stairs but the hall was in darkness. She bolted the front door at the bottom, and then at the top. She leaned against it for a moment. I'm not as I was. I'm coming from my lover. His smell is all over my body, in my hair. I shall sleep with it, as if with him. But before I greet my son in the morning, I must bathe. She smiled to herself as she went through the hall.

"Where have you been?" Justin was sitting on the chair next to the grandfather clock.

"Out," she said. "With a friend. As I told you. We had so much to talk about. You needn't have waited up for me."

Justin stood up and switched the hall light on; the light was shaped like a lantern, its bulb white and harsh. He looked at Marietta, with her hair streaming over her shoulders. "What friend is this?"

"Someone I met in America. A long time ago."

"And you stayed so late with such a one, a stranger!"

"Not a stranger," she said, and looked away.

"Mari, do you know what it is that you do?"

"I'm not a girl, Justin," she said coldly. "There's no need to warn me. There's no need to protect me. Good night." And she went upstairs.

*

356

Justin brought in her tea. He put the cup and saucer on the bedside table and drew the curtains. The sun flooded in, the high bright sun of December. He frowned down at her. "Today is Friday," he said. "You are going to Nanyuki in the evening. What clothes will you take with you?"

"I'm not going to Nanyuki."

"You told me so yesterday. You are going to Bwana Thompson."

"I've changed my mind. It wasn't definite anyway. I'll telephone the Thompsons after breakfast. If he wants to, Charlie can have Anthony sleep here tonight. He'll like that better than going to Nanyuki."

Justin stood next to her bed, hands at his sides. "What reason will you give to Bwana Thompson?"

"I shall tell him" — she yawned — "that I have malaria."

"You never suffer from malaria!"

"But he doesn't know that. I don't feel like driving all that way. I prefer to stay home."

"So you will be here this evening?"

"I shall have supper with Charlie," she said, "and then I shall go out."

"Who is this friend, this one from America?" Justin was grim-faced, insistent.

"It's no concern of yours." For a moment she stared at him in silence, then she burst out, "All my life you've shaken your head at me! 'You watch out, Mari! Do you know what you're doing?' Well, now I shall do as I please."

"And what is that?"

"It's no concern of yours," she said again, with the sheet drawn up to her chin.

"I think it is Kagia whom you go to," he said sadly. "He came here looking for you. I told him, Leave her. But he did not hear me." He bowed his head and ran his hands over his face, as if he were washing it. "He is a mongrel, that one. Not black, not white. Why do you choose him, Mari?" He sighed heavily. "You should stay with your own kind."

"He *is* my kind!" she exclaimed. "I'm a mongrel, too!" She pushed the sheet back. "See this," she said, touching the soft pale skin of her underarm. "It's a lie, Justin! When Violet and I used to fight, you'd catch the backs of our dresses and pull us apart and shake us. 'Why do you quarrel?' you'd ask, 'if you are sisters?' Then

I'd weep, 'In that case, I would have a father, too, just as she does!'
And you'd answer, 'But I have two girls, Mari, haven't I? Both are
mine.' You were right, of course," she said softly. "So what am I
now? Not white. Not black. Something of this. Something of that.
If I was your girl once, Justin, could I be a European now?"

"Drink your tea," he said. "It's almost cold already. You don't like
it cold."

"Won't you wish me happiness? I haven't been happy with my
husband." She added, "You know where he sleeps now."

Justin said quickly, "Is that what you want, then? Some man,
any man. Shall you become a wanderer? The way your mother
was!"

"Did you shake your head at her as well?" Marietta cried. "Like
some old goat! My mother knew who she wanted. Not any man. A
particular man. And once she found him, her wandering ceased. I
found the man I wanted years ago, only I didn't dare to claim him.
But I do now, Justin, and whether you wish me well or not, I shall
go to him!"

Flora drove back from Lamu with an enormous Arab door
wrapped in burlap in the back of her truck. She'd had her eye on
it for a couple of years and a client waiting in Milan. "I told him,
'I'm going down to the Coast again, but don't get your hopes too
high.' Twice I left that family empty-handed. They'd come so close
to selling. Then they'd change their minds. This time the negotiations took everything I had in me, and it was a hundred degrees in
the shade as well, but in the end I got that door, and at the price I
wanted. Quite a coup, though I do say so myself! If I air-freight it
out before the end of this week, it'll be in Milan by Christmas.

"Incidentally," she added, "what are your plans for Christmas,
Marietta? Since Jonathan's off at the back of beyond, how about
you and Charlie coming to dinner with us?" Nelson would be leaving for Geneva that night on the one o'clock plane to try to convince the Aga Khan to come up with backing for a tourist complex
near Mombasa. "We'll have plenty of time for turkey and pudding
and crackers and paper hats. It's just the family — Nelson's sister
with her twins, and two of his brothers as well. But not the archdeacon. Christmas is his peak time. He'll be preaching and praying
and blessing and singing back home in Nyanza. I'm sorry you'll
miss him. He has moral fire. Most moralists are icy, so I've found.
And oh yes, Catherine's coming, with Mattias."

358

"Whose idea is this?"

"Mine, of course. It's the only practical answer. The boys and I want Nelson to spend Christmas with us, but it being his last day here he has to see Catherine. She wouldn't go with him to Switzerland because she's got a big case coming up. And I wouldn't go with him, either. Who on earth, given the choice, would go to Europe in December? Anyway, the moths ate my winter coat ages ago and I can't leave the gallery again so soon. You'd give notice and Rose probably would, too. So Nelson's going by himself and he's not looking forward to it. He tends to have nightmares in hotels alone."

Marietta shook her head. "You're incredible! You talk as if he and she and you were three people you just happen to know. 'There's this man and two women and oh, yes, their four kids. They're reasonable, they've worked things out. Give a little, take a little. Even if the man's not completely satisfied all the time, the others are reasonably pleased.' I ask you, Flora," she added, "is it really necessary to invite Catherine to your family party?"

"But where else would she go? She just came back here recently. Her father died last August. She can't go home."

"She's not exactly short of brothers and sisters, and some of them must have migrated to Nairobi by now. Let her go to them!"

"And what sort of Christmas would that be for Mattias? He's a very British little boy, accustomed to a tree and everything. In London, Catherine boarded him out with a cockney woman. Mrs. Chase, her name was. I met her once. She was ever so cozy. Catherine's never had much time for him herself, and I don't imagine she'll have much more in the future."

"Next you'll be telling her, 'Let Mattias come and stay with his brothers, dear, so you can concentrate on your career'!"

"But Mattias and my boys aren't brothers."

"He's not Nelson's son?" Marietta exclaimed.

"Good heavens, no! He was six months old when Catherine and Nelson met. Didn't I tell you?"

"No." Marietta sank to a carved Swahili stool. "Who *is* his father, then?"

"I've never asked her, as a matter of fact. Although we're bound to cooperate a certain amount, Catherine and I usually stick to practicalities. Who goes where when and how, that sort of thing. All I know is, she was pregnant when she went to London to study for the Bar, and she'd been living in Kampala before that. So I

359

suppose she had an affair with some Ugandan. Idi Amin? No" —
Flora grinned — "not him. In those days he was only a sergeant. I
doubt she'd have given him the time of day. Frankly, I really don't
care who the father is. I'm just enormously thankful it isn't Nelson,
given how African men are about their sons."

"Not just *African* men," Marietta murmured.

"If Nelson *were* Mattias's father," Flora continued, "then he'd
hang on to him forever, and through him, on to Catherine as well,
in which case I'd probably have cut my throat by now. As it is, I'm
getting rather fond of Mattias. He's an engaging little fellow, bright
as a button. He's taught himself to read already and he's not quite
four. In his short life he's spent too much time with grownups,
though. When he comes here he'd rather hang about with me than
with the boys. Anthony's only interested in games with violent end-
ings, and Mattias isn't quite up to them yet, but he'll be going to
school in January. No doubt he'll be as rambunctious as the rest of
them after a week or two at Saint Paul's."

"He's going there too, is he?"

"By the skin of his teeth! They told his mother they had enormous waiting lists, they wouldn't have a place for him till 1976.
But I made such a nuisance of myself that they agreed to take him
in the middle of the year."

"Couldn't Catherine have done that?"

"Done what?"

"Made a nuisance of herself?"

"I'm not sure that would've done the trick."

Marietta said dryly, "D'you intend to go on making things pleasant for Catherine indefinitely?"

"It does seem odd to you, doesn't it?" Flora smiled faintly as she
unlocked a filing cabinet. It was two minutes to ten in the morning,
two minutes till opening time. A dozen Italians waited impatiently
on the pavement outside. The Casuarina Gallery was just the first
of seven stops they were scheduled to make that day. "No, I don't
intend to go on indefinitely. I shan't have to. Catherine's not going
to be around indefinitely. She's a temporary spectacle, not a permanent affliction." Flora sighed. "At least I've told myself that so
often, I'm more or less convinced it's true! No doubt Nelson will
find a replacement for her, but they say the first major diversion is
the greatest trauma. They get progressively easier after that, until
eventually they're almost routine. Besides," she added, "there's

something rather sad about Catherine underneath the gloss. I suppose that's often true of people who feel compelled to try so hard. You may snort, Marietta, when I tell you she brings out my mothering instincts; nevertheless, it's true."

Kagia said, "I'll be away for several days at Christmas time. There are meetings I have to go to, a *harambee* in the Rift."

"I wish I could go with you," Marietta said. In the darkness before dawn they lay together in Kagia's iron bed.

"People will drink *changaa* and quarrel and fight. You wouldn't find that interesting at all."

"But I don't like to sleep alone."

"Sleep?" He smiled. "Is that what you do here with me?"

"Besides," she said, "I had a plan. Flora Otieno's asked me to her house on Christmas Day. I'd decided you should get her to invite you, too. Then she'd say to me, 'I believe you know this gentleman,' and I'd say, 'Indeed I do! He's the villain of the piece.' And she'd say, 'Can't you let bygones be bygones? Life's so short! Shake hands and have some champagne!' Then we'd take a stroll together on the terrace and Flora would be perfectly delighted. She hates loose ends. Oh well, so much for that little scheme!" After a moment she said, "Will you be at Olgolulu on Christmas Day?"

"If Christmas Day is a Friday, then of course I shall. I go to Olgolulu every Friday. Why did you ask?"

"To remind myself who you are."

"And who is that?"

"My old enemy, now my friend."

"How did that come about?"

"You persuaded me."

"That was very clever of me!"

"It was very foolish of me to have delayed so long!"

Kagia lay back, hands behind his head. "When's Johnny coming?" he asked.

"On the eighth."

"And when will he go out again?"

"I'm not sure. The Germans he'd booked for later in the month have canceled."

"When he's at home, will you come to me like this?"

"I don't know."

"When are you going to tell him?"

"I don't know that either, Michael."

Kagia turned on his side, facing her. "He doesn't want you, Marietta. I do. Why should you stay with him?"

She said sadly, "Because I'm the only friend he has. Apart from Charles. But Charles is a little boy. Charles can't save him."

"From what do you hope to save him?"

"From being utterly alone."

"You can't do it!"

"I knew that's what you'd say, but I must try."

"Why? Do you love him?"

"I am enormously grateful to him."

"For what?" Kagia cried. "For enslaving you? For doing the work he should have done himself?"

"For giving me a true beginning." After a moment she added, "I can't leave him until I know where he's going and if he'll be all right."

"How long must I wait this time?"

"Perhaps not so very long." She placed one hand over his heart. "I love you, Michael, but I can't tell where we're going either, or if we'll be all right."

Marietta was driving into town. Charles sat on the back seat in a clean blue shirt, his hair slicked down. Beside him lay a parcel wrapped in shiny paper.

"We're always going out these days," he said, "especially you. You used to stay at home at night. Now you hardly ever do."

"People invite me," Marietta said. "Up at Olgolulu no one did, but down here things are different. It's nice to have some friends at last. Before, we used to be quite lonely."

"I wouldn't want to go back, would you?"

"I wanted to at first, but now," she said, smiling, "I'd rather stay."

"Would Johnny, though?"

"I don't know, love."

"I think he'd want to go back," Charles said. "He hasn't got a friend down here. I've got Anthony and you've got his mum. D'you think Johnny would get along with Anthony's father? No," he said, sighing, "he wouldn't, would he. He likes being by himself the best. Was he that way when he was small?"

"I didn't know him then, love. I didn't meet him till after he'd grown up."

362

They were on their way to Dexter Dodge's seventh birthday party. Dexter was a black American and four and a quarter inches taller than the next tallest boy in Standard Two at St. Paul's School. His father owned a Mercedes, a jeep, and a Lincoln Mercury, so Charles had reported the first time he'd been over there to play. In Dexter's house there was an electric ice cream maker, a trampoline, and a stereo with seven speakers, one of which was in the bathroom Dexter shared with his sister, Delila, aged ten. Today's invitation offered four P.M. treasure hunt, five P.M. movie, and six P.M. barbecue in the back yard, and Charles, a new arrival in these circles, was deeply awed. How could he keep up? On the third of March, when he turned seven, he'd have a party too. To this event, still months away, he was giving considerable thought. He liked best the idea of an outing in the safari truck. None of his friends had a safari truck. Then, none of them had a hunter for a father.

"Will Johnny be at home for my birthday, Mum?"

"He promised he would."

"But he isn't coming home for Christmas. Why does he like those strangers better than us?"

"There's no one in the world he likes better than you, Charlie."

"Not even you?"

"Not even me."

Charles considered this a moment, then he said, "Why does he stay away so long?"

"Because it's hundreds and hundreds of miles to the Selous. I went there once. It took us a week just getting there. The roads weren't really roads at all."

They were coming to a roundabout piled high with scarlet bougainvillea. Marietta slowed, and then swung left towards Muthaiga. A crowded city bus lumbered along in front of them. Down the twisting road they crawled. At the bottom of the hill the bus stopped and passengers struggled to get off. Mary burst out, lifting a small boy down behind her. The boy had on a baseball cap pulled down over his eyes. Mary knelt to tuck his shirt into his shorts. Then she wiped his nose, took his hand, and set off down the road. It was very hot and the little boy was tired. He dragged on Mary's hand and scuffed his shoes and stumbled, but Mary held him firmly so that he didn't quite fall. Marietta thought, I'll give them a lift to wherever they're going. It can't be much out of our way. But then she remembered, Charlie's with me. He'll ask, How d'you know her, this old woman? And Mary will say, So this is your boy. How closely he resembles you! You should bring him to visit us very soon. And in a moment a link will be forged between night and day, and I'm not ready for that. She passed the bus and accelerated, leaving Mary and the sleepy child on the hill in the afternoon sun.

In the Otienos' entrance hall stood a lavishly decorated pine tree in a brass Benares pot. Spruce boughs wreathed the banister and the ceiling was festooned with paper chains from end to end. "If only Daphne Dawson could see this!" Marietta exclaimed. "Daphne was a great one for decorations, too."

"I like a proper show at Christmas time," Flora said. "It's how it used to be at home. All the rest of the year my parents were self-denying ideologues. Then there was this one great day. The boys made all the decorations. They're ever so good with their hands. Who knows, perhaps they'll end up as surgeons, like their father." She laughed. "If they do, I hope they stick to it. They're upstairs in the playroom, Charlie. Off you go!"

The door handle rattled and a child dashed in. He was wearing gray flannel trousers and a long-sleeved shirt and a tie with a paisley pattern on it. He ran over to the tree and crouched to inspect the presents piled beneath it.

"Merry Christmas, Mattias, how are you?"

The child turned to Flora. "Is there one for me?"

"Of course there is. And when everybody's here, you shall have it."

He scrambled to his feet. "Can I go and fetch them?" Then, noticing Marietta, he added, "You're the lady we visited in Boston, aren't you?"

"That must have been someone else," Marietta said, smiling. "I've never been to Boston. I used to know your mother, though, but a long time ago, before you were born."

"Was that in England or America?"

"Right here in Kenya."

Mattias said eagerly, "Did you know my grandfather as well?"

"I certainly did."

"He lived in a big red house," said Mattias solemnly. "Only now it's brown because the paint's peeled off. My mother's sad about that," he added.

364

"Where *is* your mother?" Flora asked.

"She's lost her keys. She's outside looking for them. She can't come in until she finds them." Slipping past Marietta, Mattias raced on up the stairs.

"So that's the little prince," Marietta said.

"He's cute, isn't he? I wonder, would you mind going to help poor Catherine? I'd go myself, only I'd better make sure the cook doesn't burn the onion sauce."

Outside the evening sky was dense with stars; the moon had not yet risen. By flickering flashlight, Catherine was searching the ground for her keys. She wore a long black, tight-fitting evening dress, slit on one side to above the knee, and high-heeled patent leather sandals. Unsuitable for a family Christmas party, one might say, but Marietta, gazing into Catherine's décolletage as she bent to feel the surface of the gravel, had to admit again that the spectacular suited her. Close up she smelled of Shiraz, which came in a crystal bottle with a stopper shaped like a heart. This perfume was a steady favorite of the wives of Jonathan's richest German clients. Perhaps Otieno had bought it in Geneva last time he'd been to see the Aga Khan.

"Marietta, see the stupid thing I've done!" Catherine snapped off her flashlight. "And now these batteries are almost dead. The *askari* had to go to get some new ones." She added reproachfully, "You never came to see me. I waited and waited and never any sign of you!"

"I'm sorry. I've hardly had a moment," Marietta replied. "I've been working in Flora's gallery. Perhaps you knew that? Things are very busy in there at this time of year."

The *askari* came back from the kitchen with new batteries, and the keys were found in the car between the front seat and the door. "My son insisted that's where they'd fallen," said Catherine, smiling. "He said he'd heard them clink as they fell, but I was sure I'd dropped them on the stones. Well, I was wrong and he was right. That's often so. Have you met that boy of mine yet, Marietta? He's been beside himself with excitement since four o'clock this morning. We haven't had a moment's peace!"

"Yes," Marietta said. "I met Mattias. He's not at all shy, is he? He talked to me as if he'd known me all his life."

In the starlight Catherine smiled. "He's used to meeting many different people. He's traveled about so much already, you see. I'm so glad you came tonight!" she exclaimed as they went up the front steps. "In London you were very angry with me, weren't you? You refused to see me. You never gave me a chance to explain!"

"You nabbed my boyfriend, that's all," Marietta said dryly. "Did that require an explanation?"

"Oh, I believe it did! And I was hoping that after so many years I'd get a chance to give one. That's why, when I met you here a month ago, I invited you to come to see me. But you didn't come and you didn't telephone. So," Catherine said, sighing, "of course I knew you were still angry with me. I thought, Then I must seek you out myself. How should I do it? Should I telephone? But you might be just as unfriendly as you were before. Should I write a letter? That you might ignore. Then I had a new idea. I told Flora, 'When we were girls Marietta and I were such close friends, but later we quarreled and from that day to this we've never reconciled. You understand the need for reconciliation, Flora. Will you help me now?' 'I'll see you get your chance,' she said."

"So that's the story, is it?" Marietta added quietly, "You should know that I was far more disappointed with myself than I was with you. You were generous, you gave pleasure. I didn't. At that time I was virtually incapable of giving anything to anyone and particularly not to a man. I really wasn't angry with you, Catherine. Only jealous. Not of what you'd taken. Of what you had to give."

But Catherine wasn't listening, because she had her own speech ready. She said urgently, "What I wanted to tell you is that of all the teachers I had when I was young, you were the most important. Yes, I used to think, if I can understand Marietta, why she says what she says, why she behaves as she does, the next *mzungu* will not be so strange, the one after less so, and so on."

Marietta frowned in disbelief. "You'd known white people before me. Mrs. Tyson, for example. You'd read her books and picked her brain. You'd been the apple of her eye."

"Of course, but from her I learned facts and numbers, but very little about people. For that I needed a European my own age. I remember the first morning. I can see you even now, standing next to my sister Agnes in that Keriki school. I could scarcely believe my eyes! Ah, I thought, now I'll have what I have wished for. You didn't stay, though. You went away. But later I found you again, like a miracle, in that huge cold place with its rooms full of faces. Row upon row of flat white faces and light eyes. They stared at me with disdain, not curiosity. Their minds were made up. They had no wish to reexamine anything. They had no wish to know me as I really was. How could I learn to live among such people? But I was fortunate," she said softly, "I wasn't quite alone. You were there. It was from you that I learned."

"From me? But I had no vision, no sense of mission or responsibility. So you said."

"That was only later, Marietta, when I saw your determination to leave Africa forever, and that saddened me."

"Why did you choose me? You'd have been better off with Rosemary Fullerton. She was white. She wasn't a hybrid, a bit of this, a bit of that, like me."

"*That's* why I chose you. You were the only one who was familiar. Like me and like them, too."

A car drove over the gravel and stopped. Doors slammed. Behind them there were children's voices.

Catherine said hurriedly, "The painter, what was his name? I have forgotten. It was so long ago. I thought, He is Marietta's friend. Can't he be mine as well? Can't he be a friend to both of us? It was never my intention to take him from you." She touched Marietta's arm. "I'd hoped that, by knowing him, I'd know you better, and so be closer to you! You know, in Keriki, that is how it is." She smiled quickly. "Two sisters sometimes marry the same man. That is the arrangement many sisters prefer, in fact."

Marietta said wearily, "Yes, I've heard of that custom. Unlike you, I was an only child; I never had a sister. But had I been able to choose one, in a thousand years I'd never have chosen you. Whenever we've been together, you've taken all the limelight. I'd have been crazy to have agreed to share a man with you!"

Otieno was crossing the lighted hall in his Savile Row suit and Church's shoes. "Merry Christmas, Mrs. Sudbury! I'm sorry I didn't come to greet you earlier. I was busy sorting papers in preparation for my trip. Then all of a sudden I realized it's seven-thirty, time for our party to begin! But perhaps you didn't even notice my discourtesy." He laughed. "After all these years you two young ladies have so much to talk about, I'd only have got in the way!"

Dexter Dodge's mother had said, "Could you spare us your son for a few days? We're going down to Malindi over New Year's and Dexter would so love for Charlie to come along." So Charles went off

367

with the half-size surfboard Jonathan had brought him from Santa Barbara.

"I'll bring you seashells," he'd promised as he jumped into Dexter's father's Lincoln Mercury, "and by the time I get back, Johnny should be back as well!"

Marietta went upstairs to get ready before driving into town to work. She passed Justin in the corridor.

"Will you have supper here tonight?" he said, not looking at her.

"No, and tomorrow I'll be out as well."

Justin walked away from her, his arms full of sheets and pillowcases. "You tell Karanja, then."

Tonight I shan't come home at all, nor tomorrow. Not even the night after that. I don't care how much you frown at me, old man!

She brushed her hair and pinned it up on the top of her head. Looking at her reflection in the mirror she thought, Why does he have to judge me? Why can't he trust me, complicated though things appear to be? We all have a chance to be happy. Jonathan as well as Michael and I!

She took her handbag from the dressing table and felt about inside it for her sunglasses. She must have left them downstairs. But they weren't on the hall table, and they weren't in the pantry and they weren't on the dashboard of the Datsun, either, so they had to be in Kagia's sitting room. She could drive without them if she had to, but did she have to? Why not overlook for once the gulf between night and day? What harm could be done by going to recover at noon what she'd mislaid in the darkness? She smiled to herself. There were dozens of neat little pale blue cars like hers, dozens of women with sunstreaked hair. If she turned in at the gate in the wall with broken brown glass along the top, who would notice?

Kagia had gone at dawn to a meeting in Nyeri; he'd be back in the late afternoon. In the darkness, as she'd been about to leave him, he'd said, "Mary doesn't like it that at night you never come in time to eat her food."

"Tell her I don't like it either."

"If your son's going down to Mombasa, then please come here earlier and let Mary cook for you at last." As she drove into the city, Marietta thought, At lunchtime I'll go and fetch my glasses. I'll encourage Mary with the preparations. I'll feel the chicken: How plump it is! Those scrawny birds they're selling in the city nowadays aren't worth half the price they're asking. You must have gone to Kiambu to find a bird like this!

The gates to the Ismaili's mansion stood wide open and the guard and the Alsatian dogs were gone. Marietta drove in past servants grinding spices by the kitchen door and on down the driveway to the bungalow. A flame tree was in full flower behind it. I never noticed it before, she said to herself, but then, I never saw this garden in daylight — the pinks against the yellows, the blues, the violets, the darkest green of the pines. Whoever planted this garden had a wonderful sense of what would please in forty years.

From the kitchen came the sound of Congo music. Congo music was the latest craze. Mary was playing the radio so loudly she wouldn't have heard the car. Marietta thought, I'll go quietly and surprise her, and then, when she's over being startled, she'll make me a cup of tea.

She got out of the car and went along the veranda around the corner, under the flame tree. Bees were worrying the blossoms scattered in the grass. Thirty yards away was the kitchen, a hut of rusty corrugated iron, tilting a little to one side. In the shade next to the door stood a small black radio, and in the doorway itself, knees apart, her shirt tucked under her, Mary sat on an upturned pail. Next to her Mattias squatted in his baseball cap. He was peeling a potato. He hacked at it, dropped it, picked it up again, and threw it into a bush. At that moment he saw Marietta.

For an instant he stared; then he tugged Mary's skirt. Mary switched off the radio, wiped her hands, and eased herself to her feet. Her face was sharply disapproving as she said, "I did not expect to see you at this hour."

"I believe I left my glasses here," Marietta said. "I came to fetch them." The sun was so hot, like a hammer at her head, on the equator at the end of a bad year. "May I sit down?"

Mary took a stool and placed it in the shade, beside the radio. Marietta leaned back against the metal wall, eyes shut. "I didn't mean to trouble you."

"She's ill. She's going to be sick," Mattias said.

"She needs cold water," Mary said. "You stay here with her and I'll fetch some from the fridge." She went away across the grass to the bungalow.

Marietta heard the screen door open and slam shut. She opened

369

her eyes. Mattias was standing before her.

"You told me you were my mother's friend," he said in English. "Is Mary your friend too?"

"Yes."

"But I haven't seen you here before, and I come almost every day. Soon I'll be going to school in the mornings and then, in the afternoons, I'll have to stay with Thomas. He's our cook and" — Mattias lowered his voice — "he smokes *banghi*. And then he lies down and goes fast asleep. He never plays. I'd rather stay with Mary. She doesn't play either, but she takes me to the shops, and sometimes, if she's pleased with me, she buys me an ice lolly. D'you know what?" he went on. "My father promised to teach me how to swim. My mother can't teach me. She's never learned herself. But my father lived for a long, long time in America and there everyone knows how. Have *you* ever lived in America?"

"I went there for a visit once. Not a long visit, only a week or two," and in a low voice she added, "I met your father in America."

"When we were there," Mattias said, "it was in the cold weather. That's why I didn't learn to swim, and anyway, I was only little. Now I'm big. My father's going to take me to a pool soon. I've already got my suit. It's red." He stopped for a moment, then he asked, "Do you know Mrs. Chase as well?"

"Mrs. Chase?"

"My other mother. I lived with her in London, then my real mother took me to live with her instead." Behind him Mary was coming from the bungalow with a water bottle. "I've only had one father, though," he added, "everywhere I've been."

"Here," Mary said, "drink this. There's ice in it." She handed Marietta a cup. "I found your glasses. You should have waited, not come out here twice." Marietta drank and Mary refilled the cup and she drank again. A lizard slithered along the top of the kitchen door and down it at an angle. It dropped to the bare, hard earth under the eaves and vanished into the grass.

Marietta stood up. "Thank you for bringing me the water. Thank you for my glasses. Now I'd better go."

"Did you come by bus," Mattias asked, "or did you bring your car?"

"I came by car."

"What kind of car?"

"A Datsun," she said. "Just a small one."

"Two doors or four?"

"Only two."

"Has it got a radio? A lighter? Can I play in it before you go? Just for a little while?"

"Not today, Mattias," Marietta said. "I'm in a hurry today."

"What shall I say when he comes?" Mary said.

Marietta looked into the troubled eyes. "That his son's a fine boy," she answered softly. "That's all there is to say."

21

Katari

Justin frowned against the afternoon sun. "Who will cook your supper now? You said you would not eat at home and so Karanja went to town to meet his friend."

"I won't need supper," Marietta said.

"Are you sick? But this morning you were quite well! Do you need the doctor?"

"Not him. Nobody. Nothing."

In her room she lay down on the fern-patterned bedspread Bruce and Virginia had bought in London on their honeymoon. The ferns had reminded Bruce of the Queensland forest he'd camped in as a boy. In the glare of the tropics the colors had faded, the greens to brown, the browns to yellow. Not worth taking with us, Virginia had said. Their great bed in Malaga had a new striped cover. Spanish colors — terra cotta, purple, and white.

Ears. Eyes. Yes, they told me something, but it was from touching that I learned much more. Why guess at secrets? Why not trust that they, too, will be revealed in time? Meanwhile, how miraculous, I thought, used to think, that he had waited to know me! The only man by whom I'd wanted to be known.

A fallacy: he hadn't waited. He already had a son, a son old enough to read! And his son had a mother. A courageous woman, a fitting mother for the son of a courageous man. Like to like.

The sky blazed beyond the open window. The room grew fiercely hot. Behind her closed lids red circles whirled.

Why did he want me? I've stumbled through my life. I've lost courage, edged along, any old way. The only grand plan I ever had, I abandoned.

Did he want me for the gold in my hair? But many women have golden hair and they'd be his for the asking. Or was it to watch the pleasure he gave me — I, who'd known little pleasure before, and was craven?

No! His wanting had nothing to do with me, only with Jonathan. Whatever Jonathan had, *he* had to take away. For the sake of pillage, merely. I was one more theft. That's all. That's why he waited.

Far away she heard the the telephone, and then, on the other side of the door, Justin saying, "Will you speak?"

"Not now."

"But you *should* speak."

"I want to sleep. Say I am sleeping."

"You're not, though."

"What is it, Justin? Who can't wait?"

"It is he, Kagia. What am I to say?"

"I don't wish to speak to him. Not now, not later."

Justin went away down the passage, down the stairs.

She'd believed that old story. "For Virginia's daughter," Sophia had written on the flyleaf of the Sleeping Beauty. "May she be enchanted!" And of course she had been. She'd waited for her prince to find a way through thorns and thickets. And sure enough, at the end of a hundred years, she'd stirred and awakened and laughed to see him, after having almost lost her life in sleep.

Should she sleep again now? But what else was there to do?

Birds swarmed across the deepening sky, and in the room, as the air cooled, wood cracked. From the garden came the early sounds of night, an owl in the plantation, frogs in the ditch, dogs barking at a narrow moon.

A car was coming up the drive. Headlights sprayed across the walls of her room. But it wasn't morning, so why wake now? Why wake ever, to feel the pain in her throat and over her heart?

"He has come," Justin said, on the far side of the door. "What am I to do?"

"Is he so dangerous? Why are you afraid?" Marietta sprang from the bed. "He's only a man!" She threw the door open.

Justin stood in the corridor in the dim light, the guardian at the gate, in an old jacket of Jonathan's, collar frayed, elbows worn out.

On his feet he wore a pair of Jonathan's shoes. The furrows across his forehead were deep and sharp enough to grip a five-cent coin.

"He's only a man," she repeated. "What harm can he do? Make him welcome! Offer him a drink! Don't let him think we're not hospitable!"

She went into the bathroom and dashed water on her face. She brushed her hair fiercely over her shoulders, bending to one side, to the other. She licked her finger, smoothed her eyebrows.

From the top of the stairs she saw the light under the study door. Justin stood beneath her, next to the grandfather clock. Down she went, her sandals clattering. She turned the handle and went in.

Kagia had driven two hundred miles since the morning. All the way to Nyeri, up a rough road. All the way back. Four speeches in between. His white shirt wasn't very clean. He said, "Mary cooked, but you didn't come to eat her food."

"Am I the one who's been discourteous?" Marietta threw back her head. "Oh, my God! Was it my fault that Mary's dinner was spoiled! She couldn't explain to you why I didn't come?"

"You were there at midday, so she told me."

"And left a message for you."

Kagia nodded. "I received it."

"Your son's so very much at ease with visitors," Marietta said bitterly. "He likes to chat and tell you just what's on his mind." Her voice rose. "How long did you expect to keep your secret, Michael? You've got a very handsome family, as it turns out. So I wonder, why did you bother with me? These last few hours I've been trying to answer that question. No doubt another woman, used to having love affairs, would have asked it long go. She'd have said to herself, How charming this Kagia is. These games of hide-and-seek he plays with me are charming, too. A little intrigue brightens things up a lot. But that other woman would have wondered, Where's the hitch? Why does an ambitious politician play these games with a Settler's wife? Politicians are pragmatic. They don't waste time with leftovers from a past that everyone's doing their best to forget. Unless they stand to gain. In your case, Michael, what did you stand to gain?"

Leaning back against the door, she continued harshly, "I'm the last spoil in an old war. Isn't that it? Not that you value your spoils. Once you've won them, you don't want them. You've often been in England, so you've told me. Just once you could have taken the train to Swindon and a taxi from there. There *are* taxis, and quite cheap. It's not far to Tresham. Thirty-five minutes on a straight road, and on a bright Wiltshire day, you'd be reminded of the country around Eldonia. Home away from home." She shook her head. "But Edmund's still waiting. On mornings when the sky is wide and the wind sweeps over the Downs as it does through the Rift at the end of the rains, he thinks, Will Michael come at last? Or won't he?"

Kagia watched her steadily, his face completely still. She thought, How dark he is! He used to be much lighter. Speechmaking in marketplaces, at crossroads, on football fields, has made him black again. "You've never wanted anything of Johnny's for its own sake, have you? Your triumph lies in taking, not in keeping. You didn't want the burden of being loved by Edmund, once you'd won him. You had little use for Olgolulu, once you'd dispossessed us. Let others have it! And as for me —"

"Marietta!"

"No." She put up one hand, silencing him. "Let me say what I have to say! I came far too late to this old war to play a part of my own. But what I could offer you was one last opportunity to harm Jonathan. One last victory of a sort. From your point of view, that was the only purpose I could serve. If your goal was to make me fall in love with you in a way that I've never been in love with Jonathan, and so to punish him through me, you've succeeded, for I have loved you, Michael. But don't insist that Johnny know it! He lives at the furthermost edge of the world. He doesn't thrive, as you do, on adversity. He doesn't easily recover from defeat. Every battle you two have ever fought, you've won, but don't insist he know of this last victory. Let him be!"

Kagia gripped the back of the desk chair and in the lamplight Marietta saw how the skin stretched over the knuckles. She thought, Soon he'll go and I shan't see that head again, the set of the shoulders. Shall I keep away from public places for fear of running into him, for fear of running *to* him?

He said carefully, "You have strong opinions, Marietta. You like to make pronouncements. You have little patience for listening to others. But now you would do well to listen, for I have a story to tell you. My parents were murdered by the British. First, my mother. She was stopped at the edge of the forest by an officer who was still too young to grow a beard. This white boy believed my mother carried ammunition; he didn't examine her. He shot her first. He only examined her later and by that time she was dead. Then he discovered she was carrying not ammunition but kindling, for our supper fire. As for my father, he had more warning. His murder came as no surprise. From the day of his arrest, he knew he'd never come from jail alive." Kagia's hands dropped to his sides and he stood back against the windowsill. "These things would have been terrible enough," he said, "if I'd been innocent. But I was not.

"On that morning, when the lorries had come to take us from Olgolulu back to the reserves, I'd refused to go with my parents. 'I shall stay. I belong here now. This is my place, these are my people. I have no need of you!' That is what I told them in the larder, the small one behind the kitchen. I'd hidden there until the cook found me. My parents had never set foot inside the house before. For years I'd entered freely, and they had stayed outside, and now my mother stood before me, barefoot in her faded dress. 'You are ours,' she said. 'So many children your mother has borne,' my father pleaded, 'and all but you have died. You are our only child, our only son. We cannot part with you.' But I stopped my ears.

"In the end it was Edmund who convinced me. He told me, 'This is the regulation of the government, and although it angers us, nevertheless we must obey. One day these troubles will be over and you'll come back and we shall live together, just as before.' Then he led me to where the last of the lorries waited and watched me climb in to take my place beside the parents I had just renounced." Kagia ran his hand over his head. "As I had begun, so I continued. In that village where they sent us I thought only of returning to Olgolulu. When my father was arrested, my very first thought was, Does this mean the war will soon be over? I didn't care about the cause he'd fought for. I was thinking only of myself.

"The afternoon on which my mother died, I was in the fields. I'd gone out there to spend the few hours they allowed us between curfews with a book Edmund had given me. I was looking for a quiet place away from goats and children and old women. I'd become very proud, you see, in those years with Edmund. I was not as others were, but better, so I liked to think. I was sitting with my back to the trunk of a tree when that patrol came up the ridge with the beardless white boy leading. He didn't see me. The branches hung so low they hid me. I stayed where I was. I did not alert my mother. In that moment of peril, I betrayed her. I thought only of saving myself!" He went on slowly, "But in fact, I had betrayed her long before. My father also. I'd found someone who suited me better than they did. I'd chosen him over them." After a little while he said, "That beardless boy, a mere stranger, had killed my mother in the course of the work he was paid to do. But I, her son, who once had loved her, had renounced and then deserted her. The responsibility for her death was as much mine as that white boy's. So I believed at the time. These days" — he looked straight at Marietta — "I am less sure. But of one thing I am as certain now as I was then. I can never know Edmund face to face again."

He sighed. "You make so many accusations, Marietta. Why so little faith?" He shook his head sadly. "Well, let me see if I can answer you. Certainly you believe that I was interested in Olgolulu only because it belonged to Johnny. But you are wrong, Marietta. My interest had very little to do with Johnny. If he'd left this country at Uhuru and sold the farm to someone else, even so, when I returned to live in Kenya I'd have done my utmost to gain possession of it, whomever it belonged to!

"It was for my parents' sake that I wanted it. They never had any land of their own. All their adult lives they'd gone from place to place until finally they came to Olgolulu. But there they lost the loyalty of their son." After a moment he went on, "I realized I could never right the wrongs I'd done them. Nevertheless, I hoped that if I made it possible for other landless people like my parents to live in that house where I had entered freely and they had always been excluded, I might make my peace with them. I'm very tired," he added. "Today I've driven too far and talked to too many people. Excuse me," he said, and he sat in Jonathan's chair.

"Why did I bother with you? That's what you asked me. That's the word you used. When I first saw you dressed all in white, under a great tree in a garden in America, I marveled, How beautiful she is! Perhaps this is my imagination. When I discovered who you were, I wondered, What is she like, this girl whom Johnny has married? You were very young and even then so impatient! I thought, When she grows up, what will happen, since he's not half so lively as she is? When I get home I'll go to see what's happened." He smiled faintly. "And so I did. It was then that I saw your son. He was in the vehicle with you that day. I had imagined you were a girl, and free to come and go. But now I saw this wasn't so. I didn't want to look for trouble. I'd had a great deal of that. Why add more? Most men, not only politicians, are pragmatic. And so I went away, and I stayed away for a long time.

"Do you remember the Eldonia show? It was too hot that day. Pig after pig went by, sheep and goats were there, turkeys, too. Then you came, pulling a pale yellow cow. That cow had won the prize for cream, or was it butter? Cream, I think. It was a pretty color, with soft black eyes. A little mournful. But *your* eyes I remember much better. They were a dark strong blue. What has she seen? I wondered. What ambiguities and sorrows! And what has she understood?" He finished softly, "That's when I fell in love with you, despite the dangers. I said to myself, One day she'll tell me what she sees. Let me wait till then."

"You never waited for me!" Marietta burst out. "You were always planning what to do this year, next year, the year after. How to make the most of every opportunity. And already, on the side, you had Catherine, already you had Mattias!"

"Mattias is my son," Kagia said quietly, "and Catherine is his mother. She is not my wife, Marietta. She might deny she was ever my lover. I only served a purpose."

"What are you talking about?"

Kagia leaned back, his hands behind his head. He smiled. "Catherine is quite unusual. I believe you know that. Once you even recommended her to me yourself. She was a student at Makerere when I first went there. She was at the center of everything. I was on a committee with her, and that is how I came to know her, for she studied philosophy, not science. She was certainly fierce, just as you had described her. One day, to my surprise, she came to see me. She told me she was going to England. She had the opportunity and her professors urged her to take it. 'They tell me I am young,' she said, 'but I am not so young. My age mates in Keriki are arranging for the circumcisions of their sons and daughters, and here am I, a girl still.'"

She'd already delayed too long, she said. Six years of secondary school, three more of university, and now she was going overseas. She would wait no longer. She would have a child. After considering several possibilities, she'd decided to approach Kagia. She'd been impressed by his clarity of speech, by his reasoning, how well he argued a point. And also by his character. She'd heard that he'd overcome certain difficulties, and the strength to persevere was a quality she valued very highly. She did not mention physical proportions. Evidently his were good enough. Was he prepared to father her child? He should understand from the outset that this child, whatever the sex, would be hers alone. The upbringing would be entirely her responsibility.

"Why did I agree?" Kagia shrugged. "Because I liked her. I admired her resolution. Was I flattered? Yes, of course I was! As for her insistence that I make no claim on the child, I had no reservations about that. My mind was not on having children in those days.

"We were together half a dozen times and then she wrote to say our efforts had been successful. She did not need my services again. She was going home to say good-bye to her father, and then she would leave for London. She would write to me when the baby was born, to let me know if all was well.

"In due course a letter came. She'd had a son, whom she'd named after her own father. He was in good health. So was she. She expected to resume her studies shortly. She gave me no address.

"When we made our agreement in Kampala, I had no idea that it would present any difficulties. I had not imagined that when the time came I would think differently. But in fact, when I received the news of my son's birth, I knew at once I could not abide by our agreement. A few months later I had the chance to go to London. Finding Catherine was extremely simple. Persuading her to let me see the child was much more difficult, but in the end she conceded. She took me to the place where Mattias was staying. After that, she agreed to a different arrangement. She allowed me" — Kagia smiled faintly — "what are called rights of visitation. That's what I was doing when I went to England, Marietta, I was invoking my right to see my son." After a moment he said, "Yes, I have a son, just as you have a son, Marietta. Would it be an easy thing to let him go to his father and give up all your claims? I don't think so. I lost my family a long time ago, and my home and the right to a boyhood. Here and there I tried to make up that loss. But with time I learned better. The past is over. It cannot be made up, you cannot be a child again. Instead you should look to the future. Catherine expected nothing more of me after she left Uganda. It was I who chose to be a father to my son. His mother, though, is not my wife, nor is she my lover. She is Otieno's now. She'll be someone else's later. She is a woman I very much admire. But you, Marietta, for all your harshness and impatience, you are the one whom I love." He was silent. "Now you have to tell me," he said finally, "if I have answered well."

"Oh, yes!" She leaned across the desk and covered his hands with her own. "I'm sorry, Michael. I'm sorry I was so cruel."

"You were very hurt," he said. "I understood that." And interlacing his fingers with hers, he continued, "You called yourself a left-over. I suppose by that you meant you have no place in our new Africa. But that I don't accept. You have a place with me tonight, tomorrow, always, Marietta." He smiled. "It's very late and that houseboy of yours, that Ruba man, he doesn't care to see me here. Will you come home with me?"

From her room Marietta heard the lorry grinding up the drive, then cries of greeting and footsteps on the gravel. Below her window Justin asked, "How was your safari, bwana? It is so long since last we saw you! How happy we are at your return!"

What will he see — that one who slept has awakened? At one glance will he see that? She went along the corridor to the head of the stairs.

Jonathan stood in the hall, flanked by Justin and Karanja. Beyond them, through the open doorway, was the hard glare of afternoon. "Where's Charlie?" She heard panic in Jonathan's voice. "What in Christ's name has happened to him?"

Eyes wide and almost black, he stared up at her. She thought, Asleep, awakened, whichever I were he would not see. He's not concerned with me. Not anymore. For an instant she felt dizzy.

"Nothing's happened to Charlie," she said at last. "He went to the Coast with Dexter. They left on New Year's Eve."

"You expect me to believe that? These fellows gave me that line, too!"

Halfway down the stairs she stopped. "Why wouldn't we tell the truth?"

"Out of fear! That's why most people lie, to save their skins!"

But I'm not afraid of you, Jonathan, she tried to tell herself. Only afraid *for* you.

"He came and asked for Charlie and you let him go! You decided a high-class whore didn't deserve to be anyone's father — God only knows what he'd pass on. But this other one's industrious, altruistic, and more honorable than most. Charlie will be safe with him!"

Hand on the banister, steadying herself, Marietta said as calmly as she could manage, "I haven't the faintest idea what you're talking about. The Dodges invited Charlie, and I let him go because there wasn't much for him to do here, with no school and my being out most of the day. I expect him back today by four. Mrs. Dodge telephoned from Taita and said they were making good time." Just as she reached the bottom of the stairs, the grandfather clock struck three.

Jonathan said, "I'd expected to see him hanging on the gate watching the road. But he wasn't there and he wasn't in the garden either. I thought, I didn't get back in time to prevent it." He breathed an immense sigh. "But there *is* still time." And then, eyes narrowing, "I'm surprised *you're* still here, Marietta. I'd thought you'd gone long ago!"

"I told you I'd be staying," she said very quietly.

"But that was in the heat of the moment. Once things had cooled, I imagined you'd think better of it." He added harshly, "The Datsun's still here, too?"

"Of course."

"I'll take it, then. There's something I should do right away."

"Now?" she said incredulously. "But you've been gone six weeks!"

"There's a chap I've got to see."

"What about?"

"Old unfinished business."

"Can't it wait till Monday?"

"*I* can't wait till Monday. I tell you, I've had this on my mind."

"Do you have to leave this instant? Where are the Hillinghams?"

"They'll be in in a couple of hours. They stopped off at the Coach and Horses. They've got the Land-Rover and Kamau. You say there's petrol in the Datsun? Where's the key?"

"Where it always is." Marietta nodded at the hook by the front door. "Charlie's been counting on you being here when he gets in. Can't you wait for him?" she pleaded. "You could take him into town with you." She reached out to touch Jonathan's arm, but he stepped back abruptly. In a rush she said, "It's Friday. Whoever you've got to see may have gone off early for the weekend. He could be halfway to Mombasa by now!"

"No, he's always there on Friday, I'm sure of that. I'll change my shirt, then I'll be off." Jonathan sprang by her and on up the stairs, two at a time. Drawers rattled in the dressing room and water gushed in the bathroom sink.

In the hall Justin said, "You must not let him go again. He is not as usual, Mari."

"But how can I stop him?" Marietta cried, despairingly. "He doesn't see or hear me, Justin."

"You must try."

Jonathan was coming down the stairs again in a clean safari jacket. Marietta stood before him, barring his way. "I've been having trouble with the carburetor. It was because of that I didn't go to work at all today. I was afraid that even if I got to town, I wouldn't make it back. You shouldn't take the Datsun. If I were you, I wouldn't risk it."

"Ah, but you aren't me."

Marietta turned and ran across the hall; a second before Jonathan she reached the hook where the car key hung. Her hand closed over it. "Don't go!" she cried. "Go tomorrow, go on Monday, only not today!"

"Got plenty of iced tea for Dexter's mother? That's all she drinks on hot afternoons, so she told me. If I were you, I'd be worrying about that. At four, did she say? How long does tea take to cool? Now," Jonathan insisted, "will you give me that key!"

"Where are you going? Tell me that at least."

"What business is that of yours? You live your life, I live mine. That's how it's been. Why change things now?" He seized her wrist and pulled the key out of her hand.

As he passed out of the shadow, into the sun, Marietta went after him. "When will you be home? For tea, for dinner?" But he did not answer. She fell back.

They heard the garage doors being opened and an engine spluttering to life, and then the small blue car came round the corner of the house. Marietta ran out. "What shall I tell Charlie?" she called.

"That I love him, that I always will, regardless," Jonathan shouted back, and then, in a splatter of gravel, he sped away down the drive.

Ten minutes later Dexter Dodge's father's Lincoln Mercury deposited Charles and his surfboard and his bucket full of shells at the front door. "We drove like bats out of hell," Dexter's mother

382

said, "to get Charlie home to see his dad. All the way from Mombasa it was 'How much longer? How much longer?'"

"The lorry's here," Charles cried, "but where's Johnny? In the shower?"

Marietta brushed his hair off his forehead. "You just missed him. He came and went again. I expect him back for tea, though."

"He wouldn't wait?"

"He told me that he couldn't."

Charles flung away from Marietta. "It's thirty-seven days since I've seen Johnny," he cried, on the brink of tears, "twenty-two since I got the postcard with the leopard on it. Sixteen since the letter came, and he isn't here!"

"We'd better be getting on ourselves," said Dexter's father hastily. "I don't like to think about the mail that's come while I've been gone. That's the trouble with vacations. Well," he added to Marietta, "it's been our pleasure having Charlie with us. He has a calming influence on Dexter. Any time you can spare him, send him over to us!"

Justin came onto the veranda and rang a silver bell. Marietta had been watering the lettuces. She turned off the hose and started up to the house. "You promised he'd be back by tea," Charles said, trailing after his mother across the lawn. "But he isn't. Where is he, Mum?"

Down the road a car changed gears. "Did you hear that? It must be Johnny. It's the noise the Datsun makes," she said, and Charles dashed off towards the drive. But it was Kamau and the Hillinghams.

"You didn't hold up tea for our sakes, did you?" Valerie Hillingham cried. "It's my fault we're late, Marietta! Johnny really didn't want to stop at all, but it was so astonishing to come across an English pub in the middle of the bush. How could one resist it? Anyway, I couldn't. Johnny was as sweet as always. He gave us the Land-Rover and took the lorry himself so Patrick and I could stay and have a lovely lunch. He told us he'd made an appointment he simply had to keep. He couldn't be persuaded to stay and have a trout with us. The pace your husband goes is killing, Marietta!"

They'd had a most successful safari. Better than last year's, even, Patrick Hillingham announced. Such a pity Marietta hadn't come along. They'd really missed her! They'd had a bit of trouble with supplies. Not much petrol in Morogoro, but that hadn't daunted Johnny. "Nothing can, of course." Valerie laughed. "He kept absolutely cool with all those dreadful little clerks telling him 'Tomorrow, tomorrow.'"

They'd got their two hundred gallons in the end, and gone ahead as planned and had great sport. Next year they'd go even further afield. The Central African Republic? Congo Brazzaville? But if all turned out as hoped, Marietta would simply have to go with them. "No excuses next time," Patrick said. "It would be much more fun for Val if she had another girl to gossip with. She gets a bit sick of me and Johnny banging on about spores." It depended on soybean futures. They'd keep their fingers crossed.

"Do let us take you out to dinner," Patrick added, as they went into the dining room for tea. "What about Chez Jacques? I trust it isn't too late to make a reservation." The Hillinghams would be leaving for Gstaad in the morning. Ever since Harrow, Patrick had been forced to live abroad to avoid being reduced to penury by Her Majesty. He'd moved to Switzerland from the Bahamas when he married Valerie. She liked the mountains and the sun on the snow. Six weeks of dust and insects weren't exactly her idea of fun, but these annual jaunts to Africa were for the marriage. She believed in a degree of compromise, and give and take.

"Do you know, Marietta," she said, squeezing lemon into her tea, "this is Patrick's tenth time out with Johnny! And my eighth. I've only ever missed in order to give birth. When word was out last spring that you were off to Oregon, we were quite beside ourselves. Thank the Lord you changed your minds! For entirely selfish reasons, we hope you and Johnny stay in Africa until the day you die!"

After tea the Hillinghams began to yawn behind their hands. "We might just take a nap," Patrick said. "We were up before dawn. Do bang on the door when Johnny comes in."

Charles was perched on a stool in the pantry while Justin polished the shoes. "Why did Johnny go to town?" he said.

"I don't know."

"Didn't you ask him?"

"No. Your father doesn't like to talk about his business, Charlie."

"Why not?"

"That's the way he is."

384

"Would *you* tell me your business if I asked?"

"Only if it was good for you to hear."

"When *isn't* it good?"

Justin sighed as he put his brushes away in the pantry drawer. "Carry these black ones and that brown pair, too."

Charlie slid off the stool and took a pair of shoes in each hand. "You're trying to change the subject."

"Yes," Justin said.

Charles followed him in silence up the back stairs. In the doorway of his parents' dressing room he said bitterly, "I hate secrets. They aren't fair!"

Jonathan's shirt lay in the middle of the dressing room floor. "You don't complain when Johnny makes a mess. Only if I do," Charles grumbled.

"It wasn't I who trained your father," Justin pointed out. They put away the shoes on the racks at the bottom of the cupboard and Justin led the way into the bedroom. Seeing that the drawer in the table on Jonathan's side of the bed was pulled wide open, he went to shut it.

"That's where Johnny keeps his revolver," Charlie said.

"Revolver? No." Justin shook his head. "One of those he has not got. They are for killing people. He has only guns for killing animals and they're all downstairs in the room where the door is locked."

"But he showed it to me," Charles insisted, "before he went away. He bought it because of thieves and he put it in that drawer. Don't you want to see?" He slipped behind Justin and opened the drawer again. Inside were several notebooks, pencils, matchboxes, a dirty pocket handkerchief, but no revolver.

"I told you there wasn't one," Justin said, turning away. "You've been playing too many games with that friend of yours at Mombasa. You begin to imagine things that are not there!"

"But I saw it, I swear I did," Charles protested. "Ask Mum, she saw it too!"

At eight o'clock Valerie Hillingham sat on the drawing room sofa in pink silk knit and her traveling pearls. "We're going to have to decide," she said loudly, "whether to go without him or stay here. Couldn't we leave a note? He'll understand. He always does. Johnny's a very understanding man." She giggled. "I've got this silly craving for sailfish. One can never get it in Gstaad, you see. You don't think anything's happened to Johnny, do you?"

"I imagine he's doing business in the Norfolk Bar," Marietta replied. "That's what's happened, probably." Better his not getting back in time. Better to face him later, alone, with the Hillinghams safely in bed, than at a table for four. "If he'd run into trouble, he'd have telephoned. He'll be upset if he comes back and finds you've spent your last night in Africa hanging about waiting for him."

They drove into the city to champagne and sailfish, Molo lamb and crêpes suzette. With the cognac, Lord Hillingham proposed a toast: "To Johnny, that most skillful of hunters, that most gracious of hosts! May he put up with me and Val in future with the same tolerance and humor that he has in the past!"

When they returned to Olduvai Road a gray Land-Rover with a Government of Kenya license was at the door. "The police?" Patrick Hillingham frowned. "What would they be after at this hour? One of your boys in the clink? What a bore!"

"It could be Karanja," Marietta said. "They came here for him once before. He'd hit some woman's husband."

Light poured from the hall windows onto snapdragons and stock. She'd planted the seedlings herself two months ago and now they ran riot in the flower bed. On this still warm night the scent of the stock was almost overpowering.

The door was opened by Justin. "I didn't call you from town," he said softly. "I thought, Let them finish, let them hear in time." A captain and two sergeants stood behind him, beneath the hall light shaped like a lantern. Seeing Marietta they removed their hats and held them stiffly under their right arms. Their uniforms were crisp, their boots shone.

Marietta swung round to Justin, "Where's my son?"

"Sleeping. He drank his Horlick's. We read from his book and after that he slept. When these men came, I did not awaken him."

"Why are they here?"

The captain shifted his hat from his right arm to his left. He cleared his throat. "I came myself immediately," he said in Swahili. "I did not think it fitting to use the telephone." Perspiration stood in beads on his forehead. "When I received the news I came here straight. You weren't at home, memsahb, but even so, I waited." He fell silent, eyes immensely round.

Marietta went up to him. "What is it that you have to tell me?

Can you not say? Is it so difficult? Whatever it is, it is time I heard it."

"For God's sake, what *is* this?" Patrick demanded. "What's the fellow going on about?"

Marietta went past the policemen and sank to the bottom stair. There were scratches on the hall floor. Charlie'd made them, by jumping from the seventh step in cowboy boots Jonathan had brought him from Dallas. The boots had complicated stitching and pointed toes and heels that dug in deep.

"What happened to my husband?" she said at last. "Tell me what you heard."

The captain cleared his throat again. The sergeants stood up straighter. "It was in the forest above Moro, after the sun went down. They heard the shot. They ran and searched. Eventually they found him."

"Who found him?"

"Dorobo people. Those people live there in the forest. Once the sun has set the darkness comes so quietly. Perhaps he stumbled, your husband, and his gun went off. When the Dorobo came to him, he was already dead. They carried him to the forest edge to a place called Olgolulu. It was the people staying there who informed us. But the telephone was not so good." The captain sighed heavily. "You could not hear well. There was too much noise in the wires. What purpose your husband had in going there, perhaps you shall learn from the police at Eldonia. I was not there. I was only here. I know no more than I have told you. *Pole*, memsahb, this is very terrible! They will take the body to Eldonia, to the morgue. Soon they will have an inquest. When, I do not know for certain, since, as I have already told you, the wires were very bad. A little later when we tried to telephone again the operator said the line was dead and nothing could be expected until Monday. Tomorrow's Saturday, you see. Those telephone people never go to work on Saturday. *Pole*, memsahb, this lack of news is most unfortunate."

"Why should there have to be an inquest?" Marietta said faintly. "He's dead. What else is there to know?"

"They must decide the cause."

"He had a gun. The gun went off."

"Indeed." The captain sighed again. "But did the death happen accidentally" — he ran his tongue across his lips; his lips were black and narrow and his tongue was soft and pink — "or was it his intention to die?"

"They couldn't decide, that other time."

"What other time?" The captain frowned. "I don't understand."

"You were there, Justin. You remember. At the investigation for my father, what did they decide?"

Justin came across the room. "Up," he said gently, taking her hand. "Let us go to the kitchen. I'll make a cup of tea. This man has nothing else to tell you. You heard him, he has said as much as he knows."

But she remained on the bottom step, her eyes glued to Justin's. "What did they say about my father?" she insisted.

"They talked such a long time. From morning, Mari, until late in the afternoon. They argued but they decided nothing. How could they? How can you know for certain what another's thoughts were, once he's dead?"

"Now we shall go," the captain said. "At the station we have but the one vehicle, for the others are not working well. We cannot keep this one away any longer. If we receive more news, we shall inform you." Then he and the sergeants put on their hats and clicked their heels and filed into the darkness.

"Quick," Patrick Hillingham exclaimed. "We've got to give her brandy. Hurry, can't you!" He plucked Justin's sleeve. "Johnny keeps it in the drawing room."

Of course the Hillinghams would stay until the inquest. They wouldn't dream of letting Marietta go through that ordeal alone. Valerie's mother was coming out from England, but they'd put her off for a day or two. What difference would it make if she arrived on Wednesday night instead of Sunday morning? Valerie echoed, "We want to help in any way we can!"

As if from a great distance Marietta said, "Please don't change your plans for my sake."

"But we must!" Valerie cried. "We should! Not to would be unforgivable. Jonathan was Patrick's oldest friend! He fagged for him at Harrow twenty years ago. Patrick always told me Johnny made the most delicious scrambled eggs. Plenty of butter, a little runny, never too set. Didn't you say that, darling?"

Marietta thought, You don't realize, do you, that he sells his soul to the likes of you? So he says. *Said*. He's dead now. That's what the policeman told us. There's nothing for you to stay for. Go away!

388

"It's very good of you to offer, but of course you mustn't stay. There are people here I can rely on. I'll be okay."

"How can we be sure?" Valerie protested. "Such a bolt from the blue. Simply no warning. Of course you're in a state of shock!"

"I'll be okay," Marietta repeated. "It's a question of surviving the beginning." Her voice rose. "I know, you see, because this isn't my first death. The one before was in an air crash."

"Oh, really?" But already Valerie was flushing with relief at being let off the hook. It wasn't so much the death as what came after — *that* was what unnerved one. *How could Johnny be dead!* Wouldn't he appear at breakfast after all? And who in the world would Patrick find for next year? She opened her mouth to ask —

"We feel quite dreadful about leaving," Patrick said hurriedly. "Though we might have been more of a hindrance than a help. I do see that."

"You've got a long day's traveling ahead of you," Marietta said. "You should try to get some sleep."

"Should we? I suppose we should. You're sure you'll be all right?" Valerie retrieved her evening bag from the hall table and they went off gratefully to bed. Later when she went into the garden Marietta heard Patrick's snores rolling under the guest room door.

She'd done nothing. Something. Never enough, though. He'd come. She'd let him go again and the pace that he'd been going at had killed him. She walked down moonlit paths to the stone bench by the tennis court. She had seen, but not clearly; heard, but not well. She'd understood the need for vigilance and turned her back. How could she ever sleep again? She sat in the dew to wait for the first morning after.

She heard the car and Gelda barking and the *askari* speaking to him in the drive. But she stayed where she was, watching the hills against the dimming stars. Already from the highest hill you'd see in the east the pale sky of a new day. He was coming towards her over the grass, just as he had that other night so long ago in Chicago. She tried to count the years and could not. Johnny'd had a suit of dark green velvet. She'd worn white, drenched round the hem. For a moment she'd imagined Michael was American, but no, they'd been born, all three of them, in the Great Rift Valley. They'd shared an African past and their future would have to be shared, too, though each of them would try to avoid that. Johnny had gone to the bush and she to the farm and Michael to Uganda. But in the end there'd been no keeping them apart.

"I came as quickly as I could." Kagia was standing before her. "I'd have come sooner, but the Olgolulu people were so fearful! They wouldn't let me leave them until almost two." He took her in his arms. "I'm sorry, Marietta," he said, and he held her for a long time.

"You go to Olgolulu every Friday," she said eventually.

"That's why he went up there, to settle an old score."

"What are you saying!" Marietta pulled away. "They found him in the forest above Moro. They took him to Olgolulu only after he was dead!"

"No, Mari. He was first at Olgolulu in the early evening. It is that time I've come to tell you about."

On this, the second Friday of the new year, the two hundred share-holders of the Moro Farmers' Cooperative were crowded into the great hall of Olgolulu. There were many items on the agenda, so much to be done! They had started at three and talked until six and taken their supper and reconvened again at seven-thirty. The secretary, Matthew Mungai, was speaking of repairs to the pig pens when a tremendous commotion was heard outside. A white man burst in and slammed the door and bolted it. One of his shirt sleeves was ripped at the shoulder and his hair fell over his eyes. In the dim hall, lit only with bush lights, since the cost these days of an electric generator was more than the cooperative could bear, two hundred people stared. As the man leaned against the door to catch his breath, Kagia, seated at a massive table sixty feet away, recognized him as Jonathan Sudbury.

"Maruga!" Jonathan shouted down the length of the great room. "We have a debt to settle, you and I."

Those who had been stunned into silence rose from stools and benches and the floor itself and surged towards him. "Who is this *mzungu*? How does he dare to enter here?"

But Kagia called out, "Let him alone! I know him and if he has business with me, then let him speak of it." So the people stood back and allowed him to pass.

He walked through the patchy light to the table where Kagia waited. "I'd like a very few moments of your time," he said. "What I have to tell you, what I have to do, will be finished very soon."

390

Then he turned to face the people, who were pushing and shoving and craning necks to get a better view, and spoke to them clearly in the Kikuyu language so all could understand.

"There are very few of you here who ever knew my father, but it was he who claimed from bush the land on which you make your livelihoods. It was he also who constructed this house and all the others which you occupy. My father worked as hard as any man I've ever known. He worked on his own account and on mine as well, for Olgolulu was to be my inheritance." He paused. He went on more loudly, "Apart from his property, might not a son also expect his father's loyalty, his affection, his respect? Are these not his due? I thought so. But this one" — he swung round and pointed to Kagia — "poisoned my father's heart against me! 'Why should you remain loyal to your son, if he is quite unworthy?' That is what he told my father. 'Surely I am more deserving of your trust than he!' And in the course of time my father was persuaded. He turned to him, leaving me, his son. For that, many years ago I thought to kill this one whom nowadays you call Kagia. However, my error was that I did not kill him; I only wounded him severely. In time his wound healed, but from that day forward he thought only of revenge, and after waiting twenty years, almost to the day, he took it. He chased me from this place where I was born.

"Driven from his birthplace, a man may nevertheless live on. You all know that. Each one of you came here from somewhere else, to make a better life for yourselves and your children, since there was no chance for that at home. But without a son, without promise of a future, a man is nothing. It is as if he had never been born." Again he paused.

"First Kagia took my father from me," he said slowly, "and then my patrimony. Soon he will come to take my son. And who will dare deny him? I tell you, no one! For all have learned from my experience that he is merciless to any who stand in his path. Why invite such hatred? Better to draw back and let him take the child away! Let him complete his revenge, that is what they'd say! So there is no one to deny him, except myself." Moving a step closer to Kagia, Jonathan went on steadily, "I have looked forward to this meeting, I have planned it with some care. Should it be in Nairobi, in Parliament, for instance? Or in Eldonia? At the opening of a rural school, at a *harambee*? Each of these I have considered, but in the end I decided we should meet at home."

Out of his jacket he pulled a revolver. A gasp swept from the

391

front to the back of the crowd, and abruptly died. To Kagia he said, in English, "I want them all to see the scar, Maruga. I want them all to know our history. Take off your coat." He jerked his gun upwards. "Hurry. Twenty years is already too long a delay. We should finish our business as quickly as we can. Now roll up your sleeve, and walk the length of this room. Hold out your arm, give them the chance to get a close look. See," he said, in Kikuyu once again, "how white the skin is where the wound healed! He was so proud in those days, so ambitious! And above all else he longed to become white. But since my father wasn't a magician" — he smiled wryly — "it was up to me to do the best I could!" At the main door he told Kagia, "We haven't finished; back we go."

Again they made their way through the crowd of men and women elbowing each other to get a glimpse of Kagia's outstretched arm. Jonathan motioned Kagia onto the table. "The hero of the common man must let his adulators see him!" he said, and two hundred people waited silently as he turned to them. "I have never killed a man before," he told them. "Ten thousand animals, never a man. This will be a very special pleasure." He took aim. "I shall count to three . . ."

But suddenly he spun away from Kagia. Once he fired at the great Sudbury escutcheon over the fireplace, VIRTUTE, a unicorn rampant, three scimitars. Then he was shooting at the portraits of men and women in velvet coats and panniered skirts, at their ruined faces looking down on the panic-stricken crowd. Two on the left wall, two on the right.

His arm fell to his side. "Not such a special pleasure," Kagia heard him say to himself, and he climbed onto the table too. "None of you has been harmed," he called, and as each discovered that indeed this was true, all were as they'd been before, the crowd grew quiet again. "I've done what I came to do," Jonathan told them. "Now I shall leave you. May you and your children and your children's children thrive here." And then, quietly, to Kagia only, he said, "My ancestors are merciless and unforgiving. I've never managed to appease them. Neither I nor you nor anyone should have to bear their scrutiny. Take care of these people, Maruga. You and they are the true heirs. Make good use of your inheritance." He smiled suddenly. "How ridiculous, two grown men, standing on a table! Shall we get off it? You've got to finish your meeting and I should be on my way." Gun in hand, he slipped to the floor.

392

He passed through the crowd, unbolted the door, and walked out into the night.

A little more than two hours later his body was brought from the forest and laid on that same table where he and Kagia had stood.

"I wanted you to know this first," Kagia said. "Before the police at Eldonia. I'm going up there now to make a statement. I must be there by eight and already the dawn is breaking. But I also came here to tell you that I love you, Marietta, and regardless of the consequences of what occurred tonight, that won't change."

PART VI

1973

22

Galana

In February, Dr. Nelson Otieno, whose birthplace was on the mainland, not so far away, had smashed a bottle of champagne against the hull and gone on board for the maiden voyage of the new Galana ferry. Six cars it could carry, and a bus, two lorries. So many people had crowded on behind the minister that some cried, See! The chains will surely snap! But the wind had shifted suddenly and they'd made the crossing safely to the other shore, where Otieno had been greeted with songs and ululations and half a glass of Cutty Sark brought to him on a tin tray from the Hope Springs Eternal Bar. "Now the white people will come," he told the crowd before him, "to roast themselves upon your beaches, and you'll be cooks and cleaners in the hotels that will be built to house them." "When will this be?" the crowd shouted back. "You must be patient," Otieno told them. "This boat is the first change only. Development needs careful planning. But I promise you from this day onwards Galana will never be the same again!"

In March Violet and her six children waited as the ferry came across the channel. Spotting Justin and Marietta, the oldest, Sampson, cried out in excitement, and the baby, who'd been sleeping soundly on his mother's back, awoke and burst into tears; but his sister Juliet jiggled his plump little hand and whispered lovingly. By the time the ferry docked, his tears had dried and he was grinning toothlessly from ear to ear.

"How long will you stay with us?" Violet asked Marietta gravely.

397

"In the morning I must go back to Katari. Charles and I are leaving at the beginning of next week."

"So soon!"

"So late! We ought to have left long ago."

"Ought? What is that?" said Violet roughly.

"Now I, too, am going," Justin said. On foot, he insisted. "When I was a boy I left on foot. On foot shall I greet my place again. They will watch my boxes here until tomorrow when I send for them." So Marietta helped him loosen ropes and lift cartons down and carry them one by one into the shop with the long blue shutters and a dusty palm in front of the door. When they'd stowed all the cartons behind the counter they turned to one another.

"Now and then you'll send a picture of my boy?"

"Each year at Christmas, as I promised."

"I saw you marry. Him I shan't see marry."

"You've got so many children, Justin, apart from him and me!"

"But you I watched grow. Not them. Not even Violet. When she came to me, already she was big. But you I brought from the hospital and him I brought from the hospital. I am used to the two of you, and not so well used to those others!"

She took a hand that was rough, not from mending nets or paddling fishboats but from washing the clothes of Europeans — hers and Virginia's, Charlie's, Jonathan's, and, long ago, Charles Hamilton's, until he'd died by accident or possibly on purpose beside the lake at Songo, Tanganyika Territory. "You've taken care of me too well!" She tried to laugh, but wept instead, so that the palm tree quivered and the long blue shutters looked as if they were about to fall. "It's time I stood on my own two feet. How could I do that, with you forever holding me?" she said, and this time she laughed successfully.

Head down, looking at her sandals, Justin said, "May you settle in the White Man's Country. May you recover, Mari. May you find peace." Then he picked up his roll of blankets, a gift for Boremo. With the money orders he'd sent her month after month over many years, Boremo had built an iron-roofed house and next door a shop, which she'd stocked with Ginga cottons, Sunlight soap, Vaseline, Enfamil. All was ready for his homecoming.

He walked away between the dusty green euphorbia hedges. At the end of the rise he looked back for an instant. Then he turned and was gone.

Marietta drove across the island with Violet and the children in a solemn row behind. Violet's homestead was almost deserted. A few children played desultorily near the granary. The women slept inside, out of the burning heat. The men were working in hotels and railroad yards, on docks and ranches and cashew nut plantations, at the Coast, six hundred miles away. There was no work in Nyanza.

Quickly Violet closed her shutters against the afternoon.

"Now you will tell me," she said as soon as they were seated. "Why are you going away?" She spoke more gently than she had before.

"So that Charlie won't grow up believing he belongs where he cannot. His father believed that Africa was his home forever, despite the color of his skin. He died rather than accept the fact that it wasn't so."

"They said so at the investigation?"

"They said a great many things at the investigation. None of them were falsehoods. Yet they didn't add up to the truth."

Josiah Wangu testified that at dusk on Friday, January the eighth, nineteen hundred and seventy-three, a white man in a small blue vehicle had driven up the Olgolulu farm road. At the fork he'd turned not left to the house itself but right, towards the forest. Wangu could not say what became of him thereafter.

Andrew Ngugi had seen the headlights and jumped into the ditch, out of the way. But the car stopped just before it reached him and a man called to him. He had some business to do at the house, the man said, and he would give Ngugi two shillings to watch his vehicle meanwhile. At first Ngugi thought, This is an African. But once he had passed through the glare of the headlights, he saw to his amazement that the man was white. Why did he choose this road, Ngugi wondered, and not the other leading to the house directly? But he said nothing since he would be paid for watching, not for asking questions. Two hours after sunset the *mzungu* still had not returned. At home the evening meal would have been finished and Ngugi was hungry, and frightened also. How long does this white man need to do his business? He decided not to wait there any longer. Better to do without the money he'd been promised than to stay and be come upon by witches. And so he'd run on home.

399

I saw him, Peter Mathari said. I thought he was a stranger. But I came only recently from Kinangop. I was near the fish pond. That pond is empty. The fish all died and so we drained it. He passed close to me but did not see me because I stepped behind a bush. He went to a window and looked in. At that time inside there was a meeting. There is such a meeting every Friday evening, though this was larger yet than usual. I should have challenged the *mzungu*, but I did not because the moon had risen early and was very bright and I saw that in his hand he carried a small gun. If I called to him, certainly he'd kill me, that is what I was afraid of. He stood at that window for many minutes and then he turned and came back past where I was hiding. I did not see the gun again. He must have put it in his pocket. He went round to the front of the house, so I came from my hiding place and followed cautiously. Then I saw him quarreling with Jomo, the *askari*, who waits at the main door. He tried to prevent the *mzungu* from entering. He struggled with him, but he is not so strong, Jomo, and the *mzungu* knocked him down and forced his way inside. The events which then occurred I did not see because the door was locked. But I heard the shots, five altogether, and the people screaming. Soon the door swung open and out the white man came. He went across the gravel, across the grass, to the railing. He climbed over it and that is the last I saw. Inside the house there was a great deal of confusion. I thought, Surely he has killed many people. That is why I did not follow him, I was frightened he would kill me also, you understand. It was only later I heard he'd harmed no one. But afterwards as I was sitting at the door again with Jomo, I saw a man and a boy coming from the forest. Between them on their shoulders they carried something long and heavy. As they came nearer they called out to us, it was a body they were carrying. The head was hanging and the eyes were open and I saw immediately it was that same *mzungu*.

Towett is my name. I was coming with my son from the market at Moro. We'd been delayed. We were making our way home after sunset. It is at Laldayet we are living now, beyond the loggers' camp. We heard one shot ahead of us and then no other. I told my son, "There has been some misfortune. Let us run to see." My boy, he did not want to. "Perhaps someone has died," he said. I answered, "All the more reason why we should see." So we ran together, and at a place where the path crosses a small river my son

400

called out in terror, "It is as I had thought!" In the moonlight in the shallow water, a *mzungu* lay. We pulled him out, my son and I, but he was dead. He'd been shot through the heart. The bullet had passed through and out the other side. In the river, in the shallow water, I found his gun. The bullets had been all used up. It was the last one which had killed him. The path where it reached that river was very wet. I told my son, "Perhaps in the darkness he slipped and fell, and his gun went off." My son replied, "But why was he, a white man, in the forest after nightfall?" That I could not answer. How could I know? I told him, "Let us carry him to Olgolulu. It is the closest place," and that is what we did. The body was heavy and my son is young; he will be circumcised next December. We could not travel fast, but in the end we reached there and went inside and laid the dead man down. It was only then that I learned that he was Johnny. When he was the age my son is now, he used to come to us. We used to hunt together, in that very forest where we found him. But after that, for many years I never saw him, and when I did again, it was to see him dead.

— Mrs. Sudbury, did your husband have some special interest in Olgolulu?

— It was his home, had been his home until August of last year, when he sold it to the Moro Farmers' Cooperative. After that we settled in Katari.

— Did that change disturb him?

— How could it not? He had been born at Olgolulu. He used to say he wished to die there.

— Lately had he said that?

— Lately? No.

— In recent months, what was his mood?

— He was quiet. Occasionally he was very angry.

— Apart from leaving his old home, was his life changed in other respects? His work, for instance, did that continue as before?

— Yes, as before.

— Did he ever seem to you to be despondent, Mrs. Sudbury?

— What exactly does that mean?

— Had he, for instance, ever talked to you of suicide?

— Never.

— On that particular day, Mr. Kamau, the day of his death, did your master's mood strike you as in any way unusual?

— He was cheerful, in fact. At midday we had taken leave of one another at the Coach and Horses on the Amboseli road. No, he had not been drinking. On some mornings he did drink, but not on that one. He had business to attend to, so he said. That is why he left the white people with me and went ahead.

— What about you, Mrs. Sudbury. Did your husband's mood strike you as in any way unusual?

— Yes! My husband had been in Tanzania since the last week of November. On that day, the eighth of January, he came to our house, but he stayed only long enough to change his clothes. For the few minutes he was with me, he was different from at any other time that I had known him.

— Could you say more about that?

— It was as if he saw what others could not see.

— Do you mean he was deranged?

— He heard me, yet at the same time he was deaf. Because of this I was afraid. I attempted to dissuade him, but I was not successful. He took another vehicle and left.

— Dr. Kagia, what business did the deceased have at Olgolulu?

— It was a prank. A game that he came to play upon us. He'd left behind his ancestors. Their portraits were hanging on the walls. His family had brought them out from Europe long ago. They were still there. He told us that they'd always burdened him, and he did not want us to be burdened by them, too. It was in order to destroy their spirits that he shot them, each one of them, between the eyes. Then he went away.

— Was your husband knowledgeable about firearms, Mrs. Sudbury?

— He was an expert. He'd been a professional hunter for the past twelve years.

— In the ordinary course of his safari business, did he often use a revolver?

— No. He did not.

— Why, then, did he acquire one?

— Because of the recent burglaries in Katari.

— Where did he purchase it?

— I don't know.

— Did he have a license for it?

— No.

— Possession was therefore illegal ... Mrs. Sudbury, having

402

done what he set out to do, knowing that his wife and child and guests were waiting for him, why would your husband go into the forest?

— He loved it.

— Would you repeat what you just said?

— He loved the forest. He once said that as a boy he had been happier there, with the Dorobo people, than at any other period in his life.

There were so many questions, so many testimonies. Not a single witness. They talked, they argued, they debated, but at one o'clock they finished. So it was quicker, after all, than that other time in Songo. Cause of death undetermined, the coroner wrote. He signed the death certificate with his gold-nibbed pen.

Then the widow was free to take the body to Katari for burial between Philip Sudbury and Peter Dawson, under the jacaranda trees, and when the wind blew, purple blossoms tumbled over the new grave. By the time the blossoms had withered and Kikuyu grass was creeping over the raw red earth, Marietta had rented the house on Olduvai Road and given the servants notice. She bought two one-way tickets to London and put them in her bureau drawer.

"Do you have to do this?" Kagia asked. "Do you have to run away from me?"

"Not from you," she said despairingly. "Never from you. From Africa."

"But despite certain sorrows, you have thrived in Africa!"

"Have I? Perhaps. But others have perished. My grandparents, father, husband. Might not my son perish also?"

"Then you believe in the rage of the ancestors?"

"How can I not! None of them died well. If we stay here, Charlie and I, would they let us live in peace? How could they? There would be seasons of sunlight when they lulled us into thinking they were satisfied, we'd paid enough, we were safe, but our ancestors are never satisfied, Michael! Although at times they consider their grievances silently, their silence cannot last. Always they return to torment us. It is from dread of them that I shall take my son and go. Could I do otherwise?"

"Now, no. But one of these years," he said gently, "I shall come after you. How obstinate you can be, Marietta! There have been times when I have wondered, Must you remain deaf to me? But

I'm quite as obstinate as you, as convinced of my own truth, and so I haven't lost heart. Always, in due course, I have seen your eyes widen, and the hint of a smile, signs that you're beginning to hear me. Those signs I expect to see again, eventually."

In Galana, in the stillness of the long late afternoon, Violet said, "Is there a single truth, Mari? I don't think so. There are many, and can you know them all?"

"I'd hoped to," Marietta replied softly, looking away. They sat in silence for a moment until Violet leaned forward and touched Marietta's cheek.

"Look at me, Mari. Tell me this. It's hardly two months since you buried your husband, and yet you pack your belongings and lock your house and go. Is that a good way to leave us?"

"If I don't go now, I will never go at all."

"Why must you? This is your home."

"Yes, and I'll take it with me wherever I go."

"Where will you find other friends who love you as we do?"

"I don't expect that, Violet."

"How will you do without us, then?"

"It will be very hard."

"What kind of life will you lead?"

"An ordinary life."

"And what is that?"

"It's one without myths or special privileges. Without the burden of what happened once and of how things used to be. It's a life in which you choose what to do, the choice hasn't been made by others before you were born. That's why I'm leaving, Violet, and so quickly. Before I lose courage."

"Whom will you live with?"

"We'll live by ourselves, Charlie and I. Under a pale sky, more suitable for white people."

"Will you ever come back, Mari?"

"That I cannot say."

ABOUT THE AUTHOR

Louisa Dawkins grew up in England. She was educated at Cheltenham Ladies College, Lady Margaret Hall of Oxford University, and the University of Chicago. She has worked for extended periods in tropical Africa and Latin America and now lives in Massachusetts with her family, two cats, and a dog.